Murder on the Wind

Cheryl F Taylor

A Rock Shop Mystery

To
Greg Peterson and Jim Peterson
The rock whisperers!

Books by Cheryl Taylor

Gone to Ground

Up North Michigan Cozy Mystery Series
Up North Murder (Book One)

Rock Shop Cozy Mystery Series
Stone's Gems and Minerals (Book One)
Murder on the Wind (Book Two)

"Hey, Jackson, do you know where those new pieces of coprolite went? Pete Martin is coming in and he is interested in looking at them," Amy called out from the front counter of Stone's Gems and Minerals where she was studying the shipment manifest from a rock dealer in Tucson. It identified the coprolites but unhelpfully didn't say anything about where those particular items had been placed once they reached the shop.

A voice carried out of the small computer room to the right of the front door, "Coprolite? Isn't that the dinosaur poop?" Amy noticed two older women who had been browsing through a selection of semiprecious stone beads, suddenly look up at the word "poop" with expressions of surprise on their faces. Amy gave them a weak smile, then looked back down at the papers in her hand. The women were unfamiliar to Amy, which meant they were probably tourists, passing through Copper Springs while traveling Historic Route 66. Of course, Amy had only been back in town a few weeks herself, so it was possible that these women were some of the newer residents of the small town, brought to the area by the recent expansion in development.

"Yes," Amy called back. "It came in that shipment from Suzanne Morrison at Raining Rocks the other day. It had a particularly nice mix of red, green and white. Pete Martin said he's been looking for some."

Jackson Wolf came walking out of the computer room which was to the right of the front door of Stone's Gems and Minerals, the rock shop belonging to Nick Stone, Amy's father. Amy, herself, was running the shop while Nick was in a rehabilitation hospital in Kingman, Arizona, recovering from a badly broken leg.

"What is he planning on doing with dinosaur poop?"

Amy sighed and shook her head. "It's coprolite, Jackson." She looked over to where the two women were staring at her, apparently engrossed in the conversation. They quickly dropped their eyes, but Amy had caught the twinkle of amusement pass between the two of them.

"Right. Coprolite. Fossilized dinosaur do-do. Imagine the level of constipat... Hey!" Jackson yelped as Amy punched him in the chest. She was careful not to jar the shoulder he'd injured several weeks earlier, even though she knew darn well he'd been pulling his arm out of the sling whenever she wasn't looking (and sometimes when she was). She noticed that the older women, *definitely tourists, or at least not rock people like Dad,* were giggling and whispering.

"Be serious, Jackson," Amy scolded, giving him a stern look. "At least when there are customers in the store," she continued in a low whisper.

Jackson gave Amy a limpid, blue-eyed stare. "These ladies don't mind, do you?" He turned to the older women who had moved closer to the glass checkout counter, making a show of examining some small animals carved from various colors of soapstone and onyx. While they tried to hide their interest, it was obvious that they were fascinated by Amy and Jackson's conversation. The shorter of the two looked at Jackson and gave him a cheeky grin.

"No, we don't mind at all. Do you really carry petrified dinosaur... ah... feces?"

Her friend bent her head closer to the small green aventurine rabbit that she was turning over in her fingers, but Amy swore she could hear a snicker.

Jackson turned his brilliant grin on the woman. "Of course we do, ma'am. Petrified dino doo, petrified dino bone, petrified turtle poo, petrified wood. If you can petrify it, we carry it."

Amy scowled at Jackson and gave him a pointed look. "We just can't find where we put it?"

Jackson gave Amy a bland look. "Oh, we know exactly where we put it."

"We do? Then where the heck is it?"

"Where would you put petrified poop?" Jackson's tone dripped innocence.

Amy's violet eyes widened, and she looked toward the far corner of the front showroom where a small rest room sign was tacked to the wall. "You didn't! Jackson! What on earth? What were..."

He grinned at the look on her face and gestured toward the opposite corner of the L-shaped room, where the unpolished slabs and rough rocks were kept in boxes or bins on a huge set of shelves. "It's in the bin with the petrified dinosaur bone. Where did you think I'd put it?"

"Why didn't you tell me that to begin with?" Amy rolled her eyes.

"Because it was more fun this way." Jackson's laugh bubbled out, drawing a corresponding smile from Amy and their audience of two. Jackson Wolf had only been working for Stone's Gems and Minerals for a short time, having been hired after Carl Schrader, the shop's previous employee, was murdered. Amy had been suspect number one, and Jackson had helped clear her name, and capture the actual murderer. His left scapula and collarbone had been broken in the final struggle to survive, which was the current reason for the sling, although it didn't slow him down any from what Amy could tell.

Of course, these women didn't know anything about that. They were just responding to Jackson's infectious good cheer. He seemed to have the same effect on most of the older women he met, from what Amy could see. Even the crusty Moira Larson, Jackson's new landlady, was putty in his hands. In fact, the only woman who had failed to fall for the Jackson Wolf charm, as far as Amy knew, was Bea Hazelton, the wife of Jon Hazelton, a town council member who seemed to feel that Copper Springs was his own private fiefdom to shape as he wanted. His wife was equally disdainful of the long-time residents of the area. It amazed Amy that Hazelton had ever been elected to the council, although, come to think of it, most of the residents of the town were the "don't call us, we'll call you... *if, and when, hell freezes over*" type when it came to the government — even the local government. For all she knew, Hazelton, and the others of his ilk may have been the only ones running.

"What does one do with petrified dinosaur feces?" the taller of the two women asked, giving up her pretense of studying the small carved animals. She had a distinct British accent, Amy noticed. Definitely a tourist, although her friend sounded American enough.

"Well, some people just use them as display pieces, they can come in beautiful colors. Of course, it also makes a heck of a discussion starter," Amy said, her voice taking on a dry note, as she thought about some of the books that had been written on the subject of coprolite.

Jackson chimed in, "Yeah. You go over to a new friend's house, and they say, 'hey, do you want to see the new petrified poop I picked up?' That tends to get the ball rolling nicely."

Amy looked at Jackson with an increasingly familiar *knock-it-off stare*, which he ignored as usual. She sighed and continued her lecture.

"Others may cut it into cabochons or cabs, polish it and make jewelry or other decorations. Here, let me show you what I mean." Amy walked out from behind the glass counter, opening and carefully shutting the gate that kept Jynx, her Australian shepherd/border collie mix, and Bess, Nick's corgi, out of the main part of the store during the day. She made her way down the long log of the L-shaped main showroom, heading for the back corner where Jackson had indicated he'd put the slabs. The two women followed closely, with Jackson trailing along behind.

At the end wall, Amy studied the stacks of bins and trays, looking for ones that were labeled petrified dinosaur bone. If she stayed much longer, she was going to have to revamp her dad's organizational system. Nothing was alphabetized, nor did any of the bins have any relation to the boxes on either side, above or below, as far as she could tell. She spotted the one she was looking for and pulled it out, displaying the contents to the women.

"This is gem-quality fossilized dinosaur bone," She picked out a reddish slab and set the box back on the stack. "You can see the canals, or what used to be canals when it was actual bone." She drew her finger across the dull surface with a faint frown on her face. She raised the rock preparing to spit on the surface, then glanced at the older women who were watching in fascination and lowered the rock with a guilty feeling. She heard a snicker and looked over at Jackson, who was trying to control his expression and failing.

Because most rocks didn't show their full colors unless polished or wet, the majority of rockhounds had developed the habit of spitting on their finds to get an idea of what they were holding. Those few well-prepared souls carried bottles of water for that purpose, but even they resorted to saliva at times. Still, it wasn't exactly an approved practice in retail to spit on the merchandise.

Amy looked around blankly, then saw a spray bottle of water on the front counter. She grabbed the box of slabs again and headed to the front of the store, the two women and Jackson close behind. Amy set the rocks down on the glass surface, picked up the spray bottle and gave the petrified dinosaur bone slab a few squirts. She set the bottle back on the counter, then used her fingers to rub the water over the rock. The moisture gave the slab a polished look, intensifying colors and making the canals and web-like structures in the petrified bone stand out.

"Here, you can see them better now." Amy offered the slab to the closer of the two women, neither of whom seemed to be aware of her earlier dilemma.

The shorter of the two women took the rock slab from Amy's hand and held it up in the soft light of the showroom, pushing her glasses up her nose to get a better look. She tilted the slab from side to side, then held it up to the light and drew in a breath as the bone glowed.

"Look, Gloria," she offered the piece of petrified bone to her friend. "You can see all the compartments of the bone. It's quite beautiful." The woman with the British accent, identified as Gloria, took the piece and also studied it closely nodding in apparent fascination.

After a moment, she handed it back to Amy, glancing at her friend. "You're right, Alice. It's lovely." She looked back at Amy and smiled. "You have so many fascinating pieces here. This is your store? I was interested in the name: Stone's Gems and Minerals. I thought it must be a mistake, and that the word *Stone's* shouldn't have the apostrophe."

Amy laughed at the woman's remark. "You have no idea how often we get that question. The shop belongs to my dad, Nick Stone, hence the apostrophe 's.' I'm his daughter, Amy. He gets a kick out of playing with his last name, in more ways than one." Her voice took on a wry tone. There was no way these ladies could know that Amy's actual first name was Amethyst and that her middle name was Gem, nor that her siblings were named Opal and Jasper, and she wasn't about to tell them.

Alice, the shorter woman, and the one with the American accent, spoke up again, "Could we see what the cor... ah co... um, dinosaur feces look like?"

"Oh, yes. It's called coprolite, although not all coprolites come from dinosaurs. Coprolite just refers to petrified fecal matter, so any feces that were produced a long enough time ago, and in the correct environment, can become coprolite." Amy put the dinosaur bone slab carefully back into the box and removed a roughly hemispherical piece of stone, chalky white on the outer surface, but the cut face showing a swirl of green, red and white, with several dark green wavering lines. "Here you are. Mind you, not all coprolite looks the same. It depends on the type of animal that produced the, ah... feces, and what it ate, as well as what minerals replace or intermingle with the organic material during the petrification. This one has some beautiful patterns, though." She handed it to Alice, who took it gingerly between two fingers and looked at the flat cut surface carefully.

Gloria took the stone from her friend, Alice's, hand, and reached for the bottle of water. She sprayed the surface as she'd seen Amy do earlier with the dinosaur bone, and the swirls of red and green came to life. She looked at it for a moment, turning it over and examining the outer crust, then back as if comparing the inside colors with the plain outer crust.

"It is amazing, the difference. It makes one wonder why anyone would pick up something this plain if they saw it on the ground, yet inside all of this is hidden." Gloria's accent gave the words a lilt that made Amy work for a moment to understand. She smiled at the woman, enjoying her fascination.

"Actually coprolite is considered to be a trace fossil, since it didn't come from a living organism itself, but instead from something left behind by the living creature." Amy smiled at the woman's enjoyment. "It's found all over the world, although that piece there," she gestured at the hemisphere sitting in the woman's hand, "came from the desert in Utah."

"Really," Alice said, intensified interest shining in her eyes. "We'd planned on traveling Route 66 to Kingman, then up through Las Vegas, and make a loop, going back east through Utah." Alice paused, then looked at Gloria. "Speaking of which, we had better get going. Were you going to get that cute little T-Rex, Gloria? The one carved out of that pinkish rock?"

Gloria nodded, and the two women paid Amy for their purchases which Jackson wrapped securely in paper towels to protect them from damage, pulling his arm out of the sling for greater mobility. When Amy gave him the evil eye, he grinned.

"Physical therapy is important to healing, you know."

"So is following the doctor's instructions, and they told you to limit the use of that shoulder for a few more weeks."

With a meek look, Jackson slid his wrist back into the sling, and with a nod and a wink to the two women, he headed back to his office. Amy shook her head, certain that as soon as he entered the room the arm would be back out of the sling again.

She looked up to see Gloria watching her intently. "You can tell that one will do exactly as he wants." She gave Amy a slight smile. "He'll likely not come to any harm though. You shouldn't worry about it."

With a final smile and a wave, the two women headed out of the shop with their packages held protectively to their chests. Amy turned back to the bin of dinosaur bone and coprolite, lifting the heavy box to carry it back to its spot. There was no knowing when Pete Martin would be in today, but at least she now knew where the specimens he wanted were kept. They didn't have to clutter up the front counter any longer.

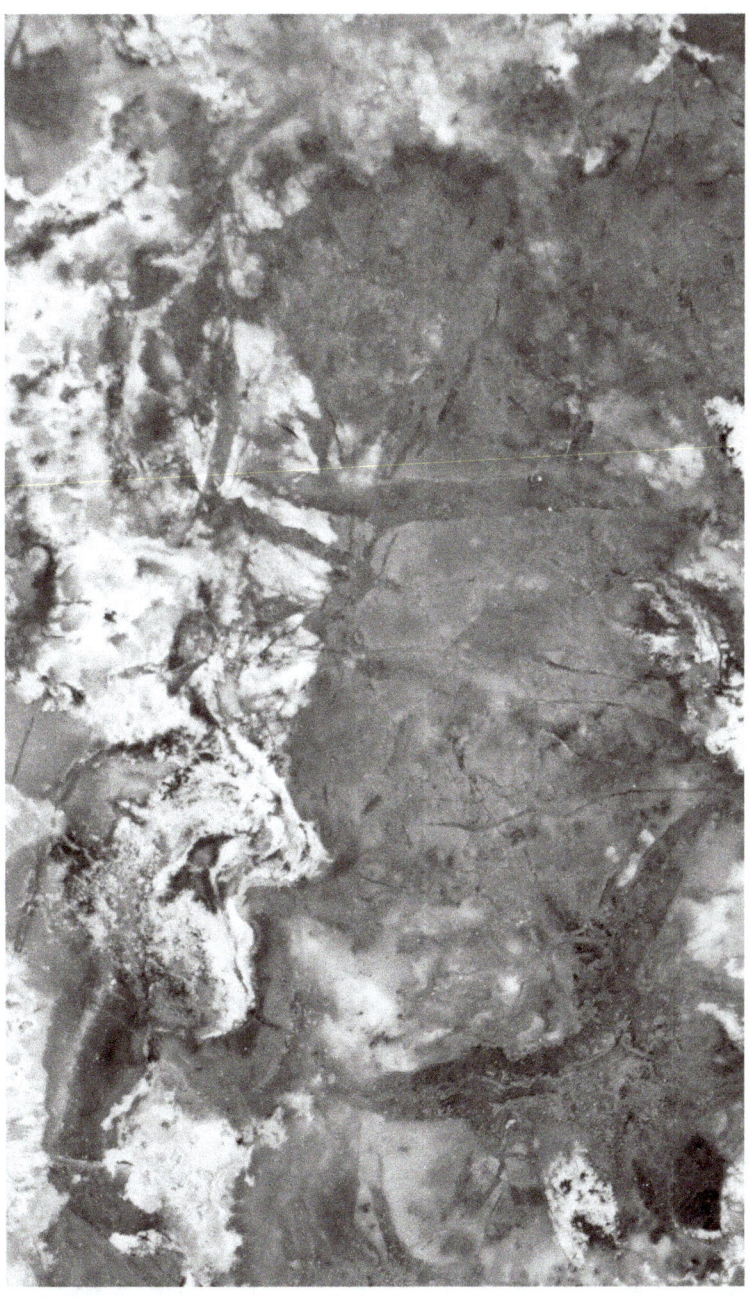

Dinosaur Coprolite, Utah

Jackson had just returned from a sandwich run to the deli in the gas station across Route 66 from Stone's Gems and Minerals when Pete Martin arrived at the shop. Amy and Jackson were divvying up the sandwiches, chips and iced teas when she heard the distinctive roar of Martin's 1962 Ford pickup pulling in to the gravel parking lot outside. Martin had a nearly new Ford F-250, which he used out on the rough ranch roads, but he enjoyed the looks he got driving the '62 restored pickup around the town of Copper Springs, and most of the residents were very familiar with its deep bass rumble. Amy looked longingly at the roast beef and Swiss sandwich, and her stomach grumbled at the impending delay.

"There's Pete," she sighed to Jackson. "Do you mind sticking my sandwich in the mini fridge in Nick's office?"

"Why? If all he's in for is the coprolite, then it shouldn't take to long." Jackson had unwrapped his own sandwich and was just preparing to take a huge bite, arm once again out of its sling.

"Have you met Pete Martin?"

"Yeah, he does like to talk, doesn't he?" Jackson grinned and nodded, scooped up Amy's sandwich with his own and headed for Nick Stone's office which was located down the front wall of the building next to the computer room.

"You don't have to wait on your lunch, Jackson. I can take care of Pete."

"Nah, you might need backup," He called out from a small room. Amy could hear the refrigerator's door open and close, but before she could answer, the wind chimes hanging in the entryway jingled as the front door was opened.

"Hello, hello!" came a booming voice from the short hallway, and Amy turned to see a tall, lanky man enter the room. Pete Martin had been a fixture in town ever since Amy could remember, and in all that time, he hadn't seemed to change at all. He always seemed to Amy to be a cross between a cowboy and a hippie, wearing Wranglers and boots, with a tan canvas vest and a beat up, sweat-stained cowboy hat, but also with a long gray ponytail to match his long gray mustache and beard.

"Hey there, Amethyst Stone. Got some rocks to show me?" Pete's deep bass voice rumbled, nearly as rough as the engine of the Ford sitting outside, and his body seemed too thin to contain such a deep sound. "I've got a commission for a necklace and earrings, and the man specified coprolite. Said he wanted to give his soon-to-be ex a piece of sh..."

"Hi, Pete. You know darn well I go by Amy, and not Amethyst," Amy said, a smile in her voice and pointedly ignoring his comment about the jewelry. She thought about the beautiful pieces of coprolite in the box and felt a wave of regret that the recipient wouldn't know the story behind the beautiful stones.

"I like the name, Amethyst." Pete gave her a wink and Amy rolled her eyes. "How's your mom and dad doing?"

"They're doing well, Pete," Amy answered. *Small town grapevine*, Amy thought. *Everyone knows everyone else's business.* "Nick's still at the rehab facility in Kingman. Mom's staying down there with him, but they're thinking he's going to make it home in the next few weeks."

"Hi, Pete." Jackson's voice came from behind the tall man. Martin's height dwarfed both he and Amy and she hadn't seen Jackson come out of Nick's office. Martin turned and put out a large rough hand.

"Hi there, Jackson Wolf, right?" He pumped Jackson's had several times. "You're Merri Thompson's brother, aren't you? The photographer?"

"That's right. We met at the Copper Springs Diner back in July. Gladys Sanchez introduced us."

"So you're working here now, huh? Becoming a rockhound?"

"More of a rockhead," Jackson laughed. "But I'm learning more every day. Amethyst, here, is a great teacher."

Pete grinned and looked back at Amy. "See, even your employee is calling you Amethyst. With those violet eyes, girl, the name fits."

"If Mr. von Wulffen wants to get his next paycheck, he's going to knock off the 'Amethyst' thing," Amy stated, giving Jackson a glare with said violet eyes, eyebrows raised, although those were probably hidden under her curly brown bangs. Jackson usually used Amy's preferred name, unless there was an audience who might appreciate the use of Amethyst, bringing it up usually when there were customers around, especially with customers who knew her father, Nick Stone, well, and were familiar with his refusal to call Amy anything other than the name on her birth certificate. Of course, Amy was equally likely to come up with interesting variations on Jackson's own name, since he'd told her upon their first meeting that he'd shortened it to Wolf, and adamantly refused to tell her his original last name. Amy would periodically test out different possibilities, but each time Jackson would laugh off her attempts.

A confused look crossed Pete's face as he looked at Jackson, and then at Amy. "I thought his last name is Wolf. That von Wulffen thing... sounds German?"

Jackson took his arm and turned him toward the back of the showroom. "Don't pay any attention to her. My last name is Wolf. Says so on my driver's license. She just gets confused sometimes, don't you Amethyst?" Jackson looked back over his shoulder as he walked Martin back to where the coprolite was kept. "You were looking for coprolite, correct? We have some amazing pieces back here."

"I sure am. Nick told me a few months ago he'd be on the lookout for some nice slabs or rough, and Amethyst told me that they'd come in when I called earlier."

"They did. Beautiful slabs," Amy heard Jackson say as he and Pete reached the back of the shop. "By the way, how is the museum doing? I heard that the town council was thinking of buying the building and moving the town office there. The person who told me mentioned that the old town building was going to be sold and turned into a bed and breakfast."

Great! Don't encourage him, Jackson, Amy thought, with an internal groan. Pete Martin was the head of the Copper Springs Historical Society, and that meant he was also in charge of the town's small museum. Unfortunately, the historical society seemed to be in constant conflict with the town council, at least according to Gladys Sanchez and Emily Jameson, owners of the Copper Springs Diner. Asking Martin about the latest series of wrongs done to the historical society by the council was akin to throwing kerosene on a fire.

Nick Stone, Amy's father, tended to stay out of the town's government, saying that if they left him alone, he'd leave them alone, an attitude that had nearly come back to bite him in the butt a few weeks ago. However, since Pete was one of the key members of the Northeastern Mohave Gem and Mineral Society, he and Nick were close friends, Nick was a frequent audience to Pete's rants about the newest members of the Copper Springs Town Council. While Amy knew Pete from her childhood, she had only recently returned to the town and all she knew about the situation was obtained secondhand through the small town grapevine or from talking to her father.

"That bunch of country western wannabes should have stayed in their big cities and left Copper Springs alone," Pete stated adamantly. Amy could have sworn an electric current had run through him. His hair, mustache and eyebrows bristled, and his blue eyes snapped in anger.

"The Mineral and Historical Museum is a valuable part of this town. You know what the council says? They say they shouldn't be spending any money on supporting the museum! Can you believe that? It's our history. We do an important job for the community. That Jon Hazelton and his wife are a blight on this community, buzzing around and wanting to make it into some fancy tourist destination." Pete's voice had started to rise, the lower tones dropping out as he got into the swing of his diatribe. It reminded Amy of an engine being revved up to a dangerous level and she expected to see smoke start leaking out from his pores as he melted down.

"I thought Hazelton was going to be kicked off the town council for his actions with Scott Branson in trying to get the rock shop closed down. How's he still got any influence on the council?" Jackson asked and Amy wanted to kick him for adding even more fuel to the blaze.

"That guy has the whole council wrapped up. Convinced them that he was Branson's victim in the whole scheme, just as much as Nick. He said Branson was now lying in hopes of getting a lighter sentence. Hazelton and his wife should be driven out of town. They should... should..." Martin stuttered to a stop, out of words for the first time since Amy met him.

Jackson looked startled by the fireworks his question had invoked. Amy had realized over the last few weeks that Jackson had no problem poking hornets nests, as the saying goes, but it appeared that this time he got more of a reaction than he intended.

Amy hurried out from behind the counter and headed to the back of the shop wracking her brain for another topic of conversation.

"Hey, Pete. I hear that the rock club is planning a field trip this coming weekend. Something about the Red Wind Mine?" Amy's kept her voice light, as though she was unaware of the current topic of conversation, and she could see the look of concern on Jackson's face replaced by one of relief.

"I heard the same thing," Jackson spoke up as he reached for the bin that contained the coprolite. "What is the Red Wind Mine?"

Completely derailed from his line of thought it took Pete a moment to switch directions. For several seconds Amy thought he would continue on his tirade, but ultimately the lure of discussing the trip to the Red Wind was too much to resist.

"The Red Wind is a mine north and west of Route 66, on an inholding up along the reservation border." Pete glanced at Jackson, then clarified his statement. "An inholding being privately owned land surrounded by publicly owned lands."

Jackson nodded at Pete's comment. "That means it's a patent mine, correct?" Amy noted a smug look on his face. Jackson had been doing a lot of research on minerals and mines since their adventure in the Skystone and Pipe Wash mines a few weeks ago, and apparently, that research was paying off.

Pete looked impressed at Jackson's use of the term. "Yes. Salina and Jania Mattheson purchased the mine a few months ago, and in this case, own both the land and the minerals. That's not that common in this state. The sisters have been living rough out there, only coming into town once a week or more. None of the modern conveniences, although they do have a solar system for refrigeration and light. I met Salina when she came into the museum about a month ago. She wanted to see if we'd be interested in buying some of the old mining equipment they found on the site when they took over. Of course, I said yes. If that damned Hazelton would..."

"Uh, what is coming out of the Red Wind these days?" Jackson spoke up in a rush as he tried to keep Martin from sliding back into his rant on the Copper Springs Town Council. Once again the opportunity to talk about the mine was too much for Pete and Amy breathed out a sigh of relief and gave Jackson an approving nod behind Pete's back. She'd much rather have Pete rambling on about the mining history of Mohave County, Arizona, than ranting about the governmental overreach of the town council.

Pete seemed to deflate slightly. *He's like a puffer fish,* Amy thought with a chuckle, *get him angry and he seems to increase in size.*

"There are a lot of different minerals in that area, but the Red Wind was known for gold, silver, lead and molybdenum over the years, although it never produced a large quantity of any of them. It was first mined back in the early 1900s by the Hanson family. It was called the Gold Doll at the time. It changed owners several times over the years and was called alternately the Lonely Lady, Deep Wash and the Cross Point. Then the claim was abandoned about thirty years ago." Pete's voice started to return to its deep timbre as he got started talking about his favorite topic.

"The girls, ah..." Pete looked at Amy guiltily, although his smile, hidden as it was in his beard and mustache, belayed the look to some degree. "Um... the ladies... took over the claim and the two have been living out there and working mine. They haven't brought out much gold or silver which was the main reason Salina told me they bought the mine. I could have talked them out of it before they bought that ant hill if I'd known. That mine was never a big producer as far as the valuable metals go, but recently they've started bringing out some nice mineral specimens and are trying to determine how to get the word out to collectors." Pete shook his head, a distant look in his blue eyes. Jackson looked over at Amy and grinned. Amy smiled in return. She recognized the sound of rockhound in full cry.

"I've seen some wulfenite equal in quality to the pieces coming from the Red Cloud Mine." Pete's voice took on reverent tones, and he looked at both Amy and Jackson, with excitement clear in his blue eyes. "You know, that old mine in the Trigo Mountains in southwestern Arizona?

The girls have also pulled out some beautiful galena samples as well as some cerussite. I even saw a little smithsonite. The wulfenite seems to be the most prolific, however. Nice gem quality crystals. Very unusual. Same bright red as the Red Cloud, although I've seen a little bit of druse covered, similar to the Finch."

Amy looked at Pete in surprise. "Really. I've seen a couple of small pieces of Red Cloud wulfenite. It's considered some of the best in the world. It's certainly gorgeous. Dad has an impressive plate in the back showroom. I hadn't heard about another find of that quality in Arizona."

"It's a small mine, and the sisters haven't been working it that long. Their main goal when they purchased the mine was silver and gold. They only hit the high-quality wulfenite this last month, although I'm told that their spoils pile can provide pretty good hunting for smaller specimens. Over the years, the various people who ran the mine weren't focused on anything except the valuable metals, so anything else wound up in the waste rock piles."

"How is the field trip going to work? Where are people meeting?" Amy asked. When she was younger, before leaving for Flagstaff to attend Northern Arizona University, she'd frequently gone on rock club field trips with Nick, and she thought this one sounded like fun, even though the club had probably gotten a lot of new members since she'd left.

Besides, she'd like to meet the mining sisters. Running a mine was hard work and she was interested in meeting the women who'd taken on the challenge. She had to admit that the opportunity to add some nice specimens to the shop's collection, or her own if she was lucky, made the field trip even more enticing. She wouldn't mind a little bit of gemy red wulfenite.

Then a thought crossed her mind... wulfenite... wulf... She glanced at Jackson from the corner of her eyes. He must have caught the look, but had no idea what it meant.

Apparently, he knew there was something up, however, as his eyes narrowed in suspicion. She could feel a smirk twist her lips and tried to get it under control. She knew that there was no way Jackson's last name could be wulfenite, could it? Even it wasn't, it would be fun to start calling him that, especially since he was now working in a rock shop.

Pete talked on, unaware of the turn Amy's thoughts had taken. "We're planning on meeting at the gas station in Copper Springs, then heading northwest from there. The road gets pretty rough in spots, but we've had good weather and you should be able to make it easily in the jeep. You're thinking of coming, right Amethyst?"

"It sounds great. I think..." She looked over at Jackson who was watching her with a grin on his face. "I think we'll probably make it. Mom was planning on coming up sometime this weekend to pick up some more books for Dad. He's getting pretty bored down there in Kingman. I'll bet she'd be more than willing to watch the shop for the day. It will give her a break as well."

Pete looked at Jackson, then back at Amy, a huge grin making a divot in his beard and mustache. "Wonderful. The ladies are charging each person twenty-five dollars to prospect, but it will be worth it, I'm sure. We've got members of the historical society coming as well, wanting to check out some of the antique equipment. I'm told there's an old stamp mill there, although I can't imagine that this mine produced enough ore to make it worthwhile. Still, one of the past owners was an engineer, and, as the story goes, bought an old broken down stamp mill, hauled it out to the mine, then fixed it up to run on a gasoline-powered lawn mower engine. It's going to be a wonderful trip." Pete nodded vigorously, beard bobbing up and down on his chest.

"Now, where's that dinosaur poop?"

A half-hour later Pete Martin walked out the door with the coprolite, as well as several slabs of petrified dinosaur bone, two slices of Laguna lace agate and a large piece of natural Royston ribbon turquoise. He'd tried diligently to talk Amy out of several of her specimens of Skystone Mine turquoise, instead of the Royston – pieces that she and Jackson had brought out before being kidnapped by Scott Branson, and nearly dying in the mine that produced those brilliant blue stones. However, since the actual ownership of that find was still in question, and there was no guarantee Amy could replace the pieces, or if she even legally owned them, she was loathed to let them go until a decision was rendered by the authorities. Because of the situation, Amy's small stock was more expensive per carat than Pete felt he could get for the jewelry he wanted to make from it and he settled for the beautiful Royston slabs instead.

Pete's exit left the room feeling larger... and silent. Amy looked at Jackson and grinned. "Whew, hasn't it gotten quiet in here?"

"You were right. Pete sure likes to talk. It's amazing how much he knows about the history of the area."

"It's always amazed me how he manages to keep all that information in his head. Saturday's field trip should be fantastic. I've been on a few with him in the past, but never on a joint historical society and rock club tour. I wonder how he'll decide to spend his time between the mine and the mining equipment."

"Should be interesting. You're sure you don't mind asking your mom to watch the store?"

"No. I'm sure she'll be glad to get out of the rehabilitation facility for a day. She's been thinking about moving back up anyway since Dad doesn't need her as much as he did at the beginning. Besides, he'll be home soon." Amy sighed at the thought of the changes in the future that were heading her way at breakneck speed.

Back in the middle of July, when Nick broke his leg falling off a ladder, Amy had just left her job with Gila Geologic Consultants and had decided to return to Copper Springs to help run the shop while Nick was in the hospital. The idea was to use that time to catch her breath, sort out her feelings and develop a plan for the future. Amy's boyfriend at the time, Jeff Donaldson, and his father had used Amy as a scapegoat on the failure of a large dam construction project. The personal and professional betrayal scalded Amy's self-confidence, as well as damaging her professional reputation in the geological world, making it more difficult to find another position.

By coming back to Stone's Gems and Minerals, Amy thought she'd be able to gain some distance and perspective, and eventually come up with a solid plan to move forward in her career. To her surprise, she found herself blending back into the small town of Copper Springs, and in spite of the murder of Carl Schrader and everything that happened afterward, including her near death at the hands of Carl's killer, Amy realized that she didn't want to leave. Nick was getting older, and the shop was more than able to support all of them. Besides, neither of her siblings had any desire to take over the business.

The only question was where to live when her parents came home, and as Jackson had pointed out weeks ago, the answer was right above their heads. Stone's Gems and Minerals was located in a two-story building, but for years the upper floor had been shut off and the entrance hidden behind a rug that hung over the door.

"I'd better get working on the upstairs apartment if I'm going to move in before Mom and Dad get back. I'm too old to live with my parents," Amy said as she thought about the room upstairs with a faint shiver. She was sure it could be cleaned up and made into a pleasant apartment. Too bad it had such a ghostly air about it right now, not to mention such close associations with the unpleasantness of a few weeks ago.

Amy looked up and saw Jackson studying her, a hint of sympathy in his eyes. He'd lived such a different life than hers, orphaned at an early age, and accepting the responsibility of raising his younger sister, Merri. Until she needed help after her husband, Lou, died and she started being harassed by Schrader, Jackson had lived a nomadic life. Now here he was, renting the bunkhouse out at Moira Larson's ranch, and seemingly adjusting to these new changes in his life without a second thought. He gave her a grin as if reading her mind.

"Changes can be difficult and you've had a lot of them in a short period of time."

"So have you!" Amy said in exasperation, a frown pinching her forehead.

"Yeah, but I'm used to changes. The bunkhouse is the first place I've lived in years that didn't have wheels and an engine. That takes a little getting used to, believe me." His smile grew even broader. "That upstairs apartment will be perfect for you... until the next thing comes along, of course."

Amy's chin tilted, her characteristic sign of determination and defiance, and Jackson laughed. "For now, why don't we focus on finishing our lunch. Sunday I'll meet you here with a couple of gallons of white paint and some rust remover, and we'll get started on your new home."

"I thought you said you were going to spring for an exorcist as well."

"Let's not get carried away with ourselves. You may find you want a little company."

Amy rolled her eyes and headed for Nick's office to retrieve their sandwiches.

Saturday morning dawned cool and clear. Arizona summers seem to last an eternity, but the early September weather was starting to favor those who didn't want to be parboiled every time they walked out the door.

Of course, since the Red Wind is over the edge of the plateau at a 4,000-foot elevation, it's still likely to get uncomfortably warm by the end of the day, Amy thought. There wasn't even much hope for a monsoon storm this time of year. *Layers. Dress in layers, and don't forget plenty of water,* Amy reminded herself upon leaving her parents' home that morning on Turquoise Hill Road, dressed in jeans and T-shirt, but carrying a long-sleeved shirt and light jacket. She had already packed two hard hats and headlamps with extra batteries into the jeep the night before, along with several five-gallon buckets and canvas rock bags. Just in case, she told herself.

Jackson's old teal Jimmy was already parked in front of Stone's Gems and Minerals when Amy pulled in to the gas station parking lot. Amy was impressed to see several 4x4s waiting in the graveled lot west of the station, various people milling around, talking, and drinking coffee as they waited for the rest of the party. Jackson broke free from a small group and started to walk over, carrying his backpack.

"Hey, good morning, Amy!" Jackson called, reaching for the passenger door of the Wrangler. He threw his pack into the bed of the jeep, shut the door and walked around the hood to the driver's side door.

"Looks like there's a good turn out," Jackson said, nodding toward the people. "Rockhound's paradise."

"Good thing there's room for a few rockheads," Amy said, laughing as she punched Jackson lightly on his good shoulder when he gave her an insulted look, which was quickly washed away by a huge smile.

Amy was pleased to see that Gladys Sanchez and Emily James, the talkative owners of the Copper Springs Diner, and star customers of the rock shop, were part of the group and Amy waved to them as she opened the door to her Wrangler and slid out.

A bright smile lit Gladys' face as she and Emily hurried over to welcome them.

"Amethyst and Jackson, hello. We're so glad to see you, aren't we Em? How is your shoulder, Jackson?" Gladys said, talking a hundred miles per hour as usual and patting Jackson on his slinged arm. She turned to look at Emily, who just beamed and nodded at Amy and Jackson. "We're so excited to get a chance to see the Red Wind Mine. They've had it locked up tight for years. There was that disappearance back in the eighties. The whole place was abandoned after that, and a heavy metal door welded in front of the mine entrance."

Amy frowned and looked at Jackson. "Pete Martin didn't mention a disappearance when we were talking about the Red Wind, did he?"

Jackson shook his head, although he looked more curious than concerned. "I don't remember him saying anything about someone going missing, just that the mine went through a few different owners, then was abandoned a number of years ago until the Mattheson sisters took over. Who disappeared?"

"It would have been before your time," Gladys said, then corrected herself. "Well, when you were very young, at least. I think it was in 1981, or 1982... early in the eighties, at least."

"What happened?" Jackson asked. In spite of his casual tone, Amy could tell that his imagination was already playing with possible scenarios. Jackson knew that Gladys was going to tell them what happened, whether they wanted to hear it or not. Gladys and Emily were key strands in the small town grapevine entwining Copper Springs. Amy often thought that there was no need of a newsletter when the proprietors of the Copper Springs Diner were on the job. Jackson, in asking Gladys for information, was merely priming the pump, so to speak, so that the information flowed a bit faster.

"My understanding is that the last person to run the mine... wasn't it called the Cross Point Mine then, Em?" Gladys turned to look at her friend then turned back to her audience without waiting for Emily's nod of assent. "Well, the last person to run the Cross Point Mine was William Powell."

Amy started at the name. "Any relation to John Wesley Powell, the geologist who explored the Colorado River?" Growing up Amy had always had a schoolgirl crush on the explorer, and secretly wished that she could have gone on some of the same adventures she'd read about. Of course, her father, Nick Stone, was also a geologist, and Amy had followed the same profession, so she considered it natural that she admired the famous explorer. At least that was the way she justified it to herself.

Gladys looked at Emily with a frown on her face. "I'm not sure. I can't actually recall if I ever met William Powell, did you, Em?" Gladys glanced back at her friend again.

Emily shook her head. "It was before I moved here," she said in a soft voice.

Gladys nodded, a look of concentration momentarily clouding her normally animated expression.

"The story goes that Powell... William mind you, and not John Wesley... bought the mine from a small company which had given up on hitting it big with this particular claim. They hadn't worked it in years and finally decided to sell. William Powell moved out there with his wife and kids and started working the claim himself. From what I remember, the wife went into town one day with the kids on some form of errand, a doctor or something, leaving Powell alone at the mine. When she returned later in the day there was no sign of him anywhere in the mine or around the property. Powell's wife called the sheriff's department, and they started a search. Many from Copper Springs went out to help, but Powell was never found." Gladys fell silent for a moment, a distant look in her eyes. Then, suddenly, she shook her head and her gaze sharpened. "Most people thought he was dead, having fallen in some hidden shaft, and then buried by a rock fall, but the search parties said they were thorough in exploring the mine. Others said he got tired and discouraged at his lack of success, and ran away, going cross country and leaving his wife and kids."

Jackson looked over toward the mountains northwest of Copper Springs. "Why would anyone do that? Surely there are a lot easier ways to abandon your family." His voice held a mix of disgust and disbelief.

"Yes, that's one of the reasons most people think he's still out there, somewhere in the mine or around the property. At least his body is." Gladys nodded abruptly, a sad look in her bright eyes overshadowing her enjoyment of the gossip.

"Was he the engineer?" Amy asked, trying to remember the timeline Pete Martin had described, and thinking about the antique stamp mill. "Pete said that one of the old owners was an engineer and rigged up an old stamp mill to work on a gasoline-powered lawn mower engine."

"Yes," Gladys' head bobbed up and down enthusiastically. "That's why the historical society is going. Salina and Jania Mattheson have offered to sell the stamp mill, as well as some of the other old equipment that Powell collected, to the town. It's causing quite a ruckus as the town council is refusing to help the society, even though the museum benefits the town. Isn't that right, Em?" Gladys tossed her head, gray wavy hair floating on the light breeze. She looked over her shoulder at something on the far side of the parking lot where another group of people had gathered.

Amy followed Gladys' gaze and felt her insides cringe. Standing with the small group of people was Jon Hazelton. His wife, Bea, was standing next to him, an acidic look on her face as usual. Suddenly, the much anticipated trip to the Red Wind Mine took on a sour note.

"What is he doing here?" asked Jackson, whose gaze had apparently followed Amy's. The tone of his voice made it clear that he was relishing the opportunity for a little quality time with the councilman as much as Amy.

"Mr. Hazelton seems to think he's the mayor, even though he's just a council member, and he wants to control everything," a voice sounded from over Amy's shoulder, making her jump. She turned and saw the Pete Martin had walked up while she and Jackson were talking with Gladys and Emily. He was looking at Hazelton, scowling, although Amy had to admit to herself it was sometimes difficult to tell which expression was hidden by the facial hair. Still, his eyes looked like they were glowering, bushy eyebrows crowding low, like furry caterpillars trying to climb down into his beard, but unable reach it.

"I went to the council a month ago to ask on the behalf of the historical society for assistance in buying the Red Wind's antique mining equipment for the museum. Hazelton doesn't believe the town should have any connection with the historical society or provide any support. They'd rather waste money on those ugly new street signs that have gone up recently. Now, here he is on this field trip, even though the society has found a grant in order to buy the pieces." Pete shook his head and walked off, heavy boots kicking up dust in the gravel parking lot.

Jackson looked at Amy and gave her a crooked smile. "This trip could become more interesting than I originally thought."

"You've got that right," Amy said as she watched Pete approach the group of men and women where Hazelton was standing. He said something that Amy couldn't hear, and she saw Hazelton turn his grayish, reptilian stare on the larger man. A shiver trickled down her back. She remembered the couple of times she'd spoken with Hazelton with a feeling of distaste.

Pete stepped away from the group and walked to the center of the parking lot where he called out in his big, booming voice, "Everyone, gather around. We're getting ready to head out. Looks like everybody is here. We're going to start over on Lincoln Road, and then back onto the unnamed forest roads. I'll lead, and Ben Darby there will bring up the rear. We've got radios and will keep in contact with each other." Pete nodded over toward a short, slight man wearing Wranglers, boots and a cream straw cowboy hat. "It should take us about forty minutes to get there. You'll pay your entry fee to Salina Mattheson when we arrive at the mine."

"What are we paying for?" A deep, gravelly voice came out from a cluster of people on the other side of Pete. Amy examined the group, looking for the speaker, unfamiliar with the voice.

A thin, balding man dressed in jeans, black T-shirt and hiking boots stepped out of the cluster of people and Amy's eyes widened in surprise. While she didn't know the man, he could have been Hazelton's brother based on his looks. She felt an instant twinge of dislike, which she squashed down firmly. Just because the guy had the bad luck to look like Hazelton didn't mean he had the same winning personality... she hoped.

Pete frowned and looked at the man. "I don't believe we've met before, Mr. um..."

"Dave Shaw. I just moved to Copper Springs, out at the old Linton place on Pipe Wash Road. I heard about the rock club and the field trip at the diner and thought I'd tag along, you know. Meet some new people and make some new friends."

"Well, Mr. Shaw, it's nice to meet you. Normally, it's only club members on these trips, but this one is special, including the Copper Springs Historical Society as well.

I'd guess it would be okay if you came along, presuming you'll become a member and pay your dues to either the historical society or the rock club, of course."

"Absolutely," Shaw said and nodded, an amenable smile spreading across his face. "I'd be happy to become a member and pay my dues to either of those organizations. In fact, if there's someone here who can collect the money, I'll do it now." He started fishing in the back pocket of his worn jeans, pulled out a worn leather wallet and opened it. Amy's violet eyes widened in surprise as she saw him casually displaying what looked to be a large sum of money. She looked at Jackson and saw he hadn't missed the display either.

"Ostentatious fella, isn't he?" Jackson murmured in her ear, making her choke back a spurt of laughter. What was Shaw thinking to bring that much money on a trip like this? It didn't make any sense. They were visiting a mine in the middle of nowhere, after all, not a big shopping center.

To Amy's surprise, Emily Jameson stepped forward. "I'm the treasurer for both groups," She said in her soft voice. "I can take your dues now, but we'll have to get you to fill out your membership application at the first meeting you attend for whichever club you choose."

"I'd be happy to oblige. What are the dues?" He started thumbing through the bills in his wallet, causing a stir among some of the people standing next to him. Amy caught a few frowns and a number of looks of amusement or astonishment flash between the others gathered for the trip.

"It is twenty-five dollars for an individual membership. I'm afraid that I don't have my receipt book with me, but I can write something out if you'd like."

"Nah, don't worry about it," He said with a smile. "I can get the receipt when I fill out the membership application. All these good people will vouch that I paid if you forget." Shaw pulled several notes from the wallet and handed them over to Emily, who stood holding them between two fingers with a questioning look.

"If you're sure?"

"Absolutely. Now, as I was asking earlier... what does the field trip fee go toward?"

"We'll be getting a tour of the works, and the opportunity to do a little searching through the various overburden piles, or spoils. I checked them out earlier in the week and there are some pretty good specimens to be found. Ms. Mattheson has promised that everyone will come away with a good sample of Red Wind wulfenite. Those of us representing the Copper Springs Historical Society will also be looking at some of the pieces of antique mining equipment which the Matthesons are interested in selling. We've got a grant to make the purchase if we agree that these pieces would be a good addition to the museum. We'll be discussing what we want to do at the meeting next week, so ask all the questions you can think of today."

Murmuring and smiles went around the circle, and Amy could feel the level of excitement increase. Several people started to split off, and walk back toward their vehicles. Amy looked at Jackson.

"You ready for some rough roads?"

"You mean we haven't gone down some rough roads already?" Jackson laughed. "After our last off-road experience, I'll trust your driving anywhere. I might even take a nap."

"Oh, you don't want to do that! You'll want to see all the landscape!" Gladys exclaimed, not realizing that Jackson was joking. She hadn't been there when murderer Scott Branson ran Amy and Jackson off the road as the two of them were driving to her parents' house several weeks before. Amy had barely avoided rolling the jeep, and it still bore the white scratches, commonly called Arizona pinstriping, caused by crashing through the brush on the way down the hill.

Jackson grinned at the older lady. "Don't worry, Gladys. I'll be wide awake for the whole trip. My camera equipment is in the back, and I'll be scouting for some new spots to photograph."

Amy could hear the same excitement in Jackson's voice as he talked about his photography, that she usually heard in Nick's when he discussed his favorite types of rocks and minerals. She guessed she was probably the same way, come to think of it.

"Okay, Ansel Adams, let's load up and head out. We'll see you at the mine, ladies," Amy joked, as she turned and walked toward the green Jeep Wrangler. Her goal was to be as close to the front of the line of vehicles as possible, considering the amount of dust that was stirred up on these small dirt roads. She knew the old saying that you had to eat a peck of dirt before you died, but she would prefer it didn't come all at once.

"Ansel Adams, huh?" Jackson said, following her closely as Gladys and Emily headed for their own vehicle. "You think I'm that good, huh?" Amy picked up a smug note in his voice.

"Just get in the jeep."

"But..."

Amy looked back at Jackson and nearly ran into Jon Hazelton as he stepped in front of her, on his way to his silver-gray SUV. She stopped short.

"Uh, excuse me, Mr. Hazelton. I wasn't paying attention to where I was going."

Hazelton glanced at Amy. "It's fine, Ms. Stone. No harm done. It looks as though it's going to be a good trip today, don't you think?"

Amy was shocked at the congenial tone in Hazelton's voice. Her past experiences with the man, when he was trying to force her father to sell the rock shop, hadn't been very pleasant. Hazelton's voice still held a faint patronizing note of condescension that made Amy's fists clench, but his words were perfectly cordial, if not exactly friendly. She glanced over at Jackson who had walked up beside her and was studying Hazelton. She could see he picked up the same underlying note of disdain in Hazelton's voice and didn't appreciate it.

"How's it going, Hazelton? Drive anyone out of

business lately?" Jackson spoke in a bland, conversational voice.

Hazelton's head whipped around so violently that Amy was afraid his scrawny neck would snap in half. His heavily lidded eyes narrowed and his muppet-mouth turned down at the corners even more. All his previous congeniality vanished and the original Jon Hazelton that everyone knew and detested, emerged written as clearly on his face as if it had been printed in ink.

"Listen here, Mr.... ah... Wolf, is it? You have a right to your own opinions about my actions, but it's obvious that the voters of Copper Springs don't agree with your assessment."

"I..., *oomph*!" Jackson started to answer, then grunted when Amy elbowed him in the ribs, narrowly missing the sling which supported his left arm.

"I'm sorry, Mr. Hazelton," Amy said stiffly. "I'm sure it's going to be a great day. I wasn't aware that you were interested in either mining or mining history."

"I'm always interested in anything that impacts the town," Hazelton said smugly. "Now it looks as though most people are ready to head out. I suppose we ought to get to our vehicles." Hazelton nodded briefly to Amy and Jackson and walked over to his vehicle, where Bea waited, face pinched in annoyance.

"Come on, you," Amy growled at Jackson as the two of them continued on to the jeep. Sliding in behind the steering wheel, she looked at him. "Why did you have to bait Hazelton? You know he'd still like to put Stone's Gems and Minerals out of business and take the store, right? There's no point in antagonizing him any more than necessary. Besides, we've got to spend the day with him."

"Yeah, I know. It's just that there's something about him that makes me want to see if I can set him off. You know, sort of like poking the flap on a mousetrap to see if you can get your finger out before it snaps closed?" Jackson climbed awkwardly into the passenger side, the sling keeping his left arm next to his side. He started to pull his hand free, then caught Amy's look and slid it back into place. Once in his seat, he reached for the safety harness, twisting his right arm awkwardly, a look of concentration on his face.

Amy gave Jackson a startled look. "That's a thing?" Her voice was incredulous.

"It was in middle school when we were building mousetrap race cars for the Science Olympiad," Jackson said with complacency. He finally snagged the buckle of the seat belt, pulled it over his lap and clicked it into place. He glanced at Amy, and as she started to open her mouth he said, "Yeah, I know, I know, there's something wrong with me. You and my sister should get matching T-shirts." He settled back into the passenger seat and made a flapping *move on* wave with his right hand.

Amy started the jeep and pulled out, ready to follow Pete. "It doesn't seem like setting off either of the Hazeltons would be much of a challenge, and it might cause them to retaliate." A frown creased her forehead as the caravan began heading out of Copper Springs, aiming the jeep toward the network of dirt tracks that would take them to the Red Wind Mine. "We're having enough trouble with the town council already. Maybe you should back off a bit before your finger gets caught in that mousetrap."

"One of those common sense things?" Jackson asked.

"Maybe for now." Amy nodded, as she navigated a large hole in the trail left behind by the removal of the boulder which currently perched at the side of the road. She tried to make sure that she was far enough behind Pete that she wasn't swallowing too much dust. The vinyl top of the jeep allowed plenty of air through, and at the moment that air was choked with Arizona's finest. "Of course, next year we can run you for town council, and when you win, you can poke the bear as much as you want."

"Deal!" Jackson said, grinning.

The drive out to the Red Wind took approximately forty-five minutes, and as the time passed Amy relaxed into motion of the jeep over the rough road. She hadn't been out in this direction for many years and had never been to the Red Wind. As they drove, she felt the familiar thrill of excitement at seeing territory that she'd never seen before. Jackson sat in the other seat, studying the landscape, occasionally making a comment about some interesting landmark, but otherwise traveling in silence. Amy could picture him mentally photographing everything they passed.

They had just rounded a pile of yellowing boulders, stacking in a seemingly impossible formation, when Jackson tapped her right arm. She looked over at him with a question, then gave him a black look as she noticed his left hand out of the sling once again.

"Put your arm...," she started.

"Look up there." Jackson gestured with his chin. "Who's that?"

Amy slowed the jeep down to a crawl, and then a stop, and leaned forward, turning her head to look out of the windshield in the direction that Jackson had indicated. It took her a moment, then a glint of sunlight flashing off a reflective surface caught her eye. A small, stick-like man was standing on the gentle slope on the right of the road. They were close enough to see the man's stubbled face and unkempt hair, blowing in the light breeze. He was dressed in battered army green and carried a rifle over his shoulder. Next to him was an equally battered red ATV. He stood without moving, next to a boulder, looking down on the jeep. That intent gaze made Amy's skin crawl, and she started the jeep into motion once again.

"That's Ol' Tom," she said, in answer to Jackson's question. She realized her voice was at almost a whisper as if she were afraid of the old man hearing her. She released the brake and started the Wrangler moving forward once again.

Jackson turned to watch as they went by the man who stood above them never moving, just watching them with that intense stare. Jackson lifted his right hand in a wave, smiled and nodded his head while saying "And who is 'Ol' Tom'?" out of the corner of his mouth.

Amy shrugged, eyes fixed on the road ahead, and soon they had rounded another curve in the road, and the battered sentry was out of sight. Tension she hadn't realized existed melted from her shoulders, and she took a deep breath.

"According to my Dad, Ol' Tom showed up in town back in the seventies. No one really knows much about him. He doesn't like people much and only comes into town when he needs supplies."

"Where's he live?" Jackson asked craning his neck to look back at the road, even though the man was no longer in sight."

"Somewhere on the forest land, or over the border onto the Hualapai Reservation. Maybe in an abandoned mine somewhere. Dad talked to him a few times when he'd come into town. He does some prospecting and he occasionally brings the gold or some interesting mineral specimens for Dad to buy. I've heard he will sometimes do odd jobs to make money, but no one knows much about him. He creeps me out a bit, to be honest," Amy laughed self-consciously and glanced over at Jackson.

After a few more questions which Amy couldn't answer, Jackson fell silent once again, studying the landscape as it bounced past.

It wasn't much longer before Amy and Jackson pulled up behind Pete's old battered jeep hardtop stopped in front of a large, rusted metal pipe gate, where a bullet hole-pocked sign hung proclaiming them to be at the "Red Wind Mine, NO TRESPASSING."

Pete was climbing out of the jeep. He walked to the gate and unhooked the chain holding the heavy pipe structure closed. He gave Amy the thumbs up as another vehicle drew up behind her and came to a stop. She waved in return. He nodded to her, climbed back into his old dusty white jeep, and continued on up the road.

Amy steered her Wrangler after him, following the two-rut track down into a sand wash, then diagonally up a rock-strewn slope and back down into a small valley on the other side where she could see several old metal buildings and the two-stamp mill. Another large sandy wash ran down the center of this fold in the earth, meandering out of sight between two large rock outcroppings at the foot of the valley. Several large spoils piles were scattered around the area, and she could see others up on the steep hillsides overlooking the valley. In spite of the evidence of mining activity, Amy couldn't pinpoint the entrance to the mine itself, and she found herself examining the hillsides, eager to see what condition the portal was in. From the sound of it, the Matthesons were new to mining, and the mine had been abandoned for more than thirty years prior to their moving to the claim. She told herself that Pete had been helping them and that he'd have never allowed them to enter an unsafe mine, but there was a small, niggling feeling of anxiety that the new mine owners wouldn't recognize a potential danger.

Within seconds Amy pulled up next to Pete in a wide open area. She slid out of the driver's seat, stretching after the ride over the rough roads. Jackson, climbing out of the other side, groaned and arched his back. Amy started to walk over to Pete as the rest of the vehicles started pulling up behind her.

One of the men Amy didn't recognize climbed out of a blue 4x4 pickup and called, "Hey Pete, did you see Ol' Tom back there on the side of the road givin' us the stink eye? I haven't heard anything about him for a while. I figured he was dead."

"Yeah, I saw him," Pete replied, chuckling. "He probably isn't very happy to see our group trouping through his land. He doesn't like the recent push to bring tourists to the area – says they pollute the place and they should stay in the cities where they belong. Still, there's no harm in him." Pete turned and looked up toward the cluster of tin building on the far side of the parking area.

"Now, I wonder where the Matthesons are. They must have heard us drive in."

He paused for a moment, scanning the area. Then his eye sharpened as he saw a tall, dark-haired woman walk out from behind the building that the sisters appeared to be using for a house. He lifted his arm and waved, and the woman started to make her way down a small slope and toward the visitors, a serious look on her face. If Amy hadn't known better, she would have thought that the group was trespassing, and were about to be kicked out on their collective butts.

When the woman got close enough, she called out, "Hi, Pete. I'm glad you made it. How many are with you?" She craned her neck, looking over toward where the road came over the hill.

"We've got about twenty-five people with us today. I told them to pay you when they got here."

Salina nodded then turned to look at Amy. Most of the other members of the club had parked and were getting out and stretching. Several were walking over toward where Amy and Jackson stood with Pete and Salina, smiling and joking with each other about the condition of the road. Amy studied Salina's face, confused by the somberness of her expression. Everything about her body language said she didn't want people there, and Amy began to wonder what made the Mattheson sisters invite the rock club and historical society in the first place.

Amy glanced over at Jackson, who shrugged and rolled his eyes. Amy turned back to Salina. "Hi, Salina. I'm Amy Stone, and this is Jackson Wolf. My dad, Nick Stone, owns Stone's Gems and Minerals in Copper Springs.

Salina nodded and gave Amy a small tight smile, holding out her hand. "I'm glad to meet you, Amy. Jackson, I'm happy to meet you as well. My sister Jania should be up here shortly. She went down in the mine this morning. She just found a new fracture with a lot of spectacular wulfenite specimens yesterday and was hoping to collect a few more before everyone got here this morning."

"That's wonderful," Amy said enthusiastically. "I'm told that the wulfenite that you're finding is equivalent to the Red Cloud and some of the other better-known mines in southern Arizona."

"That's what I'm told as well," Salina said as she gave Amy a slight smile. "My sister and I are learning a lot. We just came out looking for gold and silver, but Jania saw these beautiful crystals and started collecting them. It was Pete who told us that they might be worth something." Salina looked toward Pete with a more genuine smile on her face. "Pete said that we should talk to you or your dad at the rock shop and that you can possibly help us sell some of the specimens that we're bringing out."

"We'd be happy to look at anything you have and Jackson here can give you information on setting up online auctions and maybe a website. Right, Jackson?" Amy turned to look at Jackson, only to find that he'd wandered off toward one of the spoils piles and was studying the ground intently. The rest of the crew had pulled in and were making their way over to Pete.

"Hey, ya'll, come on over. This is Salina Mattheson, one of the owners of the Red Wind, and our host for the day. I've got a list of everyone on the group, and as you pay your entry fee, I'll check you off." Pete pulled a folded piece of paper from the front pocket of his shirt and fished in a back pocket for a short pencil stub. Since Amy was already standing next to Salina, she pulled her twenty-five dollars from her pocket and handed it over.

"Hey, Jackson," She called. When he looked up, she waved him back over. "Come on and pay your bill."

Jackson made his way back over to the group and held out his money. Salina added it to the growing pile in her hand and nodded a thank you. Once everyone had paid and was gathered around, Salina started to talk even though it was obvious that she was uncomfortable under the scrutiny of the crowd.

"Hello everyone. I'm pleased that you were able to come out. The Red Wind was started many years ago, as you can see from all the overburden. You are more than welcome to hunt through any of the piles for specimens and in a little bit we'll take you on a tour of the mine itself."

"Don't forget the antique mining equipment," Pete said, chuckling. "Not everyone here is a rockhound..." His eyes passed over the surrounding group and came to rest on the Dave Shaw. A small frown flitted across his face "... or rockhead." His voice took on a wry note, although Amy was pretty sure that their new addition to the community missed the distinction between those who were knowledgeable about the minerals and rocks they were collecting, and those who picked up anything sparkly, regardless of worth. Amy bit the inside of her cheek to keep from laughing. Shaw had certainly gotten on Pete's bad side.

"Don't worry, Pete," Salina said with a smile which seemed much more genuine than the ones that had earlier graced her face. "I'm not forgetting the equipment. In fact, I'm hoping selling it is going to keep us going until the mine is more profitable." Worry lurked in Salina's eyes, and Amy wondered what had inspired the Mattheson sisters to buy an old abandoned mine in the middle of nowhere, especially if money was hard to come by. It did answer the question of why the Matthesons allowed a bunch of strangers to trespass on their privacy, however.

Salina continued, raising her voice so that everyone could hear, "As some of you know, the Red Wind was first mined back in 1907 by Derik Hanson. He was prospecting for gold and came across a relatively rich placer deposit in the wash over to the left. He staked a claim and then later purchased the twenty acres. He felt that the surface gold was the tip of the iceberg, so to speak, and also began to mine into this hill. Hanson and his sons continued to lode mine after the placer deposit was depleted, but they never brought out much. Eventually, he sold the mine to the ANM Mining Company which felt that with more equipment and manpower, they would be able to make the underground mine start to pay off. At that time the name was changed to the Lonely Lady, supposedly because the mine foreman's wife found living on the property too remote and went a little crazy with the loneliness." Salina shrugged and gestured around at the empty hills surrounding her. Amy would have to agree that the mine property was certainly remote, and back in the early 1900s residents of the property would be even more isolated than the Mattheson sisters were now.

Salina continued on, describing the mine's transformation from the Lonely Lady to the Deep Wash as another placer deposit was discovered, then to the Cross Point when William Powell took ownership, and finally its abandonment in the 1980s. Amy's mind wandered as she studied some of the rock formations nearby, as well as the faces of the members of the field trip. Some of them were avidly listening to Mattheson, as she described the history of the mine, while others, including the Hazeltons and Dave Shaw, seemed bored and eager for the lecture to be over.

As Salina finished talking, a flicker of movement off to the left caught Amy's eye and she turned her head looking for the source. Another woman walked out from behind a large pile of rocks. This one was as blonde as Salina was dark, and tall and slender where Salina was sturdy, although the baggy black shirt and jeans made her frame take on greater bulk. Still, the shape of the face told Amy that this was the missing Jania Mattheson, Salina's sister. The blonde woman walked up to the group.

"Finally," Salina said, her voice revealing her relief. "I was afraid that you'd gotten lost down there."

Jania gave Salina a dreamy smile. "I could never get lost in the mine, Salina. You know that."

Salina snorted, "Yeah, right. Well, you're up here now. In about fifteen or twenty minutes, do you want to take a group down to tour your hole in the ground?"

Amy felt a slight shiver go through her body at the way Salina pronounced the words *hole in the ground* and she looked quickly at Jackson. His eyes met hers and she knew he was thinking about the same thing. It wasn't long ago that the Copper Springs code enforcement officer had told both she and Jackson that their next stop was a very deep hole. Amy considered it a miracle that the two of them hadn't wound up at the bottom of that hole but instead had been rescued by Mohave County deputies Kissoon and Arlen.

She'd thought that she was over that incident, and in fact had been back down in the Pipe Wash and Skystone mines with Jackson, walking the authorities through that evening's events. Something about the way Salina said hole in the ground, however, triggered fresh tremors.

Jania felt none of the discomfort that assailed Amy and Jackson based on the smile that lit her face at the mention of taking visitors into the mine.

"Absolutely." Jania nodded. "Just say when."

"You think we should take twelve people at a time, rather than the entire group? The others can hunt on the overburden or in the wash."

"That works," Jania said. Listening to her, Amy wondered if anything ever disturbed Jania's peaceful demeanor. Salina was very different, in Amy's opinion – sharp-edged and prickly compared to Jania's silk smooth personality. It was amazing that they were related at all, let alone sisters.

Salina looked back at the group and raised her voice so that everyone could hear. "If everyone would split into two groups, Jania, my sister, will take you on a tour of the mine one group at a time. While one set of people is underground, the rest of you can feel free to hunt through the spoils piles. I can tell you we've found some beautiful pieces of window pane wulfenite that were discarded by earlier miners. We've also found some good samples of botryoidal smithsonite. The bubble shapes have been very pronounced."

The group split apart, and for the next hour or more, the spoils piles around the mine, as well as the mine itself were ant hills of activity. Amy and Jackson went with the first group down into the subterranean passageways. Jania was a good tour guide, stopping at key spots and showing the visitors many of the characteristics of the old mine. In Amy's opinion, Jania understood well the differences between the older adit, drives and shafts, and the newer workings, and her audience was attentive, asking thoughtful questions.

According to Jania, the original Gold Doll Mine had been a pretty simple affair, with a horizontal adit, or tunnel, running straight into the side of the hill, then sloping down to follow a seam of mineral, with several small stopes, or pockets of ore, that had been dug out and removed. Occasional larger stopes and been mined out and propped up with timbers. The old tunnels were narrow, and Amy trailed her fingers over the tool marks left by original miners while carving out the hillside. Her headlamp, and those of the people with her, lit up the red-brown of the rock, occasionally slashed with strips of quartz or other minerals. Several places the surrounding rock turned from red-brown to grayish-white, then back again to the red-brown with streaks of yellow.

After a short distance down the main drive, other tunnels and shafts started branching off to the left or right. Several appeared to be clear, and safe, although at least one of the drives was filled in by a large rock fall. Jania explained that as later miners took over, they explored different areas of the mountainside, or were looking for different minerals altogether. Ultimately, the area had become a veritable honeycomb of tunnels, shafts and stopes. Some were in better, or worse condition, depending on the type of host rock the mine ran through.

Several times, Jania stopped and pointed out a fracture in the rock, or other irregularities, and Amy could make out several vugs, or pockets, with crystals of wulfenite or other mineral specimens which had not yet been disturbed.

"Oh! Look," Gladys gasped, as she peered at a particularly large, crystal lined pocket in the side of the mine wall. Several large window panes of bright red wulfenite glinted in the harsh light of the headlamps. "Why haven't you mined out specimens like this one?"

Jania came back and looked at the fracture, and the few vugs surrounding it. "I'm just learning right now. From what I understand, that is a valuable piece, and I want to practice on ones that are easier to get out first. It would be terrible if I chipped this one."

Gladys nodded since even a single small chip could greatly diminish a specimen's value. She turned and followed Jania as she moved on down the shaft leading the group deeper into the hillside. Before they rounded the next turn, however, Amy saw Gladys look back toward the area where the large crystals were located, and she swore that she could see longing in the older woman's eyes. Longing or lust... it was hard to tell the difference in some rockhounds. She choked back a laugh and looked up to see Jackson watching her with a grin on his face.

He moved closer and in a harsh, raspy voice whispered in her ear... "It's mine... my precious..." and the trapped laugh blew out of Amy in a gust before she could choke it back down. Jackson's mimicking of Gollum from *The Hobbit* was too perfectly in line with what she'd been thinking about Gladys' gaze of longing. She tried to control the laughter and ended up in a coughing fit. Gladys turned around and gazed at Amy with concerned eyes.

"Are you all right dear?"

"Uh, yeah," Amy said, eyes watering. She glanced at Jackson and saw he was hunched over, rubbing his hands together, with an entirely Gollum-like leer on his face, and the laughter nearly bubbled over again. She resolutely turned her back on him and faced the older woman, "I'm fine, Gladys. I guess there's a bit of dust in the air. Come on, we'd better catch up with the group."

Gladys turned and headed down the tunnel after the others. Moving a little more slowly, Amy and Jackson followed her to rejoin the group. From up ahead Amy could dimly hear the whining voice of Bea Hazelton, complaining about the conditions of the mine and her husband telling her to be quiet. Amy sighed.

"Think we could get lucky enough to get a cave in?" She whispered to Jackson.

"Nah. Although the vibrations from her voice ought to knock loose a few rocks." He peered at the low ceiling of the tunnel they were walking down. "Besides, I doubt that a cave in could quiet her... it would just give her something new to complain about. *'Jon, that rock messed up my hair. I think we should sue!'*" Jackson's whiny falsetto was so on the mark that it sent shivers down Amy's back.

"Yeah, I guess you're right. It's a miracle her voice isn't cracking all the wulfenite crystals in the mine." Amy dropped the topic as they caught up to where the group was standing, looking at an old ore chute which was protruding from the upper left side of the tunnel.

The aged wood had the number one marked on it, and a rickety ladder led up into an empty black space above. Jania was explaining that during the Lonely Lady period of the mine, greater effort had been put into the removal of silver and lead. Tracks had been laid down for ore carts, and several ore chutes like the one they were looking at had been used to bring rock down from upper stopes. Amy peered up the hollow interior of the U-shaped chute, but it was clogged with waste rock and she couldn't see into the stope beyond.

"I've been up the ladder," Jania was saying to the group, "but there's nothing up there of interest to us. All the valuable ores were removed from that stope back in the early to mid-1900s, and some of the timbers or stulls holding up the stope are in pretty bad shape"

"Don't suppose you've seen any sign of old man Powell in any of the nooks and crannies of this mine have you?" someone asked.

Amy couldn't identify the speaker from the group, other than it was a man. She was still adjusting to being back in Copper Springs and renewing her acquaintances with many of the old-time residents, as well as getting to know many new arrivals. Besides, voices sounded strange in the close confines of the mines.

A frown crossed Jania's normally peaceful face, surprising Amy.

"My understanding is that Mr. Powell probably took off on his own and abandoned the mine. Neither Salina, nor I, have seen anything of him left around here, except for the equipment, of course." Her voice was clipped, a marked difference from her smooth, silky tones.

Ending that topic of conversation abruptly, Jania turned and led the group off into some side tunnels where they could see a fracture which showed signs of being mined recently. Jania explained that she'd seen the crack, and noticed that it seemed to be lined with small crystals. Upon opening it up, she found a large pocket, or vug, lined with much larger wulfenite window panes, as well as some mimetite and smithsonite from what Amy could see, the yellow and aqua coloring standing out against the red-orange of the wulfenite.

The sight of this fracture effectively ended all discussion of the missing Mr. Powell and focused everyone back on the treasures that could be found in the depths of the Red Wind Mine.

The mine tour lasted close to an hour, and as Amy made her way out of the claustrophobic environment of the narrow passageways she shielded her eyes against the bright sunlight. The rapidly warming air outside was a welcome change after the cooler air of the mine and she shivered slightly with the change in temperature. Looking around she saw the others of the group doing the same.

Pete let out a yell, and the members of the second group started to clamber off the piles of overburden, and made their way over to the portal of the mine, while those people who'd already been down into the subterranean world made their way to their vehicles for water, or headed out for their turns on the various spoils piles, in a hunt for specimens that may have been discarded years ago when the miners were solely interested in gold, silver and lead. At that time the bright red crystals were of interest, but not really seen as valuable and many were discarded with the rest of the waste rock.

As Amy was pulling over a large boulder, she glanced up and saw Salina Mattheson come walking by. She stopped as the rock Amy was moving finally let loose and rolled down the pile, landing just in front of her feet. She looked up at Amy and gave her a small smile.

"I'm so sorry, Salina," Amy gasped, out of breath at the effort it had taken to move the large stone. "I didn't expect it to let go like that. It must have rolled off the hillside and onto the spoils pile." Amy wiped her forehead with her sleeve. Her dark curly hair was matted to her head, making it itch.

"Don't worry... ah Amy, right?" Salina shielded her eyes and looked up at the hill that rose above that particular spoils pile. "You're probably right about where the rock came from. It wouldn't have been carried out of the mine that size. Besides, it's got a fair amount of desert varnish, she said, referring to the yellow-brown patina covering what had been the upper surface of the boulder. "Was there anything underneath worth looking at?"

Amy stared down at her feet, looking for the flash of red she'd seen when looking around the boulder originally. Ah, there it was. Amy stooped and picked up a three-inch piece of matrix, on which twenty or thirty bright red crystals sprouted. "Yes, here's a pretty good piece. Several other rocks protected it from the weight of the larger rock, although there are a few broken or chipped crystals," she said and held it up for Salina to see.

"Will it matter a great deal if some of the crystals are chipped?" Salina asked as she started to make her way up the spoils pile to examine the specimen more closely.

Amy was surprised since Jania had clearly understood the difference. Still, the blonde sister seemed to be the miner of the family.

"Yes, it matters quite a bit to collectors. They want perfect crystals, and large ones are obviously better than small ones. This piece is pretty good, however. Only a few appear to be broken, and it's very translucent, or gemy, with great color." She handed the piece over to Salina, who examined it carefully, then handed it back to Amy, who wrapped it carefully in some tissue and stored it in a square sandwich box which she then tucked into her pack.

Amy stood looking at the surrounding hillsides, noting the gray-green swaths of loose rock cascading down the slopes, marking the positions of various other shafts or test holes. Most of the rock club members were focusing on those piles down near the mine portal, but she'd noticed earlier that there were other piles much farther uphill. She looked for Jackson and saw that he was on the far side of the wash, inspecting an interesting outcropping of rock.

"Why are there so many piles of overburden so far from the mine?" Amy asked, looking back at Salina who was following her gaze.

"There are a number of other shafts around the property. None of them as big as the main mine, and some of them seem to be test holes," Salina replied as she also examined the hillsides, following Amy's lead.

Suddenly, to Amy's surprise, a huge grin split Salina's normally somber face. "I'll be honest, this place reminds me of a prairie dog town, with holes dug everywhere. I keep expecting miner heads to start popping up and down, like a god sized version of 'wackamole'."

Amy laughed at the image. "'Wackaminer.' Do any of them connect to the main mine... an open stope or something like that?"

"I don't really know. Jania and I have spent most of our time down here, and haven't bothered much with those upper layers." Salina looked at Amy, the serious expression returning to her face. "The entire property is twenty acres, and from what I'm told, there are shafts hidden all over. I guess some of them could connect. We haven't mapped all the passageways of the Red Wind yet and there are some old tunnels blocked from collapses in the past. If those areas up there are abandoned, it was probably because there was nothing there worthwhile, and it was too much of a pain to fill in the holes, right?"

Amy nodded. She was familiar with many of the mining areas of Arizona, which was arguably one of the most mined states in the nation. One had to be careful whenever out in the backlands because abandoned mine shafts and open stopes could be anywhere, and there was no law mandating that they be marked. There were multiple stories of horseback riders, ATV riders or hikers falling into hidden shafts, and not being found until much later. The rule of thumb when going through the Arizona wilderness was never to put your feet, your horse's feet, or your ATV where you couldn't see the ground in front of you. Of course, there were also those who eagerly sought out abandoned mines with the sole intention of exploring the subterranean realms. Some made it out, other's didn't.

A commotion from the entrance to the mine drew Amy's attention, and when she looked over, she saw the second group emerging, blinking and shading their eyes, much the same way she had done not long before. Pete had apparently also noticed the others' emergence from the netherworld, and started to walk over, hailing the rest of the members of the field trip and waving them over.

"Hey, all! Before we have some lunch, those of us in the historical society, and of course any rockhounds who are interested, are going to take a look at some of the equipment that the Matthesons are thinking of selling. If you're not interested in looking at rusty pieces of metal and old wood, of course, feel free to keep hunting for the perfect rock." Pete chuckled as he, Salina and Jania headed off toward the stamp mill closely followed by most of the members of the field trip.

It was only about a hundred yards from the mine itself to the where the stamp mill stood on a flat area to the right of the wash. A small cluster of old buildings bordered the area, one of which the Matthesons were obviously using as their home. Several other old pieces of mining equipment stood nearby: a broken ore cart, something that appeared to be an old sluice box, as well as a scattering of rusted cogs and other pieces of machinery.

When the group reached the stamp mill in question, they came to a stop as one and stood looking at the tall piece of equipment, momentarily silent. Finally, Pete stepped forward and started walking around the stamp mill, reached out and fingered the shafts. He examined the wooden chute leading down to the stamps. Seemingly satisfied, Pete looked back at the group and grinned at Salina.

"It's in really great shape." He said and gestured up toward the flywheel. "You can see how Powell converted it to run on the gasoline motor, but other than that everything looks original. I'd bet we could get it working again if we wanted to."

"How exactly does it work," David Shaw's voice came from the back of the group. This time, instead of being irritated, Pete welcomed the invitation to talk about one of his passions.

"Well, this is a two stamp mill. You can see that there are two shafts. At the bottom are heavy metal 'shoes' which are what crush the rock." Pete pointed at the large blocks of iron rest on the base of the chute.

"Up above," he continued, indicating another part of the stamp mill, "that horizontal shaft you see turns, rotating the cams, which in turn push up on the tappets. Those are the large metal pieces that are attached to each shaft. That movement causes the shaft to rise about three to four inches and then drop. These ones probably weigh around five-hundred pounds or so, although many go up to a thousand. Ideally, when they fall, they crush the rock into small pieces, starting at two to three inches, and breaking it down to around to less than a quarter of an inch. At that size, it's easy to get the gold out, although we no longer use the mercury that was used back when the mill was first built in the early 1900s."

"What exactly are the Matthesons asking for this gigantic chunk of rusty iron?" Hazelton's equally rusty voice emerged from the audience. He advanced, his lizard eyes hidden behind some oversized sunglasses, which, in Amy's opinion did little for his overall appearance. She looked around, but couldn't see Bea anywhere. That surprised her, as she couldn't imagine the woman being so fascinated with rock hunting that she would have stayed searching for wulfenite on the overburden.

"What does it matter to you, Mr. Hazelton?" Pete spoke sharply, his irritation clear in his tone, and in the chopping movement of his hands. "The town council made it clear that they had no intention of backing the museum, and the Arizona Mining Foundation has awarded us a grant to purchase and restore the stamp mill and any other equipment, should we be able to negotiate an appropriate price."

"I'm here to make sure that the society doesn't make any decisions which will end up becoming a liability for the town. Considering the drain that the historical society has been on the town's finances in order to rent the old Mohave National Bank building and keep up on the maintenance, I'm not sure it should be taking on any additional expenses, grant or no grant."

Pete's face had turned as red as an Arizona sunset, and Amy worried about his blood pressure. Silence had fallen over the crowd for a moment, as what had started as a fun outing looked like it was taking a turn into stormy waters. Amy looked around the group and noticed frowning faces, and feet shuffling in the rocky soil. Salina Mattheson didn't appear to know what to do about the conflict and Jania was nowhere to be seen. She must have slipped away while Salina was talking.

"When was the last time it was used?" A voice from beside Amy broke the silence. Jackson stepped forward, a curious look on his face as he approached the stamp mill, and rested his hand on one of the shoes. A little of the tension went out of the air. The remainder of the group started to approach the mill as well, some of them moving over to examine some of the other pieces of equipment that were scattered around the flat area.

Salina glanced at Pete, then raised her voice to be heard over others in the group who had started talking among themselves. The conversations quieted quickly. "We were told that William Powell bought the old stamp mill shortly after he purchased the mine. He was able to get it running on a gasoline-powered engine, and I'm told that he used it often before his disappearance. Jania and I haven't used it since we got here because we haven't been able to get the engine started. Since we're now focusing on other minerals that don't require us to break down the ore, we thought it might be better off preserved in a museum."

Amy remembered Salina's comment about the income from the equipment getting she and her sister through and was sure there was some other motive behind Salina's words. She wasn't quite able to pick up on what it was, however. Several of the others nodded, smiling. It made sense to them. On the other hand, Amy could see Hazelton heading in Pete's direction, anger clear on his face. From Pete's stance, Amy was afraid a war was about to ensue. Amy started in their direction, then stopped as several other men claimed Pete's attention, pulling it away from Hazelton. Jon stopped, then turned and stomped off toward the group of people still gathered around the stamp mill. They looked uncomfortable at the councilman's approach and Amy could understand why.

Gradually, the group broke up as people wandered off to look at the various pieces of antique equipment that had collected over the years.

Amy looked at Jackson who was examining a large single cam sitting over by an even larger rock. "What do you think? Should the museum buy the stamp mill?" She looked at the huge piece of iron. Hazelton had a point when he called it a large, rusty piece of metal. Getting it over the rough road and back to town wouldn't be cheap. And neither would the renovations. Amy wondered briefly if the grant included those expenses or was it just for the purchase of the mill itself.

Jackson walked around the mill as he studied the tall shafts with their tappets, those bulges which the cams pushed on to raise the stamp a few inches every time they spun around, then letting them drop as cams continued around the camshaft. Amy could see Salina standing over toward the tin building that the Matthesons were using as their headquarters, while Jania was still missing in action. Amy wondered briefly if she'd escaped back to her "hole in the ground" as Salina called the mine.

"I don't know much about stamp mills, but it's pretty impressive." Jackson gestured toward the old electric motor sticking on a welded tray out behind the flywheel. "That thing is an eyesore, of course... sort of like a cancerous tumor stuck on the side, but I suppose it could be removed, and the mill restored to its original operating condition. It's got some great photography potential." Jackson's voice trailed off, and his eyes took on a distant look, Amy thought, almost as though his mind was working too rapidly to bother with controlling his facial muscles.

Amy pushed him lightly on his uninjured shoulder. "Hey, Jackson, come back to planet Earth. Before we leave, you can talk to Salina about coming back when the light's better, or there are clouds in the sky, or an amazing sunset is promised, or whatever else you artistic types need. Right now, let's head up to some of those spoils piles farther up the hill across the wash. Salina said there were test holes and smaller shafts all over the property, and I'll bet those ones farther away from easy parking haven't been picked over as much as these closer ones. Go grab you pack."

Jackson looked up the steep slope to where Amy was pointing. "I get it," he said, and his shoulders took on a dejected slump, although Amy could see the ever present laugh lurking in his eyes. "You just want to use me as a beast of burden. A rock packer. A litho lifter. A boulder booster. A... a..."

"Pebble pusher?" Amy said, laughing. "You've got it. Bring those powerful arms... well, arm... and strong back and follow me."

"Yes, ma'am," Jackson said and headed off with Amy, a cheerful bounce to his step.

A sudden explosion of voices, raised in anger brought her to a sudden stop and she looked around trying to determine where the noise was coming from.

The breeze that had been blowing all day died down briefly, and Amy could make out the words, "You have no right! The council has no right!" It was Pete's voice, and Amy could guess the target of his anger. Jackson nodded in the direction of the flattened area where everyone had parked. Amy had seen Hazelton heading that way and it appeared that Pete had followed.

Pete was squared off with Jon Hazelton. Even though Amy couldn't hear Hazelton's response, it was clear from his body language, that his temper was flaring as much as Pete's, and she had a momentary concern that the peaceful enjoyment of the day would be interrupted by a plain old fist fight. Considering the difference in size between Pete and Hazelton, she had no doubt who would come off the winner.

Jackson started to walk in their direction, but Amy put out a hand to stop him. She wasn't sure that this was a case of "the more the merrier." Then just as quickly as it had blown up, the argument ended. Hazelton turned and stalked away from Pete, heading toward the mine portal. Pete stood watching him, his body radiating fury, fists clenched at his side. Slowly he relaxed and stretched out his fingers. Two other men approached him, and they began talking, then turned and started to walk off up the wash from the mine.

"What do you think that was all about?" Jackson asked, watching Pete, then looking over to where Hazelton was standing next to his SUV.

"I've got no idea," Amy said, blowing out a breath. "It sounded like Hazelton is continuing to stick his nose in places where it doesn't belong. Do you think Pete deliberately followed Hazelton to continue the argument?" She paused as she watched the group of three men disappear around a curve in the wash. "Still, it's calmed down for now. Come on, our mountain awaits."

Reluctantly, Jackson took a step back, eyes still on the end of the wash where the men had been a few moments before, then turned and followed Amy, shaking his head.

"I don't know if he followed, itching for a fight," he said, "or whether they just wound up together, but it's a good thing there were others around. I think that one could have gotten a lot uglier."

The two of them were partway up the steep hillside, heading for the largest of several spoils piles when Amy began to doubt the wisdom of their quest. Sweat was trickling down her neck. Her short, curly, dark brown hair was damp and itchy. Twice, when she stumbled on loose rocks, she considered telling Jackson that they should just call it good and head back down. However, the mental image of that one perfect wulfenite window pane that they'd seen in the main mine kept flashing into her memory. No matter how much she told herself that there was no way something like that would be in any of the spoils piles, that image kept driving her forward. Besides, after glancing over and seeing Jackson practically skipping through the rocks and brush, she was determined not to let him show her up.

A scream ripped through the warm September afternoon air. Amy whipped around, searching for the source. Her foot slipped on the loose footing and her arms windmilled as she tried to catch herself. She overbalanced, and landed on her butt, narrowly missing a large cholla cactus.

A groan from her right told her that Jackson hadn't been as fortunate. When Amy lost her balance, her arm had swung out, and the canvas rock bag she'd been carrying in her hand had slammed Jackson across the face, causing him to take a step backward. A head-sized rock rolled from under his heel and he twisted as he fell, trying to avoid landing on his injured shoulder. He wasn't quite as lucky as Amy in his landing point, however, and Amy could see him wince as he pulled his right leg back, several sections of the cactus nailing his jeans to the underlying flesh of his thigh. His movement stopped abruptly and he squeezed his eyes shut. Amy could see his lips moving as his brow furrowed in concentration, but no sound came out.

The same couldn't be said for the person who'd uttered the original scream. Amy cautiously rose to her feet, trying not to dislodge any other rocks. She glanced down at Jackson but he was still lying on the ground, apparently deep in internal contemplation of his life choices. She turned back to the valley below her and tried to determine the source of the screams, but the sound bounced off so many hills that she couldn't be sure where, or who, the screamer was.

Other members of the group who had stayed in the low areas along the wash and near the portal to the main mine had also heard the noise and were looking around, apparently trying to pinpoint the sound as well. She could see them starting to gravitate toward one another, as if reassuring themselves that all was well, but they were so far from Amy and Jackson's position on the hillside that she couldn't be sure who was who, or more importantly, who was missing.

She turned back to Jackson and knelt, checking first that no additional segments of the cholla cactus were laying where she put her knees. The damned things seemed to be everywhere around the mother plants, and she'd been skewered enough times in the past to have a healthy respect for them.

"Jackson, are you all right?" Amy asked, her eyes moving over his injured shoulder in concern.

He opened his bright blue eyes and gave Amy a disgusted look. "I have about a thousand cactus spines that have driven themselves into my leg to the bone as well as being perilously close to even more sensitive areas, and you're asking me if I'm okay?"

"You have about twenty cactus spines. About an eighth of an inch into your leg, and nowhere near those more 'sensitive areas' as you're claiming, although I'm sure your story will get better and better with time. Come on, we've got to get back down the hill and find out what's going on." Amy started to push herself to her feet, relieved that Jackson hadn't reinjured his shoulder.

The screams had changed in timbre and now Amy could hear words, although, with the echoes and distortions from the hills, she couldn't quite make them out. It was a woman's voice, however. Amy looked again at where the group had gathered, but she was too far away to be able to tell if someone was missing. She saw one person point up toward them and she waved back, trying to tell them that she and Jackson were okay.

"Jackson, get up. We need to get back down there," Amy said in exasperation as she turned back toward Jackson.

"Fine. Why is Bea Hazelton carrying on anyway? She see a packrat?" Jackson's voice sounded distracted.

Amy looked at Jackson, her mouth dropping open in surprise. "How do you know it's Hazelton's wife? I can't even understand what she's saying... I can't tell anything other than it's a woman's voice."

Jackson had pushed himself into a sitting position and had started hunting through his pack. He looked up at Amy and a ghost of a smile crossed his face. "Mrs. Hazelton's dulcet tones are unmistakable, even at this distance. Mark my words, we'll get back down there, and find that Ms. Bea has seen a lizard and thinks the world is coming to an end. Ha, there they are!" He pulled a pair of needle nose pliers from his pack and started pulling out several of the spines, one at a time, wincing as each barb let go of his skin with reluctance. Small spots of blood stained the denim above the wounds.

"Give me that," Amy said, impatient to get back to the group and find out what was happening. The screams had quieted, but it was obvious that people still didn't know what was happening.

Jackson paused in his spine pulling and looked at Amy with a question in his eyes. Those blue eyes widened in surprise as Amy snatched the tool from his hand. In one seamless move, Amy slid the pliers between the segment of cactus and Jackson's jeans and closed the jaws. Jackson's eyes grew huge as he realized what Amy was about to do a moment too late.

"Wait, Amy! Stop! You can't...Yow! Oh..."

Amy had yanked upward, hard and fast, ripping all the spines from Jackson's leg in a sweeping move, throwing the offending piece of cholla cactus off to the side. Jackson was sitting, holding his leg in his good arm, rattling off a litany of curse words that would get him thrown into timeout by his sister for at least a year if she heard them. Weeks ago Jackson had told Amy that he was trying hard to watch his language because he had two young nephews who were highly impressionable, and because his sister would mete out the same consequences to him, that she would to her sons if the rules on appropriate language weren't followed. It appeared that while he was usually in control of his words, unknown depths boiled beneath the politically correct exterior.

"Come on, Jackson. It's a long way from the heart. You'll live. Let's get back down to the others." She held out a hand to pull him to his feet.

Jackson looked up with accusation in his eyes. "Did you have to do that? It feels like you've ripped off half my leg, as well as..."

"... other more sensitive areas? Come on. I know it hurts, but it's a lot better to pull them all out at once than one at a time. It hurts less."

"Yeah, that's what you think!" Jackson put out his right hand and accepted Amy's help to rise. She handed him the pliers, and the two of them headed back down the unstable footing of the hillside, moving much more quickly than they'd gone up.

At the bottom of the hill, Amy ran into Pete and most of the others heading down the wash in the direction from which the screams had emanated. Everyone had worried looks on their faces, and Amy heard several murmuring among themselves. The shrieks had ended and there had been several minutes of silence, which were almost more chilling than the screams had been. The normal sounds of the high desert had returned, the quail *chip-churring*, and the raucous scolding of the pinyon jay. A light breeze had picked up, and the yucca leaves rattled against each other.

"Pete, who was that screaming?" Amy asked, out of breath from her precipitous descent of the hill. Jackson scrambled after her, slightly delayed by his injured shoulder, as well as the pain in his leg. Glancing back at him, she noticed the staining of blood where the cactus spines had been removed and felt a momentary pang of guilt which she firmly squashed.

"We don't know, Amethyst. A few people are missing, and we think they went back down the mine, or over to the other wash to explore some spoils piles over there. They..."

Pete was interrupted in what he was going to say when Bea Hazelton came staggering out from behind the rock outcropping that marked the end of the small valley. Struggling to run in the sandy bed of the wash, she tripped and nearly fell, caught her balance and continued on toward them. Amy could see that she'd been crying. Heavy black streaks of mascara ran down her gaunt cheeks and her normally sour expression was even more haggard than usual. Her straw-like hair, which was usually worn in a tall beehive, had pulled loose and was hanging off the side of her head like a lopsided ice cream cone.

Amy started forward, Pete beside her, when she saw the woman look up, eyes momentarily unfocused, then sharpening as she saw the people.

"Help! It's Jon. He's fallen and I think he's dead! You've got to help him," she cried out, a note of desperation in her voice. In spite of Amy's dislike of Bea Hazelton, she couldn't help a feeling of sympathy, with an equal dose of horror, that an accident of this nature happened on their field trip.

Pete pushed forward, hand stretched out. "Mrs. Hazelton, what are you talking about? Your husband is right here." He looked back over his shoulder, craning his neck as if looking for someone.

Bea Hazelton recoiled from Pete's hand. "Nooo! He's dead. He's fallen. I saw him! You pushed him in a hole. He..." Mrs. Hazelton sank to her knees in the hot sand, sobbing.

At Mrs. Hazelton's words, Pete jerked back, a look of utter complete shock widening his eyes, and causing his mouth to drop open, creating a gap in the gray beard. A shudder ran through his body, breaking the momentary paralysis, and he looked around wildly. "I didn't push anyone! I wasn't even down the wash!" His eyes fixed on Salina Mattheson who was watching the drama with a slight frown on her face. "It wasn't me. I was over by the portal looking for Jania." He looked at the others in the group, "When was the last time anyone saw Jon Hazelton?"

A voice spoke up from in back of the crowd. "I saw him heading up the hill next to the mine entrance about twenty or twenty-five minutes ago." Amy craned her neck, trying to see who'd said the words, but couldn't identify the speaker.

"Amy, we'd better go check," Jackson said. He was standing slightly behind her shoulder, practically vibrating with impatience, a look of concern clouding his eyes. "I'll head down the wash toward the spot where Bea saw Jon. You go back and get some ropes and a flashlight just in case."

Amy nodded, distracted by the sight of Bea Hazelton whose sobs had subsided. She was still huddled on the ground, arms wrapped around her body. Her teeth chattered.

Shock, thought Amy. She was familiar with the feeling. Someone in the clustered group pushed forward and handed the older woman a bottle of water which she took with a shaking hand. Someone else helped her to her feet.

"Amy!" Jackson's low voice held a note of increased intensity. "Come on, we need to go."

Amy took a deep breath, then reached out and took Pete's arm. "We need to go check. If Jon Hazelton's fallen into a mine shaft, he may need help." *That is, if he isn't already dead*, Amy thought, thinking of the debris often littering the bottom of old shafts. If he didn't break his neck, or crack his head open, he very well could have impaled himself on iron spikes, or other pieces of discarded metal. "I'm going to grab some stuff from the jeep, and Jackson is going to start down the wash." Amy turned to look at Bea Hazelton. "Where did you say the hole was?"

The woman looked at Amy, her eyes still streaming. She dug in the pocket of her slacks, pulled out a tissue, and started to wipe her face, which didn't do much for the state of her makeup. "It's around that pile of rocks there." She gestured toward the outcropping at the end of the wash. "I was looking for Jon. I was waiting in the car, but it was hot and he had the keys. Someone said they'd seen him head that direction, so I walked down there." Bea Hazelton's voice started to rise, becoming higher as panic started to break through the shock once again. She looked over at the group clustered around. "You pushed Jon. I saw you! How did you get here before me? I saw you...!" Her voice ended on a screech.

"I wasn't even over there, Mrs. Hazelton!" Pete said, anger and concern warring in his voice.

"Mrs. Hazelton... Bea...," Amy said, willing her voice into deeper tones in an attempt to sooth the woman. "I need you to go with Jackson and Pete. Show them where the mine shaft is. I'll be coming right behind with some equipment."

Pete fumbled his cell phone from a small case snapped on his belt and glanced at it. "I haven't got a signal." He looked around the gathering. "If anyone has a signal, call 911. It will take them a long time to get a rescue team out here and I'd rather have to call them off, than..."

"Let's wait a few minutes, Pete," Jackson said, a look of impatience crossing his face. "They'll send the helicopter if someone is hurt, and that's harder to call off. Let's go make sure Hazelton isn't just sitting on a rock at the bottom of a shallow test hole with a sprained ankle. Come on!"

Jackson turned and headed off through the sand toward the far end of the wash, not bothering to look back to see if the others were following. Amy scrambled up the rock-strewn bank and jogged over to the jeep. She always kept some basic emergency supplies in a toolbox in the bed, and a large flashlight with fresh batteries under the front seat.

Amy grabbed the light, as well as a coil of nylon climbing rope and her first aid kit. She paused for a moment, then also reached for two hard hats and headlamps. Just in case, she told herself, hoping it was a case of "if you've got it you don't need it." She turned and jogged back toward the others who were just disappearing around the rock outcropping at the end of the wash.

Amy caught up with the group, breathing heavily as the deep sand sucked at her feet. On the far side of the rock outcropping, the wash took a small jog to the left, dropping down over a ten-foot pile of boulders of the same material as the exposed bedrock from the side of the hills. Amy briefly wondered about a possible fault line running down the canyon, before her mind was jerked back to the problem at hand.

"It's over there," Bea Hazelton said, pointing over at a small shelf about thirty feet up from the floor of the wash and fifty yards from where the group was standing. "Where you see that pile of gray rocks. Jon was standing on that level spot, and Pete came from around that boulder, and pushed him." She whipped around and looked accusingly at Pete. "It was you. I saw you." Mrs. Hazelton's panic was being replaced by anger and Amy moved closer to her, afraid that she was going to throw herself at Pete, attacking him physically as well as verbally.

"Come on, Pete," Jackson spoke up, breaking the growing tension. "Let's get up there. Where's Salina?" Jackson looked around trying to find the mine owner who had remained surprisingly quiet amid the chaos.

The dark haired woman stepped out of the cluster of club members. "I'm here. What do you need?"

"What's up there?"

She shrugged slightly. "I'm not sure. I've never been there. Jania said the trail wasn't safe. I'm guessing that there will be an open shaft or a test hole. There are tons of them all over the property." She gestured toward the surrounding hills. "Jania would know better than me." She paused and looked around, but her blonde sister wasn't anywhere in sight. "She's probably back down in the mine. If you want I can go look for her, but she knows the mine a lot better than I do, and I'm not sure I'll find her."

"It doesn't matter. We'll see soon enough what we're facing," Amy said and Jackson nodded. "Let's go."

It didn't take long for the small group to make their way over the pile of boulders, and down the wash, the hundred-fifty or so feet to just below the slope, covered with the waste rock from the shaft. Jackson moved to the side of the wash and was just getting ready to step onto the rocky incline when Amy put out her arm.

"Jackson, stop! Everyone quiet!" Amy commanded.

Silence fell over the group. Jackson looked back at Amy with a question in his eyes. She put a finger to her lips. For a moment all she could hear was the breeze rattling the leaves of a nearby yucca. The falling notes of a canyon wren sounded off down the wash. Then, Amy heard another sound, vague and indistinct. A muffled voice, words indecipherable, drifted down from the ledge above.

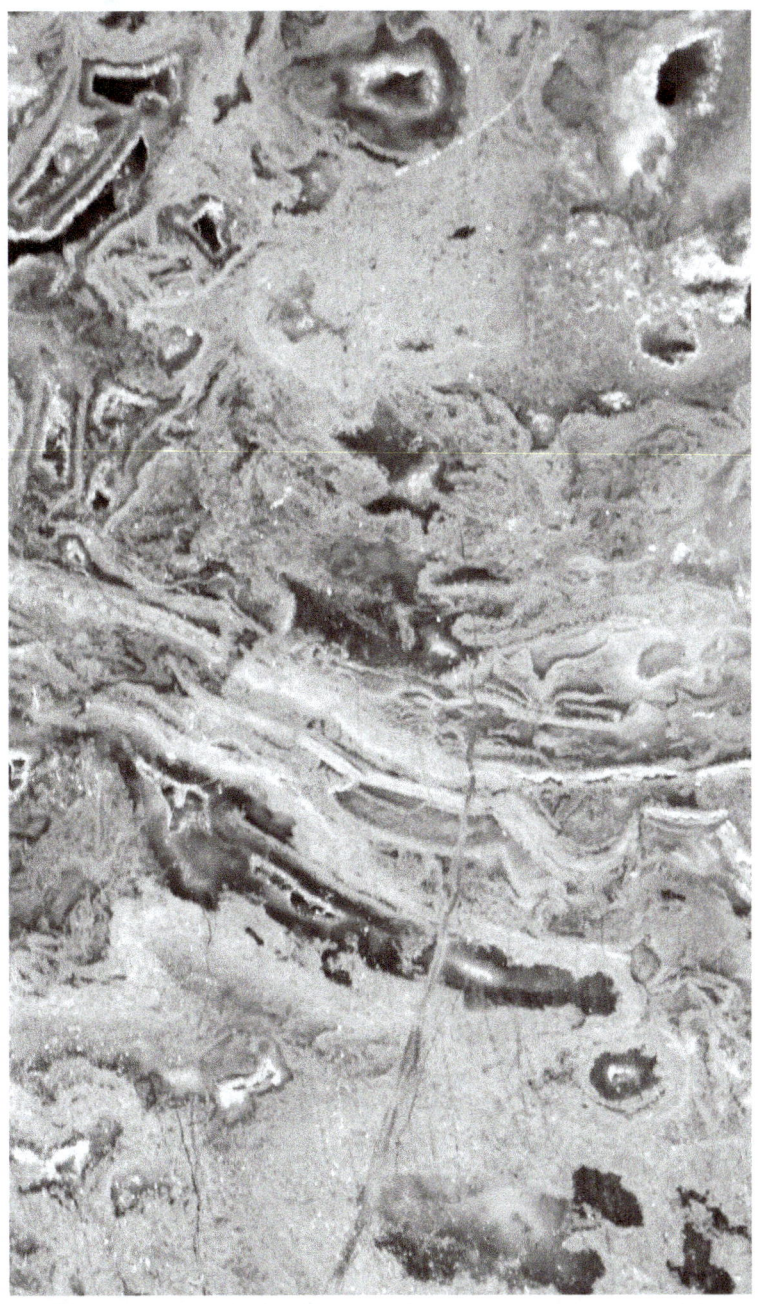

Cady Mountain Agate, California

A my's eyes met Jackson's for a fraction of a second, then he turned and started to scramble up the loose talus slope. Amy hesitated for only a moment more before she was climbing the steep hillside after him. The sound of falling rocks, rattling and clicking against one another behind her, were evidence of others following. She stopped for a second, gasping for air, and saw that Pete was close behind, followed but a number of the others.

"Hey Pete," she called out, causing him to stop and look up at her. "Get everyone to wait at the bottom until we see what's up there. I don't know how much room there is, and we don't want anyone else falling into a shaft, or knocking rocks in on Hazelton."

Pete nodded, turned to the members of the club who were following him up the pile of loose rock and shooed them back down into the wash. Amy turned and tried to catch up with Jackson who had almost reached the rocky shelf while she'd been talking to Pete. Of course, his arm was out of its sling once again, although this time she couldn't blame him.

Seconds later, she was at the top of the tailings pile and stepping onto the wide terrace covered with the same dull gray-green waste rock that covered the slope. A short distance away she could see the edge of the open shaft through a surrounding growth of catclaw and oak brush. Several t-posts and broken wire showed where previous owners had made some attempt at safety.

"Hello," Amy called out. "Mr. Hazelton, can you hear me?"

A muffled shout answered her call, and she and Jackson hurried toward the shaft. Maybe it was just a shallow hole, although the barbed wire and t-posts suggested otherwise, not to mention the sheer amount of overburden covering the area. That much rock had to have come from a pretty big hole.

Amy and Jackson pushed their way through the catclaw bushes, careful not to move too quickly. The edges of most of these abandoned shafts tended to be unstable, covered with loose rock and debris, and Amy didn't want to join Jon Hazelton at the bottom of the hole, no matter how shallow it was.

Amy's heart sank as she saw the edge of the shaft clearly - a deep, close to vertical wall dropping down into nothingness. However, as she got closer, she could see that while the side of the shaft closest to where she had emerged onto the terrace was a chisel-straight wall, the downhill side, the one farthest from Amy and Jackson was steeply sloped and covered with loose gravel and sand.

Jackson, closer to the sloped end of the shaft than she, grabbed a convenient t-post in his right hand, and leaned out over the abyss, causing Amy to gasp.

"Jackson, careful! I don't want to be hauling your butt out of that pit!"

"It's fine." He grinned back over his shoulder at her. "This post is solid, and the hole is shallow at this end. I don't think I could get hurt if I tried." He looked back down the incline. "I don't see him. Mr. Hazelton? Jon?" Jackson called out.

"Get me the hell out of here!" came a voice, still muffled, but the words this time understandable.

Pete had come up behind Amy and Jackson, breathing heavily from the exertion of climbing the loose rock. "Can you see him? Is he okay?"

Jackson had moved around the end of the shaft to the edge closest to the incline, pulling his clothes free of the catclaw as he went. Amy could see several deep red lines scoring his arm and hands where the thorns had gotten skin instead of cloth.

"The shaft doglegs at the bottom, shifting back under the mountain. Hazelton must have rolled down there when he fell," Jackson said studying the slope with an intense expression in his eyes. "Hey Jon, are you okay?"

"I can't move my damned leg. Hurts like hell. Get me out of here," came the faint reply from the dark entrance to the underground portion of the shaft. The muffling of his voice did nothing to make it more pleasant. Amy glanced at Jackson, and he shrugged.

"Tie the rope off to that big catclaw there," he gestured toward an extremely robust acacia bush about three feet from the edge of the incline. "It's not like we'll actually be climbing. That slope is steep, but it doesn't look too bad. The rope will just help us keep traction."

Amy did as he suggested, but when Jackson slipped over the edge of the shaft, grabbing the rope for balance, and standing on the upper margin of the loose rock slope, she told him to stop.

"Let me go first, Jackson. You don't know if the footing is unstable, and you shouldn't be putting that kind of pressure on your shoulder. I'll go ahead and let you know how good the footing is."

Jackson hesitated, obviously not wanting to give up his position... either that, Amy thought, or he was afraid she might take advantage of the situation to kill Hazelton with no witnesses. Then, obviously accepting the wisdom of her assessment, he climbed back up onto the edge of the shaft, and let Amy take his position on the rubble.

Amy placed her hard hat on her head, leaving the chin strap unbuckled. She pulled her leather gloves from her back pocket, slipped them on, and took a grip on the green nylon rope with her right hand. Jackson's assessment of the slope was accurate, and while the rope provided some security and balance, it wasn't really necessary. The surface of the inclined winze was unstable, but underneath the rock chips and sand, the footing was solid. She faced the right side of the shaft, planted the edge of her foot, and let herself down one step, then another, and another. The sideways placement of her feet gave her a broader base, much as a skier might sidestep up or down a slope. She moved slowly, as she tried to disturb as few of the rocks as possible.

She'd learned long ago on hikes with her father that if she tried to descend steep slopes of unstable rock and sand with her toes pointed straight downward, she was likely to end up with her feet sliding out from under her, much like skis, and she would land on her butt, usually on a sharp rock... or a cactus.

As much as she tried to avoid it, a few rocks rolled out from under her feet as she made her way down the slope to the bottom of the shaft where a five-by-five foot area created a slight landing before the slope turned to the right and disappeared into the darkness of the mountain roots.

Amy moved to the opening in the side of the shaft where the adit punched a hole in the wall. She showed the flashlight into the blackness. The floor of the adit continued to slope downward, although the angle was much gentler than in the open shaft. Broken boards and random pieces of rusty metal littered the ground but there was no sign of a collapse from the roof. She angled the flashlight downward, and there she saw Jon Hazelton looking back up at her, blinking in the bright light from the flashlight. He was about fifty feet in, laying in a widened area of the adit.

Amy picked her way over the weathered boards, placing her feet carefully to avoid knocking any of the debris down the incline and onto Hazelton, who seemed to be laying back against a pile of boards and other rubble heaped against the rough-hewn wall. She examined the sides and ceiling of the tunnel, looking for any signs of instability, but was reassured at the sight of the solid rock with few fractures. Likewise, the detritus that covered the floor seemed to be either mining refuse or ore from other areas.

She reached the bottom of the incline and shown the light past Hazelton. Shortly past the widened area where Hazelton was sprawled, the tunnel narrowed again and disappeared into a darkness that even her flashlight couldn't penetrate.

"It's about time someone got here. Do you have the emergency crews coming? I doubt you're capable of handling this type of situation." Hazelton's rusty voice jerked her attention back to his predicament. In spite of what must have been a considerable amount of pain, Hazelton managed to keep that condescending note in his voice that always put Amy's teeth on edge.

"Not yet," Amy said, struggling to keep her voice calm. "We wanted to see exactly what we were dealing with. You said you couldn't move your leg."

"Yes, dammit. I was pushed down here. When I landed, I rolled down into the shaft. Knocked myself out, so I don't remember much, but when I woke up, I couldn't move my leg. Can we get on with this?"

"I..."

The rattle of falling rocks announced Jackson's arrival at the bottom of the shaft. A second later, his flashlight cut through the dusty air, illuminating Amy and Hazelton.

"How's it going down there?" came his voice, distorted by the mine walls.

"I was just getting ready to see what we're dealing with. Where are the others?" Amy called back.

Jackson's body filled the portal, blocking what little light had been entering that way. "Pete's at the top with Mrs. Hazelton. The others are still at the bottom in the wash. Darby has gone back to the parking area in order to call for a rescue team and the sheriff's department. Is it safe to come in?"

"Yeah, I didn't see any nails in the lumber there at the entrance, and the rest of the floor is pretty clear. Are you sure it's wise to leave Pete alone with Mrs. Hazelton?"

Amy called up, shooting a glance toward where Jon Hazelton was laying, eyes closed.

Jackson moved with care over the weathered boards covering the floor of the entrance, his headlamp bouncing over the floor and walls of the tunnel. He stopped and looked up briefly at Amy, his light temporarily blinding her before he redirected the beam.

"What's she going to do to him? Besides, I'm tired of..." He glanced at Hazelton and stopped talking abruptly mid-sentence then started again. "... Ah, waiting to see if you need help."

Amy snorted. Not one of Jackson's better saves.

"If you two are done, I'd like to get out of here," Hazelton said, the crusty note in his voice making it clear that he'd understood Jackson with perfect clarity.

Amy turned back to Hazelton. "I'm sorry, Mr. Hazelton." She cast the flashlight beam over his body where he sprawled on a pile of wooden boards and rusty metal debris which had collected next to the rough-hewn walls of the adit. "Which leg..." She ground to a stop.

A few inches of rusty iron which had broken with the edge forming a spear-like point had ripped through the man's jeans several inches above his knee. Dark blood stained the denim around the spot where the metal had torn its way out. Amy felt impressed in spite of herself. Hazelton must have fallen on it with some force for it to puncture through the tough material, as well as the flesh of his leg in that manner.

Amy chewed on her lip, debating the best plan of action. Hazelton looked down at his leg, able to see for the first time the nature of the problem, and his face drained of what little color it had to begin with, the harsh light of the headlamp and flashlight casting strange jumping shadows. He looked up at Amy and Jackson, his eyes wide, for the first time showing more fear than irritation.

"Wow," Jackson breathed, looking over her shoulder. "That'll leave a mark."

"Jackson!" Amy hissed.

"Sorry." The light made it difficult to tell, but Amy thought he actually looked repentant for once.

The man was as scrawny as a starved chicken, she thought, maybe the iron bar had just grazed his leg or possibly went through skin and a little bit of muscle. "I'm going to cut your jeans so that we can see what's going on. Okay?"

Hazelton nodded and leaned his head back. Amy pulled out her pocket knife, an old one her grandfather gave her when she was ten, and as gently as she could, started cutting the denim. In spite of her care, Hazelton hissed as the cloth pulled on the piece of rusty metal.

"Damn," Amy muttered under her breath.

Hazelton's skin was the color of a dead frog's belly... a dead frog belly covered in blood and black hair, but still shockingly greenish-white. The long piece of sharpened metal had ripped through the skin and muscle dangerously near the bone. Hazelton shivered, and Amy showed the flashlight upward, into his face. His skin was pale and clammy looking. *Shock*, she thought. *We need to get him warm, lay him down and raise his legs.* She looked at the leg again and realized that at least the laying down and raising the legs part of the that wasn't going to happen.

"Jackson, go call up and tell Pete to get us a blanket from my jeep. And tell him to find another hard hat for Hazelton and maybe some extra batteries. I don't know how long these will last."

He nodded once, then turned and climbed back up the short slope to the portal where she could hear him calling orders back up to Pete at the top of the shaft. A few moments later he was sliding back down the slope and squatted next to Amy as she continued to study the leg.

"Is that chunk of metal attached to something?" Jackson asked, speaking in a whisper. "Can we move him without removing the spike? He doesn't look good."

"I don't know. I know," Amy muttered, "Here, hold the flashlight." She handed the tool to Jackson. "Mr. Hazelton, I'm going to check underneath you."

He nodded briefly without opening his eyes. "Feels like I'm sitting on a bunch of sticks and boulders, he muttered with only a trace of his normal pugnaciousness. He shifted slightly, then winced as the iron pulled at the wound.

Amy held the denim and tried to stabilize Hazelton's leg. "Show the light under here," she said. "I see some sticks and the metal seems to be tangled in them." She held the leg with her left hand, and reached behind Hazelton with her right, trying to see if she could shift some of the debris and free the end of the spike. "Let me see if I can move... What the... !" Amy gasped and looked over at Jackson as she lifted her hand. She felt the blood drain from her head.

"It's a rib bone," Jackson said flatly, as he examined the curving brown piece of bone between Amy's fingers. His face was devoid of expression. Amy looked up at Hazelton who had opened his eyes, the reflected light of the flashlight making his naturally bony face into a caricature of a death mask. The pupils of his eyes were huge, and he was staring at the stained bone in Amy's hand.

"Some animal," Hazelton croaked. "Something crawled down here to die. Hope I'm not next."

Amy shook her head, moved around behind Hazelton, and farther down the tunnel. "Give me the flashlight, Jackson. You support his body."

Jackson knelt, handed Amy the flashlight and stabilized Hazelton's leg and hip, while Amy peered behind his back. More ribs, she thought, as she moved several more browned bones aside. The rusty metal seemed to go right through the middle of the ribs. Whatever this was, it seemed that the piece of iron was the end of its life. She couldn't think of any other way that the creature could have gotten into that position. Scraps of material... denim jeans. Her heart was in her throat. Not an animal after all. The only way that there would be the remains of clothing would be if the owner of the ribs was human.

She pushed lightly on Hazelton's shoulder, moving him forward. Something round was poking into his back, and as he moved aside Amy's stomach, which had already migrated into her throat, plunged back down again. A human skull was revealed. Scraps of leathery, dry skin and hair covered part of the rounded dome which was marred by a series of radiating cracks. The empty eye-sockets of the skull stared back at her.

Amy pulled back, turned and looked at Jackson. He nodded slightly at her. It was obvious that he'd seen the macabre backrest.

"Mr. William Powell..?" Jackson started, a strained note in his voice.

"I presume," Amy finished, her tone matching his.

"I didn't say that," Jackson stated, a slight smile twisting his lips.

"Yeah, but you were thinking it."

"Okay, I'll give you that," Jackson nodded in a matter-of-fact manner.

"What are the two of you talking about?" Hazelton grumbled.

Amy looked at Jackson, and he cleared his throat. "It appears that the skeleton is human. A miner disappeared back in the eighties, and it would be quite a coincidence... uh." Jackson came to a stop at the sound of rocks falling outside the opening to the mine. Several rolled on down the incline and struck Amy in the foot, kicking up fresh gouts of dust. All three heads turned in that direction, squinting against the bright light. Two indistinct figures came into view, one reaching out for the other, who shook off the touch and rushed to the entrance of the adit.

"Jon? Jon are you down there? Are you okay?" Bea Hazelton's high pitched voice had the same reaction on Amy as fingernails on a chalkboard. She looked at Jackson and rolled her eyes. What's she doing down here? She mouthed.

He shrugged and turned to stand, careful of the low, jagged roof of the mine adit.

"Yes, Bea, I'm here. You know that perfectly well," Hazelton called, his face showing no enjoyment at his wife's appearance.

The light at the entrance to the mine dimmed as the two silhouetted bodies filled the narrow space, and small rocks pelted down on Hazelton, Amy and Jackson as the newcomers made their way down the incline. The silhouettes resolved into Pete Martin and Bea Hazelton as they stepped into the beams from Amy and Jackson's headlamps.

They brought two large, high powered flashlights with them and Pete was also holding a blanket and a battered blue hard hat. When he reached the bottom of the incline where Amy, Jackson and Hazelton were waiting, he turned sideways and edged around Mrs. Hazelton, holding both items out to Amy.

"Here's the blanket from your jeep, Amethyst and my extra hat. Emergency crews are on their way, but you know how it is out here. It's going to be a little while. How's he doing?" Pete stared down at the man lying at his feet. The harsh shadows of the flashlights made it difficult to tell, but Amy couldn't see any sympathy on his face.

Amy shrugged. "He's got a piece of rusty metal jammed through his leg, and I'm worried about shock." She took the blanket and laid it over the older man, then set the helmet on is head.

"Why can't we get him out of here!" Bea Hazelton demanded. "He'd be much warmer, not to mention much more comfortable out of this filthy hole." She looked around the alcove, the harsh lighting and the look of distaste on her face turning it into a grotesque mask.

"We can't pull the iron bar out. It's not bleeding too badly right now, but it will start if we pull that thing back through his leg... not to mention the damage it will do to the muscle. Plus we don't know if he has any other injuries," Amy said, trying to soothe the woman. "We've got to wait for emergency crews."

Hazelton nodded, the light of the flashlight making

the furrows in his face deepen. His lizard-like eyes were hidden behind the heavy lids. He frowned and shifted his weight, then jerked to a stop. "They're right, Bea. We'll just have to wait." His voice was weaker than Amy was comfortable with, Hazelton's perpetual tones of condescension and irritation on the wane.

"I told you we shouldn't have come here," Mrs. Hazelton's previous grief at her husband's presumed demise was quickly being replaced by annoyance. "Who in their right mind wants to spend a perfectly nice day digging around in the dirt and looking at rusty old metal? I said I wanted to stay home, but no, you insisted that it was important for your position that we be part of the town's activities. Well, see where it got you?" The whine in Bea Hazelton's voice had the same annoying quality of a drone and gave Amy the same feeling: that she wanted to shoot it out of the sky and stamp on it until it was in a million pieces.

Amy flicked the flashlight's beam toward Hazelton and saw that he'd leaned back against the wall of the cave, eyes closed. She couldn't tell if the expression on his face was pain or annoyance. As Bea continued complaining about having to come on the field trip, and now wait until help arrived, Amy didn't think it was possible, but she felt sorry for Hazelton.

She glanced at the illuminated screen of her cell phone. Another forty-five minutes at least until the cavalry arrived. Another burst of condemnation sounded from Bea Hazelton and Amy cringed. She had the feeling that it was going to be a very long forty-five minutes.

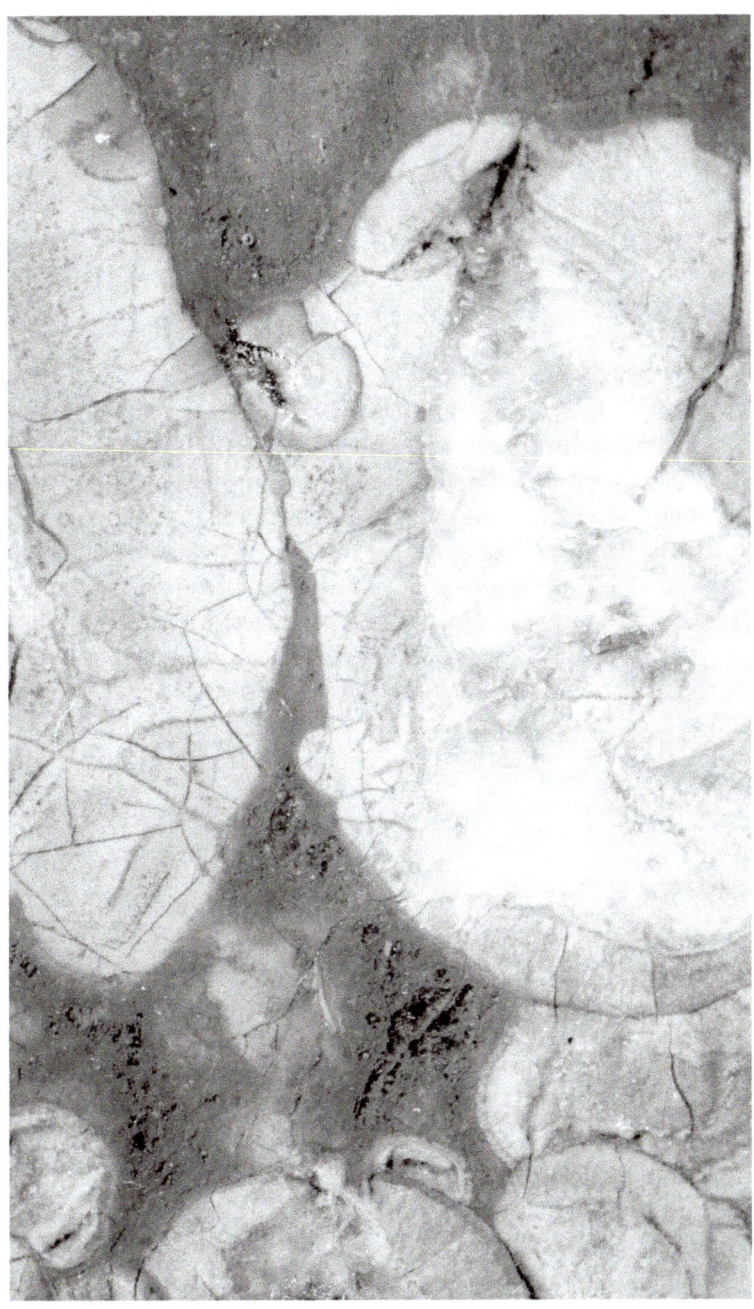

Mushroom Jasper, Arizona

In the end, it was closer to an hour before Amy heard voices outside the mine portal, announcing the arrival of the rescue team. Pete had waited with Amy and Jackson for a short time, but as Mrs. Hazelton's list of complaints continued, he began to edge his way toward the mine's entrance. Finally, he said that he would return to the parking area to wait for the emergency personnel, as well as let the others know what was happening. He turned and scrambled back up the slope and out of the mine, falling rocks rolling down in his wake, pelting those who still sat at the bottom of the incline and stirring up even more dust.

Several times, either Amy or Jackson suggested to Bea Hazelton that she also return to the surface and the relative comfort of her vehicle while they waited, at which point the older woman proclaimed loudly that she would never leave her beloved husband. Amy glanced back at Jackson who had taken up a perch on the pile of debris. It was hard to tell in the given light, but she was sure she saw his eyes roll. She wondered if he was learning the gesture from her, or if she was learning it from him.

Eventually, even Bea's complaints ground to a halt and the four of them sat in silence. The deadened air had an almost tangible quality. At one point a low groan sounded, making Bea Hazelton gasp and look wildly around. Jackson and Amy's eyes met and he started to open his mouth.

Amy jumped in before he could start spinning any tales of William Powell's ghost haunting the location of his violent (presumably in Jackson's world) death, seeking revenge on all who had wronged him or tried to steal his gold.

"It's okay, Mrs. Hazelton," Amy said in as matter-of-fact tones as possible. "It's just the earth moving and settling. Nothing to worry about. These walls are solid as are the ceilings."

"Are you sure?" the older woman asked with a quiver in her voice.

"Absolutely," Amy responded, catching the crestfallen look on Jackson's face. That's just what they need, she thought: Hazelton's wife in a panic over an imaginary haunting. Amy checked Jon Hazelton again. He seemed to be drifting in and out of consciousness, and she prayed that help would arrive soon. She pulled out her phone and checked the time once again.

Finally, voices, and another cascade of loose rubble, announced the arrival of the first of the emergency crew. Amy looked toward Jackson and he started to rise to his feet.

Before Jackson was able to move toward the portal, a body once again filled the opening to the mine, making their dark hole seem even darker in spite of their own headlamps and the now waning flashlight. A new, heavy-duty flashlight beam cut through the dusty air, causing Amy to blink and duck her head.

"Hey!"

The beam of light was immediately turned toward the sloping floor.

"Sorry, Amy, Jackson. How's everything going down there?" called a familiar voice, Tommy Kissoon. Make that Mohave County Sheriff's Deputy Tommy Kissoon, Amy's high school boyfriend, and brother to her best friend Maria Kissoon. When Amy had returned to Copper Springs to help her father, she learned the hard way that Tommy had joined the Mohave County Sheriff's department when she was suspect *numero uno* in Schrader's murder. Still, she didn't hold it against him, especially since it was he, along with another deputy, who saved her and Jackson in the Skystone Mine.

Tommy made his way down the slope, placing his feet with care, yet knocking the inevitable barrage of pebbles down on the group clustered at the bottom. Many of the old mines weren't very wide at the best of times, and even though the original miners had done some extra digging in this area, probably to remove a pocket of minerals, things were still getting pretty crowded.

Tommy reached the small group in short order, and stood for a second, shining his light on Hazelton who had roused to a small degree at the deputy's appearance.

"Pete said that Mr. Hazelton fell on a piece of rusty metal and couldn't be moved," he said.

Amy nodded and gestured toward Hazelton's leg where the torn denim indicated the location of the wound. "It's got a sharpened end that ripped through the muscle of his thigh. It looks pretty close to the bone and I'm afraid if we try to pull the metal out and move him, we might hit an artery or a vein. Right now the metal is plugging the hole."

"The rescue team is only a few minutes behind me, and they'll have something to cut through that and the big wheel to get him back out of the mine." Tommy gestured back toward the portal to the mine.

"A 'big wheel'? What is that?" Bea Hazelton piped up. "You can't mean a child's toy." Scorn sounded in her voice.

"It's a litter with a large single wheel, which makes it easier to get it over rough terrain," Tommy explained with more patience than Amy ever hoped to possess. "They'll have to lift it over the boulder pile at the end there, but the rest should be easy. We've called for the helicopter, and it will be able to meet us in the parking area. It's too narrow down here in the canyon."

To Amy's surprise, Bea Hazelton had no argument or other questions to offer, seeming to accept the deputy's statement.

"There is something else..." Jackson said from behind Amy's shoulder, where he'd been sitting on the pile of old timbers.

It was hard to tell in the dark mine, but a half smile seemed to briefly settle on Tommy's face. "Yeah, Pete told me. Another body. What are you guys doing, starting a collection?"

"Hey, it's not my collection," Amy protested. "This one has been here a long time."

"We think it might be a miner who disappeared back in the 80s; William Powell," Jackson said.

"We'll certainly be looking into it, but I think your pile of bones is a little past needing the emergency crews. We'll worry about Hazelton first, then start an investigation on who the remains were when they were a living, breathing person."

"What about arresting the man who pushed Jon?" Bea Hazelton spoke up, the anger and annoyance back in her voice. "I saw Pete Martin push my husband into this filthy hole, and he should be arrested for assault! He...." Her voice was rapidly increasing in volume and vehemence, echoing off the walls of the mine.

At the start of Bea's rant, Amy saw Tommy stiffen and he glanced at Amy and Jackson before turning his attention back to the older woman who had risen to her feet as though pulled up by strings.

"I'm sorry, Mrs. Hazelton. I was under the impression that your husband had slipped on the edge of the mine shaft and fallen in. I wasn't informed that he was pushed. Mr. Hazelton? Can you tell me what happened?" Tommy fished his notebook from the breast pocket of his uniform shirt.

Jon Hazelton hadn't moved, although his wife's screeching voice had elicited an expression on his face that reminded Amy of a baby suffering from an extreme case of flatulence.

"I can't tell you much," Hazelton said, his voice barely audible. Tommy squatted down next to the man.

"I was looking for something... or maybe someone, I think, and followed a path over the hill. I can't remember what I was looking for..." A frown settled on his face and his voice faded into nothing.

"He's hit his head!" Mrs. Hazelton exclaimed. "He's got a head injury and here you are questioning him. I'll tell you what happened. I saw it all!"

Tommy took a deep breath and rose to his feet. "Okay, Mrs. Hazelton, why don't you tell me what you saw. Just start with..."

The sound of voices and rocks rolling wafted in from the shaft outside, telling the current mine occupants that the emergency crew had arrived. There was the now familiar darkening at the portal and a new beam from a headlamp illuminated the now crowded tunnel.

The leader of the rescue team, a tall woman dressed in a uniform which identified her as a member of the Wild Land Search and Rescue, approached the group at the bottom of the incline, carefully sidestepping down the unstable stone and debris strewn slope. Two men followed close behind, all packing heavy red duffle bags and moving with a surefootedness which spoke to plenty of training in rough terrain.

"What do we have here?" the female EMT asked in a matter-of-fact voice as she approached the group crowded around the debris pile. "We got a call that someone fell into a mine shaft and broke his leg?" As she got closer Amy could see a piece of white tape on her helmet identifying her as Montez, J. in black marker. She still couldn't see the names on the helmets of the other two members of the team.

"I don't know if it's broken," Amy spoke up, "But he's got a chunk of sharpened iron through his thigh, and we were afraid to pull it out."

"It's a good thing you didn't. We'll take it from here," the woman said brusquely as she played her flashlight beam over Hazelton. Amy could see a frown of concentration cross the woman's face as she studied the man. "Now, there are too many people. It's too crowded down here. We need everyone to leave the mine, please."

The woman knelt at Hazelton's side and started talking to him, asking his name, and age, and whether he had any underlying health conditions. Hazelton only opened his eyes for a moment to look at the new arrivals, then closed them, but Amy could hear him answering clearly in his dry voice. The other two members of the rescue team moved in around Hazelton, forcing Amy and Jackson back farther down the drive, toward the interior of the mountain. Amy caught a brief whiff of something old and damp. The mountain breathing she thought. At least this mine had good ventilation, although it smelled as though it may have some flooded drives farther down.

Funny how in the middle of a desert, where water is in short supply, you can still have flooded mines and caves. Amy directed the beam of her flashlight down the tunnel, trying to see if there was an indication of moisture. Nothing. *Still, there's that huge system of lakes and rivers under Death Valley. Just because I don't see it here, doesn't mean it isn't farther back.*

"Come on Amy. Jackson. Mrs. Hazelton. Let's head up top," Tommy said, his voice pulling Amy's attention back to the tableau in front of her. He held out his arm to usher their small group out of the adit. "I'll get your accounts of what happened up at the top. Pete is waiting at the parking area so that he could direct the EMTs. I need to call and make sure that no one else who may have witnessed anything has left."

Bea Hazelton rose to her feet and turned to face Tommy, her body radiating outrage. "I should stay with my husband!"

"Ma'am, you can't help your husband right now, and we need room to work," said the woman labeled Montez, J. in firm tones while also rising to her feet. "We need you and the others to leave the mine so we can help your husband."

Bea only spared a momentary glance at the tall woman and her two partners, then stared back at Tommy. "But, you'll arrest that Pete Martin, right? He's the one who pushed Jon. I saw it!" Her voice reverberated off the walls making the drift feel even smaller than it was. Amy saw the woman shoot a quick look at her partners, the frown lines deepening on her face.

"The report I had said that this man had just fallen into an abandoned shaft..." Martinez started, looking to Tommy for confirmation. "If this was a crime..."

"It is! It's an assault! And Pete Martin is the one who...," Bea started.

"Stop it now!" Tommy's voice held a level of authority that Amy had never heard in it before. In her mind, he was the bright, cheerful teenager who hung out with his sister, Maria, and Amy after school, and who wandered the wilderness with them on the weekends.

He turned to the EMTs. "At this point we'll have to presume a crime has been committed. Obviously, Mr. Hazelton's well-being is your priority, but if you see anything that looks as though it could be evidence, preserve it if you can." He turned and held out his arm once again to usher the others out of the mine, then hesitated and turned back. "Oh, and in case the dispatcher didn't tell you, there's another body underneath Mr. Hazelton."

The woman, who had returned her attention to Hazelton, whipped her head back around and stared at Tommy, then at Amy and Jackson, with her mouth open, eyes wide with shock in the bouncing beams from the headlamps.

"Another body? Where?" she snapped.

"An old one... We think it may be a man who disappeared in this area about thirty years ago," Tommy answered continuing to make shooing motions with his arm toward the others.

"I take it this is the guy in question?" One of the male EMTs had moved around Hazelton and had knelt beside him. He held up a long bone. Probably a leg bone, Amy thought.

"I'd say so. Obviously, Mr. Hazelton is more important, but just be aware that this may be both a new crime scene and an old one. Now everyone out of the mine." Tommy's tone left no room for argument.

Amy and Jackson had moved back when the EMTs arrived, and now Amy flattened herself against the rough stone of the far wall of the adit and edged her way past where the EMTs were starting to work on Hazelton without sparing another moment's attention for the others. Jackson followed close enough behind that she could feel the brush of his arm several times when she hesitated.

Bea Hazelton pushed past Tommy, cutting off Amy and Jackson, and headed up the incline toward the portal. Dislodged rocks rolled and bounced, several pelting Amy in the legs, and causing the EMT to call out to be more careful. Amy glanced back over her shoulder to glance at Jackson who was standing close behind. In the dim light of the opening, she could see him make a face, then he jerked his chin, indicating that Amy should follow.

Sighing, Amy started picking her way up the incline.

A few minutes later, the small group stood on the flat area at the top of the mine shaft. Amy blinked in the bright light, and took a deep breath of the warm air, trying to get the damp, musty- mine smell out of her nostrils. She could taste the dust and must, and wished for something acidic to wash it away. She looked at Jackson and noticed that his face had accumulated a fresh coating of dirt, and several cobwebs had tangled themselves in his sandy-colored hair. He flashed her a grin and gestured toward his face then pointed at her, which she interpreted to mean that she had gained a similar collection of grime and cobwebs.

Tommy was the last to pull himself over the lip of the shaft, and he stood for a second, catching his breath from the climb up the unstable stone and sand of the inclined shaft. Then he pulled out the notebook and turned to the small group.

"I'm going to need to get everyone's report, but I also need to stay here in case the EMTs need anything. If you don't mind, I'll get your stories right now, then when I'm done talking to each person, you can head back to the..." The crackle of a radio interrupted Tommy, and he reached down to the transmitter on the shoulder of his uniform shirt.

He glanced at the others, then took several steps away and started talking into the handpiece. Amy looked at Jackson and he shrugged. Mrs. Hazelton was becoming more agitated while waiting and finally began to make her way back toward the shaft, with the obvious intent of returning to her husband.

"Mrs. Hazelton..." Jackson started, moving toward her, arm outstretched. "I know you're worried about your husband, but it's very crowded down there. I'm sure they'll be able to get him out soon, but you don't want to get in the way."

Bea Hazelton turned her sour expression on Jackson. "You don't know anything, Mr... Wolf was it? You think I'm crazy, and that I didn't see Martin push Jon. You're friends with that man. You both are." She favored Amy with an equally disgusted look. "Now I'm going back to be with Jon," She said with determination.

Just as Bea reached the edge of the shaft, Tommy finished his discussion with whoever was on the other end of the radio and returned to the small group.

"Mrs. Hazelton, please stay here. We'll wait for them to get your husband to the surface. They're going to airlift him to the trauma center in Flagstaff. Do you have someone who can drive you?"

Bea looked at Tommy, then over at Amy and Jackson. "What do you mean, drive me? I intend to ride with him." Her voice held a rock-solid conviction, and when Amy glanced at Jackson, she saw a wisp of a smile.

He leaned over and whispered into Amy's ear, "You've got to admire her tenacity."

"Only when it's aimed at someone else," Amy muttered back, remembering the woman's conviction that the rock shop was going to be condemned and that the

Hazeltons would be able to take it over for a business of their own.

Meanwhile, Tommy had fixed Bea Hazelton with a sympathetic gaze. "I'm so sorry, Mrs. Hazelton, but there isn't room on the helicopter. Is there someone in the group who can drive you. Maybe a friend in town?"

An even deeper frown rested on Bea's face. "I don't know or associate with any of these people. Jon only wanted to come because he said it was important for his position on the council. I suppose that I could call Alice." She looked at Amy and Jackson. "You know, Alice Roberts? Her husband, Dennis Roberts, is on the council with Jon. They're our close friends." A note was evident in her voice that told Amy the friendship of the Roberts was something to be envied.

Amy hesitated and looked again at Jackson. A slight frown pulled at her forehead and she rubbed her nose with a dirty hand as she tried to picture the Alice and Dennis Roberts in question. A vague image of a long, pale yellow walrus mustache flashed into her mind. She looked back at Bea and nodded slightly. "He's one of the newer residents of the town, right? I remember seeing him at council meetings, and I've probably seen his wife, but I don't know them well. I haven't been back all that long."

Before Amy moved back to Copper Springs, her parents had told her about the growing pains of the community. In their minds, the newcomers wanted the small town to step up, capitalize on its location on Route 66 and proximity to many of the state's most popular tourist locations. They envisioned tourist dollars flowing into the community and property values skyrocketing. They felt it was important for the town council to take on the aspect of a quasi-HOA, implementing many of the same types of ordinances. On the other side of the wall were the old time residents, who, while they didn't mind visitors to their town, wanted to keep the small town flavor and sensibilities. They enjoyed the slightly dilapidated face of the community, boasting on its historical significance. As long as safety wasn't an issue, they believed in a "live and let live" atmosphere.

Amy had realized upon first meeting Jon Hazelton and his wife that they were solidly in the "progress or die" camp. She'd learned from talking to Nick, her dad, that Hazelton and several of his cronies had gotten themselves elected to the council and ever since that moment, the old-time residents had been fighting an uphill battle to keep unbridled growth at bay. She'd heard Roberts' name mentioned in conjunction with Hazeltons' by several people, and not usually in glowing terms.

"Let me get your stories, and then the three of you head back to the parking area. Mrs. Hazelton can call her friend and see if she's able to help." Tommy turned his attention back to Bea. "Do you think you can drive your car back to Copper Springs, or maybe Amy or Jackson can help you out since they rode together?"

Amy quenched an internal shiver and gave Jackson an apologetic look. "Jackson can drive, and I'll follow since he's not familiar with my jeep."

She saw Jackson try to suppress wince and give her an accusatory glare. However, her sense of self-preservation won out. There was no way she wanted to be trapped in a car with Bea Hazelton all the way back to Copper Springs. She'd probably be looking for a cliff to drive over before they got a hundred yards and she couldn't remember any handy ones along the route. *Maybe if Ol' Tom is still around...* She shook her self mentally out of that line of thought.

"I'd be happy to help," Jackson was saying, giving Bea a sympathetic look, while behind his back, he gesticulated wildly at Amy. In spite of the seriousness of the situation, Amy had to fight down a laugh. Mrs. Hazelton gave Jackson a look of disfavor, apparently taking in his blood-stained jeans and grubby T-shirt, but then grudgingly nodded.

"Great," Tommy said. "Jackson and Amy, if you don't mind, please have a seat on any handy rock, I'd like to talk to each of you while we're waiting for the rescue team to get ready to move Mr. Hazelton out."

"Okay," Amy answered, a frown of concentration once again on her face. "But I don't think either Jackson or I can be of much help. We were both up on the side of the mountain above the parking area when we heard Mrs. Hazelton's screams. We didn't see anything. Heck, I didn't even realize who was screaming until Jackson said it was Mrs. Hazelton."

Tommy looked surprised and gave Jackson a long look.

"I recognized her voice," Jackson said with a sheepish look on his face.

Amy bit her lip a little harder, trying to suppress an inappropriate laugh at the thought of the reason he gave for recognizing the screamer.

Tommy nodded, apparently taking Jackson's comment at face value. "Did you happen to notice where anyone else was when you heard the screams?" He jotted a couple of notes down on his pad of paper.

"I told you...!" Bea Hazelton started, then stopped abruptly at a look from Tommy.

I've got to work on that look, Amy thought to herself, impressed at Tommy's ability to control the situation. In her experience, Bea Hazelton spared her comments for no one.

Jackson's eyes narrowed as he focused on Tommy's question, then shook his head, a look of regret on his face. "No, I'm afraid not. We were too far away from the parking area. There were some people scattered around on the spoils piles, as well as over by the old machinery, and I think some had gone over the ridge to explore the far wash, but I couldn't tell who was who."

"Amy, how about you? Did you notice anything, or anyone, where they shouldn't have been?"

Bea Hazelton, unable to contain herself any longer, broke out again in a strident voice. "It was that Pete Hazelton, I tell you. I came around the pile of rocks, and I saw him go up behind Jon and shove him into the shaft. It was him, I recognized the braid down his back... disgusting habit on a man." She sounded almost more upset about Pete's hair than about his supposed actions.

"I'm sorry Tommy," Amy said when Bea stopped to draw in a fresh breath. "I couldn't tell where anyone was for sure. When we'd left, Pete was heading up the wash with a couple of other men, but I'm not sure who they were." She hesitated, then added, "Pete and Hazelton had been fighting, though. Those two men came and pulled Pete away from the argument."

Tommy jotted a few words into his notebook, then looked back up at Jackson and Amy, the muscles of his face tightened in concentration, dark eyes serious. "Okay, thanks you two. Now, go ahead and have that seat while I talk to Mrs. Hazelton."

Amy and Jackson walked over toward several large boulders which had tumbled down from the hillside above. Amy moved slowly and headed toward the nearest of the rocks, determined to hear exactly what Bea Hazelton was telling Tommy.

"I want to thank you for volunteering me to drive Bea," Jackson said in a low voice so that the other two couldn't hear him. "Want to tell me what I've done to piss you off?" His voice held a hint of a laugh, and Amy knew him well enough at this point to realize he wasn't truly angry. For that matter, he probably would have volunteered himself if she hadn't done it already.

"*Shhh*, I want to hear what she has to say," Amy hissed back at him. The two of them settled on the large rock. Amy held her breath, trying to hear Bea Hazelton's story. She needn't have bothered, she thought after a few moments, as it became clear that the older woman's voice carried to the far side of the terrace quite well.

"You said that you saw Mr. Martin push Mr. Hazelton into the mine shaft, correct?" Tommy asked, writing in his notepad. "Why don't you go through your story from the beginning. Why were you and your husband over here, so far away from the rest of the group?"

"I wasn't with Jon. I had no desire to look at that piece of rusty junk that everyone was arguing about, so I went back to the car when they went to look at it. Jon said it would only be a few minutes, but he was taking forever, the car was hot and I was tired of waiting. When he didn't show up, I decided to go find him." Bea's bony arms were crossed across her chest and her head thrust forward at an aggressive tilt. Her face was still streaked with the remnants of her mascara, and the lopsided beehive gave her an evil clown appearance. "There were several people down on one of those rock piles, and one said he thought that he'd seen Jon head in this direction, so I walked down the wash."

"So you didn't come down here with him? Do you remember who told you they'd seen your husband head in this direction?" Tommy prompted, pencil moving across the paper in his notebook.

"I don't know who it was." Mrs. Hazelton sounded exasperated, as though Tommy was missing the point of the story. "It was a man. I don't know if I've ever seen him before. Why does it matter? It wasn't Martin." She glared at Tommy as though he was deliberately wasting time.

"When I got to that pile of the rocks at the end of the gully there, I heard a shout. I looked up at this flat area here and saw Pete Martin shove Jon. He disappeared and Martin turned and ran back that way." Mrs. Hazelton pointed at Amy and Jackson.

Amy's eyes widened, and she and Jackson scrambled to their feet.

"What..." Amy said, but Jackson took her arm and pointed to the hillside behind where they had been sitting. A narrow worn pathway was barely visible, vanishing over the shoulder of the hill. Amy nodded, understanding, and settled back on her rock. She tried to remember if she had seen anyone coming down from the top part of the hill when she and Jackson had heard the screaming. She narrowed her eyes, concentrating, then ran her fingers through her short, dark hair. She shook her head, certain that she'd seen no one in the upper area of the mountain.

"Did you see anyone up here?" she whispered to Jackson, leaning back so that he could hear her more easily. He shook his head and shrugged. Amy turned to examine the trail but didn't rise to approach it. If there was such a thing as footprint evidence like they showed on TV, she wasn't going to be the one to disrupt it. She became aware that Tommy had asked another question.

"I screamed, of course, and ran back to the parking area to get help," Bea said.

Amy could picture a thought balloon over Mrs. Hazelton's head saying *"Duh"* at Tommy's question. "Now are you going to go arrest Martin?"

"You said you were all the way over there?" Tommy pointed toward the boulder pile at the end of the wash. "And that your husband and this other person who pushed..."

"Pete Martin pushed my husband!"

Tommy's entire person radiated calm as he waited for Bea to stop talking. "...the person who pushed your husband were here." He gestured at the deepest end of the mine shaft. "However, you said you recognized Pete Martin?"

"Yes! That disgusting ponytail of his whipped out when he rushed Jon and pushed him."

"You couldn't see his face?"

"Not from that distance, but the sloppy black shirt and jeans, and that long, scraggly ponytail are unmistakable." She sniffed in disdain. "It's only luck that Jon didn't die in that fall. You are going to arrest Martin, aren't you, and charge him with attempted murder?

"Mrs. Hazelton, I can assure you that...," Tommy started

A commotion from the bottom of the shaft interrupted Tommy's words, and he and Mrs. Hazelton turned to look down the inclined slope of the shaft. Amy scrambled to her feet and moved to the upper end of the hole, followed closely by Jackson. She peered over the edge, careful not to move too close and knock loose rocks from the edge down into the pit.

One of the male members of the rescue crew was emerging, carrying the end of the litter. Jon Hazelton's head was visible above a blanket. Several straps secured him to the litter to prevent him from sliding off.

Amy pulled Jackson back with her, and they quickly made their way around the edge of the mine to the shallow end where Tommy and Mrs. Hazelton had stepped back to give the EMTs room to maneuver the litter up the steep slope and out of the shaft.

In a few minutes, everyone was up out of the mine and standing on the plateau. Out of the cool underground air, and with an IV in his arm, Hazelton appeared to have more life in his withered body, and his cheeks had more color, having turned from gray-green to gray-pink. A blanket covered his body, but a sharp protrusion showed where the metal remained in his leg, the rescue team having cut it off at the root. They'd determined in short order that it would better to take it with them and allow the surgical team to remove it once he was in the sterile environment of an operating room.

"Okay," Montez, J. said, catching her breath. "The hard part is over. Just a quick jaunt to the parking area, and a helicopter ride, and you'll be good as new, Jon." She put her hand comfortingly on the older man's shoulder.

"Do you need anything from me?" Tommy asked, studying the man laying on the litter.

"No, we've got it," said one of the male members of the rescue team. Amy could see the patch on his uniform which identified him as "Harrison, J." She shook her head with a wry smile. She ought to ask them their first names, she thought, but she couldn't help but think of them by the names on their patches.

"Thanks," Tommy said, then turned to the other three. "Mrs. Hazelton, Amy and Jackson, let's head back to the

Cheryl F Taylor

parking area." He motioned with his arm, ushering them toward the bank of the terrace and away from the mine shaft. Amy looked back over her shoulder, the barely visible hole in the ground and its trampled brush. She chewed her lip, a slight frown tightened her forehead.

Why on earth did Hazelton come all the way back here? He's got no interest in old mines. She shook her head and turned to watch her feet as she made her way down the loose slope. She was sure that Pete hadn't pushed Hazelton, but if he hadn't done it, then who had?

It was a quiet walk back to the flat parking area in front of the Red Wind Mine. Bea Hazelton had finally sailed her river of complaints to the end and trudged back through the sand, head bowed. Jackson and Amy walked a little ahead of the older woman.

Fifteen minutes later, the group found themselves standing in the flattened parking area in front of the main mine portal, watching the rescue team load Hazelton into the waiting helicopter. The other members of the rock club and the historical society milled around, watching the action. Two other sheriff's department SUVs had joined Tommy's in the parking area, and it was evident that the deputies had been detaining the others from leaving due to the report from Tommy that the situation might involve more than just a simple accident.

Tommy reached out and touched Amy lightly on the shoulder. "I already have your and Jackson's stories, so why don't you guys head out?" He dropped his hand and directed his words to Jackson. "You said you'd drive Mrs. Hazelton? If you'll get her into town, they're taking Hazelton up to Flagstaff, and she can call her friends and see if they'll help her get the rest of the way."

"Do you need me to stay?" Amy asked. She felt torn. She was glad to be released, but she felt a burning curiosity deep down in her gut. If she left, she'd have to rely on others for a report. *Crap!* she thought. *I'm just as bad as Gladys and Em, wanting to know all the dirt in the town first hand!* She supposed it was the same urge that made people rubberneck at an accident as they drove past. Amy looked over at Jackson and could tell that he was fighting his own internal battle.

"No, I have your statement, and if you have nothing to add, the two of you might as well go so that Mrs. Hazelton can get up to Flag to be with her husband." He shook his head, a half smile on his face. "Heaven knows how that marriage has lasted. I know I would have thrown myself down a mine shaft a long time ago if I'd been married to her."

"Well, I probably would have thrown myself into a mine shaft and set a charge at the opening to cause a cave in if I'd been married to him!" Amy said. She heard Jackson choke back a laugh behind her.

"No accounting for taste, I guess." Tommy's voice held a smile that didn't appear on his face. "Go ahead and take off. I'll let you know if we need anything else."

"I...," Amy started, looking over toward the cluster of people standing over by the mining equipment, the other deputies separating people and starting to talk to individuals. "I don't mind staying if I'm any help. Jackson can drive Mrs. Hazelton back to the rock shop, and maybe her friends can meet her there."

Jackson looked at Amy over Tommy's shoulder, pantomiming *what the heck* then pointing at her, making it clear that he thought she was throwing him under the bus. Amy sucked her lower lip between her teeth.

This is a serious situation, she reminded herself.

"Go ahead and take off, Amy. I think that the fewer people we have milling around here, the better." He gave her a smile that held a faint note of sadness. "If I we have any more questions, someone will contact you. If either of you thinks of anything else, give us a call." He looked up to include Jackson in the statement.

"Okay," Amy said, stomping down the urge that made her want to stay regardless of what Tommy said. "What's going to happen with Pete?" She looked over her shoulder to check that Bea Hazelton wasn't in earshot. She was over near the helicopter which was starting to make noises as though it were getting ready to start up or explode; Amy wasn't sure which. From the look on Bea's face, she might also be getting ready to explode as the EMTs closed the door of the machine, forcing the older woman to back up.

Amy turned back to Tommy and Jackson moved in more closely to hear his answer.

"It's an ongoing investigation, Amy, and I'm not going to discuss it with you. However, you've heard Mrs. Hazelton."

Amy started to protest, but Tommy cut her off.

"You and Mr. Wolf here had your ears pricked like bats back there at the mine, so I have no doubt you heard what she told me. Besides, from what I'm told, she's been claiming that Pete did it all along. Unless one of the others can give him an alibi, I imagine he'll be taken for questioning."

"Tommy, you know Pete! He's been in the area since we were kids. You know he didn't do anything like that!" Amy protested, her voice starting to rise.

"I know nothing of the kind, Amy." Tommy's voice was icy in its reserve. "It's surprising what some people will do when provoked enough, and I've heard that Hazelton and Pete have had several loud and angry arguments recently."

Amy felt a frisson of doubt scamper up her spine as she thought about Pete following Hazelton to the parking area earlier in the day. *Still*, she thought, *this is Pete we're talking about here. I know Pete.*

"But..."

"No, Amy. I'm not talking about this any longer. If you remember something, give me a call. Now, if you'll get Mrs. Hazelton into town, I'd appreciate it." Tommy's voice had risen as the helicopter had gotten over its initial groaning and squalling and the rotors had achieved full speed. Gradually it started to rise from the ground, dust exploding from the downdraft. It picked up height, then sped off to the east.

Tommy turned away from Amy and Jackson and started to head over to the remainder of the field trip group, but Amy reached out and grabbed his arm. He turned back with a question in his eyes.

"What about the bones of William Powell?" Amy asked, annoyed at the frustration she heard in her voice.

"The possible bones of William Powell, you mean?"

"You saw them, they're definitely bones," Jackson said in a helpful manner. Amy elbowed him in the side.

"Knock it off, Jackson. Come on, Tommy, who else can they belong too?" Amy exclaimed.

"I'll admit, it would be a heck of a coincidence if someone else was dead on the property, but we're going to have to wait for tests to determine for sure if those are Powell's remains. Don't worry, I'll be making a call and someone will be out to collect the skeleton soon. Now if you don't mind..." Tommy gestured toward the waiting people. "It's already going to be a long day, and besides Mrs. Hazelton's waiting." Tommy turned again and walked toward the group.

Amy looked back toward where the helicopter had rested only a short time before and saw Bea Hazelton standing in the empty area, looking at Jackson with impatience.

"We'd better get moving," Jackson said, sighing. "M'lady awaits." He turned and headed toward the older woman. "Are you ready to go, Mrs. Hazelton?" he said with forced cheerfulness. "If you'll give me your keys, we'll get you into town in a jiffy, and then your friend Alice can get you over to Flag in no time."

Bea Hazelton gave the rapidly departing helicopter one last look then walked over to Jackson. She pulled a set of keys from the pocket of her grubby tan slacks and held them out to Jackson, pinched between her fingers like the tail of a dead rat. "You will be careful, right? Jon is very particular about who drives his vehicles. You haven't had any accidents or tickets, correct?"

Jackson hesitated for a moment and looked back over his shoulder at Amy, closed his eyes in an exaggerated manner, head tilted to the sky as though he was praying. He then focused back on Bea with a brilliant smile. "No, ma'am. I have a pristine driving record. You and your husband's SUV will make it home without a dent or a scratch." He glanced down at Mrs. Hazelton's mine-soiled tan slacks, then back at her face. "Well, without any more dents or scratches than you already have." He took the keys and gestured for Bea to proceed him to the car.

"I'll see you back at the shop, Amy," he called.

Amy gave one last, longing look at the remainder of the group and her heart sank as she saw Tommy leading Pete to one of the Mohave County Sheriff's Department SUVs. She started to turn to walk back to the cluster of people.

"Amy," Jackson's voice pulled her attention away from the scene. He came jogging over as Mrs. Hazelton continued on toward the Hazelton's silver-gray SUV.

"Come on, Amy. Tommy's right. You can't do anything right now to help Pete. Trust Tommy. He's going to make sure Pete gets a fair shake." Jackson put his hand on Amy's shoulder and pulled her toward the vehicles.

With one final hesitation, Amy turned and followed Jackson back to where she'd parked the jeep. She felt the same knot of confusion and fear that had assailed her when she had been accused of murder such a short time ago. She'd known Pete since she was a child, and while he could be a bit hot-tempered, she couldn't imagine him losing control to the point that he'd have lured Hazelton out away from everyone, and then pushed him into a mine shaft. It just wasn't possible.

Jackson started Hazelton's SUV, gave Amy a jaunty wave and headed up the two-rut track at a turtle's pace. Amy sighed and started the jeep. *Time to swallow a few more pounds of dust,* she thought.

As she pulled up the little ridge and away from the Red Wind Mine, she searched for something to occupy her mind. It came to rest on the second body in the shaft. Was it William Powell? If so, did it have any relationship to Hazelton's attack, or was it all one huge coincidence? The rest of the trip back into town seemed to pick up speed as she mulled over the possible reasons why that skeleton was down there - but only a little.

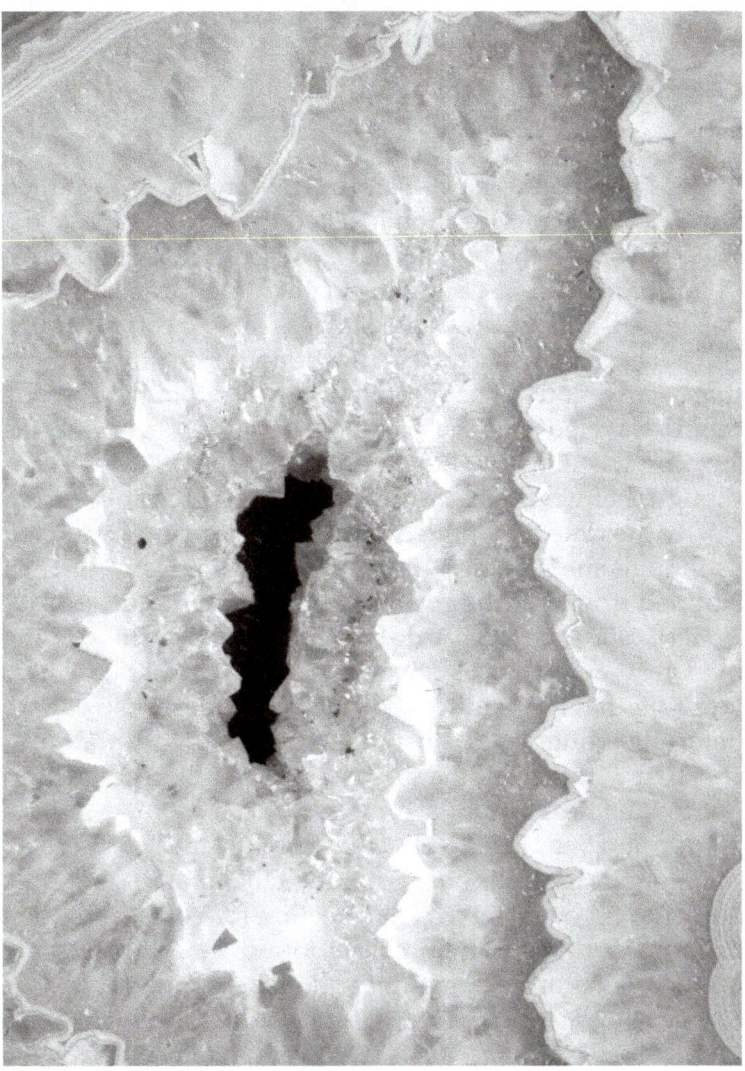

Brazilian Agate

6

It was past four o'clock before Amy and Jackson pulled into town. Mrs. Hazelton insisted that Jackson drive the SUV at a speed that would have earned him second place in a race against anything faster than a garden slug. The benefit for Amy was that she had less dust to eat on the trip since Jackson wasn't moving fast enough to stir up more than a tiny cloud. The disadvantage was that by the time they'd traveled half the distance, Amy was gripping the steering wheel with white knuckles, pushing it forward as though that would make the Hazelton's SUV move faster.

By the time they pulled into Copper Springs, Amy felt as though she'd carried the jeep the entire distance. They stopped briefly at the rock shop, intending to meet Alice Roberts and her husband, Dennis, and turn the driving over to them. Mrs. Hazelton had other ideas, however, insisting that she had to return to her home and clean up before heading to the hospital. As a result, after a quick check in with her mother, Crystal, Amy followed Jackson out to the Hazelton's place.

Jon and Bea Hazelton lived a short distance northeast of town, in the foothills bordering the Hualapai Reservation. Amy hadn't been out in that direction for years, and upon driving around the final curve, found herself slamming on the brakes and staring at the house in front of her.

Wow! Whatever Hazelton did before moving to the backwoods of Arizona must have been pretty lucrative, she thought, admiring the wrought iron gates and stone entrance. The house itself was a large cedar and granite affair, not much different than her parents' home, albeit twice as big and with a large, rounded front room with floor to ceiling windows. A flagstone walk led to the elaborate redwood slab front door complete with large, black, wrought iron strap hinges. Huge clumps of pampas grass were planted on either side of the walkway, their feathery cream plumes dancing in the breeze.

There must have been a remote in the Hazelton's SUV, as the gates started to swing open with ponderous dignity. Jackson drove through and up to the front walk. Amy started to follow, then paused, noticing a small sign mounted next to the front gate.

"Hazelton Hacienda?" She asked herself, reading the ornate lettering aloud. She groaned. It was so cute it was nauseating. Shaking her head she followed the silver SUV up to the house and parked behind it on the wide, asphalted drive.

Jackson got out and looked at Amy. Surreptitiously, he pointed a finger at her and mouthed you owe me! A voice from inside the vehicle pulled his attention back to his passenger, and he walked around the hood and opened her door. Amy bit her lip to keep from laughing. After all, the woman had been through a lot today.

Mrs. Hazelton stepped out and took several unsteady steps toward the front walkway of the house, then turned and looked back toward Jackson and Amy.

"I... um..." A frown pleated her forehead as she stuttered to a stop. "Uh... Thank you for driving me... I never would have found my way back to town on that maze of trails they call roads." The sour note was hard won at the end, but Mrs. Hazelton managed it. Still, Amy wondered if the unfamiliar words of gratitude would cause an implosion.

"No worries, Mrs. Hazelton," Jackson spoke up, giving her a warm smile. "The Roberts should be here soon, so if you don't need us any longer, we'll head back into town."

"That would be fine," Bea said. The woman seemed to

have aged ten years in the last few hours, as though the trauma of the day had sucked what little moisture was left out of her body. She turned away from them and slowly walked toward the front entrance of the house.

The smooth growl of an engine sounded from the road, and a slate blue Range Rover pulled into the driveway and up alongside Amy's jeep, making the dusty Wrangler look even rougher than normal.

"Come on, Jackson," Amy muttered. She walked to the driver's side door, put her right foot on the floorboard of the jeep, and started to lift herself in as the Range Rover disgorged a couple approximately the same age as the Hazeltons. *That must be Dennis Roberts and his wife Alice,* Amy thought as she paused, and studied the two newcomers, trying not to make it obvious that she was staring.

The man looked vaguely familiar, and she was sure she'd seen him around town. The blond to gray hair and huge mutton-chop whiskers were hard to miss. He was dressed in jeans and boots, although something about him projected more of the "cowboy wannabe" vibe than the "wealthy rancher" feel she was sure he was after. His wife also gave off a stereotypical "western cowgirl" air. They were the type who called forty acres a ranch, even if the grass growing there had never seen a cow and their saddles had more silver than scratches. She felt her lip curl in disgust.

Alice Roberts hurried up the walk toward Bea Hazelton and enveloped her in a hug. "Oh, honey! This is just so terrible! I knew Pete Martin was no good after the way he talked to Jon and Dennis at the last council meeting. At least they caught him and he'll pay for what he did!"

Dennis Roberts followed close behind his wife, glancing back over his shoulder at Amy and Jackson standing by the jeep. He turned back to Bea. "Come on ladies. Let's get into the house, and you can get cleaned up Bea. Then Alice will drive with you up to the hospital in Flagstaff. I'll follow behind in the Rover. That way you can stay there as long as needed since Alice can ride home with me. We can discuss what happened later..." He looked back over his shoulder again, a frown on his face.

"*Psst!* Amy!" Jackson's hiss pulled her attention from Mrs. Hazelton and the two Roberts. "Stop giving the Roberts the evil eye, and let's get back into town."

Amy mentally shook herself and finished climbing into the jeep as Jackson settled himself into the passenger seat, buckling the seatbelt. She pulled out her cell phone and noted the time: just after four o'clock. She knew her mother would be closing up the shop and driving back to Kingman, but Amy was reluctant to head home yet. What she really wanted was to know what had happened back out at the mine.

She turned to Jackson. "What do you say we head back to the shop? It's too early for dinner and..."

"And Gladys Jameson and Emily Sanchez won't be back at the Copper Springs Diner, yet." Jackson's eyebrow rose.

"Shut up!" Amy said in mock annoyance. "You know darned well you want to find out what happened after we left as much as I do!" Amy started the jeep and slammed it into reverse, kicking up gravel as the tires spun the Wrangler backward. She glanced over at Jackson and saw him watching her with a huge grin on his face.

"Okay, fine, know-it-all! I want to know if Pete is okay and what they've found out. I'm pretty sure that Tommy won't tell me if I called, but Gladys and Emily have to know something, and they'll tell all they know. So are you with me or not?" Amy asked.

"Heck yeah, I'm with you," Jackson said, laughing, not fooled by Amy's grouchy tone. "I'm not ashamed to admit being a bit worried about Pete, and more than a little curious about the skeleton in the closet.. err... mine."

"He couldn't have done it," Amy muttered under her breath, willing it to be true. "Sure, Pete and Jon weren't getting along, but there's no way he'd have done something like that."

"I totally agree," Jackson said, "Pete's more of a shoot-you-in-your-face type of guy, but everyone saw them arguing earlier in the day, and saw Pete follow Hazelton to the parking area to continue the fight. Most people in town know there's bad blood between them. What was Hazelton doing back there at that old shaft anyway?"

"I don't know. Maybe Gladys or Emily will know something." Amy sighed.

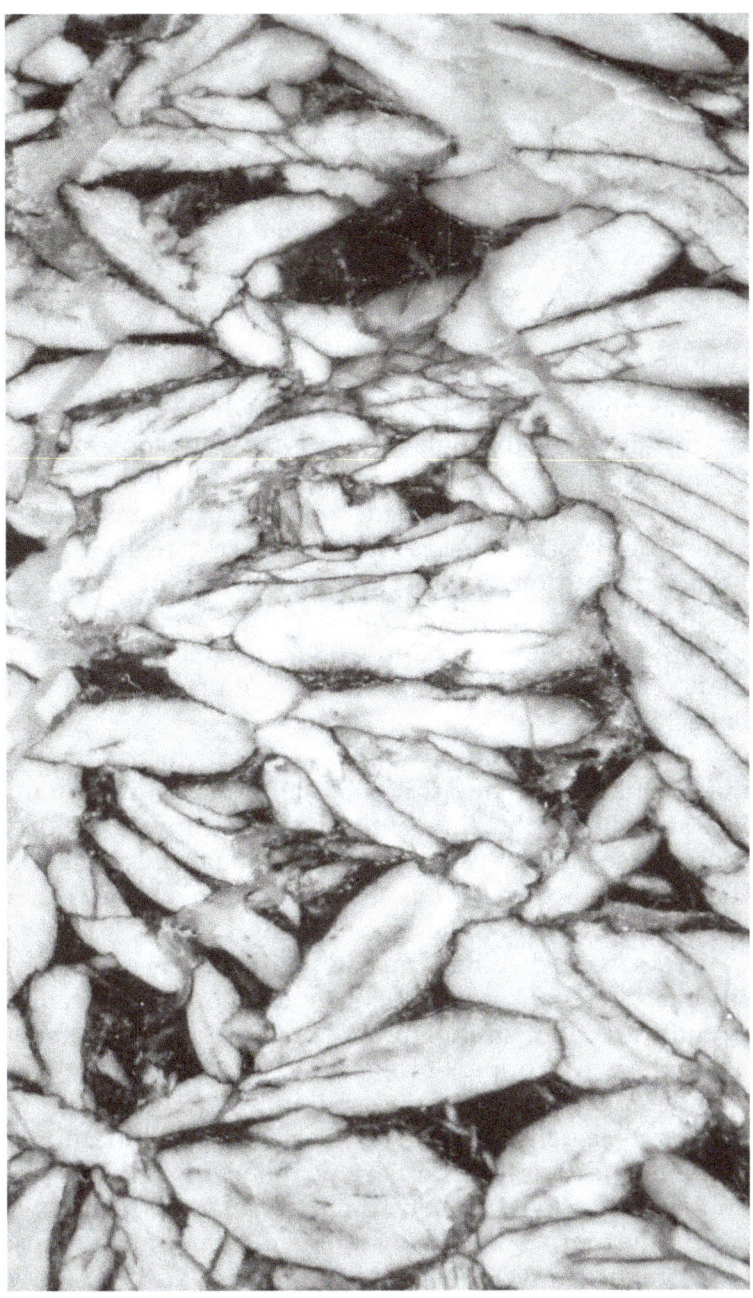

Pinolith, Austria

It was shortly after seven o'clock when Jackson and Amy walked through the glass front door of the Copper Springs Diner. Delicious smells drifted through the doorway when it opened, smells that validated their claims of "World Famous" food, and Amy realized how hungry she'd gotten. Other than an energy bar at noon, just before she and Jackson ventured up the hill toward the upper spoils piles, she hadn't eaten anything since early that morning, and her stomach growled in complaint and expectation.

The tourist traffic was slowing a bit with the approaching fall, but the small fifties-style restaurant was still busy at this time of the evening. Amy stood for a moment, scanning the large room, once again appreciating the strange juxtaposition of fifties kitsch and Arizona mining history and mineral specimens.

Jackson touched her arm and nodded his head toward the bar where two seats had just opened up. Amy headed in that direction, smiling at a couple of locals she knew along the way. Copper Springs wasn't large, and the diner was the most popular eating spot in town, so the diner's occupants usually represented a slightly off-kilter mix of cultures and languages. There were local ranchers, Supi and Havasu tribe members, preppers and survivalists, as well as the tourists and their various cultural contributions.

Tonight, Amy found herself sitting next to a family who appeared to be from Germany while Jackson, to her left, had introduced himself to the young Japanese boy sitting on the adjoining stool. Amy couldn't figure out what they were talking about, although it involved a lot of hand gestures and head bobbing. For that matter, she wasn't entirely sure that Jackson knew what they were talking about, but he seemed to be enjoying himself immensely.

Amy was watching Jackson and the little boy, trying to figure out if the topic of discussion was baseball or the Grand Canyon when she heard her name and turned back to the far side of the counter.

"Hi Amy, What can I get for you?" Merri Thompson, Jackson's younger sister asked, giving Amy a wide smile, an exact copy of her brother's. It was the type of smile that practically forced one to smile back.

"Hey, Merri. I'll have a Route 66 Burger and fries. I deserve some extra calories after today," Amy answered, then looked over toward the kitchen door. "I don't suppose that Gladys and Emily have come in yet, have they? I'd really like to talk to them."

"They came in about fifteen minutes ago." The sunny expression on Merri's face dimmed momentarily. "It's so terrible what's happened to Pete Martin. He came over after Lou was killed and told me if there was anything I needed, to just call. I just can't believe that he assaulted Jon Hazelton. Not that someone assaulting Mr. Hazelton is a surprise, but I can't believe Pete would have done it."

Amy's heart sank at Merri's words. All the way into town she had told herself that there had been a mistake, and Pete hadn't been arrested as it appeared. Now it sounded like it was exactly what it looked like when she and Jackson were leaving. *Damn.*

"Don't say hi, Sis. It's not that I'm your favorite brother or anything like that, right?" Jackson's young friend had left with his family and Jackson had turned his attention to his younger sibling. "How are the boys today?"

"Get over it, Jack," Merri said, the smile returning in a flash. "You were busy discussing the state of the universe

with that kid and didn't even realize that I'd walked up."
She laughed at the hurt expression on her brother's face.
"Besides, I've got no choice in the favorite brother thing.
You're the only one I've got, so that makes you by default
my favorite, no matter how big a jerk you've been to me
over the years." Merri laughed at the crestfallen look on
Jackson's face.

"The boys are fine, by the way," Merri said, referring
to her two young sons. "They're spending the evening at
Mike Crozier's. The three of them are probably driving
Mike's parents up the walls. I'll pick them up on the way
home. Are you still coming over tomorrow for dinner?
They miss Uncle Jack living in the driveway."

Jackson looked over at Amy. "We still starting the
renovations on the penthouse suite?" He grinned at her
look of resignation.

"Yes, I thought we could start painting. Mom and Dad
have several old cans of paint out in the barn. There should
be something there that will work," Amy answered.

Jackson looked back at Merri. "So, if you don't mind a
paint-stained brother, I can come over when we're done."

"That sounds great! Amy, do you want to come, too?
It'll be noisy, but the food is good I'm told, and Lucy's
puppies are at the totally adorable stage right now." Merri
turned her bright smile on Amy, and Amy couldn't help
but grin back. Lucy was Merri's border collie/Australian
shepherd, similar to Jynx. She had just produced five
puppies a few weeks earlier and Amy had been looking
forward to seeing them after hearing Jackson's stories.

"You bet, Merri! That sounds like a lot of fun, way
better than going back to an empty house at any rate,"
Amy answered with pleasure.

Just at that moment, Gladys emerged from the kitchen
door, and the memory of why she and Jackson had come
crashed back down. Amy felt the smile slip away as
she studied the older woman's face, noting the somber
expression in her eyes, and the wrinkles which seemed
more deeply etched into her skin.

Gladys looked around the restaurant for a moment, then her eyes came to rest on Amy and Jackson and a wisp of a smile curved her lips. She started over, then braked to a stop when someone from inside the kitchen called her name through the pass-through window.

Merri set two glasses of iced tea with lemon down in front of Amy and Jackson, and whispered, "This situation with Pete and the rock club sure seems to have hit both Gladys and Emily hard. I hope you can cheer them up." She stepped away from the two, heading down to the far end of the counter where a customer was calling for a refill on his Coke.

"I hope someone can cheer *me* up," Amy muttered to herself.

In spite of her soft voice, Jackson heard her words and patted her leg under the counter. "It will work out," he murmured. "We know Pete didn't do it. Have faith that they'll find out what happened."

Gladys had just stepped back away from the pass-through and was heading in Amy and Jackson's direction when a loud voice spoke from behind Amy's shoulder, making her jump.

"Well, hello there! Long time no see!"

Amy jerked around and saw David Shaw slipping onto the newly emptied stool next to Jackson. She looked up and saw Gladys hesitate for a moment, then turn and scurry back toward the kitchen door.

Shaw seemed oblivious to Gladys' abrupt change of direction, turned toward Jackson and clapped him on the shoulder, making him wince. "That was something today, wasn't it? I had no idea that the Copper Springs social scene could be so exciting." He signaled for Merri, who nodded and held up an index finger, letting him know it would be a moment.

Shaw turned back to Jackson and Amy. He truly did look like Jon Hazelton's twin, Amy thought. However, it appeared that this was the twin who got all the personality, maybe too much. Even Jackson, who normally handled people with a skill which Amy envied, was leaning away from Shaw. *Strange,* she thought, *Hazelton and Shaw are complete opposites, but both have the total creep factor.* She shook her head slightly, thinking about their differences and similarities. What was it about Copper Springs that it was drawing new residents like these guys?

Amy leaned on the counter in order to see around Jackson's shoulder and looked at Shaw who was busy popping toothpicks from the complimentary dispenser. By the looks of things, Merri would need to be refilling it soon. She looked toward the kitchen door, but Gladys had disappeared and there was no sign of her reappearing any time soon. The curiosity was eating at her guts like a coyote in the winter. In spite of Shaw's obnoxiousness, she asked, "What happened after we left?"

Shaw looked over at her and popped one of the toothpicks into his mouth, then slid the others into the front pocket of his shirt. He tongued the sliver of wood into the corner of his cheek and grinned at Amy giving her an internal quiver. If Hazelton was a dried up lizard, then Shaw was a slimy toad. The same eyes, though, she thought.

"There was a lot of confusion," Shaw said. He paused, gnawing on the toothpick. He pulled it out and looked at it, then popped it back into his mouth on the opposite side. "The deputies talked with everyone, wrote down where each person was when the old lady started screaming..."

Amy nearly choked on Shaw's casual identification of Bea Hazelton as the "old lady," especially as she didn't think Shaw could be much younger than the Hazeltons himself.

"And they arrested that fella with the ponytail. That seemed to upset everyone quite a bit. Everyone started arguing with the deputies. I thought there was going to be a heck of a riot for a little bit." Shaw gestured toward Merri again, trying to get her attention. She finished setting a glass of iced tea down in front of a diner farther down the counter, then walked over.

"Honey, I'd like to get a burger and fries to go," Shaw said, studying the menu.

Merri made several notes on her pad and told him the price. He pulled out the wallet, and once again Amy caught sight of a huge stack of bank notes as he pulled out the money to pay for his order. "Keep the change as your tip, honey," Shaw said, giving Merri a huge, turd-eating grin which made Amy's stomach clench.

Apparently, it made Merri uncomfortable as well, and she looked at the bills in her hand, her eyes widening. "I'm afraid you made a mistake, Mr. Shaw. Your bill was fifteen forty-five. This is a fifty dollar bill. That's too generous," she stammered.

"You've got to reward great service, honey. You keep it. I know waitresses aren't paid much."

"I... uh," Merri started. Amy could tell she was torn between not wanting to accept the money from this man, and being grateful for the bounty. "I appreciate it, Mr. Shaw. We'll have your order right up. Thanks again!" Merri hurried away to turn in Shaw's order.

Shaw turned back to Jackson and Amy. "Where was I? Oh, yeah. Anyway, the man who was arrested... Martin, right? Martin something?..."

"Pete Martin," Jackson interjected, the sharp note in his voice surprising Amy. She couldn't remember a time where she'd seen Jackson's feathers ruffled. In fact, his perpetual calm tended to irritate her at times. Shaw's attention toward Merri had seemed to touch a nerve, however. "He's the head of the local Northeastern Mohave Gem and Mineral Society, as well as the Copper Springs Historical Society."

"Oh yeah. Pete Martin. Seemed like a great guy when I talked to him out at the mine. Very knowledgeable." Shaw paused for a second, took out the toothpick and examined it, then wrapped it in a napkin, set it on the counter, and put a new toothpick in his mouth. "Anyway, Pete Martin apparently told the deputies that he was with a couple of other guys down the wash in the opposite direction from where Mr. Hazelton was pushed into that mine shaft. Problem was that those guys that Martin said he was with were no longer around. It seems they took off before everything hit the fan, as the saying goes."

"They still arrested him, though? Even though he has an alibi?" Amy blurted. She could feel her stomach clench, and her appetite disappeared.

Shaw let out a bark of laughter. "You've been watching those crime shows too much Miss... uh?"

"Amy Stone. My father, Nick Stone, owns Stone's Gems and Minerals. It's the rock shop down the road about a quarter of a mile from here."

"Yeah, I've seen it. Haven't been in, but I haven't been in town that long, either." Shaw gave Jackson a questioning look, inviting him to introduce himself as well.

Jackson was still frowning, obviously irritated by the attention that Shaw had been paid to Merri, and Amy could just picture him as the protective older brother. After all, Jackson had taken custody of Merri when their parents died, not to mention moving to Copper Springs after Merri's husband was killed and Merri was being harassed by Carl Schrader, the rock shop's former employee. The moment stretched out, and Amy was just opening her mouth to introduce Jackson when he spoke up for himself.

"Jackson Wolf. Merri's brother." He bit off the words sharply, leaving Amy in no doubt that he was very suspicious of Shaw's motivation in handing his sister such a large tip. "I work with Amy at the rock shop."

Shaw seemed oblivious to the annoyance his actions had caused in some quarters and thrust out his hand to shake Jackson's. Hesitating for a moment, Jackson put out his hand toward Shaw.

"Pleased to meet you, Jackson and Amy. I should have introduced myself during the trip to the mine," Shaw said.

"Will they be charging Pete, do you think?" Jackson asked, bringing the subject of the conversation back to the topic of the arrest. "I mean if he has someone to give him an alibi."

Shaw shrugged, "I couldn't say. I imagine it will depend on what those fellas say when the deputies track them down." Shaw seemed to lose interest in the topic and craned his head to look at the pass through, then down at his watch.

"Are you in a hurry?" Amy asked, curious. The town was small, and she hadn't seen Shaw at any time prior to the field trip, although he must work somewhere or maybe have a family who lived in the town.

"No, not really, I guess. It's just been a long day." Shaw grinned at her.

"It's a small town. I'm surprised I haven't run into you earlier. You said you just moved out to the old Linton place, right? What made you move to Copper Springs?" Jackson asked, sounding to Amy as though he was regaining his normal *sang-froid*. She couldn't see his expression from where she was sitting, but his shoulders had dropped, and some of the tension had left his neck.

Shaw checked his watch and looked toward the pass-through again, then back at Jackson and Amy. It appeared as though he was thinking about what to say, and Amy's suspicions rose. Still, he looked nothing like Pete, and Mrs. Hazelton was dead sure that the assailant had been a tall man with a ponytail. Shaw was none of those things.

"I've been here since the first of the month. I used to know some people who lived 'round here. They used to speak highly of the place. Ah, there it is!" Shaw started to rise as he saw Merri retrieve a Styrofoam box from the pass-through shelf and head in his direction.

"It was awful nice talking to the two of you. I'm sure we'll be seeing each other again. Like you say, it's a small town." Shaw grabbed the take-out box, turned and strode toward the front door, only pausing as a family of four hurried in talking in something that sounded to Amy like Italian, or maybe Portuguese – not that she knew the difference.

Jackson turned to Amy. He raised an eyebrow and jerked his chin toward the door. "I guess he had some important things to take care of. You know how busy things get in this town." He turned and gave the new occupant of Shaw's stool a brilliant smile and a nod of welcome. The father of the Italian, Portuguese or another country unknown family smiling back at Jackson and then turning his attention to his children and wife.

Jackson looked back at Amy. "If Pete has people who will verify that they were with him when Hazelton was pushed into the mine, then he should be released pretty quickly."

"But what if they can't?" Amy asked, eyes unfocused as she thought.

"Don't borrow trouble, Amy," Jackson scolded, although the tone of his voice and his smile told her that he was teasing. "Pete didn't do anything, and we both know it. It shouldn't take long before the sheriff's department figures it out as well." His grin grew even broader. "Besides, knowing Pete, he's going to end up using this experience to develop a whole new series of tales to tell everyone."

Amy choked back a laugh. *Jackson is right*, she had to admit to herself. Pete did love to tell stories, and "My time in prison as a murder suspect" would be top of his list for years to come... that was assuming he didn't have to stay there too long.

Amy sighed.

A flurry of movement at the kitchen door caught her attention and she looked up in time to see Gladys emerge. She glanced around the diner's main room, then hurried down to where Amy and Jackson were sitting.

"Is that man gone?" Gladys' face was uncharacteristically serious, her eyes troubled.

"You mean Shaw?" Jackson asked. "Yeah, he's gone. Why? What has he done?" Jackson gave Gladys a puzzled look and Amy understood why. There weren't many people whom Gladys didn't like... Hazelton and Roberts being obvious exceptions to her "everyone's a friend" outlook on life.

"There's something about him," Gladys said, a frown on her face. "I can't put my finger on it. Maybe it's just that he looks so much like Hazelton." She gazed at the door of the diner for a moment, then shook her head. "You can't blame the man for genetic bad luck, I guess."

"Can you tell us any more about Pete?" Amy asked, pulling Gladys' attention back to the people in front of her.

"No, I don't know much. Pete was taken in, but he says he was with Clint McGinnis and Alex Sanders when Bea Hazelton started screaming. The problem is that Clint and Alex rode together to the mine, and they left when they and Pete returned to the parking area before Bea Hazelton started screaming."

"Why did they leave early?" Jackson asked, putting voice to the question in Amy's mind. Jackson had leaned over the counter and was studying the woman with interest.

"Clint was always planning on leaving early," Gladys said, her face clearing. This part of the story at least held no mystery. "He drives a livestock transport truck, and he had to leave for a pickup over at the Slash SJ Ranch on the east side of the state, hauling a load of Angus yearling heifers over to New Mexico. He said he wanted to get there this evening so that they could load and be out of there first thing in the morning. Alex is going with him so that they have two drivers."

"No one was able to reach them by phone?" Amy asked.

"Not that I know of. Cell service is pretty poor in some spots, and who knows where they were when the call was made. I'm sure Clint will call as soon as he gets the message. That will clear up all of this baloney that Pete pushed Hazelton down a mine shaft. " Gladys put a lot of confidence into her voice. She beamed at Amy, then turned her smile on Jackson who gave her a warm smile in return.

"Not that Hazelton doesn't deserve to be pushed down a mine shaft," Gladys went on to say, her face taking on a thoughtful expression. Then her eyes sharpened again. "It's just that Pete wouldn't have done it." Her voice had a sharpened edge to it that Amy seldom heard from the older woman. Her brown eyes were intense, brows furrowed into a frown of determination, as though Gladys thought that Pete could be declared innocent by sheer willpower.

"Who do you think Bea Hazelton saw, then?" Amy asked.

Gladys shook her head, her steel gray curls bouncing. "I have no idea. For all I know she saw Hazelton's shadow on the side of the cliff and just thought she saw someone standing there." Her lips twisted in derision. "The old bat."

Amy bit the side of her cheek, trying to keep from laughing. Gladys easily had five to ten years on Bea Hazelton. She glanced at Jackson and saw that Gladys' comment had caught his imagination and he was trying to envision the terrace around the mine shaft, trying to remember if the sun was shining in such a way that a shadow, either of Hazelton or a piece of brush, could have fooled Bea in the heat of the moment.

"Bea was pretty adamant that it was Pete's ponytail flying out that caught her attention," Amy said. "You wouldn't see that in a shadow."

Gladys made a flapping motion with her hand and rolled her eyes. "So she saw a branch of catclaw moving in the breeze at the same time. I'll bet she's not able to see her hand in front of her face without glasses and is one of those women who's too vain to wear them."

Jackson had just taken a sip of his ice tea, and at that comment started to choke. He grabbed for a napkin from the nearby holder and began to cough. Amy looked at him, surprised and a little bit concerned.

Finally, after the paroxysm stilled, he mopped his face and looked up at Gladys with a rueful smile. "Actually, you might be right, Gladys. I hadn't thought of it, but Bea was complaining on the way into town about having me drive, but that she couldn't see well enough. I asked her if she had glasses, and she gave me a disgusted look and said that it wasn't a question 'one should ask a lady.'" The smile became his normal grin. "I dropped the conversation right there, but she must wear glasses or contacts, although all I ever remember seeing her in are those fancy sunglasses."

"That's right," Amy exclaimed. "Gucci sunglasses. I wonder what happened to them. Surely she had them today for the field trip."

Jackson gave her an impressed look. "Really? Gucci? I'm not sure what surprises me more... that she had Gucci sunglasses, or that you knew they were Gucci sunglasses." He laughed.

"Yeah, well, it's hard to miss the logo on the side. Besides, I was behind her in the grocery one day and she was on the phone talking about them," Amy said.

"Now you're eavesdropping?" Jackson teased. He shook his head in mock reproach. A lock of his sandy hair sliding down his forehead. He pushed it back into place, apparently without thought. "I'm thinking that small town life is having a bad effect on your character, Ms. Stone."

"Shut up, Jackson," Amy said and poked him in the side. "She made sure everyone in the whole store could hear her. I don't even know if anyone was even on the other end of the phone call, or if she was just pretending so that she could advertise to all of us peons that she was wearing glasses that cost more than some of these people make in a week."

Jackson nodded, then turned his attention back to Gladys. "Still, you're right that she might not have been able to see Hazelton's attacker as clearly as she let on to the sheriff's department. Do you think I should call Tommy and let him know?"

Gladys nodded, but it was Amy who said, "I think it would probably be a good idea, especially if they aren't able to reach Clint right away. It might put enough doubt on Bea's story that the sheriff's department will let him go." She started to pull her phone from her pocket.

The sound of the front door banging open caused Amy to jump. Jackson reached out and grabbed the hand that was fishing for the phone and she looked at him in surprise. Jackson's eyes were fixed on the front door and Amy turned to follow his gaze.

Pete Martin was standing just inside the door of the diner, wearing the same clothes he'd had on during the field trip, but looking considerably the worse for wear. He looked around the crowded dining room. His gaze alighted on Amy and Jackson, and he made his way over. A frown drew his busy eyebrows closer to his beard, making it look as though hair was going to swallow his face.

"Amy. Jackson," Pete said abruptly his voice tense.

"Pete, are you okay?" Gladys asked and Pete turned his look on her and he nodded abruptly.

"I'm fine, Gladys. They've let me go without charging me with anything... Yet."

Amy let out a breath she didn't realize she'd been holding. "Yet?"

Pete looked at her with a ghost of a smile parting his beard. "Yeah, yet. They questioned me, but they want to talk to Clint first. I just hope..." His voice trailed off.

"Surely he'll give you an alibi," Jackson said, then a slight frown crossed his face. "That is if..." He shrugged and gave Pete a look out of the corner of his eyes.

"If I'm telling the truth and he was with me in the opposite direction from where Bea Hazelton says she saw me?" Pete barked. "He was. After the argument with Hazelton, Clint and Alex walked with me up the wash, talking me out of my temper. The problem is that we had turned and walked back toward the mine's main entrance shortly before we heard the screams." The worried frown settled on his face again. He stood for a moment in silence, looking at his dusty boots, then looked up again, first at Amy, and then at Jackson. "There's no way I could have made it over to where Hazelton fell, though. There wasn't enough time, and I would have had to go by Bea in order to get there."

Amy thought about that trail that headed from the terrace and up over the saddle of the hill, back toward the main mine, but didn't say anything out loud.

"What were you doing when Bea said that Jon was pushed?" Jackson asked. There was no note of accusation in Jackson's voice that Amy could hear, but the frown on Pete's face deepened.

"I didn't touch that pencil-necked, land-baron wannabe." Pete snapped.

Jackson put his hands up, palms toward Pete. "Hey, Pete. I know you wouldn't have pushed Hazelton down the mine shaft no matter how much he deserved it."

"Jackson," Amy growled, looking around the room. A few heads had started to turn in their direction, although Amy couldn't see any familiar faces. Still, no point in feeding the rumor mill any more than necessary. "Knock it off! People will start thinking you did it," Amy hissed.

Jackson looked over at Amy. "But you're my alibi, remember? We were up on a mountainside. I couldn't have done it." He gave her a wink.

"And if you don't straighten out, I might start denying it," Amy growled.

Pete chuckled his expression lightening for a moment, but only for a moment. Then the thunder clouds began to settle again. "I was over by the mine portal looking for Jania." A sheepish look replaced the frown. "I was very much hoping to get my hands on that huge wulfenite specimen we saw today. The one by the mine chute? I thought if I talked to her now, I might be able to grab it at a good price before it went up for auction. Collectors would kill to get their hands on one like that..." Pete choked off his words, surprise causing his face, or what could be seen of it, to flush bright red.

Amy's violet eyes flew open wide, and Jackson started laughing.

"You might not want to word it quite that way to the detectives," Jackson said, still choking back chuckles, "although I doubt that Hazelton could be described as a collector."

"Actually," Pete said, his eyes taking on a faraway look. "I'm not so sure about that. Have you seen that fancy house of his out there east of town?"

"We drove Bea out there, but weren't invited in," Jackson said. "The Roberts arrived just after we did and took over. Why? Have you?" He asked, his head tipped to the side and curiosity practically dripping from his pores.

Pete nodded, the thoughtful expression still in his eyes. "I was, if you must know, shortly after it was built and the Hazelton's moved in. That had to be... what... six or seven years ago?" He made it sound like a question although Amy had no idea when the Hazeltons had moved to Copper Springs. She did remember her dad, Nick, had told her it was shortly after she'd left for college and a life in the big city.

"Well, Jon and Bea Hazelton have quite a collection of 'valuables' up there at the Hazelton Hacienda. I'm not sure how many of them are authentic, and how many are just good replications, but they seem to be into collecting a number of things, such as Navajo blankets and weavings, pottery and the like. Hazelton went on about the appreciation in value of one of the blankets. If he thought there was money to be had in mineral specimens, I wouldn't put it past him to try and grab some of the best ones for himself, and to use his clout as a council member to do so."

"The mine's not even in Copper Springs," Amy said in disgust. "There can't be any clout to be had."

"You never know. Honestly, if he just offered Salina and Jania fifty or sixty bucks for a specimen, they might take it, not knowing what the piece is really worth, and money being tight for them," Pete shook his head. "That big cluster is easily worth close to a thousand if not more considering it's a new find, and they'll have full control over how much hits the market."

"And that's what you were going to offer them, right?" Jackson said with a huge grin.

"Well, maybe not that much, but I'd sure offer a lot

more than that skinflint Hazelton would have offered," Pete said in disgust.

"Salina said she wanted to talk to me about marketing some of the specimens that are coming out of the Red Wind... Sounds like maybe I should give her a call before all the vultures swoop in and scoop up the good stuff," Amy said with a smile. She knew Pete and was certain that he would have offered the Mattheson sisters a good price, but it couldn't hurt to give the women a few lessons on the value of their property.

Pete nodded, but the distant look had taken over his gaze again. "I went looking for Jania over in the mine. Salina said she'd gone back in, and I was hoping if I could find her, maybe I could help her remove that cluster of crystals." He shrugged. "I didn't go too far down the adit since I wasn't sure exactly where she was. I intended to go at least as far as that vug, but the batteries started to die on my headlamp, and the last thing I wanted was to wind up down there with no light."

Amy looked at him in surprise. "You didn't take an extra battery pack or a handheld flashlight?"

"Nah," he shrugged again and tucked his chin into his chest, the beard flopping on his overalls. "Originally I hadn't planned on going back in. Then I told myself I wouldn't go in too far. I was just looking for Jania. I went a little farther than I intended, but when the battery indicator went yellow, I turned around and headed back for the portal."

Amy was shocked. Pete had been around too long to make such a rookie mistake. No one went into a mine without having extra batteries and a hand-held flashlight or lantern, no matter how well he knew the mine. Amy's father, Nick, had taught all of his children that from their first mine and cave explorations. People got separated, lost and died in mines doing stupid things like that. She caught Jackson's eye and saw that he'd understood the magnitude of Pete's foolishness as well.

"So, no one saw you go down into the mine? You

didn't find Jania?" Jackson asked. He gave Amy a *this isn't good* look this turned his eyes back on the older man

Pete didn't seem aware of Amy and Jackson's thoughts. "No. Well, yes, I did find Jania, or she found me, but it wasn't until I was back out to the portal. I was standing outside the mine wondering what was happening when Jania came up behind me and asked what all the commotion was about."

"So Jania can say that you weren't down in the wash with Hazelton," Amy asked, a spark of hope lighting in her chest.

"Yes and no. I mean she wasn't with me when the screaming started, obviously, but there is no way I could have gotten back to the front of the mine before Bea Hazelton. Don't worry kids, the sheriff's deputies will get it all straightened out." He gave Amy and Jackson a huge smile, but Amy could hear the note of strain in his voice and she was sure she knew where it came from. The hillside was covered with trails and riddled with shafts. If Bea Hazelton had run toward where she'd seen Jon fall before she ran back to the main parking area, giving the perpetrator extra time to escape. If Pete knew the trails, it would be possible for him to make it back to the portal in time. Amy glanced back at Gladys and saw that Emily was standing at the doorway to the kitchen and had been listening to Pete's story as well. The two older women were uncharacteristically silent, but Amy could tell that they were worried.

"What about Powell?" Jackson asked, diverting everyone's attention.

"Do you really think it's William Powell down there?" Gladys asked, her eyes lit with excitement. "You saw the remains, Amy... Jackson...? What happened to him?" Emily had emerged from the kitchen and stood behind Gladys' shoulder, expression curious as well.

"Well... uh... We saw a skeleton with some rags of material and scraps of hair. It might have been Powell, but it's not like he was carrying ID or anything like that,"

Amy said. She shot Jackson a look. Not that she wasn't happy to be off the subject of Pete's alibi, or lack thereof, but the identity of the skeleton in the mine wasn't exactly where she wanted to go.

"But could you tell how he died?" Gladys went on, breathless in her excitement. Obviously, a cold case murder was a lot less disturbing than current assaults credited to close friends.

"It looked like the same iron that went through Hazelton's leg had also gone through the rib cage of Mr... uh..." Jackson looked at Amy. "...of the skeleton. It was hard to say how much Hazelton had disrupted the bones, but I'm guessing that something like that would be fatal."

"That poor family," Emily said, shaking her head. "Didn't you say that he had a wife and children, Gladys?"

Gladys nodded, her sun-weathered face crinkled with a frown. "Yes, from what I remember, William Powell's wife and children had gone into Kingman to see a doctor or something like that, and when they came home that evening, they couldn't find him. I wonder where they are now."

"I'm sure the authorities will track them down," Amy said. "They'll want to do some sort of DNA testing or something else to see if this is Powell."

"It shouldn't be too hard to find them," Jackson said with confidence. "The Matthesons probably bought the mine from the family... either the wife or his children. The kids would be in... what," Jackson concentrated for a moment, "their late thirties or early forties, depending on how old they were at the time. Do you know how old they were when their father disappeared, Gladys?"

"Oh, my," said Gladys, a look of concentration on her face. "Young weren't they, Pete?"

Pete paused and thought for a moment. "Under five probably. Powell was only in his thirties and same for his wife. Of course, that wasn't a lot younger than my wife and I were at that time." He fell silent again, a smile played around his lips and his eyes took on a distant look as he remembered those days long past. Amy could only vaguely remember Pete's wife, Lil. She'd passed away from cancer when Amy was around ten. The picture in Amy's mind held a round, laughing lady, who was right there beside her husband on rock hunting trips, laughing excitedly when she found a particularly good piece of jasper or agate.

Pete shook his head, and his eyes came back to the present. "You're right, though, Jackson. It should be fairly easy to find the family, as long as the property hasn't changed hands multiple times since Powell disappeared. I doubt it since we never saw anyone else out there. Even if it did, there should be a paper trail, just a little harder to follow. I'm sure it will be a weight off Powell's kids to know what happened, as sad as it is. I can't imagine there is anything worse than to grow up with everyone saying your father abandoned you."

Amy was watching Jackson and saw the flash of pain in his blue eyes. He had been eighteen when his parents died, and Merri was fifteen. He may not have been abandoned, but he knew what it felt like to lose the support of family. It was only a moment, and he quickly covered it with a smile, but Amy was sure she'd gotten a brief look at the well of sadness that lurked deep within.

Pete hadn't noticed the momentary change in Jackson's mood, involved as he was in the contemplation of the skeleton which may or may not be the solution to the mystery of William Powell's disappearance.

"I suppose we'll never know how he wound up there down in the mine, even if it does turn out to be Powell," Emily said.

Gladys shook her head, but a smile played on her lips. "No, not likely. But I would think the ghost stories that will result might help the Matthesons if they ever decide to make the Red Wind into a tourist attraction."

Pete snorted. There were no shortage of ghost stories in the old towns of the west, and no shortage of opportunists willing to cash in on those stories, romanticizing the past, no matter how dirty or violent it was in actuality.

"That's what we need is more tourists," Pete growled.

Gladys laughed, "That's exactly what Hazelton and Roberts are saying. Makes the land prices go up, keeps the businesses busy. It sure hasn't hurt us anyway." She gestured around the packed restaurant.

"Yeah, well I liked it better in the old days," Pete muttered.

Amy felt a qualm... a deep shiver in her chest. The investigators wouldn't have to do much investigating to find plenty of animosity between Pete and Hazelton. She watched him from the corner of her eye, talking with Jackson about the evils of unbridled expansion.

For that matter, she thought as she looked over toward Gladys and Emily, *there are a lot of people here, Dad included, who are benefiting from more traffic. We could wind up with a war on our hands in the near future.*

An image of Ol' Tom standing on the side of the road, watching the stream of field trip visitors go by, flashed into Amy's mind. There was someone else who wouldn't be happy to see more tourists.

"Hey Pete, you know the Mattheson's better than any of us. Have they said anything about making the mine a tourist mecca?" Amy asked. She thought about Jania's shyness and Salina's icy reserve. She couldn't imagine either of the women being eager to have strangers tramping across their land on a daily basis.

Pete shrugged, the movement compressing his beard like a hairy scarf. "They've never mentioned developing the mine that way. I had to do some fancy talking to get them to open it up to the rock club on that single trip, and I don't think they'd have done it if they weren't so short of cash. Now, I think I'd better head on home. I just didn't want you worrying about me." He gave Gladys and Emily a wink, and patted Amy on the shoulder, then turned and made his way out the front door.

The sound of plates clinking on the Formica counter made Amy jump, and she turned to see that Merri had set a burger and fries in front of her, and was setting a similarly heaped plate in front of Jackson. She closed her eyes and inhaled deeply, all thoughts of ghosts and mines disappearing as her stomach renewed a hunger driven assault of its own.

She took a deep breath and dug in. Tomorrow would be soon enough to worry about Pete and Hazelton, let alone William Powell.

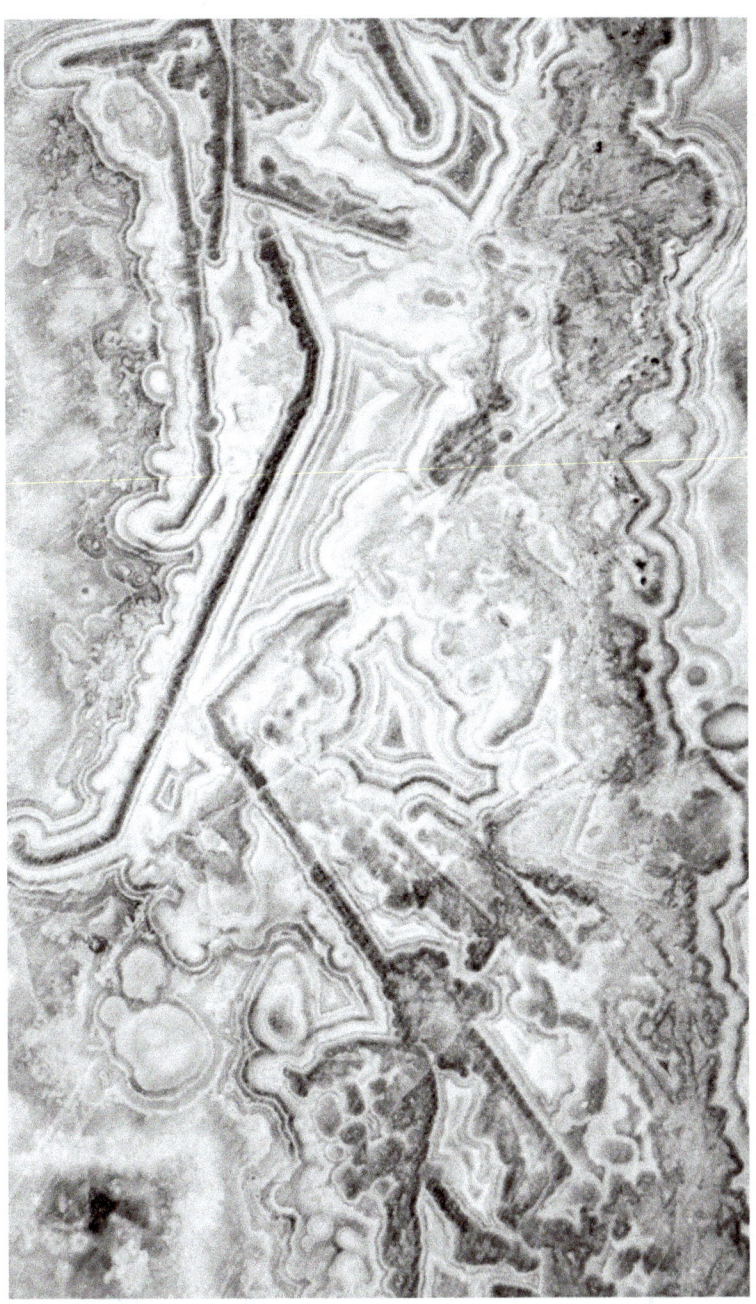

Crazy Lace Agate, Mexico

8

"What do you think?" Jackson stepped back from the wall where he'd administered a final swipe with his roller. He looked around the second-floor apartment critically. "I think any self-respecting ghost would be proud to live here."

Amy looked around at the freshly painted walls and nodded. Jackson had been correct that a fresh coat of paint would brighten the place up. "It's looking pretty good, Jackson."

"Yep, it's taking shape for sure." He nodded in satisfaction. He looked down and toed a loose flap of the ancient, cracked vinyl flooring, probably as old as the building itself "Of course this stuff isn't adding to the ambiance much."

"Do you think it's going to be hard to remove?" Amy asked. She squatted and grabbed another piece of grubby flooring and pulled. It came up with a ripping sound, displaying the wood floor below.

Jackson shook his head. "It shouldn't be too hard. It's not glued very well. We'll get it pulled up, then rent a sander and sand down any glue that is left. Then a bit of wax, a little polish, and you'll be good to go," he said in a cheerful voice.

Amy gave Jackson a lopsided smile, certain that it wasn't going to be quite as easy as he made it sound. More than likely it was going to be a hard, sweaty job that would make her long to set the apartment on fire before she was done. She stood again and looked around the room, trying to imagine it with bright curtains and squishy, comfortable furniture. The white walls helped, but the exercise in visualization was still a stretch. She thought back to her apartment in Phoenix... a large windowed, modern space. Thoughts of her life in Phoenix automatically brought up thoughts of Jeffery Donaldson, her ex-boyfriend, and the man who, with the help of his father, had torpedoed her career. She shook her head, banishing her ghosts back to the past.

"It'll work out," she said, forcing her voice to take on a determined tone and was proud to hear no wavering. She looked over at Jackson and saw that she hadn't fooled him, but that he wasn't going to let on.

Searching for a new topic, she said, "How do you think Hazelton's doing?"

Jackson shrugged and a small smile twisted his lip. He ran his fingers through his sandy hair. "Hard to say. He's not young, and that was a pretty severe injury, but if his leg wasn't broken, and no major vessels were damaged, they will want to get him out of there without delay thanks to the nuances of modern insurance." Jackson looked at her. "Not today, of course, but I wouldn't be surprised if he were back in the *Hazelton Hacienda* by tomorrow or the next day."

Amy made a face. "You saw that sign, did you? Good grief."

"Oh, yeah. I saw it. Threw up a little in my mouth." Jackson said, making a face, then laughed.

Amy grinned back at him, then broke into a laugh herself, feeling some of the tension of the weekend melt from her shoulders.

Jackson's expression became a little more thoughtful. "The house looks pretty fancy from the outside, though. Maybe it deserves its name. Their architect knew what he was doing, at least based on the exterior. I wouldn't mind a look around the inside. Pete seemed impressed by it."

Amy rolled her eyes. "Now you're into architecture?"

"Unplumbed depths, Amy. Unplumbed depths," Jackson said then broke into a laugh at her expression.

Amy shook her head and couldn't help smiling at his foolishness. She bent and started pulling up another chunk of vinyl flooring, then tossed it a few feet away. She pulled another piece, and added it to the pile. A short distance away, Jackson began the same process, tugging on a flap, then when it cracked loose from the larger sheet, tossing it over onto the growing pile. The two worked in companionable silence for a few minutes. Finally, Amy rocked back on her heels and surveyed the floor that had been uncovered, and nodded to herself. Already a large area of the wooden floor was exposed. Whoever had installed the original flooring had skimped on the adhesive, and it appeared that relatively little sanding would be needed to get it ready to wax.

She looked over at Jackson, who had just pulled up an exceptionally large chunk of the grubby white and green checked vinyl and was levering it onto the trash pile, where it smothered the other, smaller pieces.

"How would you feel about running out to visit the Hazeltons? When Jon is home from the hospital, I mean. Just to say hello and see how he's doing," Amy asked, trying to keep her voice neutral.

Jackson turned his head and looked at her, not fooled by her tone. A smile played around his lips, although Amy could tell he was gnawing on the inside of his cheek... probably to keep from laughing.

After a beat, he said, "Because you're such good friends, right?"

"Well, we did spend quite a bit of time down in that mine together. It sort of builds a bond," Amy said, then wanted to kick herself at the self-righteousness in her voice.

Jackson started laughing. "Oh, without a doubt. I'm sure you're motivated by concern for Hazelton, and the opportunity to quiz him about what he remembers has absolutely nothing to do with it."

Amy grabbed a small chunk of flooring and flung it like a Frisbee toward Jackson. He ducked just in time to avoid the rough edge of the vinyl taking his head off.

"Hey! Careful there, blood stains are heck to get out of a hardwood floor!"

"I'll take the chance," Amy growled.

Jackson picked up the piece that Amy had thrown and tossed it onto the trash pile. "So I take it that you don't trust Tommy to get to the bottom of this mine shaft assault so to speak?"

"Pun intended?"

"Totally." He grinned at her.

Amy frowned, chewing her lip. "It's not that I don't trust him to investigate. It's just that..."

"That it's Pete, and you're worried about him? That sitting here doing nothing is driving you up the wall?" Jackson gave her a sympathetic look.

"Yes to all of the above." Amy laughed, then threw her head back and groaned. "I feel like I'm turning into Gladys and I've got to know what's going on or I'll explode."

"Nah, you don't have the hair, nor the..." He gave her a critical look that made her laugh. "...to be Gladys. Besides, if you were Gladys, that would make me Emily, and that's just not happening." He batted his eyelashes at her as he dropped his voice close to inaudible levels.

"However," he continued in a normal voice, "in the interest of keeping you from exploding, and thereby keeping my job, I say we give Bea a call to see how Jon is doing."

"You said he wouldn't be home from the hospital yet," Amy said, giving him a startled look.

"No, but I happen to have her cell number." He pulled his old cracked phone from a clip at his belt and brandished it in front of Amy.

"You do? When did that happen? Your trip back from the Red Wind must have been more interesting than you'd let on." Amy looked at him, impressed. She'd thought Bea Hazelton one of the only females on the planet impervious to Jackson's charm, but maybe even the old bat... uh... woman, was susceptible. Although for the life of her, Amy couldn't figure out why Jackson would want her to be.

"It wasn't a ride I care to repeat any time soon," Jackson's voice held a wry note, "but I did feel sorry for her. Did you know they've been married for almost forty years? Their anniversary is next month."

Amy sat gaping at Jackson, her mouth moving but no sound came out.

Jackson's face held a rueful smile and he gave her a lopsided shrug. "It was a very long drive. The stress made her talkative, at least after the first few minutes, and I just let her ramble on. She spit out a few nuggets of information in between her complaints about how I was driving, and that I was trying to hit every single rock in Arizona."

"So how did you get her number?"

"She is worried about how she'll manage if Jon is out of commission for very long, and I told her to call if she needed anything. I gave her my number and she accidentally hit send instead of save after putting it into her phone."

"You actually told her... The woman who tried to drive my family out of... You volunteered..." Amy stuttered to a stop, at a loss for words. She might be able to dredge up a modicum of sympathy for Bea Hazelton. It wasn't long ago that Amy's mother was in a similar situation, after all. Her husband had been injured, leaving her to hold down the fort. Still, Crystal Stone met every challenge with a calm, peaceful strength, while Bea Hazelton seemed to meet every situation with icy condescension or bristling antagonism.

"Yeah, well," his smile became even more rueful. "She may not be a very nice person, but she is a person, and she was scared. Besides, I figured it was more like a security blanket and that she'd never actually call."

Amy had to admit there was a good chance he was right and that Bea Hazelton would never willingly call on Jackson. Still, his offer now made it easier for them to call and see how Jon was doing.

"Make the call, Jackson," Amy said with a sigh, gesturing toward his phone. "I know I'm going to regret it, but make the call."

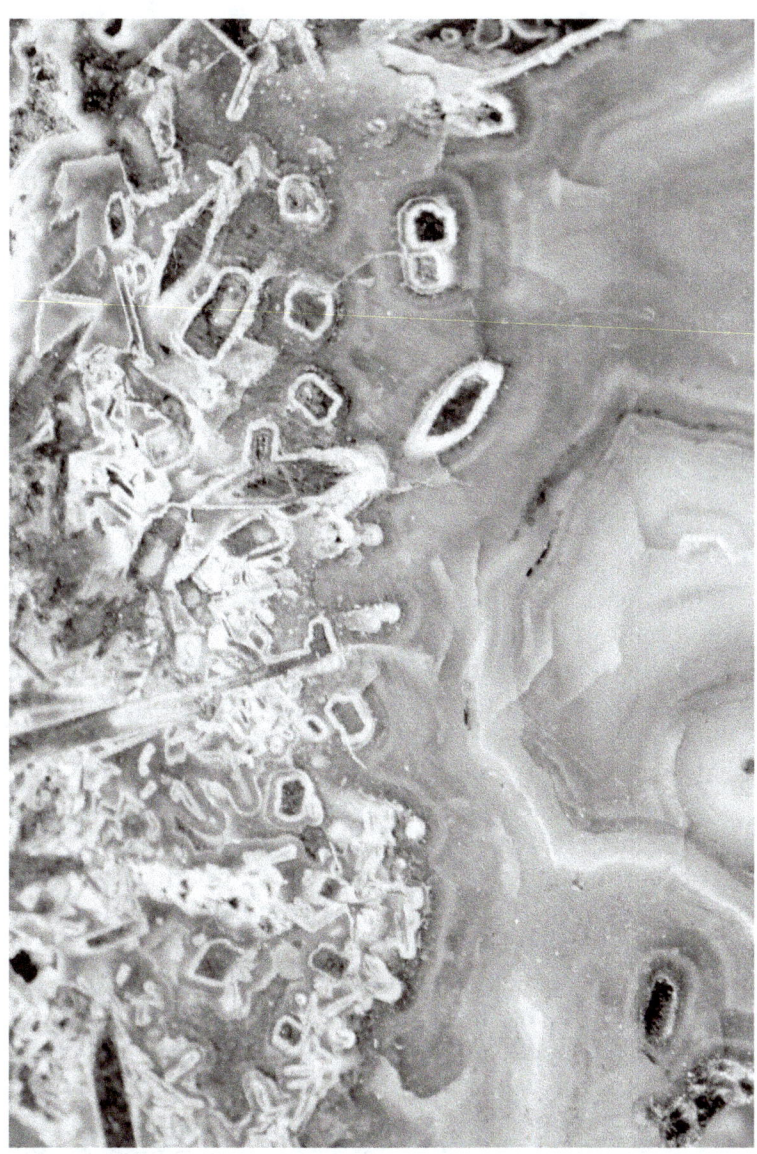

Turkish Stick Agate Pseudomorph

9

Jackson left a message for Bea, which did absolutely nothing to staunch Amy's growing curiosity, especially since she was positive that the distaff side of the Hazelton duo would never bother to return the call. To her surprise, Jackson's phone chirped its standard *Don't Worry Be Happy* ringtone at five o'clock that afternoon, just as they were cleaning up to go to Merri's house for dinner.

Jackson looked at the screen, and a huge smile split his face. He held up the phone and set it on speaker.

"Hi, Mrs. Hazelton," Jackson winked at Amy. She rolled her eyes and shook her head.

"Hello uh... Ja... Um... Mr. Wolf,," came Bea Hazelton's voice, obviously uncomfortable deciding what to call Jackson. "I received a call from you asking about Jon's health and I just wanted to get back with you."

"Thank you so much. Amy and I were worried about both of you. How is Mr. Hazelton doing?" Jackson's voice had a soothing mix of lightness and sympathy that Amy envied.

"I appreciate your concern, uh.. Jackson. Jon is doing very well, all things considered. His doctors say that his leg wasn't broken, and that piece of metal missed any important blood vessels. Shock seemed to be their greatest concern, and that has been resolved." She sniffed, and it sounded as though she wasn't convinced that the doctors in question were qualified to render an opinion. "They intend to discharge him Monday, which I think is much too early." The disapproval radiated through the air.

Amy spoke up, directing her words toward the phone in Jackson's hand. "Hello Mrs. Hazelton, this is Amy Stone. I'm glad that Mr. Hazelton is doing better. We've been pretty worried about him."

"Thank you, Ms. Stone." The formality in Bea's voice was unabated. "We... I mean... Well, I appreciate all your assistance down in that hole. The doctors said that without your care, it's very likely that Jon would have been in much worse shape."

"It was nothing, Bea," Jackson slipped in Mrs. Hazelton's given name. He glanced at Amy and raised his eyebrows. "I'm glad we were able to help, and that it sounds like Jon is going to be okay. I don't suppose he's available?"

"No. He's sleeping at the moment. He's been sleeping a great deal since he got here. The medication they have him on makes him tired. The doctors assure us, however, that it is a normal reaction to the pain medication, and that there is no sign of infection. Now, I do need to go if that's everything. Thank you again for calling to check on us." Bea's voice became more distant, as though her mind was already on other things.

"That's fine," Amy said. "Maybe Jackson and I could come out and visit when you get back? I'd love to see how your husband is doing."

"I suppose that would be okay," There was a hesitation in Bea's voice. Amy wasn't sure if it was because she didn't want Jackson and Amy tramping through her house, or if she couldn't figure out why they would want to see her husband. As far as Amy was concerned, it didn't matter.

The call ended and Jackson was left holding the silent phone. His eyes met Amy's and he gave her a crooked smile. "It looks as though we've got an audience with the king and queen."

"Yeah," Amy said, her voice making it clear that she wasn't sure if it was a good thing or a bad thing. "I wonder if Pete has heard anything more since we talked with him last night."

"You mean if he's been arrested and charged with the assault?" Jackson said, his voice as dry as the desert, lacking the usual humor that underlaid most of his statements.

"Well, there is that." Amy sighed, then pulled out her phone and looked for Pete's number, pushing the send. She set the phone on speaker but all that rang out through the small apartment were the lyrics of the Eagles *Take It Easy* as they waited for the call to be answered. Finally, two notes sounded and Amy was sent to voicemail.

She looked at Jackson and shrugged. "Hey Pete, this is Amy. I just wanted to see how you were doing, and if you'd heard anything. Has the sheriff's department been able to talk to Clint yet? Give me a call when you get the message."

She pressed the "end" icon and stood for a moment holding the phone.

"What do you think that means?" Jackson asked, tipping his chin toward the device in Amy's hand.

"Probably that he just doesn't want to talk to anyone," Amy said. "He might be out in the shop, though. He usually puts the phone on silent when he's working on delicate pieces. He says that the phone going off at the wrong time can cause him to jump. He claims he lost a beautiful piece of moldavite he had just finished faceting. He jumped, the stone flew, and he hasn't found it to this day."

Jackson frowned, obviously thinking. "Moldavite is that the green glass that was formed when a meteorite hit the ground in the Czech Republic or Germany, right? The green stuff."

"Yes, the 'green stuff,'" Amy said, "found only one place in the world, and not something you want to lose just because you were startled by the phone." Amy studied the blank screen for a moment then hit several buttons, and pressed send again. This time Tommy's voice floated out into the dry air.

"Tom Kissoon here."

"Hey, Tommy; it's Amy. I was just calling to..."

"To see if I'll tell you anything about our investigation?" Tommy finished. Amy couldn't miss the exasperated note in his voice and she made a face at Jackson. He looked back at her and gave his head the merest hint of a shake.

"Uh... yes, then, I thought maybe you could tell me if you'd been able to talk to Clint and what he'd said."

A deep sigh came out of the speaker and Jackson pinched lips with a thumb and forefinger. Amy was certain it was to keep from laughing and she was tempted to wing another piece of flooring at him.

"I don't suppose it can hurt. Yes, I spoke with Clint McGinnis and Alex Sanders, and just as Pete said, the three of them had gone up the wash after Pete and Hazelton's argument. However, according to them, they had also returned to the parking area well before Bea Hazelton started screaming. They split up, and Pete headed over toward the mine. Clint and Alex left, so they have no idea if Pete had time to make it to the mine shaft and back before Bea Hazelton showed up or not. The best he's got going for him is that Clint and Alex both stated that Pete had seemed over the argument and more interested in obtaining some large piece of rock he'd seen."

Amy grinned, "It was actually a crystal about the size of your thumb, but that's big for that type of crystal. So, Pete isn't cleared yet, then?"

"No, he isn't cleared." Tommy paused, the silence making Amy wonder if the call had been dropped, but then his voice sounded once again. "Amy, I know you are worried about Pete, but you need to trust us to do the investigating."

"I'm not investigating," Amy protested. "I just wanted to..."

"I know. You just wanted to know what we'd found out. Remember what happened with Schrader. I am pretty good at my job, Amy. Let me do it."

Amy felt as though she'd been slapped in the face. Her chin jutted out in defiance. "Tommy, I do trust you, but this is Pete. I want to know he's going to be okay." She looked up and saw Jackson studying her.

"I know you care for Pete, Amy. We will find out exactly what happened. You have to understand, though, that if Pete broke the law, he will be arrested."

"He..." Amy started but Tommy cut her off abruptly.

"And if he's innocent, we'll find that out as well."

Amy wanted to argue, but Jackson had started shaking his head and mouthing the words, *say thank you and hang up.*

She took a deep breath and struggled to squash the rising rebellion in her chest. She knew Tommy. She'd known him for a very long time and she knew she could trust him. Hell, he was the one who saved both Jackson and her from the mines, with a little help from the dogs, Jynx and Bess. *I can trust him to do this, she told herself firmly.*

"Okay, Tommy. Thanks for talking with me. Say hi to Maria and your folks when you see them next."

"Will do, Amy. They'd love to see you if you get down in the canyon," Tommy said, referring to the branch of the Grand Canyon where his parents lived in Supai on the Havasupai reservation. Amy knew they hadn't been doing well in recent months. Maybe that was why he was so tense.

Amy heard a flurry of sound coming over the phone's speaker. Several other voices, indistinct, and a high piercing whine. "Amy, I've got to go. I promise you that we'll get to the bottom of everything. Just take care of the shop and try not to worry."

"Wait, Tommy, have you heard anything about the skeleton...?"

She was too late. The call was ended abruptly and Amy looked at Jackson.

"What do you think, Jackson?"

"I think he sounded busy. We did hand him two bodies at the same time, after all."

"Yeah, I guess," Amy shook her head and slumped momentarily, then pulled herself upright.

"So, should I call and cancel with the Hazelton's?" Jackson asked. A sly smile twitched across his face.

"No, we'll still go. Just because I told Tommy we wouldn't investigate doesn't mean we can't go and say hello to Hazelton and see how he's doing."

"It would only be polite," Jackson said, keeping his expression bland.

This time Amy did tug up another slab of flooring and flung it at him.

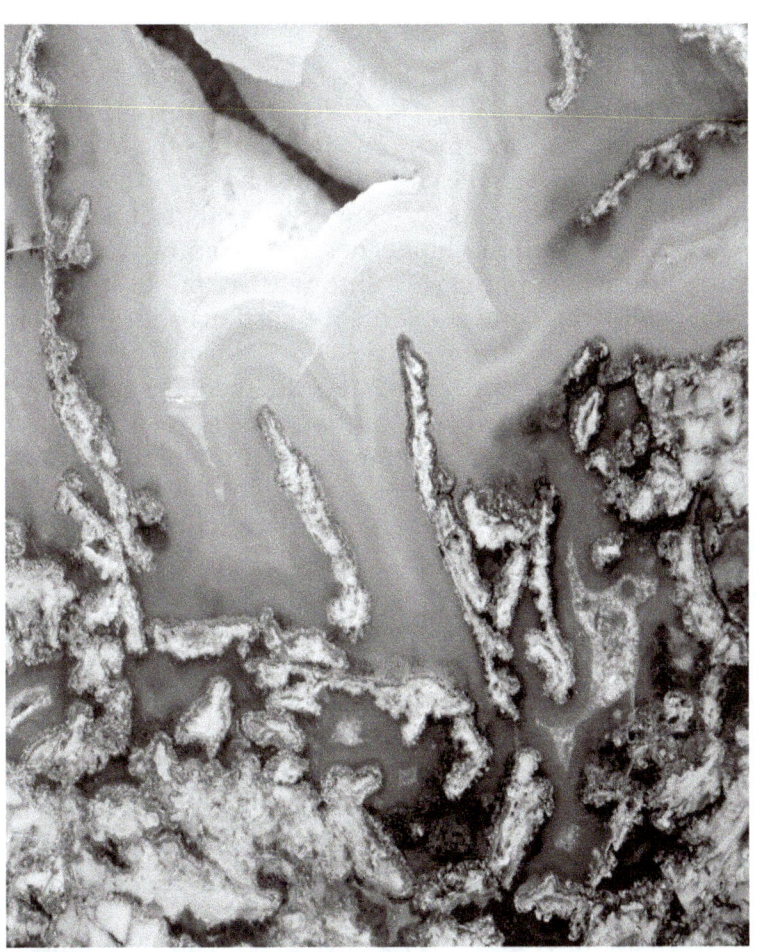

Becon Hill Agate, Idaho

10

Tuesday at one, Amy flipped the closed sign on the shop's door, set the "We'll be back at" sign for two o'clock, and she and Jackson climbed into the Wrangler and headed toward the *Hazelton Hacienda*.

Amy gripped the steering wheel tightly as they raced toward the Hazelton's home, her mind spinning. She kept running different scenarios through her mind - playing out the meeting, and thinking of questions she could ask that might help Pete.

Periodically she'd give herself a mental shake. *This isn't my job. The sheriff's department would have gone over everything with them,* went the internal dialogue. *I'm just going to check and see how Jon is doing. He looked so ill down in the mine. I told Tommy I wouldn't investigate.* Then she'd lose focus, and she'd be back in the Hazelton's living room grilling Jon and Bea like prime Arizona steaks.

"Buck seventy-five for your thoughts." Jackson's voice penetrated Amy's distraction. "I would like to live to see my grandchildren," he added conversationally and Amy realized that her physical speed had increased as her mind had raced.

"A dollar and seventy-five cents?" Amy shot him an exasperated look from the corner of her eye as she dropped her speed back to a reasonable level for the small road.

"Inflation, you know. I'd have given you two dollars, but my boss is a skinflint and I just don't have the money to spare." He gave her a serious look which cracked into a smile after a few seconds.

Amy choked back a laugh. Jackson had the ability to start a nonsensical discussion about almost anything and the person targeted would often find herself invested in the conversation before realizing that they had taken a major detour into the weird. Amy had to admit, however, that these ridiculous discussions served their purpose, as the victims of these diversions from reality tended to become totally distracted and forgot whatever they were doing before Jackson opened his mouth.

Amy felt some of the tension drop from her shoulders, and the jeep's speed dropped closer to a safe level. A furry head popped over her shoulder and gave her a warm lick on the cheek. Apparently, Jynx, who had come along for the ride, appreciated the more sedate pace as well.

"I don't know what I'm expecting. Maybe Hazelton will have remembered something, such as why he was back at that mine shaft to begin with. Maybe now that Bea has had a chance to calm down she'll remember something about the attack," Amy said, with a sigh.

They still hadn't heard from Pete since seeing him at the diner Saturday evening. Amy tried to call him several additional times, but the phone had gone straight to voicemail each time, not even giving an encore of *Take It Easy*, and Pete hadn't called back. She had considered driving out to his place that evening, but in the end, decided against it. She wouldn't be able to do more than offer the same platitudes she'd offered the night before, and it was obvious that he was blocking people out.

"What about the sheriff's department, and your talk with Tommy on Sunday?" Jackson asked, giving her a curious look.

"I'm not investigating anything," Amy protested, and she could feel her chin taking on that telltale tilt. She glanced at Jackson and knew he saw it too.

"Hmmm. Yeah, okay. Asking questions about what someone knows about an assault is defiantly not investigating."

"Shut up." Amy stared straight ahead.

"Yes ma'am," came his replay. Amy refused to look at him, but she could tell he was laughing quietly.

A few minutes later the dusty green jeep was pulling up to the security keypad in front of the gate to the *Hazelton Hacienda*. Amy reached out and punched the silver call button.

Nothing happened.

Amy looked at Jackson with a question in her eyes. "Do you think it's broken? How did she get in when you were driving?"

"There was a remote in the SUV. I didn't even have to enter a code into the box," Jackson said. "Give her a chance. She might be in the bathroom."

"Okay, okay," Amy sat staring at the call box, willing Bea's voice to emerge. Finally after what seemed to be many minutes, but was likely only one or two, she reached through the window to push the button again. Just as her finger caressed the brushed stainless steel, the gates groaned and started to swing open. Amy snatched her hand back inside the jeep and nosed the vehicle through the open portal.

She pulled up in front of the walkway and turned the key and sat for a moment in silence.

"You ready for this?" Jackson asked, looking at her, his eyes crinkling with his smile. "We can always just say hello, pay our respects and then retreat unscathed..." He glanced at the granite and redwood facade of the house. "Well, hopefully unscathed." He looked back over toward Amy. "After all, you aren't..."

"Investigating. I know, I know." She popped the door, climbed out and walked around the Wrangler, meeting Jackson on the flagstones on the far side. The two made their way to the ornate front entrance, but before Jackson could press the doorbell, Bea Hazelton pulled the huge redwood slab open.

It had been three days since Amy had seen Bea, and it hadn't been under the best of circumstances. The intervening days had returned the older woman to her former glory - straw-blonde beehive hairdo firmly in place, makeup slathered on thickly, and sour expression firmly settled on her features. There was no sign of the vulnerability that she had evidenced on Saturday afternoon.

Jackson, as usual, seemed unaffected, giving Bea a smile that lit up his entire face, bright blue eyes sparkling. Amy and Bea's hellos were not nearly as carefree, both exhibiting the wariness of two strange cats meeting for the first time.

The door opened into a large, airy front room decorated with Navajo woven wall hangings, traditional southwest pottery and kachina dolls. Other Navajo style rugs were spread out on the Saltillo tile floor, their earthy tones blending well with the red clay tiles. Everything had a studied rustic air in keeping with the front of the house. Amy remembered Pete's comment about the Hazeltons' collections, and she subtly studied the weavings, trying to determine if they were authentic or not.

Bea led the way back through the living room and to a set of double glass doors leading into a large Arizona room, as these sunrooms were called in this part of the country. Amy looked down the length of the room and saw Jon Hazelton stretched out in a tan leather recliner placed strategically in front of one of the largest flat screen televisions that Amy had ever seen.

"Jon? Amy Stone and Jackson Wolf are here to see you," Bea said, with no enjoyment in her voice. There was no additional annoyance either, so Amy decided that maybe the older woman was warming to them.

Jackson looked over at Amy and winked, then stepped into the room. "Hey Jon, you're looking a lot better than the last time we saw you," he said genially, as though he hadn't accused the older man of trying to steal businesses

Saturday morning. He took the man's hand and gave it a brief shake.

Amy followed close behind, and also took Hazelton's hand. "I'm so glad that you're back home. We were pretty worried about you on Saturday."

Jon Hazelton gave them a small smile that didn't quite reach his eyes. Try as she might, Amy couldn't keep from picturing him in the sun, like a lizard, waiting for a tempting morsel to wander by, and she wondered if Jackson and she were next on the menu.

"Bea and I wanted to thank you for everything you did for us Saturday. The doctors in Flagstaff tell me that I would have been in much worse shape without your care." His voice held its normal dry tone, but Amy thought she detected more warmth than usual when talking with Hazelton... at least when he wasn't trying to get something out of them. He gestured at a padded window bench kitty-corner to the recliner and Amy and Jackson took seats. Bea sat in an overstuffed chair a few feet away.

Amy glanced at Jackson. He gave her a *what are you waiting for... ask* look with a barely perceptible jerk of the chin in Hazelton's direction.

She took a deep breath, then said, "Considering the injury, I was surprised that the doctor sent you home so soon." Maybe if she made it sound as if he had been on the brink of death and was showing miraculous healing powers, he'd warm up even more.

"Humph!" The sound came from Bea and both Amy and Jackson turned their eyes toward the older woman. "If you ask me, Jon should still be in the hospital, or at least a rehab facility, where they can supply the assistance he needs, rather than sending him here and just having a nurse check on him once in a while. That's what you get with the health care in this country, though. It's deplorable."

Amy took a deep breath. That was a can of worms she hadn't meant to open, especially considering that her own father was in one of those rehabilitation facilities that Bea felt was being denied to Jon.

"It is sad," Jackson said in a sincere voice, stepping into the breach. "On the other hand, Amy's father has said repeatedly that he'd be healing faster at home. Not to mention that he hates being stuck around a bunch of 'crazy old farts' as he calls them, so maybe it's for the best."

Bea gave him a withering look and Amy decided that any thawing of the Hazelton ice flow was going to refreeze in short order.

Jon, on the other hand, looked thoughtful. "You may be right, young man. It would be difficult to sleep in one of those places with the nurses always waking you up. The hospital was terrible that way. Besides, I can get around with that thing there." He gestured toward an aluminum walker parked discreetly to the side of the chair. "They said they'll have me start PT in a week or two and within two months I should be as good as new."

"That's wonderful news," Amy said. "Um... I was wondering.." She shot a quick glance at Jackson and was rewarded with a slight nod. "When we were talking down in the mine, you said you couldn't remember why you'd gone back there in the first place. Have you remembered anything more?"

Hazelton nodded slowly, his eyelids drooping, reinforcing the lizard resemblance. "Yes. I told this to that deputy when he called yesterday. I wanted to talk to those Mattheson girls, and I thought I saw one of them on that trail over the hill."

Amy wasn't expecting that answer, and from the look on Jackson's face, she could tell he was surprised, as well.

"I didn't know you were interested in minerals and mining." Amy blurted out, regretting her words as she saw a frown cross Jon's face.

"I'm not particularly. However, I am interested in bringing in tourist opportunities to the area. I thought those girls did a good job with their little tour, and I wanted to talk to them about potentially developing the mine tours more fully. Of course, it would be in their best interest to maintain ownership of any mining memorabilia..." He let the last word hang. The final *and not sell the stamp mill or anything else to the historical society* hanging unsaid.

If Amy had been surprised before, she was floored now. *I shouldn't be surprised,* she admonished herself, *since Hazelton is always looking to make a buck.*

"Which of the Matthesons did you follow?" Jackson asked.

"I don't know. I don't remember their names," Hazelton said, waving a hand in the air, making it clear that his interest in the topic was waning.

"Salina and Jania," Jackson said in helpful tones.

"I don't know," Hazelton said in exasperated tones. "The one who was in charge."

"Salina," Amy said, nodding. "It must have been her then. Did you find her?"

"No. I hiked to the top of that little ridge, but couldn't see where she went. I saw the opening to the mine shaft and thought she might have gone back underground, so I walked down. I was looking into the hole, and someone hit me from behind. Next thing I know I was opening my eyes to darkness down in the mine." Jon Hazelton closed his eyes and sat in silence for a moment, his face twisting at the memories that were flashing through his mind.

"You didn't see who pushed you?" Amy asked, feeling her stomach clench. What if Jon pointed the finger at Pete? Pete might fuss about the tourists, but he'd always be in favor of educating others about Arizona's mining history. If Hazelton identified Pete as his assailant then there would be nothing anyone could do to save him.

"No," Hazelton snapped. "Whoever it was hit me from behind like a coward."

"I've told you, and told you that it was Martin," Bea said, anger and exasperation evident in her voice. "No one seems to believe me. The sheriff's department released

Martin. How do we know that he won't come back after Jon now that he's home?"

"I...." Amy stuttered to a stop. What could she say? That Pete didn't assault Jon? That wouldn't solve anything. Nothing would convince Bea Hazelton that Pete hadn't pushed Jon other than to find the person who did.

"I don't think you have to worry," Jackson said in confident tones. "There's no way the sheriff's department would have released Pete if they'd thought there was any danger to you or your husband. I'm sure they'll get to the bottom of this whole thing before too long."

"*Humph!*" Bea's short retort making clear her opinion of the sheriff's department, Jackson's assurances and the entire situation in general. She stood abruptly. "It's been kind of you to visit Jon, but he does need to rest. He's still very weak," she said, gesturing toward the door.

Amy and Jackson started to rise, but Jon's next words caused them to pause, and sink back down onto the cushioned bench.

"What about the skeleton? The one I joined in the mine shaft?"

"We haven't heard for sure," Jackson answered. "The presumption is that it's William Powell, the mine owner who disappeared back in the eighties when it was called the Cross Point mine. They're trying to track down his family through the property records so that they can do a DNA test."

Hazelton nodded. "That will make it even better for advertising, having a real mine ghost," he muttered to himself, almost as if unaware that other people were listening.

Amy was shocked, although she told herself she shouldn't be. Hazelton always seemed to be on the lookout for ways to advance his goal of making Copper Springs into an up and coming tourist attraction.

She stood once again and said, "Come on, Jackson. We should let Mr. Hazelton get some rest."

"Absolutely," Jackson said, smiling as though he

hadn't heard Hazelton's comment. "I'm glad to see that you're healing, Jon. Take care of yourself, and give us a call if you need anything." He took Hazelton's offered had and gave it a swift shake, then turned to follow Amy and Bea out of the room and back to the front of the house.

They were ushered out with hardly a word from Bea, the large door closing behind them with a soft *whump*.

"Well, that was fun, wasn't it?" Jackson said, shaking his head. He glanced at his watch. "I guess it's back to the grindstone." He started walking toward the jeep parked in the driveway.

Amy looked back at the doorway and noticed a slight quivering of the curtains at the sidelight to the right of the slab of redwood. Bea Hazelton must still be watching them. Amy turned her back and hurried down the walkway, catching up with Jackson just as he was putting his hand on the passenger door.

"Come to think of it, I think grindstones are the only thing you don't carry in the shop," Jackson said.

"Huh?" Amy said, momentarily confused, pulled out of her contemplation of Hazelton's words.

"I said it was time to get back to the grindstone. Meaning back to work? Then I realized that we probably didn't have any grindstones to get back to... a lot of jasper, agate and turquoise, but no grindstones. Why is that?" He pulled open the Wrangler's door and climbed in, settling himself in the passenger seat as he gave Jynx a scratch behind the ears.

Amy shook her head as she walked around the hood of the jeep and climbed inside. "Probably because there's not a lot of demand for grindstones these days." She started up the engine and put the jeep in reverse. "Most people tend to just either throw away or buy new tools when they need to be sharpened. Besides, they're not very attractive."

"I've seen some of the rock you've got stashed behind the shop. *Pffft!* Some of that's not very attractive!" Jackson snorted.

Amy could feel Jackson pulling her into another one of those nonsensical discussions to take her mind off the meeting with the Hazeltons and she laughed and shook her head. He grinned back at her.

"Feel better?" he asked.

"Yeah, thanks." She took in a deep breath, then put the jeep into gear, and the tires spit up gravel as she rushed out of the open gate.

After they'd traveled almost five minutes in silence, Jackson asked, "So, Sherlock, what did we find out?"

Amy took her eyes off the road for a moment to glance at Jackson. He was watching her, the intensity in his blue eyes belying the casual tone in his voice.

"That the *Hazelton Hacienda* is as impressive from the inside as it is from the outside?" Amy said, matching Jackson's tones.

"Yeah, there is that. Do you think all those Navajo weavings are real? Not to mention the pots. It's pretty remarkable."

"Probably Mexican knock-offs," Amy said laughing, "But they're good ones."

"I meant, what did we learn about the assault and Pete's role in it."

"Pete has no role in it," Amy snapped, her voice tight. She could feel her jaw clench and consciously tried to relax her muscles.

"I know," Jackson said in soothing tones. "That's what you want to believe, and I want to believe. Now, what did we learn?"

"That Hazelton was following someone he thought was Salina in order to talk to her about turning the Red Wind into a tourist trap."

"Do you think Pete found out about his plan?" Jackson asked. "How would he feel about it?"

Amy sat in silence for a moment, eyes on the road as she thought about Jackson's question.

Finally, she said, "I don't know. He's usually in favor of anything that promotes the history of the area. He might not trust Hazelton's motives, but I'd think he'd be excited about the potential regardless of the way he was talking Saturday evening. There are a few other mines in the country, even several in Arizona, where the owners have started offering tours. There are caves and caverns as well, such as the Grand Canyon Caverns on the other side of Peach Springs. The insurance has to be astronomical, though. I wonder how they'd pay for that."

"I visited the caverns when I first moved up here and I've been to Bisbee's Copper Queen mine. That's pretty amazing," Jackson said.

"The Copper Queen is one of the bigger mines that offers tours. There's another in Michigan, the Adventure Mine, where the mine is more of a network of adits, drives, winzes and shafts. I visited it a few years ago when I went to Michigan's upper peninsula on vacation with... uh...," She trailed off and didn't finish the sentence, although Jackson probably figured out that the vacation had been with her boyfriend at the time. The boyfriend who had tanked her career.

"So Hazelton wanting to turn the mine into a tourist mecca isn't likely to send Pete on a murderous rage," Jackson said in thoughtful tones.

"No, not in itself, although the way someone like Jon Hazelton would want to accomplish this task would likely raise Pete's blood pressure to dangerous levels. Pete would more than likely suggest that the historical society and the Matthesons partner somehow. He does seem pretty protective of the sisters."

There was a moment of silence as each contemplated the information they'd gotten from Hazelton and its implications.

"You know who might object strongly to Hazelton's idea? Ol' Tom," Amy said in a tense voice, feeling in her chest that she'd unlocked the key to the mystery. "Ol' Tom might go to some lengths to stop something like turning the mine into a tourist trap from happening. There's no way he'd want all those people traipsing back and forth over what he thinks of as his land."

Jackson was silent, eyes narrowed in a frown as he thought about Amy's statement. Finally, he looked at her and said, "I'll agree with you that Ol' Tom might be a few fries short of a Happy Meal, but how do you think he would have found out about Hazelton's secret plan?"

Amy felt as though cold water had been thrown in her face at his comment. "But you've got to admit, Jackson, that Ol' Tom fits the role of eco avenger perfectly," she said, knowing as she said it that Jackson's point was valid. Still, she didn't want to let go of a theory that tied the mystery in a neat little bow and exonerated Pete.

A few moments passed where neither said anything, then Amy drew a deep breath and glanced over at Jackson who was looking out at the scenery. They were approaching the town of Copper Springs and more houses dotted the high Sonoran desert landscape.

"Say Ol' Tom did find out about Hazelton's plan," Amy stated, determined to follow her theory to the end. "The Matthesons could also be on the target list? They've been living out there for a few months now, and no mention of Tom harassing them. They might be in danger."

"True," Jackson answered, sounding patient but unconvinced. "If he was able to read Hazelton's mind and knew about his plan, and if he is a homicidal maniac who assaulted one person, and is looking to keep the streak going."

"But if Ol' Tom did attack Hazelton..."

"Big if."

"Granted," Amy said in clipped tones. "You've made your point. But if he did attack Hazelton, do you think the sisters are in danger now?" Amy frowned in concentration. "Maybe Ol' Tom became upset about the crowd of people invading what he thought of as his domain."

"When did you say that Ol' Tom came to the Copper Springs area?" Jackson asked, surprising Amy with the abrupt swing away from the Matthesons.

She glanced over at him, frowning. "I don't know,"

she said in exasperation. "I think Pete said sometime in the seventies."

"And who disappeared from the area in the eighties?" Jackson said, as though talking to someone who was a bit slow.

A bolt of lightning flashed through Amy's mind. "William Powell," she gasped, as she realized where Jackson was going with his train of thought.

"Maybe Ol' Tom decided that he didn't want Powell digging up that particular part of Arizona, and attacked him in that mine shaft to keep it from happening," Jackson said. "And, maybe the reason he attacked Hazelton wasn't because he didn't like the tourist plan, maybe it was because he was afraid Hazelton would discover the body."

Amy felt a surge of hope in her chest once again, which was squashed by Jackson's next words a few seconds later.

"Of course, that doesn't explain why he hasn't attacked the Matthesons for the same reason," Jackson said in reasonable tones. "Or why Bea said she saw a big man with a ponytail. She may not have had her glasses, but there's no way I would have described Ol' Tom as big or even average."

"Maybe Bea's eyes are worse than we thought, or her imagination made the assailant look larger than he actually was." Amy determined to hold on to her theory. "Maybe he's waiting to see what Salina and Jania do. They haven't been very inviting to people in the area until last weekend. He could have been willing to coexist peacefully until more people started invading the neighborhood, so to speak."

Amy glanced over at Jackson. "This has to be it, Jackson. It all fits."

"I'm not sure I'd go as far as it fitting, but I guess it's possible." Jackson's voice still held some doubt, but he didn't bring up any additional arguments against the idea.

"We've got to tell Tommy." Amy pulled the jeep to a flat area on the side of the road, twisted around and pulled her backpack out of the bed of the jeep and into her lap so that she could retrieve her phone. She hit send, knowing that Tommy was the last person she'd called and that his number would automatically appear on the screen once again. She put the phone on speaker so that Jackson could hear the conversation as well.

Four rings and Amy was getting ready to leave a message, when Tommy's voice came over the speaker.

"Hi, Amy. What can I do for you?"

A note of exasperation in his voice stopped Amy in her tracks. She looked at Jackson, and he shrugged and jerked his chin toward the phone. *Say something*, he mouthed.

"Uh... Hi, Tommy. I'm sorry to be bothering you again but I... uh..." Crap, Amy thought. How do I tell him I learned something without him saying that I've been investigating?

"Amy, not that I'm not glad to hear from you," came Tommy's voice, "but we're sort of swamped right now. If you're calling to find out where we are on the investigation, I told you everything I could tell you earlier..."

"It's not that," Amy interjected, stopping Tommy in mid-sentence. She gave Jackson a wide-eyed look, mouthing the words, *now what?*

Jackson just shook his head and shrugged.

Amy took a deep breath and started, "Tommy, Jackson and I are just heading home from visiting the Hazelton's."

"What?" Tommy's voice took on a hard edge that Amy had never heard from him before. "I thought we discussed you *investigating* this situation."

Amy felt her chin lift in its stubborn tilt, her jaw muscles tightening. Jackson was shaking his head at her, realizing that she was on a slow boil.

"It's not like that, Tommy," she spluttered. "We wanted to see how he was doing. After all, he was looking pretty tough down there in the mine." She took a deep breath, then in an attempt to be more conciliatory she added, "Besides, Jackson and Bea bonded a bit on the drive into town, and he was worried about her."

Jackson, who had been taking a drink, choked and started coughing at Amy's words, water spraying out everywhere. Amy looked at him with concern as his face turned a mottled red, eyes squeezed shut.

"What's going on there?" Tommy asked.

"Jackson just choked on some water. He's fine." Amy answered, although she was not sure about that at all. The coughing stilled, but Jackson's face still was an alarming color, and tears streamed from his eyes as he gave her an offended look.

"So what did you learn," Tommy had continued.

Amy jerked her attention back to the phone. "Well, did you know that Hazelton has plans for turning the Red Wind into a tourist attraction? That's what he was doing back at that abandoned shaft. He was looking for Salina."

"No, I hadn't heard that," Tommy said, a tinge of interest creeping into his voice. "But, how does that affect the investigation? Who else would have known about the plan?"

"He said he hadn't told anyone about his idea," Amy had to admit, "But Jackson and I got thinking on the way home that the only person we know that would be totally against something like this would be Ol' Tom. You remember him don't you, Tommy."

A sigh from the phone's speaker. "Yes, I remember Ol' Tom. Creepy guy who occasionally came into town when we were kids. And you think he found out about Hazelton's plan how?" Tommy said in conversational tones.

Amy frowned and looked back at Jackson. Tommy had picked up on that flaw in the plan pretty quickly. "He couldn't have. I know that. But, maybe he was upset about everyone driving to the mine that day."

"Amy, you know darned well that Ol' Tom may have the creep factor in the triple digits, but he has never, in all the years he's been in the area, been accused of violence. You're stretching here. On the other hand, I did hear that the other night in the diner, Pete Martin was saying how he liked things the 'old way' when tourism was brought up."

Amy's heart sank. She'd been trying to clear Pete and instead pointed the finger straight back on him. "I know. I was there," she said, frustration clear in her voice. "You know Pete, though. He grumbles about change, but he's always pushing things that are good for teaching about the area's history."

William Powell Jackson mouthed at her, eyebrows raised.

"Maybe Ol' Tom didn't push Hazelton, but how about William Powell?"

"What has Ol' Tom done to you?" Tommy asked. "You're trying to pin every Copper Springs crime since the seventies on him."

"Listen to me," Amy said in exasperation. "We know Ol' Tom is antisocial. How do you know he didn't run across Powell and fight with him about the mine."

"How do you know he did?" Tommy countered.

"Think about it, Tommy. That mine was abandoned long before Ol' Tom arrived in the area. He's probably had most of that part of the county to himself. Then Powell shows up with a wife and two little kids. It had to annoy him." Amy heard a wheedling tone in her voice that irritated her.

"Okay, Amy. You may have a point, although it's a slim connection. I'll call the guy who's looking into the remains, see if the sheriff's department talked to Ol' Tom back when Powell disappeared."

"Thanks, Tommy." Amy felt deflated, frustrated, and angry.

"I know you're worried about Pete, but as I've told you before, this is our job, not yours."

"I know. Thanks, Tommy. I'll talk to you later." Amy hit the end icon on her phone and sat looking at the screen, as though it held the clue she needed to save Pete.

"Now what?" Jackson asked, looking at her, face serious.

Amy glanced at him, then stared off into space for a moment. Finally, she straightened her shoulders and shifted the jeep into drive.

"Now 'what' is we're going to go find Ol' Tom and talk to him."

Jackson's eyebrows migrated toward the top of his head at an alarming rate, but his voice was conversational. "So, we're going to go out to find the man you think has killed one person, and possibly tried to kill another. Huh?" He gave her a crooked grin. "This one of those 'other duties as assigned' things?" he said referring to the common phrase from many employment contracts.

Amy looked at him, violet eyes narrowed. "I can drop you at the shop if you prefer. Someone should be there this afternoon, and I don't know how long this is going to take."

"No, no!" Jackson exclaimed, putting his hands up, palms outward in a *"stop"* motion. "I'm in. I'm just trying to figure out what type of hostess gift one brings to a potential murderer. Emily Post just doesn't cover that situation."

Amy glanced over at him for a moment, mouth hanging open, temporarily at a loss for words.

"I ordered the T-shirts. They'll be here on Monday." Jackson said complacently, then added at Amy's confused look. "You know, the ones that say 'There's something wrong with you' for you and my sister. I hope I got the right sizes." He studied Amy's slim figure critically.

Amy groaned, and stepped on the gas pedal, heading for Lincoln Road on the edge of town, and Ol' Tom's lair.

Brecciated Mookaite, Australia

11

"Do you actually know where we're going?" Jackson asked, as the jeep jolted over another boulder protruding from the faint two-rut road.

"Dad said Ol' Tom lived out here somewhere, maybe in an abandoned mine or camp shack. I know of three or four old mines and a couple of ruined miner shacks in the area. Maybe we'll get lucky. The first one should be up this trail a little farther.

Jackson nodded, and grabbed for the door as the jeep jolted roughly to the left. "I hope we find him soon, or the jeep is going to need a bolt transplant."

Amy had to admit that the old Wrangler had developed a definite squeak over the last few minutes, and this quixotic mission to find Ol' Tom had started to lose its luster. Amy slowed even more as they rounded a large pile of boulders and saw a dilapidated wood cabin with a rusted tin roof. About fifty feet behind the shed were the remaining timbers of the mine frame, looking like a fallen pile of pick-up sticks. She braked to a stop in front of the shed, and climbed out of the jeep.

Jynx wriggled up to the front seat, jumped out of the Wrangler and ran, nose to the ground.

Jackson walked around the hood of the jeep and stood next to Amy, surveying the hillside around the mine. "I don't see any sign of Ol' Tom, or anyone else living here."

"No," Amy sighed.

"Giving up?" Jackson looked at her with a crooked smile.

"No," Amy said again, only with more determination. She whistled for Jynx, and turned to climb back into the jeep.

Jackson moved back to his side and climbed back in, wincing as he reached out with his left hand.

"Why aren't you wearing your sling?" Amy said

"You just noticed? I haven't been wearing it most of the day. You must really be distracted." Jackson chuckled, and finished settling into the passenger seat of the jeep.

Amy shifted the Wrangler into drive, turned and headed back down the two-rut road. It was only a short distance to the next mine that Amy remembered, but the condition of the road ate up the minutes. The squeak from the undercarriage grew more pronounced and Amy tried to remember when she had last taken it in for servicing.

Three mines and three strikes later, Amy was feeling deflated as she steered the jeep down the worst track yet. She cringed at a loud bang which emanated from under the vehicle, glad that her dad had insisted on her installing skid plates when she bought the jeep.

"That one hurt," Jackson said. His right hand was still gripping the door, and his feet were braced on the floorboards.

"Maybe we should just turn around," Amy said, voice tight with tension. She looked over at Jackson. "I was an idiot to think we'd just drive out here and find Ol' Tom. When we get up to the next wide spot, I'll turn around and..."

"Look!" Jackson hissed, his eyes fixed out through the dirty windshield. He jerked his chin toward the front of the jeep, off to the driver's side where a tall pile of boulders kissed the side of the track.

Amy's head whipped around, and she looked at the boulders. She frowned. "I don't see any..." She fell silent as she saw Ol' Tom, standing in a cleft of the large rocks, looking exactly the way he had on the day of the field trip. She blew out a breath, and eased her foot off the brake, allowing the jeep to creep forward until they reached a relatively level area. Amy shifted into park and turned the key. The silence was sudden, and gave Amy a case of the jitters. She could see Ol' Tom watching them, but he made no move to hale them in friendship or in threat.

"Are you sure you want to turn the jeep off?" Jackson whispered out of the side of his mouth, eyes fixed ahead on Ol' Tom. "What if we have to make a quick getaway?"

"Going anywhere quick on this road is out of the question," Amy whispered back, "so we'd better hope that Ol' Tom is in a good mood."

"I'm thinking we maybe should have thought this plan through a little better before we headed out here," Jackson said, then opened the passenger side door of the jeep and climbed out.

"Hi there," he called up to the old man, still standing motionless on the wind sculpted pile of boulders. If it weren't for the slight breeze blowing his jacket and lifting his gray hair, Amy would have almost thought he was a statue, carved from the cream-colored rock itself.

Amy popped her door, and slid out of the jeep.

Jackson walked to the front of the jeep and stood in the middle of the track.

"My name is Jackson Wolf," Jackson called. "You're Ol' Tom, right? We were hoping to talk to you about some friends of ours."

No answer from the man statue, and Amy felt the knot in her stomach start to grow to basketball proportions. She walked forward and stood next to Jackson.

"Ol' Tom, my name is Amy Stone. I think you know my father, Nick Stone? You've brought mineral and rock specimens in for him from time to time."

Still no response. Amy glanced over at Jackson, afraid to take her eyes of Ol' Tom for too long in case he went for the rifle which was slung across his back.

Now what? He mouthed.

Just as Amy was trying to come up with another conversational tidbit that might pry words out of the old man, he moved. Amy wouldn't have been more surprised if the statue of the cowboy on the edge of town had slapped his chapped leg and started calling to the cattle frozen in front of it.

"Nick Stone, did you say? I know your dad. Good man." His voice sounded rusty, as though it hadn't been used in a while. Then Ol' Tom turned and disappeared through the crack in the rock, turning to the side so that his rifle didn't catch on either side of the narrow passageway.

Amy looked at Jackson. She realized her mouth was hanging open like a baby bird, and she clamped her teeth shut with a snap.

"Not a very talkative fella, is he? Was that all the audience we're going to get?" Jackson asked, his voice echoing the wonderment that was stamped across his face.

"I don't know. What should we do?" Amy stared up at the crevice in the boulder, and the turned to look at the two rut road. No sign. If she hadn't known better, and had Jackson to back her up, she might have thought that she'd imagined the whole meeting. She thought of that line from *A Christmas Carol* by Dickens... an undigested bit of beef, a piece of underdone potato, or something along those lines.

"Let's keep going," she said to Jackson, turning back, and walking to the driver door. "There's an old mine camp just up the trail another hundred yards or so. That's got to be where he's staying." She climbed in and started the jeep, waiting for a moment until Jackson was settled, and then started to inch forward again.

In a few seconds, they had moved around the rocks, and emerged into a wide, flat area. Another small wooden shack with a tin roof sat next to the trail. Amy couldn't see the mine portal, but if she remembered correctly, it was off to the east, around a small shoulder of the hill.

Ol' Tom was waiting in front of the shack. He watched the jeep approach without showing any reaction, the rifle still slung over his shoulder. Even when Amy pulled up to within a few feet of the front of the building and stopped the jeep, he didn't move. It wasn't until Amy and Jackson climbed out of the vehicle and walked over to the front of the shack did the old man show any reaction to their presence other than a never wavering stare.

Amy didn't think she'd ever been in as uncomfortable situation as she was at that moment. Even the worst first date, and she'd been on a few real stinkers, hadn't held this complete vacuum of communication. She looked over at Jackson, and could tell he was feeling the same way, no matter how much he tried to hide it. Ol' Tom just stood there, looking at the pair of them, apparently comfortable with the silence.

Several more moments passed as Amy searched frantically for the words she wanted to say, but they stubbornly refused to come.

"Nice place you have here," Jackson ventured. "Have you lived here long?"

Ol' Tom looked at Jackson, and Amy thought he wasn't going to answer the opening gambit.

Then, to her surprise, the rusty voice came again. "No, not really."

Amy found herself leaning forward, almost as though she could draw more words out of the old man by shear will. Jackson looked at her, eyebrows cocked, and a half shrug that said, *your turn.*

Before she could say anything, however, Ol' Tom spoke again. "You said your father is Nick Stone. He's a good man. How's he doing?"

"Ah... He's doing well. He broke his leg a while ago, and has been in Kingman recovering, but he'll be home soon."

"I heard something 'bout that last time I was in for supplies. Glad he's doing okay."

One of those uncomfortable silences fell again. Amy heard a noise from behind her and she turned to look back at the jeep. Jynx, tired of being left behind had jumped through the open driver's side window and was checking out the local news, canine style – sniffing at various clumps of brush and piles of debris.

"Nice dog there," Ol' Tom said. "I used to have a dog like that. Died last winter though."

Amy heard sadness in the man's voice and for some reason it surprised her, as though love didn't fit into the image of the old hermit. When she thought back, though, she seemed to remember Ol' Tom having a dog; a gray shadow that followed him everywhere, and was no more welcoming to strangers than Tom himself.

Amy whistled and Jynx ran over, intelligent golden-brown eyes avid, tail wagging. She sat and stared up at Ol' Tom. A bony hand reached out. Jynx sniffed it then submitted to having her head scratched. Ol' Tom squatted and started giving Jynx an all-over petting. In Aussie style, she turned her butt for a good scratch, tied herself into a knot and looked over her shoulder at the old man as she wriggled excitedly.

Ol' Tom stood slowly, a smile on his lips. "Good dog. What kind is she?"

"She's a border collie/Australian shepherd cross. She likes you." Amy smiled. It was a lot harder to think of Ol' Tom as someone who might have assaulted Hazelton or murdered William Powell when Jynx seemed to trust him. *Dammit!*

Jackson seemed to feel the same break in tension, and he bent down to give Jynx a quick pat. "Did you happen to hear about the happenings at the Red Wind Mine last weekend?"

Ol' Tom's eyes sharpened as he looked at Jackson. "I know a lot of people was heading out in that direction a few days ago. A lot of uproar those girls caused."

"You know the Matthesons?" Amy asked in surprise.

"Met them when they came. I was living out there at that mine when they showed up one day and said they owned the place, so I took off."

Amy looked at Jackson and could tell he was as surprised as she.

"You lived there? At the mine?" Jackson blurted out.

"No one lived there after that family left... that one where the father went missing. It sat empty for years, falling apart, so I moved in. When them girls showed up, I told them I'd leave," Ol' Tom said without emotion.

Amy felt as though a rug had been pulled out from under her. She'd never thought about the Matthesons actually having met Ol' Tom, but she wasn't sure if that made him more or less likely to be Hazelton's assailant.

"Didn't it make you angry that you had to leave like that," Jackson asked curiously. "Had you been there very long?"

Ol' Tom moved to sit on one of several stumps placed near the front of the shack. He pulled the rifle from his shoulder and sat it beside him, then snapped his fingers for Jynx, who appeared more than happy to get some more attention. "Angry? Nah. No point. I'd been there a few years, but I've lived in a lot of different places 'round here." He nodded at the shack behind him. "This is the third time I've stayed here. Sometimes the Game and Fish people come and tell me to move to a different spot, or forest rangers, or the police, and I move. No point in fighting it. The girls' mine was nice that way. It was private land, but no one ever came along, so I got to stay longer there than anywhere else."

Amy met Jackson's eyes, and she knew he was feeling the same thing she was. Would this man who seemed so accepting of people just coming in and moving him along, get angry enough over people coming into his territory that he'd attack one and push him down a mine shaft or kill another? She remembered Pete saying that there "wasn't any harm to him."

"So you didn't go to the mine on Saturday, when there were a group of us there for the field trip?" Jackson asked. He sat down on another stump near Ol' Tom and kicked out his legs, crossing his ankles.

"Nah." The old man shook his head, making a face. "I got no reason to be around groups of like that. Bad enough when I have to go into town for supplies, I don't care to see 'em out here as well, but I got plenty of places to get away from them groups. Most of the time they go through and don't even know I'm there." He looked at Amy and Jackson with a knowing glint in his eyes. "I watch, though. I al'us watch."

Jackson frowned. "Do you remember when William Powell, the father you were talking about, disappeared?"

Amy moved over to another stump and sat down, leaning forward, eager to hear Tom's response.

Ol' Tom sat in silence for a moment, his face screwed up in concentration. "Yeah, I remember that man. He seemed like a good father from what I saw, them little girls hanging on his hands and laughing. I was sorry to hear he disappeared like that, leaving them little kids."

"We may have found him, you know," Jackson said casually. "There was a skeleton down in the mine shaft where the man got hurt last Saturday."

Ol' Tom lifted his head and looked at Jackson sharply. "I didn't hear about someone getting hurt, although I did see that helicopter take off. Thought something might have happened. You said they found a skeleton. Think it might be that father what disappeared?"

"They're doing tests," Amy said. "But, it would be a huge coincidence if it was someone else. No one else has been reported missing in the area that I know of. I don't suppose you remember that day. Maybe you were watching the road again like you did the other day?"

Tom frowned and shook his head. "I'm not sure. It was a long time ago. Maybe some times I saw a truck drive in there that didn't belong to either the man or the woman, but I couldn't swear that it was there that day." He shrugged and bent back to Jynx, running his fingers through her ruff. Jynx rolled over on her back with a complete lack of dignity, begging for a tummy rub. "This is a nice dog. I had a dog like this, but it died last winter," Ol' Tom said again.

"Tom, did you ever talk to the sheriff's department

about the truck," Amy asked, watching his callused fingers caress Jynx.

Ol' Tom looked up at her sharply, hazel eyes narrowed in sudden suspicion. "No one came looking for me, and I didn't go looking for them." He bit off his words sharply.

"Okay, I get it," Jackson said in soothing tones. "I sure wouldn't want anyone butting into my business." He gave Ol' Tom a wide smile. "Some of those guys are alright, though."

Tom gave Jackson a skeptical look, then looked back down at the dog.

Jackson caught Amy's eye behind Tom's back and raised his eyebrows in question.

"I guess we ought to get going, Tom. It was nice to meet you. I'll tell my dad that I ran into you today." Amy stood and stretched. She caught Jackson's eye and jerked her head toward the jeep. Jackson got up, and put out his hand to Ol' Tom, who took it and rose to his feet as well.

"Hope we see you at the shop one day," Jackson said, then headed for the jeep. Amy whistled for Jynx, who scrambled to her feet and headed for the vehicle at a run. Without waiting for Amy to open the door, she jumped in through the window.

"That's a nice dog," Ol' Tom muttered, so softly that Amy almost didn't hear him. "I had a dog like that, but it died last winter." He turned, picked up the rifle, slung it over his shoulder and headed off behind the shack.

Amy climbed back into the Wrangler, then waited for Jackson to get settled before turning the key and shifting the jeep into drive. She did a three-point turn, and headed back down the two-rut road toward town.

There was silence for a few minutes, then Jackson took a deep breath and turned to look at Amy. "So, what did we learn, other than these roads are pretty rough and Ol' Tom used to have a dog like Jynx, but it died last winter?"

"Wasn't that sad?" Amy said without thought. "When he said that again right at the end, I thought I was going to start crying. It broke my heart."

"Yeah. I wonder..." Jackson's voice faded off.

"Wonder what?" Amy asked after waiting for a moment to see if Jackson would clarify his thoughts without prodding.

Jackson pursed his lips and shook his head. "Nothing. I need to think about it."

"Do you think he did it?"

"Which one? Pushed Hazelton or murdered Powell? I don't think he did either." Jackson said in matter-of-fact tones. His blue eyes met Amy's violet ones, and he lifted his shoulders in a shrug, then winced. "I have got to stop doing that."

"He didn't seem to like the sheriff's department much."

"No. But he also seemed to be pretty philosophical about being moved around. I just don't see him deliberately going closer to the mine when there were so many people hanging around."

"Even to 'watch'?" Amy asked.

Jackson's face looked as though it had been set in concrete, a frown clouding his eyes. "No, not even to 'watch.'"

"What about Powell. After all, he did get a place to live when Powell disappeared. A place where forestry officials weren't constantly moving him along."

"He couldn't know that no one else would come and run the mine, or even that Powell's wife wouldn't stay. So no, I don't see him killing Powell for a house. Besides, he seemed upset that Powell's kids were left without a father."

"Upset?" Amy said. "He didn't seem to have a lot of emotion about anything other than the sheriff's department and his dog."

"The man doesn't talk about things. That he said he said he was sorry that the kids were left without a father says a lot. It made an impact on him."

"Maybe it made an impact because he's the reason the kids were left without a father," Amy said stubbornly, even though she had the same feelings herself. She didn't want Pete guilty, but now she didn't want Ol' Tom guilty either.

"Trust me," Jackson said. "He didn't do it. He's just a sad, old man."

"Sad old men commit murder every day," Amy huffed, even though she felt in her heart that Jackson was right, and the Ol' Tom angle was a dead end.

Amy and Jackson rode back into town in silence, a slight feeling of discord making Amy feel uncomfortable. She trusted Jackson's gut feelings, and she wasn't convinced that Ol' Tom would have attacked anyone. She just so desperately wanted Pete in the clear, and Tom had been such an easy replacement. That was, until she met him.

As they approached the edge of town, Jackson spoke up once again. "You know, I don't recall Salina disappearing from the group for any length of time. Think Hazelton might have followed someone else by accident?"

It took Amy a moment to shift her thoughts away from Ol' Tom and back to their visit with the Hazeltons earlier in the afternoon. She thought for a moment, trying to remember who she'd seen where after the group had finished viewing the mining equipment.

"I don't remember. I know I talked to her a few minutes before we went to see the stamp mill, and I saw her talking to some people afterward. She was also with the group that headed down the wash, right? We didn't pick her up along the way. Still, Hazelton seemed pretty certain about who he was following. She must have left at some point," Amy said.

"Actually, Hazelton wasn't clear about who he was following," Jackson said, giving Amy a serious stare. "He said it was *one* of the Matthesons. *The one who was in charge.*"

"Right," Amy said, exasperation and frustration finally

running over and dripping from her voice. "That would be Salina. She's the one who met us and collected the money. She's the oldest one."

"Not necessarily," Jackson said, and held up his hand as Amy started to protest. "Listen to me. Jania was the one who led us around the mine. He's interested in the tours. He may consider her to be in charge."

Amy groaned. Jackson was right, She never thought to ask what the woman Hazelton was following looked like... long dark hair, or long silver blonde hair.

She looked over at Jackson. "Why didn't you bring this up when we were talking to Jon and Bea?"

"I didn't think of it until just now, truthfully. I was like you. The person in charge in my mind is Salina, so when he said that, my mind automatically went to her. It wasn't until afterward that I realized that his view of 'in charge' might be different than ours."

The jeep rolled to a stop at Route 66 on the edge of Copper Springs. Amy signaled, then turned toward the shop, fighting the urge to turn around and drive right back out to the *Hazelton Hacienda*.

"Would you call Bea and ask her to ask Jon if the woman he followed was blonde or dark haired?" she asked.

Amy's request was answered with a skeptical look, but Jackson pulled out the phone, dialed the number, then set the phone to speaker. The call went straight to voicemail. Jackson left a message, asking about the hair color of the woman whom he'd followed over the hill, then hit the "end" button.

"Happy now?" His eyebrows rose so high they nearly met with his sandy hair.

"Not until she answers," Amy retorted.

"Does it matter, though? I mean does it matter if he followed Jania instead of Salina?" Jackson asked as Amy slowed, and turned into the shop's gravel parking lot. "Bea identified Jon's assailant as a man in dark clothing with a ponytail. That's pretty specific."

"And, she didn't have her glasses."

Amy opened the door to the jeep and held it for Jynx to jump out. The dog trotted over to the patch of grama grass on the side of the building where she took care of business, then ran to the front door of the shop where she sat patiently and waited for Amy to let her in.

"So, are you thinking Salina or Jania would have pushed Hazelton into the mine shaft, even though he was going to try and help them make the mine into a booming business? From what Pete said, the sisters need money. What would have been the motive for either of them to attack someone who was going to help them?"

Amy looked at her phone and noticed the time. The afternoon was gone, and there was only an hour left until closing time. The odds of someone coming at that point was small and she had a strong desire to just go home. Instead she pushed the door open, flipped the "closed" sign to "open" and stood back for Jackson to enter.

"I don't know, but it does mean that one of the girls was in that area. Maybe whichever one of the Matthesons Jon followed didn't like the way he acted. Hell, I'd like to push him into a mine shaft on a frequent basis." Amy could hear the frustration in her voice, and knew that her chin had the defiant tilt that it usually took when she was challenged. Her father told her it was her greatest tell, which just increased her annoyance whenever he pointed it out.

"So you've accepted that Ol' Tom didn't push Hazelton?"

"It's not likely," Amy admitted grudgingly. "That doesn't mean he didn't kill Powell, though," she said, still unwilling to give all the points to Jackson.

Jackson let that statement slide by without comment. He frowned and studied the stained ceiling of the shop, as if the answer was written in the myriad lines. He leaned on the front counter, resting his elbows on the glass. His gaze returned to Amy's face and he shook his head. "I don't think that Salina or Jania being the assailant fits the scenario either, although I suppose it could be possible. If one of them didn't want Hazelton to investigate the mine shaft, why push him into it instead of talking to him and leading him away from the area? By pushing Hazelton in, she'd pretty much be guaranteeing that people would be tramping all over the area. Besides, the only thing in there that someone might want to hide was Powell's body, and neither of the Matthesons could have killed him, so why hide the skeleton?"

"You're right," Amy sighed. She could think of no reason why the Matthesons would have kept the existence of a human skeleton hidden.

"That's another thing," Jackson said, "Or maybe a totally different thing, but didn't Gladys say that searchers came out to look for Powell after he disappeared? That shaft isn't very hidden from sight. It's close to the main portal and a trail leads right to it. How could have anyone missed seeing it and investigating during the search?"

Amy gave him a puzzled look, eyebrows knitted. "Yes, that's what she said if I remember right. But, how does that have anything to do with Hazelton and the Matthesons?"

"It probably doesn't have anything with to do them, but it is strange that two men wound up in the same spot," Jackson said. "Whoever pushed Hazelton couldn't have done it intending to kill him. There was a good chance he'd die in the fall, but no guarantee, obviously."

Amy chewed her lip, her violet eyes looking off into the distance as she pictured the mine shaft. "Powell didn't just fall on that stake that killed him, either. Maybe whoever pushed Hazelton intended to go down into the shaft to finish the job, but heard Bea scream and took off instead."

"So, you're still thinking that the same person attacked both men? Who was around during both time periods? Pete... and Ol' Tom."

"I didn't say that!" Amy protested. She saw a look of smug satisfaction on Jackson's face, and blurted, "I said Ol' Tom attacking Hazelton was 'unlikely' not impossible, and there are others who were around back at Powell's time."

"How many were around during both time periods, and even more important, how many of the ones were at the mine on Saturday?" Jackson asked. He started to hold up fingers. "Pete, Ol' Tom, Gladys, maybe a few of the others. Which one are you pointing a finger at now, or am I missing something on your trail of deduction?"

Amy ran her fingers through her dark, curly hair, wishing she could pull her thoughts straight. She put her elbows on the glass counter and rested her forehead in her hands for a moment, overwhelmed by the scenes running through her mind. Jynx and Bess crowded around her legs seemingly aware of her discomfort.

She hated the thought of any of the people she knew being a murderer, but she had to admit that Jackson had a point. If the two incidents were connected, then it would have to be one of the older members of the community who had come out on the field trip.

After a moment, Amy lifted her head and looked at Jackson, a rueful expression twisting her face. Jackson gazed back at her, face torn between amusement and curiosity.

"I guess I got carried away with this investigating thing, huh?"

"I have to admit it's a heck of a coincidence, Hazelton winding up in the same mine shaft as Powell. But it has to be just that... a coincidence." Jackson's face took on more of a thoughtful expression. "I suppose that Ol' Tom doesn't have to be the only one who is 'al'us' watching, but I think that's stretching credibility."

Amy's lips twisted. "I think I'm at the point where if you suggested that aliens had come down and killed Powell for going too close to the mother ship, I'd believe you."

"Still, we keep spinning in circles and winding up in same spot," Jackson continued. "It's too big of a coincidence to think that the two events aren't related, but it also makes no sense to think they are related as we'd almost certainly find Hazelton, and therefore Powell, pretty quickly. None of it makes sense."

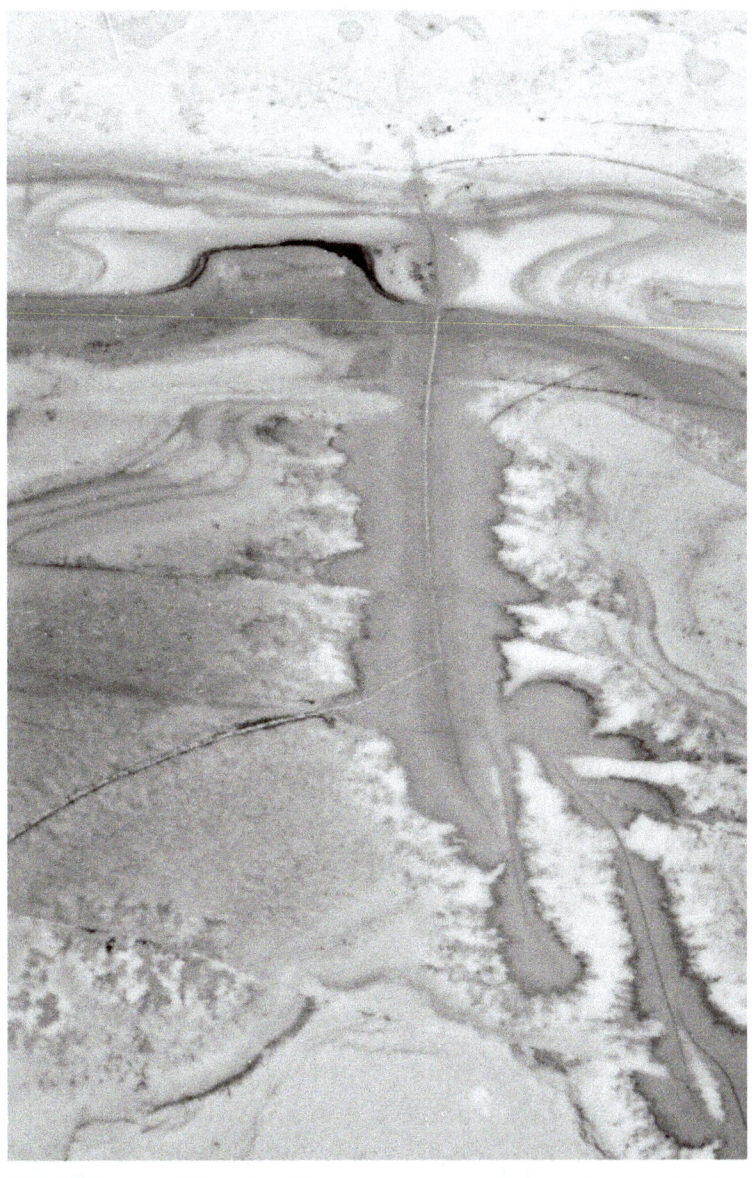

Owyhee Jasper, Nevada

12

Wednesday and Thursday seemed to Amy to drag so slowly that a second Grand Canyon could have been eroded away. No matter what she did, she couldn't seem to get her mind off the events of Saturday, the visit to Ol' Tom, and the information they'd gotten from Hazelton. The shop wasn't busy and she had a list of things she wanted to do before Nick came home from Kingman, but she couldn't seem to get her mind to focus. She frequently caught herself standing there, staring into space with a strand of beads or the pages of an invoice in her hands, running through scenarios in her mind.

Pete hadn't called back, and she was reaching the point where she didn't care about his privacy, she was ready to drive out to his place. There had been no word from Tommy either, and by the time Friday rolled around, Amy felt stretched as thin as fishing line.

Jackson, on the other hand, seemed perfectly content, working in the office, updating various online listings, sending invoices and packing stones for shipment to far flung locations. Amy caught herself resenting Jackson's calm, and fought hard to squash the feeling into submission.

Friday morning Amy found Jackson already hard at work when she pulled into the small parking lot at eight o'clock, fighting a headache, and hugging a fresh cup of coffee from the deli to her chest. She hoped the caffeine, not to mention the four ibuprofen she'd taken earlier, would tone down the kettledrums banging in her head. She turned the key and killed the engine, then just sat, listening to the morning sounds. She took a deep breath and blew it out, counting to ten and trying to release the tension from her neck and shoulders. Then, taking another deep breath, she grabbed a second cup of coffee, which had been resting in the cup holder, got out, and headed for the entrance to the shop, Jynx and Bess close behind.

The front door was unlocked. She pushed it open, and stood aside for the dogs who charged past her and down the short hallway to the main showroom. They disappeared to the right, claws skidding on the wooden floor, the sound making Amy cringe.

She followed the dogs more slowly, heard a muffled shout of surprise, and grinned. It felt good, she realized, and laughed, feeling the tension in her neck loosen. As she entered the main showroom of the shop, she turned to the right, and walked to the door of the computer office. Jackson was sitting in the swiveling chair in front of a computer monitor, the two dogs vying for his attention, a pair of noise canceling headphones around his neck.

"Morning, Jackson," Amy said, holding out one of the cups toward him and nodding. "Want some caffeine?"

"Hey there, Amy. After these two scared the crap out of me, I shouldn't need it, but never say no to coffee is my motto." He accepted the cup and inhaled the aroma. "Thanks."

"Why here so early?" Amy asked as she leaned against the door jamb and sipped the hot liquid. "The door was unlocked. Anyone could have walked in and cleared out the place, and with those things on," she gestured toward the headphones, "you'd have been none the wiser."

"As to the why, that's pretty easy. Miss Moira showed up at my door bright and early this morning, with a huge list of 'honey do's.'"

"So you told her you had to go into work early?" Amy

started laughing. "Why, I thought that you liked helping her out."

"Sure, but she was in one of her chatty moods, and I knew if I waited until this afternoon to attack the chores, I could get them all finished while she was napping. I'll get done in half the time without her looking over my shoulder and correcting every move I make." There was a harried note to Jackson's voice and his eyes looked a little wild. "Did I tell you that when I painted the bunkhouse, she told me I'd done it wrong, made me scrape it down and start all over again?"

Amy snorted in laughter. "The honeymoon's over, huh?"

"Yeah, well, it's still a great place to live, but we're definitely going through one of those relationship challenges." He gave her a rueful grin.

Amy set herself the task of completing a thorough inventory of the shop's beads and jewelry findings. Nick didn't care much for that part of the business and avoided inventorying the stock for as long as possible. When he broke his leg, he'd already been behind and Amy was determined that it would be caught up before he came back. She'd often tried to convince him to use one of the newer point-of-sale programs which would keep track of inventory for him, but he'd been resisting for years. It would have meant giving up his old cash-box-and-paper-receipt-book style of business, and he would have none of it.

The day dragged. Amy would check the clock, thinking that hours had passed, only to find that fifteen or twenty minutes had crawled by. The cheerful humming which emanated from the computer room grated on her nerves. Although she usually enjoyed Jackson's musical forays, his taste in music was eclectic, bouncing around from country to rock with stops in every decade since the fifties. Today he seemed to be on a Kansas kick, although Amy picked up the occasional Eagles medley. He had just segued from

Peaceful Easy Feeling to something that sounded remotely like the chorus from *Dust In The Wind*. She sighed.

It seemed as though she was no closer to getting the inventory finished when the jangle of the wind chime at the front door saved her.

Amy turned toward the short hallway leading from the front door, a smile on her face as she prepared to welcome her rescuer, and her eyes widened in surprise as David Shaw stepped into the front room of the shop.

The man paused and looked around the L-shaped front room. His eyes came to rest on Amy where she stood behind the front counter, the strings of semi-precious beads she'd been sorting lying forgotten in front of her. So many things had happened in recent days that Amy had forgotten the new resident of Copper Springs.

"Hey there, Amy," Shaw said, giving her an ingratiating smile which didn't quite reach his mud-colored eyes. "I was passing by and thought I'd stop in to check this place out." He looked around again, ran a hand over his thin, graying comb-over, then took a couple of steps to where a large pair of Zuni bears stood on the floor. He picked up one of the banded onyx bears and examined the glossy finish and the warm honey and cream stripes. He looked over at Amy and held up the statue. "Beautiful piece. Zuni, right?"

Amy squashed a feeling of distaste. After all it wasn't his fault he looked like Hazelton. She smiled and stepped out from behind the counter, carefully shutting the dog gate behind her. "Yes, it's a Zuni bear, and was actually made by an artist on the Zuni reservation over in New Mexico. His name is carved into the base."

She reached out and took the large sculpture from Shaw's hands. She turned it over and ran her finger over the artist's mark on the bottom of the front feet – a feather sitting on a swirl that looked like wind – the initials AB beneath that.

Shaw took the bear back and examined the mark, then turned the sculpture upright and held it at a distance, squinting. He squatted and set it on the ground next to its mate, running his fingers lightly over the stone. He stood again and turned to face Amy. "You've got an interesting place here," he said, nodding at the room.

"Thanks, Mr..."

"Dave," Shaw protested stepping closer her to her, the dead-eyed grin firmly on his face.

Amy caught herself taking a step back, a small frown on her face. It wasn't that Shaw was threatening or anything, Amy told herself sternly. Different people have different comfort levels with personal space.

"Okay...," Amy started, then paused when she saw Shaw start almost imperceptibly, as though something surprised him. He took a hurried step backward and turned toward the computer office as though expecting an attack. Jackson had just emerged, several packages in his hands and stood looking at the man, a question on his face.

Shaw recovered quickly from his surprise. "Hey, Jackson. Good to see you, too. I didn't realize you were here. I was just telling Amy here that I like the shop."

"Hi Dave," Jackson gave the newcomer a smile, although Amy could see a hint of reserve in his features. "The field trip must have made a heck of an impact on you. It looks like you might have gotten bitten by the rock bug," Jackson said, placing his load of boxes and envelopes on a clear area of the counter. He studied Shaw. "You thinking of starting your own collection?"

"Could be. That mine was something," Shaw said in contemplative tones as he looked around the front area of the shop once again. "I don't suppose you've heard from the Mattheson girls since the field trip, have you? I've got to admit that trip into the bowels of the earth has stoked my interest. I thought I'll call them to see if I could visit the mine again, but no one seems to have a phone number for them. I tried calling the club leader... Marin, Martin? But I didn't get an answer." The turd-eating grin was still plastered to his lips, but his flat eyes were avid.

"Martin. Pete Martin," Amy said grudgingly. "He's

the head of both the rock club and the historical society." She frowned, and turned her head away, kicking herself internally. She wanted to know how things were going at the mine as well, but this stranger expressing the same curiosity irritated her for some reason and she couldn't figure out why.

"Haven't heard from either the Matthesons or Pete,." Jackson said, and Amy could hear a underlying note of concern in his voice as well, and it gave her some comfort that she wasn't the only one worried.

"We don't know the Mattheson's very well, though," Amy said. "They know Pete Martin better, but we haven't spoken to him since the evening of the field trip." Amy could hear the faint note of irritation in her voice, but thought it unlikely that Shaw would pick it up. "Still, it's Pete. He's probably in 'mountain man' mode at the moment. He'll show up." She forced a chuckle, trying to quell the worry that insisted on tying her stomach into knots.

Jackson reached behind the counter and pulled out a white United States Post Office bin. He set it on the counter beside him and started piling the boxes and padded envelopes into it, preparing for the Copper Springs post woman's daily visit. He paused and lifted his head as the sound of the low rumble of an engine floated in from the parking lot.

"Speak of the devil," Jackson said, jerking his chin toward the door. The faint cloud of worry lifted and disappeared.

"What are you talking about?" Shaw asked, looking at Jackson in confusion.

"You haven't run into Pete Martin's Ford, I take it?" Jackson said, then he laughed at the surprised look on Shaw's face. "Not literally, I mean. That sound you just heard from outside is an old, grumpy truck, which belongs to our old grumpy friend, Pete Martin."

The jangle at the front door punctuated Jackson's statement.

"Hello, hello," boomed Pete's typical greeting from the doorway. Less than a second later, Pete himself emerged into the front room, a huge smile on his face, and Amy felt the knot of tension that had been haunting her for days start to dissolve.

"Dang it, Pete! We've been worried about you," Amy exclaimed. "Where have you been and why haven't you been answering your phone?"

A sheepish look crossed Pete's face, and he tucked his chin down into his chest. "Ah, I'm sorry, Amethyst. My phone suffered a slight... um.... mishap. I never got the message, and I've been busy trying to get ahead on getting stock finished for the Gem and Mineral Show and haven't gotten down to Kingman to pick up a new one.

"Mishap, huh?" Jackson said with a chuckle. "Was it run it over, drowned or cut in half?

Pete emitted a deep rumble of laughter, his blue eyes twinkling beneath the caterpillar eyebrows. "Run over. Sunday morning I caught a ride out to the Red Wind with Ben Darby to pick up my jeep. Damned thing had a flat when I got there, and I set the phone on the bumper while I was changing the tire. Forgot I put it there, of course, started the jeep and took off. You can guess what happened next."

Jackson winced in sympathy at the mental image of the resulting damage.

"How were Salina and Jania doing when you were out at the mine?" Amy asked, curious about how the sisters were handling the chaos of Saturday.

"They're shaken, of course," Pete said, sucking in his mustache, as if contemplating his words. Then he brightened. "Did I mention Salina's meeting me here today?"

Amy shook her head, laughing. "No, you didn't happen to mention that, Pete."

"Hmm. Early senility I guess."

"Looks like you're going to get to quench your curiosity, Dave," Jackson said, looking over at Shaw who had been standing quietly, partially concealed by the partition which ran down the middle of the short leg of the L-shaped shop, covered with stings of various semiprecious beads.

Martin looked surprised at Shaw's presence. "I'm sorry. I didn't see you there, Shaw," he said, giving the man a smile, and a nod of the head, then stepped forward with his hand thrust out. "Good to see you again."

Dave Shaw took Martin's hand and gave it a quick shake. "I enjoyed listening to you on the field trip. I learned a lot." He paused for a moment, then said, "I'm glad to see that you're not sitting in a jail cell in Kingman."

Amy flinched at the blunt statement, but it appeared that Pete had no such feelings, and that he'd gotten over the majority of his ire regarding the situation during the intervening days.

"I'm right there with you," he laughed. "I haven't heard from them this week. I guess they've decided that someone else took a shot at Hazelton." Pete ginned at his audience. "Or that he just tripped, fell, and made up the rest of the story." Pete chuckled to himself.

"Or, they've left you numerous messages to call them, and you'll find out they're looking for you when you pick up that new phone," Jackson said with a wry note in voice, but a smile on his face.

Pete shrugged, the grin on his face increasing in width. "They know where to find me if they want me." He chuckled, all the stress and anger from Saturday having seemingly melted away with the passage of time.

"You said that Salina Mattheson was coming to meet you here?" Shaw said. "Are both the sisters coming, or just Salina?"

Pete shrugged, then turned toward the door where the rough roar of an engine and the crunch of tires on gravel announced the presumed arrival of one or more of the Mattheson sisters. The engine coughed and died, and Pete shook his head. "We've got to look at that truck," he muttered to himself, then he looked up at the others with a smile.

"It's probably just Salina today. She said it's hard to get Jania out of the mine. There's something strange about that girl." A slight frown crossed his face, and he shook his head, as though thinking about something that eluded the rest of them.

A moment later, the wind chimes on the front door tinkled, and Salina walked into the shop, brushing her fingers through her long, dark hair.

"Hi Pete," she said, walking up to the older man, a slight smile on her normally serious face. "Looks like a late monsoon storm is brewing. The wind sure has picked up." She looked around the room, her eyes drifting over Shaw and Jackson, and coming to rest briefly on Amy. "Hi. Amy, right? And Jackson?" She looked at Shaw again, a slight frown settling on her features. "I remember you from the field trip, but I'm sorry, I don't remember your name."

"David Shaw." Shaw gave Salina smile and thrust out his hand. Salina hesitated for a moment, then put out her own hand, which Shaw shook twice then released, the smile fixed firmly in place, although it was clear to Amy that he'd picked up on Salina's hesitation. "Your sister didn't come with you? I was hoping to thank her again for the tour on Saturday."

Salina frowned, and gave her head a slight shake. "Uh..., no. Jania prefers to stay out at the mine." Her face cleared momentarily, a small smile crossing her lips. "She's become a real mole since moving to the Red Wind. I don't know how she remembers all those different shafts and tunnels, but..." Salina's voice tailed off, and she looked around the shop.

Amy looked over at Jackson and saw he was watching Salina intently. As though he felt Amy's gaze, he glanced over at her. He started to shrug, then stopped himself abruptly and made a face. Amy squelched a laugh at Jackson's action, sure that Salina would see it as aimed toward her, that is if she noticed at all. Ol' Tom might have been the king of the introverts, but the Mattheson sisters had to be the princesses. She wondered what had brought Salina in to town.

Pete, seemingly oblivious to the byplay between Jackson and Amy, brought a large hand down on Salina's shoulder. "We need your expertise, you two. Salina here has brought in some gorgeous mineral specimens which she needs to get photographed and listed for sale. I thought maybe you could give her a hand setting up a website and the like. I'm not much good on that type of stuff. Damned computers run the world these days."

Amy choked back a laugh. She knew that Pete was perfectly capable of using a computer, and frequented many of the rock sale groups on social media, but grumbled about every minute of it, except when he was crowing over a particularly outstanding slab or piece of rough.

"We'd love to help you, Salina. I can give you a hand with pricing, but Jackson here is the magician with the camera and the website. Do you have internet out at the mine?" Amy asked, giving Salina a warm smile. "We might even be interested in buying a few pieces for the shop... if we can agree on a price." She laughed, feeling a little self-conscious. Her father was usually the one buying stock for the shop, and he'd told her not to buy anything "fancy" while he was gone, but she wouldn't mind him coming back from the rehabilitation facility to find that his daughter had done him proud.

"Thanks," Salina said, her expression gradually expanding into a genuine smile. "We appreciate it." She hesitated and gestured back toward the front door of the shop. "I have a couple of boxes of crystals and minerals out in the truck. Should I bring them in?" Her voice became tentative and reserved once again, and Amy's curiosity about the woman intensified.

"I've got to take off," Shaw interrupted, surprising Amy.

She could have never walked away from the chance to see the proceeds of a new mine. She glanced at Jackson and saw that he was also looking forward to the treat. She gave herself an internal shrug, everyone was different, or maybe Shaw just had an appointment. He never had mentioned what he did for a living here in the small town of Copper Springs.

Jackson had turned to Shaw. "It was good to see you again. Come back when you get a chance, and we'll get you totally hooked into the rockhound world." He grinned at Shaw. Amy noticed that his previous animosity over Merri had shelved for the time being,

Shaw nodded, a distant smile on his face. "Maybe I will, if I get a chance. Thanks for your time, Amy. Jackson." He turned to Pete. "It was good to see you again too, Pete, and you, Salina. Hopefully I'll get the chance to come back out to the mine soon and get another tour."

Salina gave Shaw a surprised look, but then gave him her small, tight smile and nodded. "I think we could arrange that. Give me a call and we can set up a time." She rattled off a series of numbers and Shaw typed them into his phone then hit "save contact," completing the now-familiar sharing of digits. Amy wondered what anthropologists in the future would think of this ritual. Shaw stuffed his phone back into a pocket, and turned toward the front entrance, clearly eager to leave. Pete was standing next to the counter, blocking the tiny hallway that led to the front door. Amy saw Shaw stiffen, and a look Amy couldn't identify flashed in his muddy eyes.

"Good seeing you again, Shaw," Pete said and put out his hand. Tension seemed to flow out of Shaw's body, and he seemed smaller to Amy, back to the strange, affable man they'd met originally. He took the proffered hand, shook it and said his goodbyes to Pete, then made his way out the front door. Amy heard an engine roar to life as Shaw sped out of the parking lot, spitting gravel.

A half hour later, Pete and Amy were in their element, examining a variety of mineral specimens which Salina had carefully packed into several beat up cardboard boxes.

Jackson had taken Salina into the computer room to help her set up accounts for the mine on several social media sites, as well as give her some tips on selling through social media.

Amy had just picked up a large, bright orange windowpane crystal of wulfenite with a surge of longing in her heart, when her cell phone rang. She jumped and almost dropped the specimen. With shaking hands she set the gem and its rock matrix on the counter with the wulfenite crystal protruding upward from the ugly, red-orange stone base and fished her phone out of her pocket.

"Hello?" Amy noticed her voice was shaking after the close call. That crystal was easily worth $700 and it would almost certainly have broken if she had dropped it on the hard floor or the glass counter top. She stepped back even farther, as though afraid that just her breathing on it would cause damage.

"Hi, Amy. This is Tommy." The deep voice rumbled over the line, surprising her. In her shaken condition she'd forgotten to look at the caller ID. Pulling the phone away from her ear, she looked now: Mohave County Sheriff's Department. He was calling from his work number, and her heart sped up. She put the phone back to her ear.

"Hi, Tommy. Have you learned anything new about Hazelton?" The words came out in a rush, and Amy gave Pete a guilty look.

He had looked up at the world "Hazelton" and Amy could see him studying her, a slight frown stamped on the landscape between his eyes. Amy shook her head and shrugged.

"You sound shook and out of breath. Is everything okay?" Tommy was asking, concern evident in his voice.

"Everything is fine. I was just looking at some amazing wulfenite crystals and nearly dropped one when the phone rang, Did you need something?" Amy answered, not mentioning that she was dying of curiosity about why he was calling, or her fear that it was something that boded ill for Pete.

"I was calling to see if you'd heard from Pete, or either of the Matthesons. I've been trying to reach them for several days. I just left the Red Wind. No one was there, or I couldn't find them if they were. Went by Pete's too, and his truck isn't there." Tommy sounded frustrated with the difficulties in locating his witnesses... or was that suspects?

"Pete's standing right here. He said he broke his phone and hasn't gotten down to Kingman to replace it," Amy said, a clutch of fear in her chest. She squashed it down, and continued, "Salina Mattheson's here, too. She brought in a bunch of minerals to show us, and to get some lessons in selling online."

Pete was staring at her, his blue eyes boring a hole in her forehead.

She turned her back on him and continued, "Why do you need them? Have you found out who pushed Jon Hazelton?"

"We're still looking into that," Tommy said. "What I really need Pete for is some historical information. May I speak with him?"

Amy pushed an icon, then held out the phone. "I've put you on speaker." She heard him sigh over the phone.

"What can I do for you, Tommy? Other than confess, of course," Pete chuckled

"I'm actually calling for information about the Red Wind," Tommy said.

Amy caught movement from the corner of her eye and saw Jackson and Salina emerge from the computer room with matching questioning looks on their faces.

"What do you need to know?" asked Pete. Amy figured that by the time Pete was done, Tommy would have learned much more than he needed to know, if her past experiences with Pete were anything to go by.

"Did you get to know Powell when he and his wife took over the mine?" Tommy's voice floated out of the speaker. Amy's heart rate increased another few notches.

"Does that mean the body is..." she started, but Pete cut in.

"I met him a couple of times, but he kept pretty much to himself," Pete said. "He's the one who put in that heavy duty iron gate. Neither of them shopped in town much as far as I know." Pete paused and thought.

"Come to think of it, I don't know that I ever saw him at the gas station or anywhere else in town, for that matter. It was his wife... Damn, I can't remember her name. Pretty little blonde thing. Looked tired all the time. It would have been a hard life out there and..."

"Pete, back on subject," snapped out Tommy's voice.

Pete chuckled. He always took being called out on his verbal scenic routes with good humor, and redirected his words without argument. "I went out when I heard he'd bought the mine. He hadn't put in the gate yet, and when I pulled into the flat area in front of the portal, he came out of one of the tin sheds carrying a rifle. Seemed a bit put out that I'd just shown up. Still, he didn't threaten me. Wasn't friendly, exactly. Just seemed a bit nervous, but I've seen other miners that way. They get the idea that they're sitting on the mother lode and that everyone is out to steal it." Pete grinned and shook his head, knowing how many times the "mother lode" actually came true.

"The family wasn't there long. Probably not more than six months or a year. He called me once or twice to ask about mining, and came over once to see a sluice box I had sitting out back. Next thing I know, I hear he's disappeared."

"Did you help with the search?"

"No...," Pete's voice tailed off as he thought back close to thirty years. "Lil and I had gone out of town." His voice took on a sad note and his eyes looked into the distant past. "It was the first time she got sick, and we'd gone down to Phoenix for a few days for some tests."

Everyone was quiet for a moment. Amy thought again of Lil Martin, Pete's wife, a round, friendly woman as excited about rocks as Pete was. She'd been gone for what must be fifteen years now, but it was clear the pain at the memories of her illness was as fresh today as it was all those years ago.

Pete visibly shook himself, then continued. "When we got home, we heard the story of the search. Sounded like most of the town was out looking for him, but there was no sign in the mine or out. If I remember, the wife and kids packed up and moved away within a week. There was a padlock on the gate, and we haven't seen anyone there until the Mattheson's bought the place a few months ago."

"Ol' Tom lived there for awhile," Jackson blurted out, and Amy looked at Salina to judge her reaction.

"Really," Pete said, but he didn't sound too surprised. "That man has always moved around from one spot to another. I guess the opportunity to squat in a bunch of abandoned buildings must have been tempting."

Salina remained silent, declining to mention her meeting with Ol' Tom when she and Jania took possession of the mine. Amy looked at her, but couldn't see any emotion other than a touch of wariness on the woman's face. Still, as Jackson had pointed out earlier, Ol' Tom's living at the mine only showed that he saw an opportunity and took it, not that he'd done anything to create that opportunity.

"Why do you need to know all this, Tommy?" Amy broke in, concern forming a lump in her chest. "Was the body Powell's? Do they know what happened to him?" She looked at the various faces surrounding her, wildly different expressions on their faces.

Jackson seemed as eager as she was to learn why Tommy was suddenly so interested in their pile of bones. Pete also seemed curious, although his curiosity seemed to be more tempered, maybe by reluctance to remember that painful time.

Salina's wariness remained and Amy wondered briefly why, although when she thought about it, she supposed that having a body found on one's property could cause a number of complications, and the sisters were already struggling to make a living.

"We're still trying to determine if the body is Powell's, but we have traced the ownership of the mine and we...

"You found his wife and children?" Jackson broke in. "Where are they? Can you do a DNA comparison to determine if the body is Powell's?"

"Jackson, shut up!" Amy said, scowling at him across the phone. "I want to hear, too." She saw Pete move in closer. Salina on the other hand had taken a step back, her face pale. Amy frowned. *She almost looks scared* Amy thought.

"Powell's wife, Maria Powell, nee Kritenden, passed away about a year ago." Tommy said stiffly, as thought he were reading from a report. Amy could vaguely hear paper rustling in the background. "However, she maintained ownership of the mine until her death."

Amy nodded almost to herself. Mind racing ahead. *The kids inherited the mine as part of the estate and probably sold it for what they could get.* Briefly her mind touched on what would happen when her parents passed away. Would Amy, Jasper and Opal keep the shop or would it also be sold for whatever it brought, the proceeds split between the three of them? She shuddered. The idea of Stone's Gems and Minerals passing into someone else's hands, or being dissolved completely, made her vaguely nauseous.

Amy realized that Tommy had continued on, his words trickling out of the phone and falling like a boulder into a pond, creating ripples.

"What?" Amy exclaimed, sure she'd heard the end of that sentence wrong. "Repeat that, I didn't catch it." She looked around. Jackson and Pete were staring at Salina, eyes wide.

Tommy sighed, "Salina and Jania Mattheson inherited the mine from Maria, their mother."

The room whirled around for a moment, and Amy put out her hand and rested it on the glass counter, catching her balance. Salina had retreated another few steps and was looking at the other three as though she was an animal trapped in a cage.

Amy studied Salina's face. Her mouth was set in a straight line, and a canyon carved the skin between her eyebrows. Her body radiated anxiety, creating an almost palpable cloud which extended out as far as the watchers.

Tommy, unaware of the silent dialogue in the shop, continued on, "So, we're going to need to get a DNA sample from either Salina or Jania to make a positive identification of the remains. If you don't mind, Salina, someone could stop by the mine, or if you're going to be in Kingman anytime in the next day or two, it would save us the trip."

Three sets of eyes watched Salina as she fought to form the words. "That would be fine," Salina finally said in a tight voice. "I was planning on coming to Kingman to go shopping next Monday if that would work for you." She sighed, and her shoulders slumped, the tension breaking without warning. "I'm pretty sure that the skeleton will be my father's. I've been expecting this since you first discovered it, Amy." Salina ducked her head, but not before Amy caught the glint of a tear. Jackson reached out and put his hand on her shoulder. Salina stiffened again for a moment, and then seemed to collapse in on herself.

Tommy's voice emerged from the phone's speaker once again. "Thanks, we appreciate it. One other thing: are you familiar with any allegations against your father, regarding theft from his place of employment prior to buying the mine?"

"Not that I can think of," Salina said too softly to be heard easily.

"I'm sorry, I didn't get that," Tommy said.

Salina increased her volume. "My mother told us a little bit when Jania and I were old enough to ask questions about Daddy. She didn't tell us too much. She didn't like to speak of him. Why?"

"Just a mention in the file. A lot of money went missing from your father's place of employment. There was a belief that it was a team... an insider and someone on the outside. A man was arrested, but there were suspicions that he was working with an inside man, and most of the money was never found. If this skeleton is the remains of your father, and it sounds like it probably is, then maybe he and his partner had a falling out. I don't suppose you'd remember anyone hanging around when you were a child?"

Salina shook her head violently. "Our mother said that our father didn't steal anything," she blurted out, then paused for a moment. "I don't remember much from when we lived at the mine when I was little. I was only five or six and Jania is two years younger than me." She stopped talking again and crossed her arms over her chest in a unconscious sign of defiance.

For several beats there was silence in the shop .

Finally, deciding that Salina was done talking for the moment, Tommy's voice floated out of the phone's speaker once again. "Well, be sure to let us know if you remember anything from that time, Ms. Mattheson." The formal "sheriff's deputy" tone more pronounced. "We'll see you on Monday," he said, making it clear that it was not a simple request.

Amy frowned for a second, not sure if he could coerce DNA or not in this type of situation. Then the frown shifted into a rueful look. Jackson was right. She'd watched too many crime shows. Besides she was sure that Salina and Jania would both want to know for certain what happened to their father.

The cell phone went dead and Amy reached toward the device, then paused. She, Pete and Jackson couldn't seem to take their eyes off Salina, who was standing, rigid, staring back at them.

Predictably, it was Jackson who broke the silence. "So, this is awkward. Are you okay, Salina?" Amy saw a look of compassion in his eyes, and the corner of Amy's mouth twitched in a smile. Jackson seemed always willing to give people the benefit of the doubt.

Salina gave Jackson a slight smile, and some of the tension melted from her shoulders, arms dropping to her sides, her hands loosening from clenched fists, fingers extending slowly.

"I'm fine. I just didn't figure that they'd be able to trace Jania and my history so quickly."

"You're really William Powell's daughter?" Amy asked while Pete remained uncharacteristically silent, watching Salina with sad expression on his face.

Salina paused for a second, then nodded. "Yes, William Powell was my father. After he disappeared, Mom, Jania and I moved back down to Phoenix, and Mom got a job in the cafeteria of a local school. A few months later, she met Robert Mattheson. They moved in together, and when enough time passed, she had our father declared dead and she and Robert got married. Robert adopted Jania and me, which is why we go by his last name." She shrugged. "Jania was so young when our father died, and I was fine with the change. By that time we'd been with Robert longer than we'd been with our own father." Her face crinkled as though she'd smelled a dead rat. Amy remembered what Pete had said about Powell meeting him with a gun. Still, Ol' Tom seemed to think he was a good father and his children loved him.

"Didn't you wonder what happened to him?" Jackson asked, his voice soft and gentle.

"When we were older, we asked about our father, or at least I know I did. Jania and I loved Robert, but we couldn't help being curious about William. Mom didn't like talking about it. She always thought that he had been killed, although when we asked, she was sort of vague about why." Salina's voice faded away. She looked into the distant past, her eyes unfocused. Then suddenly her gaze refocused on her small audience.

"One time, when I was a teenager and hanging out with the wrong crowd, I got arrested and taken to juvenile detention. My mother came to get me out, but she was furious, naturally. I remember on the way home we were arguing, and she said that it was 'hanging out with the wrong crowd got your father into plenty of trouble, and look at what happened.' She shut up after that, and I was never able to get her to talk about it again."

"Gladys said that you and your sister had gone into town with your mother the day your father disappeared," Jackson said, eyes curious. "You don't remember anyone coming to visit your father at other times?"

"I was the only one with my mother that day. I'd gone with her into town for a doctor's appointment. Jania loved going in the mine with our father and had stayed with him." A small wistful smile slipped across her lips. "He even got her a tiny hard hat. I had one too, but I didn't like going underground as much as my sister did. When my mother and I got home that afternoon, Jania was asleep on the front porch. The police asked her about our father, but she didn't say a thing. She was only three at the time and I don't know if she didn't know what happened to our father, didn't understand, or just couldn't say." Salina paused for a moment, looking at each of the three faces in turn, dark eyes wide and haunted. "I've asked her several times since then if she remembers anything about that day, but she's never said a word, and well, you've seen her." A wry expression crossed her face. "She can be a bit..." Salina searched for the correct word. "... fey, I guess. Not attached to this world." Salina halted her narrative, and silence fell over the shop.

Finally, Amy took a deep breath, and said, "Well, we've got some wulfenite specimens to get photographed and priced."

Salina gave her a grateful look.

An hour later, the front counter of the shop was covered with various mineral specimens, many of which caused Amy's heart to beat a little faster. She and Pete had been making a list, describing each piece, and debating good-naturedly on reasonable prices. Jackson and Salina had retreated into the computer room where he continued to help her set up a website and create pages on the various social medias.

Pete was examining a large, particularly bright, reddish-orange piece of wulfenite sprinkled liberally with botryoidal, or ball shaped, yellow mimetite when he jerked his head up. Asking what time it was, he swore, and rushed out the front door of the shop, calling back that his dino poo customer was coming to pick up the finished piece in fifteen minutes, and he would call them later.

It felt as though all the air had been sucked out of the shop with Pete's rushed departure, and Amy stood there, a large crystal cupped in her hands, a bemused look on her face. Placing the piece on the counter, being careful not to hit any of the delicate edges, Amy headed for the computer room. There, she found Salina and Jackson sitting side by side, staring at an over-sized computer monitor, a large image of a wulfenite crystal cluster against a soft gray background in front of them.

"Hey guys," Amy said from the doorway. "Pete's left for an appointment. How's it going in here?"

"Almost done for today," Jackson answered, looking back over his shoulder and giving Amy a brilliant smile. "These images came out fantastic. I think Salina has a handle on the basic part of uploading photos, updating auctions and such. Don't you?" He looked over at Salina who looked up from the monitor.

"I don't know about 'enough' but I think that I've absorbed as much as I can at the moment." She ran her fingers through her heavy dark hair, brushing it back from her face. She pushed the chair back from the work desk and started to rise when her phone rang: a straight up, old fashioned phone ring. Nothing whimsical, just like the woman herself, Amy thought.

Salina picked up the phone and hit the green phone icon. "Hello." She paused listening, a frown on her face. "Hello," a stronger voice this time. She stood still for a second, then pulled the phone away from her ear and looked at the screen. Her expression turned from one of annoyance to one of concern. She looked at Jackson and Amy as she put the phone back to her ear.

"What is it?" Jackson asked, his expression mirroring Salina's.

Salina shook her head sharply. "Hello. Jania, are you there? Jania!" Finally she gave up and hit the end icon, then send. No answer. "Dammit, Jania," she muttered to herself. Then she looked up and gave Jackson and Amy a crooked smile, the left side of her lips twisting upward, and she shrugged. "I told you... a little bit fey. She probably butt dialed me, or hit the button as she was setting the phone on a nearby rock, then walked off and left it. I can't tell you how many phones she's lost over the..."

Her voice faded, and she gave a little laugh, but Amy could tell that Salina was worried. *If I got a strange phone call from my sister who was alone in the place where my father had disappeared years ago, I guess I'd be a little worried, too,* she thought.

Salina shoved the phone back into her pocket, "I better get headed back out to the mine and see what's going on." She stared at the flats of mineral specimens with a frown. "I don't..."

"Why don't you leave the minerals here?" Amy and Salina spoke at the same time but Amy continued. "We'll put them in a safe place, and it will give Jackson a chance to finish getting them photographed for your website. I'll identify a few that the shop would like to buy, and list some suggested prices. Then we could go over the inventory when you're back in town next week."

Salina's relief showed on her face and she gave Amy one of her rare, genuine smiles. "Thank you. I can't tell you how much I appreciate it." She turned and headed out of the shop, hitting the release bar on the door so hard that Amy thought it would break. Salina headed toward the right front fender of an old, two-toned Chevy pickup that Amy could see through the clear glass door.

Amy looked at Jackson and noticed his eyes were following Salina, a frown causing unaccustomed furrows in his normally carefree face. He turned and looked at Amy.

"Do you think everything is okay with Jania?"

Amy shrugged. "I hope so." She looked out into the parking lot to where Salina had slammed the door of the old Chevy.

She heard the decrepit vehicle try to turn over, uttering a low grumble and a higher pitched squeal, then nothing. Another grumble groan, and the truck shook. For a moment it caught, shifting into a rough rumble. Salina shifted the truck into reverse and it started to crunch across the gravel. The engine died again, and the truck drifted to a stop only a few feet from where it began. Jackson started to walk to the front door, followed closely by Amy. They heard the grumble groan of the truck as Salina tried to start it again. There was no catch this time, and the engine refused to turn over.

They heard the driver's door open and slam closed. As Jackson opened the front door of the shop, they heard Salina opening the hood of the truck with a loud screech.

"You piece of sh...," Amy heard Salina muttering.

"What's up?" Jackson said, walking over to stand next to her, staring into the huge engine compartment. Amy followed, although she knew very little about the internal combustion engine, other than what the terms meant — explosions inside the engine.

"The truck has been acting up the last few weeks. Pete said he'd take a look at it, but he must have forgotten." She reached up and slammed the hood down so hard the entire truck shook. She looked at Jackson and Amy with a mix of anger and misery in her dark eyes.

Why is she so scared? thought Amy. The she remembered. *Father disappeared from the same mine years ago. Mother dead. Stepfather dead. Jania is all she has left of family. No wonder she's terrified.*

"Why don't I give you a ride out to the Red Wind?"

Jackson was saying, sympathy in his eyes. "It will be faster than trying to get someone over here to fix the truck. Do you have any other transportation out at the mine?"

Salina turned to him, a frown of concentration on her face. "We have an old quad." Her face cleared, and expression of relief taking place of the worry and frustration. "We could drive it into town, and then load it in the back of the truck when it's fixed."

"Great," Amy said, speaking before Jackson was able to open his mouth. "We'll take my jeep. It's almost closing time, and it's been dead today any..." She hesitated a moment, suppressing an internal shiver. *A goose walked over my grave,* came the phrase from nowhere. She couldn't remember where she'd heard it, and she'd always wondered where it came from.

"Anyway," she finished. "We might as well lock up. Who knows, you might need some help."

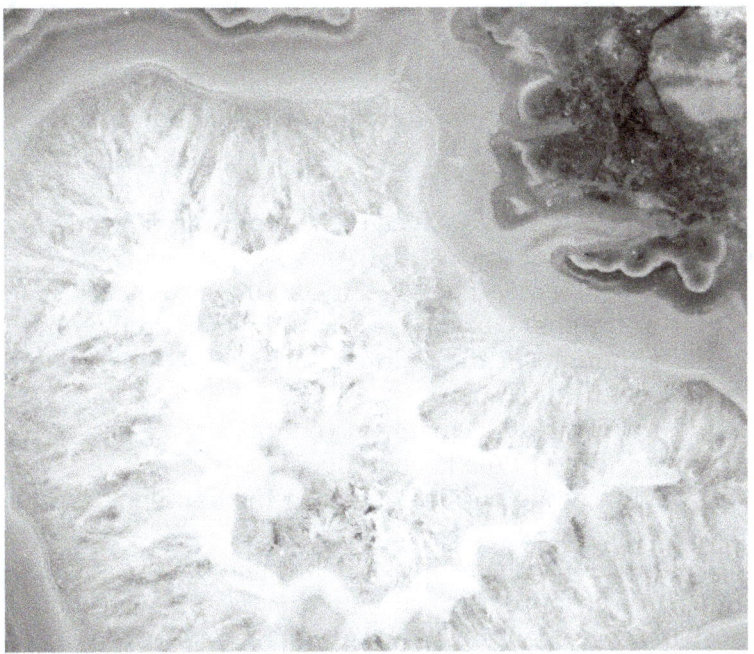

Brazilian Agate

13

Fifty minutes later Jackson pulled his 1999 teal GMC Jimmy to a stop in front of iron pipe gate of the Red Wind Mine. There had been discussion back at the shop over which vehicle to use, Amy's jeep, or Jackson's old Jimmy. The Jimmy won, but not because it was better suited for the road. It wasn't, being only a 2-wheel drive and, as Amy put it, "older than the dirt Moses was buried in." It won only because it had a second row of seats, while the Wrangler, almost as old as the Jimmy, as Jackson pointed out, had only two seats. That meant that either Jackson or Salina would have to sit in the bed of the jeep with the dogs.

In the end, the GMC got unanimous, if grudging, approval and the dogs stayed in the shop, happily chewing on some rawhide bones that Amy's father kept there in case of doggy emergencies. Amy, sitting in the back seat, had to admit that Jackson was a good driver on the rough roads, although she didn't intend to tell him that any time in the near future.

Salina fumbled at the inside handle on the passenger door, trying to get the latch to open.

"Pull in while you're squeezing the handle," Jackson prompted. "It sticks a bit."

Salina hauled back on the door handle and squeezed, and the latch popped open with a *thunk*, allowing her to push the door open and climb out. She eased the door closed careful not to let it latch, and headed for the pipe gate.

"You going to get your door fixed any time soon?" Amy asked from the back seat. "One of these days you're going to give a passenger a hernia trying to open that thing."

"Hey, it's a safety feature," Jackson said with mock seriousness. "What if I'm carrying a little kid and I don't want him to jump out into traffic?"

"Childproof doors, huh? What if there's an accident and the rescue crew needs to get in?"

"They..." Jackson's answer was interrupted by Salina opening the door and sliding back into the seat, a frown on her face.

"Everything okay?" Jackson asked, turning to look at the woman.

"I don't know. I..." She paused, ran her hands over her dark hair, then continued. "When I left, I put the padlock back into place, but I didn't snap it closed. I just made it look that way, you know." She looked over at Jackson, then back at Amy. "But now it's hanging wide open." She stopped and rubbed her face for a moment, her discomfort obvious. "I could have sworn I put it back so that it looked locked. I always do it that way if I'm not going to be gone long and Jania is staying at the mine," Salina talked in a low voice, almost as though she was trying to convince herself.

"Maybe the wind blew the chain around and dislodged the padlock," Amy suggested, although the wind hadn't been blowing noticeably that day. "Or someone out off-roading checked the lock and changed its position. It doesn't mean anything bad has happened. Did you see any unfamiliar tire tracks?"

"I didn't look. I probably wouldn't know if the tracks weren't mine. I've never paid attention to that type of thing." Salina's voice sounded distant and her eyes were fixed on the ridge across the wash. "We'll leave the gate open. Just drive through." She settled back into the passenger seat and took a deep breath.

Jackson glanced back at Amy. She nodded and he

drove through the gateway, then turned into the sandy wash, following the tracks put down by the passage of previous vehicles.

When the GMC topped the stone ridge overlooking the small valley where the portal to the Red Wind was located, Jackson braked, bringing the vehicle to a stop. Only one truck sat in the flat area which had been filled with vehicles last Saturday; an old, deep red four-by-four that Amy didn't recognize.

"Do you know who drives that truck?" Jackson asked, jerking his chin toward the crew cab pickup in the distance. It was unclear whether he was asking Amy or Salina, but Salina answered.

"I don't remember seeing it before. It's not ours, that's for sure."

"How 'bout you Amy?"

Amy squinted but it was difficult to tell anything from a distance. She thought she might have seen a red truck similar to that one, but she wasn't sure. "Wasn't there a red pickup on the field trip?" she asked, continuing to study the vehicle.

"Hmmm." Jackson took a second look, leaning forward as though those few inches would gain him inspiration. "Maybe. I just don't know. Only one way to find out, though." He took his foot off the brake and started to roll down the hill.

A few moments later Jackson pulled the Jimmy alongside what turned out to be a 1979 Ford F-150 crew cab four-wheel drive with a mismatched camper shell. Neither Jania, nor the driver of the truck, were in sight.

After another brief struggle with the door, Salina climbed out slowly, looking around the area in front of the mine, eyes intense, face frozen in concentration. Jackson popped open his door, then pulled the front seat forward to allow Amy egress.

"Do you see anyone, Salina?" Amy asked, shading her eyes and looking at the sides of the valley, then over toward the cluster of tin buildings and rusting equipment.

"No. No one." Worry was written clearly on her face and in her voice.

Jackson had walked over to the red pickup and was peering in the driver side window, hand cupped around his eyes to cut the glare. "Whoever it belongs to has a gun rack in the back window complete with a hunting rifle. I suppose it's a good thing that the rifle is in there, though, instead of being pointed at someone out here." Jackson stood up, and cast his gaze around the valley, then walked over to where Salina and Amy were still standing next to the Jimmy. "Maybe it's a lost hunter."

"It's not hunting season. At least not deer or elk, although I supposed they could be scouting," Amy said, continuing to examine the terrain, staring as if her eyes had the power to make Jania materialize out of thin air.

"Jania! Hello Jania! Are you there?" Salina called loudly, causing Amy to jump. The echo of her voice refracted off the sides of the valley.

Silence. No response to the yell.

"Jania! Can you hear me?" Salina called again, and again the only sounds were local birds, and a distant jet heading for Las Vegas.

"Maybe the truck belongs to someone from the field trip. They could have been out four-wheeling and stopped by to see if Jania would take them down into the mine again. After all, Hazelton was talking about..." Amy stopped abruptly, remembering that Hazelton had never gotten the chance to bring up the subject of opening a tourist attraction. *Not my information to share,* she thought, but she glanced at Salina and wondered if anyone else might have approached her with that idea.

"They've got to be down in the mine," Jackson said, looking around the surrounding hills. He turned and looked at Salina. "Do you know the passages well enough to search for her down there?

Salina shook her head, not taking her eyes off the hillsides to look at Jackson. "Jania is the mole in the family. I've been down in the mine, but not as far in as Jania. I usually stay on the surface, cleaning the minerals and doing some panning in the wash for some of the placer gold."

Then she stiffened, and her head whipped around to look at Jackson and Amy. "Jania did start to make a map for me, though. I don't know how much of it she got done, but maybe there's enough for us to use it to find her." Salina turned and headed for the house at a jog, leaving Amy and Jackson standing in the parking area looking at each other.

"I don't suppose you have helmets or headlamps in the Jimmy, do you? Amy said in conversational tones, knowing the answer and wishing that she'd thought to throw some equipment into Jackson's SUV before they'd left the shop.

Jackson gave a half shrug and shook his head. "Didn't know I was going to be a mine rat today or I would have grabbed some. Hopefully, Salina has extras." They both looked up toward the tin building the Mattheson sisters used as a house in time to see Salina come hurrying out, carrying what appeared to be a paper road map. A battered yellow hard hat was perched on her dark hair, and two others hung over her arm by their chin straps, banging and clicking together.

"I have the map," Salina said out of breath as she hurried up to where Jackson and Amy stood waiting. "And I brought some of the extra hard hats and lamps we found in the cabin when we got here. The batteries are good." She thrust out her arm toward Amy and Jackson, the old, blue helmets swinging even more violently, crashing together and making a racket.

Hats distributed, Salina set the accordion-folded stack of paper on the hood of Jackson's GMC and tried to flatten it, unfolding and pushing at the corners which kept lifting in the heavy breeze, stubbornly refusing to stay in place. Jackson and Amy crowded around Salina, leaning in to examine the lines that had been sketched on the smudged white surface.

Amy's brow furrowed as she looked at the map. "Do you understand the drawing?" she asked no one in particular. To her, it looked like a bunch of lines with no rhyme or reason and her heart sank. How would they ever be able to find Jania and whoever she was with if they were in the depths of the mine?

"I think this is the main portal here," Salina said, pointing to a crudely drawn star with the helpful label "E." Her voice sounded anything but certain.

"That would make sense," Jackson said, his voice expressing some of the same concerns that Amy was feeling.

Salina looked as though her whole world was crashing down. Maybe Jania, who was always down in that maze of tunnels understood this map, but Amy sure didn't.

"It looks like Jania tried to indicate different levels of the mine with different colors, and the shafts with that slashing symbol." Jackson pointed to several slash-marked tracks which joined lines of two different colors. "Look, there's the ore chute, and I think I remember that blocked tunnel there," he said, indicating a short perpendicular line ending in a large red X, which led off a heavy black line. "Maybe we should just head in, and the map will make more sense."

Salina looked up at Jackson, brown eyes wide, and desperate hope now written across her face. "If you think so..."

"Remember, we still don't even know if Jania is in trouble," Amy reminded them, trying to convince herself that the statement was true. "We could be jumping the gun here. Maybe we should wait to see if she and her visitor come back out. She might just be leading another tour." She knew from the look on the others faces that she hadn't convinced them any more than she had herself.

"If she's just leading a tour, then there's no harm in our tagging along," Jackson said in matter-of-fact tones, but Amy thought she could see concern lurking in his clear blue eyes. "I sure wouldn't mind seeing the mine again. I've been reading about mine photography and..."

Amy gave him a look and he stopped abruptly but gave Amy a wink. She felt an eye roll take over and hoped that Salina hadn't noticed.

"I'd feel better if we went looking for her," Salina said, still studying the map, unaware of the byplay between Amy and Jackson. She looked up. "We can take the map. If we get down in the mine and it doesn't make sense, we can always come back out."

Salina struggled to refold the map along the original creases, then finally a gave up and reduced the paper to a manageable size without worrying about how it was originally folded. She pushed the map into a back pocket of her jeans, then spun on her heel and headed for the portal of the mine. After a moment's hesitation, Amy and Jackson followed close behind. Salina was right. As long as they marked, or paid attention at the intersections, they could always come back out if they couldn't find Jania.

The group was almost to the mine's entrance when a flash of something bright from farther up the hillside to the right of the portal brought Amy to a sudden stop. Jackson, walking beside her, turned with a question on his face.

"Did you see that? Up the trail there. Something flashed in the sunlight." Amy jerked her chin in the direction of the faint trail which headed up toward the saddle, or dip, between two high points on the mountainside.

"I didn't see anything." Jackson craned his head back and forth, trying to pick the same flash of reflected sunlight that Amy had seen.

Salina had continued on toward the mine portal, not realizing that her companions were no longer following. She stopped and turned before entering the mine itself, and saw that the others were still back at the shoulder of the mountain where it came met the valley floor. Frowning, she retraced her steps.

"What's going on? What are you looking at?" Salina turned to stare in the same direction that Amy and Jackson were looking.

"I don't know." Amy started up the trail, scrambling over the loose rocks and stopping every few steps to scrutinize the trail above her.

There.

Something hot pink and black was on the ground next to a boulder halfway up the hillside. Amy rushed the last few feet, losing sight of the black spot temporarily. She moved around the large rock and there it was on the ground next to her feet: a cell phone in a pink and black silicone case, the screen shattered.

She picked it up, staring at the large phone, turning it over in her hands. She pressed the power button, and the screen lit, but nothing but streaks of colors overlaid by liquid black lines were visible.

"What did you find?" Jackson asked from behind her right shoulder, causing her to jump. She hadn't heard him coming up the hillside behind her. He was breathing heavily and sweat dampened his sandy hair. Salina was only a few feet behind Jackson. Her dark brown eyes widened at the site of the phone in Amy's hand. Her face went pale, two red spots glowing in her cheeks.

"That's Jania's phone," Salina gasped. "I recognize her case."

Amy held it out toward Salina, screen facing her. "It's been shattered. I saw the flash of sunlight off the screen." Amy looked up the trail toward the spot where the trail disappeared over the edge of the mountain, then turned back to her companions. "Isn't this the trail that goes to the mine shaft where Hazelton was attacked?"

"I think so," Jackson answered, then turned back to Salina for confirmation. Salina nodded, eyes glued to the edge of the hill where the trail disappeared.

"Why would her phone be up here?" Salina said, almost to herself. Then she looked at Jackson and Amy, her brows folding together in confusion and anxiety. "Jania never goes up this way. She says there are bad vibes on this trail. She says that it isn't safe."

Jackson frowned and glanced back at Amy. "Didn't

Hazelton say that he followed Salina up this trail?"

Amy shook her head. "He said he followed the 'one who was in charge.'" Amy made air quotes as she said the words "one who was in charge." "We didn't think to ask him who that was until after we left, remember? We thought it was Salina at the time."

"I've never gone up this trail. Jania said she'd explored and it wasn't safe." Salina stopped abruptly, the sudden absence of words leaving the silence ringing in their ears as they absorbed what she said.

"Then why would Hazelton say he'd followed one of you up this trail on the day of the field trip?" Jackson asked. His blue eyes were clouded in a frown of concern.

Salina didn't answer, but instead started making her way up the trail. Amy glanced at Jackson and then both turned and started climbing as well.

It took only a few minutes for the three of them to reach the saddle, and stand looking down toward the small terrace that had become so familiar. The mine shaft that Hazelton had been pushed into was easily visible in its screen of catclaw, but no people were in sight.

Salina pulled off her helmet and pushed her heavy dark hair back from her face, the increasing wind picking it up like a banner.

"I don't see her. Maybe she didn't go this way," she said, hope in her voice, as though she was trying to convince herself. Her wide dark eyes still holding desperation on the edge of panic.

"Then why would the phone, which she called you on, by the way, be lying broken on the trail nowhere near the main mine?" Jackson asked, shielding his eyes as he scanned the mountain side. He looked back at Salina and Amy, "I say we go down and take a closer look." With that he started to make his way down the trail, stepping sideways and picking his way through the loose rocks.

Amy took a deep breath and followed him, Salina

close behind, emerging a short time later on the trail that Amy and Jackson had identified while waiting for Tommy the previous Saturday. Jackson strode over to the mine shaft, making his way through the sharp, snagging thorns of the catclaw to the shallow end. He stood for a moment studying the slope before him, then turned and looked up at Salina and Amy who were making their way over to him, moving a bit more gingerly through the catclaw.

"Someone's been here. They left a rope," Jackson said, nodding his head toward the shaft. "That's not the green rope you had, Amy, this one is black. It looks like the type of rope you'd pick up at the local hardware store, not climbing rope like yours."

"You're sure it doesn't belong to the sheriff's department? Maybe they left their rope since they're still investigating the case." Amy knew as she said it that none of the deputies she'd met would ever carelessly leave their equipment behind like that, especially equipment which would encourage or help others get into trouble, the way that an inviting rope down an abandoned mine shaft might.

"I doubt it," Jackson said echoing her thoughts. He walked around to the shallow end, and looked at the loose gravel slope."I can't tell if someone went down here recently or not. Damn!" He looked up at Salina. "You have that map. Did Jania show this shaft, or any of the tunnels connected to it?"

"I told you Jania didn't come this way. She said it wasn't safe." Salina's anxiety leaked out as irritation in her voice.

"Let's just take another look," Jackson said, refusing to react to Salina's sharp tone, and once again, Amy envied his ability to keep his cool, regardless of what was going on around him. She wished she had that much control.

Salina conceded, although her body language radiated impatience. She looked around, then walked over toward the pile of boulders where Amy and Jackson had sat while waiting to talk with Tommy after Hazelton's accident.

Amy and Jackson clustered close as Salina unfolded the wad of paper in front of them.

"See, it's just the main mine," Salina said. Her hair fell over her shoulder and she pushed it back in annoyance.

Amy looked at the series of lines, Xs and slashes, no more able to figure out Jania's strategy than before. She wished that Jania had included some form of legend or key on her map.

"There's nothing here." Salina started folding the paper again, moving so agitatedly that Amy thought the paper would be torn to shreds before she got it refolded.

"Wait," Jackson put out a hand and stopped Salina. She looked at him with wide brown eyes, making her look like a wild animal and Amy thought she was going to rip the map away from Jackson's hands.

"Wait," he said again with intensity, his blue eyes meeting Salina's brown ones. "I think I saw something on the back of the map."

He gently took the paper out of Salina's white fingers and laid it on the rock again, this time with the back of the map facing upward. In the bright sunlight, Amy could clearly see where a series of lines had been incompletely erased.

"Look at this drawing," Jackson said, tracing the partial lines with a finger.

"So, Jania started a map on one side of the paper, didn't like it and started again on the other side." Salina reached for the map again, but Jackson pushed her hand away as he examined the sketch.

"No, that's not it," Amy said studying the faint lines with curiosity. "Look here. Jania drew a slashed line, and then a ninety-degree dogleg to the right. That's where she wrote the 'E' for entrance. In the drawing on the other side, the one of the main mine, she just started with a straight solid line and the letter 'E.' This one matches an external shaft with the portal at the bottom, just like the mine here." Amy traced her finger over the drawing, then patted her pockets. "Does anyone have a pencil or a pen?"

Jackson and Salina both started checking their own pockets. Salina dropped her hands and shook her head. Jackson, on the other hand, pulled a small stub of a pencil from the breast pocket of his red T-shirt and handed it over to Amy, who started tracing over the erased lines.

"See here," she started. "On the drawing of the main mine - the one on the other side of the paper - she used a slashed line to indicate inclined winzes dropping to another level. This side has those same slashed lines for this short area before and after the letter 'E.'" She drew in the lines, then studied the rest of the sketch.

"Can you make out the rest of the map?" asked Jackson, who was looking over her shoulder.

Amy paused, then shook her head. "There is an adit here, and several branches off it. There's a weird symbol here, with this squiggly line, and the mine changes directions. I don't know what this square means. It might be a stope or something else totally." She pointed to what appeared to be the main drive, the large shaded-in area near the end.

Amy looked back up at Salina and Jackson, then down at the map again and lips folded as she thought.

"You know this means that Jania wasn't telling you the truth when she said she didn't come this way," Jackson said, as he continued to study the map. You said you didn't usually go into the mines with her. You might not have realized that she was coming up here once in a while instead of going into the main mine. She probably did it when you were in town, like today."

It was left unsaid that Jania almost certainly knew that there was a body near the portal of the mine. The only one who knew whether Jania realized that the skeleton belonged to her father was Jania herself.

Amy looked back at Salina, who was standing, staring down at the map, lips pursed. She raised her eyes to meet Amy and Jackson's gazes, her dark eyes glinted with unshed tears. She jerked her head in a sharp nod and took the map out of Amy's hands. She started to refold it, this time with the newly darkened drawing on the outside.

Finally, Salina took a deep, shaky breath. "If Jania didn't tell me the truth about coming in this direction, she must have had a good reason. It doesn't really matter. What matters is that she's missing, and it looks like she went into this shaft with some stranger and we need to go after her." Salina's voice strengthened as she spoke, and by the time she ended her sentence Amy could hear a new level of determination in her tones and knew nothing would dissuade her.

"All right," Amy said, "But before we do this, I'm calling the sheriff's department."

"What are you going to tell them?" Jackson asked, head tilted to the side, reminding Amy of Jynx when she saw something that made her wonder.

Amy could feel her chin start to take its stubborn tilt, and deliberately relaxed the muscles of her neck and face. She knew Jackson was right. They had no evidence that Jania was in trouble, as she herself had pointed out earlier.

"At the very least, if something happens to us, someone will know where we are going," she said. "Even if the sheriff's department doesn't come out right away, there will be a record of my calling. It's not like we can call if we get into trouble while we're underground."

Jackson nodded in agreement, and Amy turned and started up the trail, back toward the saddle, checking the screen of her cell phone every few steps, looking for the tell-tale bars which indicated that she was in range of a signal.

She was nearly at the top of the trail before the phone suddenly switched from a persistent "no signal" indicator to a strong four bars. Amy stopped and stood, staring at the screen. She punched in the 9, then 1, then she hesitated. Jackson was right, they had no proof that there was an emergency, and the sheriff's department wasn't likely to take a "hinky feeling" as a strong indicator of an emergency. She cleared the two numbers she'd already entered, then tapped in Tommy's number. The phone rang. Amy looked back down at the terrace and saw

Salina and Jackson staring up the hill at her. Salina's body language radiated impatience, while Jackson appeared relaxed.

Tommy's voicemail clicked on, and Amy ground her teeth. "Tommy. It's Amy. Jackson and I are out at the Red Wind with Salina Mattheson. She got a disturbing call from Jania's phone. Uh... well, it was actually like a butt dial, but then it went dead and Salina couldn't reach Jania when she tried to call back." Amy thought frantically, wondering how long the voicemail would record. "When we got out here we found a strange truck, and Jania's phone is smashed. We're going down the shaft where Hazelton was attacked to look for her." She paused, wondering what to say when the line beeped and the message was ended. She pressed end, and stood looking at the phone, then shoved it in her pocket, turned and hurried back down the trail.

Amy pulled to a stop next to where Jackson and Salina were waiting. Salina's body seemed to vibrate with impatience, her hand fisted at her sides. Jackson, on the other hand, appeared at ease, although his eyebrows were quirked in curiosity.

"What did they say?" he asked. He was perfecting the innocent, puppy dog look, Amy noted, and it irritated her.

"I didn't call 9-1-1," she said in clipped tones, then softened her voice at the surprised look on Jackson's face, his eyes widened and head jerked back as though slapped. None of this was his fault. "I called Tommy instead." Her lips twisted. "You were right. We don't have enough information to convince emergency personnel."

"How about Tommy?"

"I got his voicemail." Amy sighed. "Hopefully he'll get the message. Let's go." Amy started walking toward the mine, effectively ending the conversation.

Helmets and headlamps firmly in place, Jackson ducked under a strip of bright yellow "caution" tape and led the way down the steep incline of the shaft, lightly holding the rope that had apparently been left behind by Jania and her companion.

No sling. Again, Amy realized watching him navigate the loose footing with ease. *Fine. He's a grown man. Let him permanently cripple himself. I've got enough to worry about,* she grumbled to herself.

Salina waited until Jackson was halfway down the slope before she started over the loose surface. It was obvious from her tentative movements that she was much less comfortable with the unstable footing than was Jackson. She took several halting steps, then, mimicking Jackson, turned sideways to the slope and began side stepping to the bottom, gripping the rope much more tightly than had Jackson.

Amy waited for Salina to reach the base of the slope, then ducked under the caution tape, stepped off the solid edge of the shaft and made her way down to where the other two were standing in front of the mine portal.

Jackson moved to the gaping entrance, and examined the ground at his feet, then peered inside the dark hole.

"Do you see anything?" Amy asked.

Jackson continued to study the opening of the mine for a moment, looked back at the ground, then stood straight and shook his head. "No... I'm not sure. I can't tell if any of these tracks are from today, or from last week." He looked back over his shoulder at Amy and Salina, a frown on his face. He was right. Down in the shaft, protected from wind, and with no rain during the past week, there was nothing except possible rodent or snake activity that might have overlaid older tracks to help them determine if someone had recently passed.

It appeared they were out of luck in the pack rat department, Amy thought. From what she could see around Jackson's feet, nothing but human activity had disturbed the entrance to the mine recently.

"I don't suppose you know what type of shoes or boots Jania was wearing," Jackson asked, looking at Salina. He moved aside so the woman could move up and examine the soft dirt at the entrance to the tunnel.

"No," Salina said, staring at the ground, "Just something she got at Walmart or Tractor Supply or some place like that. I have no idea what the tread looks like." She started to take a step forward when Jackson put out his right arm, halting her.

"Wait." He moved a few feet into the mine, moving down the adit, and stopping, shining his headlamp over the floor. "The tracks are all jumbled up, but here it looks like the freshest sets head downward instead of upward. At least I think they're the freshest. They seem to be overlaying the others right here, and down there as well," Jackson twitched his chin toward a spot just past a small pile of debris.

"That means that whoever left those prints is still down here," Amy said with more confidence than she felt. " And, we can follow them, and not rely totally on Jania's map."

"Maybe," Jackson said, and Amy could hear the doubt in his voice, but he started to inch forward, placing each foot with care, watching the ground in front of him, then lifting his head to shine the light farther down the adit.

Amy glanced over at Salina and saw that she was staring at the ground as well, her hands fisting then loosening, fisting then loosening, over and over. Amy felt a frisson of doubt shiver down her spine. What did she truly know about Salina? She'd already proven secretive. Could they rely on her if things went badly? Amy took a deep breath, and adjusted her helmet and headlamp, then started to make her way down the slope.

A glint of yellow caught Amy's eye. More warning tape was strewn over the pile of mine refuse where Hazelton and Powell had fallen. *Just in case people didn't pay attention to the yellow ribbon at the top of the shaft,* Amy thought, her lips twisting in a grim smile, *like us.* Amy paused for a second, staring at the pile of lumber and metal that had been Powell's last resting place, then she glanced back at

Salina, remembering that this had been her father. Salina had her head down and seemed to avoid looking in the direction of the mound of debris. A twinge of sympathy overtook Amy's doubts. She turned back to the slope and made her way the rest of the way down to the bottom of the adit.

The three gathered in the widened area at the base of the incline, not far from where Hazelton had lain less than a week ago.

"The tracks seem to be leading down the tunnel, so it's probably them. They're only pointing in one direction, so whoever made them didn't come down and just go back out again," Jackson said.

The adit narrowed drastically a few feet past the widened area at the portal. Amy remembered the whiff of damp she'd gotten when sitting with Hazelton and sniffed the air, trying to pick up the same odor she'd smelled at that time. It was there, faint but distinct, and Amy again wondered if there were flooded drives or stopes back in this portion of the mine.

The air had the dead, heavy quality she was familiar with from the other mines and caves she'd explored. However, there was a slight draft, indicating that the mine had some natural ventilation. That was good since it made it less likely that they would run into any areas of low oxygen or poisonous gases. Still, they were heading down into possibly long-abandoned areas, and old timbers rotting and rusting metal could eat up the oxygen in the air. If they ventured into a side passage, or onto another level, the air might not be stirred up by the mountain breathing. That could allow pockets of bad air to form. If they wandered themselves in one of these areas, they could find themselves incapacitated before they realized what was happening.

She put her hand on Jackson's shoulder. "Do you have any matches or a lighter?"

Jackson shook his head, knowing why she was asking. Amy looked back at Salina and asked her the same question. Salina frowned, fished in her pocket and pulled out a large, fluorescent green lighter and handed it to Amy who flicked it, causing a flame to jump to life. The light wavered indicating the slight movement of air. She released the trigger and the flame died.

"What do you think?" Jackson asked, although he'd seen the flame burning healthily.

"It should be fine. If you don't mind, though, I'll keep the lighter for a little while. It's possible that these works are connected with the main mine, and the air is transferring that way since there's no sign of ventilation tubing, or there could be open stopes or shafts up there somewhere. Still, there could be dead ends and pockets of air that aren't getting stirred up. If any of you start feeling short of breath or develop a headache, let me know right away. Don't ignore them." She gave Salina a stern look. "You won't help Jania if you pass out and die from carbon dioxide poisoning."

"I understand," Salina said in a tense voice, but Amy could see that the woman's anxiety was increasing, as was her impatience; her hands in almost constant movement at her sides. Impatience made people careless, and she realized that it would most likely be she or Jackson who identified the bad air before Salina did. Amy also remembered Salina saying that Jania was the mole in the family, and wondered if Salina's anxiety wasn't just for her sister, or if there was a level of claustrophobia as well.

It was left unsaid that if their group ran into bad air, Jania and whomever she was with would have as well, and if they hadn't come back it might be because they couldn't. Still, if the erased map was anything to go by, Jania was familiar with this branch of the mine, and she hadn't succumbed to carbon dioxide, or any other form of poisonous atmosphere.

Jackson started walking slowly down the adit, moving the beam of his headlamp over the floor, then over the walls. Occasionally he would pause, squat and examine the floor of the tunnel. The rough-hewn walls closed in, and Amy found herself walking single file behind him, with Salina bringing up the rear.

They had traveled approximately a hundred yards down the adit when it forked. Jackson came to a stop and Amy stepped up beside him in the wider junction. They shined the beams of their headlamps on the floor and then down each of the two legs of the tunnel.

"What do you think?" Salina asked from behind Jackson and Amy.

Jackson started to shake his head and then stopped when the beam from the headlamp started jumping wildly with his movement.

"The floor of the tunnel isn't taking tracks well here. What does the map show?" he asked, turning back toward the woman.

Salina pulled the folded map from her back pocket and shook it open, illuminating it with the beam of her headlamp.

After a moment of contemplation, Salina said, "I don't know. I think we're here." She pointed to a spot on the paper. "It's the first fork that I can see on the map, at any rate. That would mean we need to go to the right, but that sure doesn't look like the best way."

All three of them aimed their headlamps down the right-hand fork. It squeezed in tighter than before, much tighter than the left-hand fork, and a pile of rocks and dirt indicated that at some point in the past the drive had experienced a minor collapse. In Amy's mind, a collapse in the past meant a possible collapse in the future, and if she had a preference, she'd prefer her head not be underneath at the time.

Amy pulled out the lighter and brought it to life with a flick of the thumb. The flame burned brightly, indicating that there was abundant oxygen. On the other hand, the flame leaned away from the left-hand fork, indicating that some air was moving from that branch. Amy walked a few feet down the right-hand passageway and the flame steadied but continued to burn just as strong.

Amy took her finger off the lighter's trigger and the flame died. She looked back at Jackson and Salina. "It could be that there's a ventilation shaft down this branch." She frowned and reached up, adjusting the helmet, sweat making her dark hair mat to her head. It itched. These older helmets were heavier than her own, and not nearly as comfortable.

Suddenly, she reached into her pocket and pulled out her keys. For years, she'd used a small nylon strap mounted with two small compasses as a key fob. Her father had given it to her as a joke upon her leaving for college. He'd said it was so that she'd always be able to find home. She'd never had the occasion to use the compass, but she'd tested them out against a larger version and had been pleased to see that the little tools were fairly accurate. As long as there were no strongly magnetic minerals in the area, they should work underground. Some cell phones had a magnetometer, which allowed the phone itself to act as a compass, but hers was not one of those, and her GPS was useless in the mine.

Amy brought the little compass closer to her face so that she could read the dial. She rotated it until the arrow was pointing north, then closed her eyes and stood thinking.

After a moment, she opened her eyes and looked at Jackson who was studying her, his body radiating curiosity.

"I think that the left-hand fork connects with the main mine. It's probably one of those drives we saw that experienced a big fall, blocking the tunnel. I never checked a compass when we were in the main mine, but I'm thinking that this drive parallels the main tunnel in the other mine, and maybe joins up farther down." She shifted her attention to Salina. "You're sure that Jania never mentioned these two mines connecting?"

Salina shook her head. "No. Absolutely not." She started

to push around Jackson, making for the tunnel to the right.

"Wait. Let Jackson or I go first. You're not used to the mines and we have a little more experience." Amy moved in front of Salina, blocking her way.

Salina jerked to a stop. "Fine, but let's go."

Amy sensed that Salina was reaching a boiling point, and again wondered if she was going to be an asset or a liability. She met Jackson's eyes and twitched her chin toward the passageway on the right.

"Do you want me to lead? Give you a break?"

"Lead on, MacDuff," Jackson said amiably. "I'll bring up the rear."

"You know that's supposed to be 'lay on' right? Like we're attacking?" Amy said, giving him a critical look.

Jackson nodded with a half smile. "That could be more appropriate than we know." He gestured for Amy to go ahead of him.

Amy turned and stepped up on the pile of rubble and timbers that had partially blocked the floor of the drive. Her breathing was loud, and she could hear the others behind her. Still, there seemed to be adequate oxygen. She touched the rough, yellow-tan rock sides. Small glints indicated the presence of some metallic mineral. Maybe gold. Maybe silver. She didn't take the time to find out.

A bang and a muffled grunt sounded from behind her and made her jump. She paused and looked back toward the other two, the beam from her headlamp causing Salina and Jackson to blink.

"What was that?" Amy said, she could feel her heart beating so hard it felt as though it was going to burst out of her chest.

"I hit my head on the roof," Jackson said, dipping his chin so that the top of his helmet was visible. A fresh dent and several scratches had appeared on the battered landscape of the hard hat immediately above his headlamp.

"Watch it, okay?" Amy said. "I need you with your head intact."

"Got it, boss. I'll attempt to keep my brain between my ears." He grinned at Amy.

"I think it's more important that you don't damage that headlamp," Amy said, a laugh of nervousness fighting to squeeze its way out. "We don't have any spares." *Which is a big no-no in the abandoned mine exploration world,* she thought as she turned and started down the tunnel again.

They continued down the drive for ten more minutes. The footing was largely gravel and larger stones, but occasionally Amy was rewarded by the sight of a partial footprint in an area of soft dirt, always pointed farther into the mine. Amy also became aware of an increase in humidity, the smell of dampness becoming more pronounced, confirming Amy's suspicion that there was water somewhere in the mine. The footing so far remained dry, however.

Several times the group stopped, listening for the sounds of Jania and her companion somewhere ahead of them. Nothing. At one point they turned off their headlamps and waited for their eyes to adjust to the darkness, scanning the passageway in front of them for any tell-tale glow from other headlamps.

Again, nothing.

The blackness was so complete that even after several minutes Amy still couldn't see her hand in front of her face and she fumbled to find the button which turned on her headlamp once again.

She looked back at Salina and Jackson. Even though they hadn't been able to pick up the sound of any voices or the glow of light from other headlamps, she felt the pressure to keep her voice low. She wasn't sure who was with Jania, but her gut feeling told her that they needed to keep their pursuit hidden as long as possible.

She paused and flicked the lighter. The flame continued to burn steadily, the yellow area comprising over half the height of the flare, topping the blue portion which started immediately above the gas outlet of the lighter. She had seen mines before where the flame showed an extended blue area, the yellow portion taking up a smaller percentage of the flame's height, indicating that there was slightly lower oxygen available. In those cases, you could move the lighter up and down, and watch the yellow portion of the flame expanded and retract depending on the amount of oxygen was reaching the fire. Oxygen was lighter than carbon dioxide, so the lower the lighter was held in those conditions, the smaller the yellow portion of the flame became and the longer the blue area. In situations like that, it was time to leave for areas with more oxygen.

"What do you think?" Jackson said, his voice soft. He was looking around Salina who was waiting impatiently.

"We're still good," Amy said. "Salina, any indication where we are on the map?"

"It's hard to tell, but I think we're almost to that strange symbol that Jania drew in, and then we'll have to change directions. I suppose we'll know what it is when we see it."

Amy took a deep breath. Her eyes were feeling strained, and she felt a slight headache starting at the base of her skull. She knew it wasn't due to bad air, as the lighter had proven there was plenty. Just stress.

"Want me to take the lead?" Jackson asked, clearly aware of her discomfort.

Amy hesitated then shook her head. "I'm fine. Thanks." She turned and started back down the passageway, moving with care.

A hundred yards farther on the adit seemed to make a slight turn to the left, although telling directions underground was always difficult. The tunnel widened with a small alcove on the right-hand side. Amy took another step, and to her surprise, saw the floor of the passageway ahead of her move and she heard rocks falling.

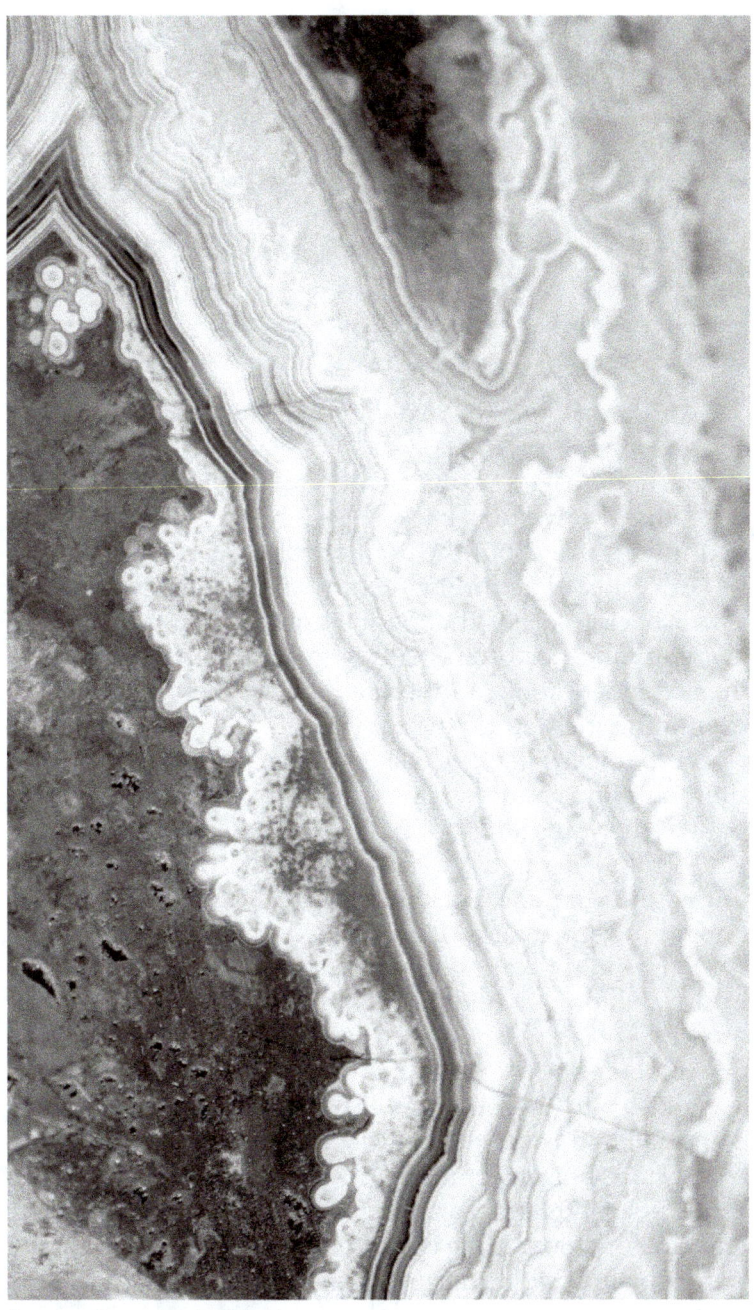

Laguna Lace Agate, Mexico

14

Amy froze, one foot extended out in front of her in an aborted step.

"What?" asked Salina. "Did you hear something?"

"Take a few steps back," Amy hissed. "Don't crowd in. I'm not sure about the floor ahead."

Amy heard shuffling behind her. A slight cooling at her back told her that Salina and Jackson had backed away, giving her room. Amy gently took her weight off the extended foot, and pulled back, then stood there examining the floor of the tunnel.

"What is it?" Jackson asked. He'd moved up to Amy's right shoulder and was looking around her, shining his light at the walls and footing.

"I think it might be a false floor. There are boards under the dirt and rocks at least," Amy said. "I don't know how sturdy it is. It moved when I stepped on it."

False floors were one of the many potential dangers in an abandoned mine. Sometimes when a deep shaft or winze was dug, but the upper passageway continued on, miners would place planks over the shaft, creating a walkway to the other side. Over time, dirt and rocks could fall and cover the boards, hiding them. At the same time, those boards could begin to rot and weaken. Mine explorers might step onto a false floor, only to hear the cracking of wood as the rotted planks broke, dropping the unfortunate adventurer into a shaft sometimes hundreds of feet deep.

"Jania and whoever she's with have already walked across. It must be fine," Salina said and started to push past Amy.

"You don't know that," Amy said sharply, and put out her arm, blocking the woman. It didn't matter if Salina was scared. Amy refused to let her impatience put the others in danger.

Amy started to examine the passageway more closely. They were in another area where the tunnel forked, although the left-hand fork this time only went in about six feet and stopped. When she showed the headlamp on the floor, they could all clearly see the edge of a shaft, pitch black in the surrounding dirt, rock and lumber debris covering the boards of the false floor.

"The passage is undercut right here." Amy started to move closer to the shaft, followed by Salina and Jackson. As they approached the edge, the light from the headlamps started to illuminate part of the shaft itself and a ladder became visible.

Gingerly, Amy made her way to the very edge, careful to stay on the solid rock of the mine floor, and not on the boards spanning the winze, any more than necessary. She heard several more rocks fall into the shaft and this time heard the distinct sound of them hitting water far below.

"Did Jania go down the ladder, or across the planks?" Salina asked and Amy could hear the desperation in her voice.

"I don't know. We don't have any ropes, and I'm afraid to cross the false floor without having some security, especially not knowing whether Jania and her companion went across already and whether it's had to hold their weight. Besides, walking across false floors can be like playing Russian roulette – you never know when the next step will be your last."

Suddenly Jackson crouched down beside her. "Look at this." He plucked something from the dirt at Amy's feet and held it up for her and Salina to see. "It's a wooden toothpick. There are several of them here." He plucked several more from the dirt.

"That doesn't prove that they went down the ladder or across the floor, though," Amy hissed, exasperated with the situation.

"You're right," Jackson answered in a soft voice. "Look at the ladder, though. Look at the rungs."

Amy leaned closer to the shaft and examined the ladder. Jackson was right. While the uprights of the ladder appeared to be old, weathered wood, it was obvious that some of the rungs had been replaced with newer wood, the heads of the nails shining brightly in the headlamp beam.

Amy shook her head and closed her eyes. While she'd been in caves and mines her entire life, she hated the ladders, even ones like this that weren't completely vertical, and appeared to be in good condition.

"Someone has gone down this ladder recently," Jackson whispered. Even at such a soft volume, his voice held an intensity that drove into her chest.

"If Jania went down the ladder, we need to..." Salina started, pushing in closer to Amy and Jackson. The irrational feeling that she was going to fall into the shaft caused Amy's heart to leap into her throat, and she pushed back against Salina.

She was on the verge of snapping at the woman when an extraneous noise penetrated her fear. She froze for a moment. Salina opened her mouth, angry at the delay.

"*Shhh!*" Amy grabbed Jackson's arm, and looked over at Salina, giving her a death glare.

Tink, tink, tink, tink came from the shaft. The sound stopped, then started again *tink, tink, thunk.*

"I guess that answers that question," Jackson murmured.

Amy felt her heart sink into her feet and her stomach do a flip-flop. For a moment, she thought about telling the others that they needed to go back to the surface and call the sheriff's department again. She discarded that idea, knowing there was no chance that they'd be able to talk Salina into walking away. Besides, they still had no more evidence that Jania was a captive than they did before.

Before Amy could decide what to do next, Salina pushed in between Amy and Jackson and called loudly, "Jania! Jania! Can you hear me?"

Amy and Jackson froze and looked at each other. The shaft was silent.

"Jania. It's me, Salina! Are you there?" The desperation in Salina's voice stabbed through Amy's fear and broke her heart.

Suddenly, a voice floated out of the dark shaft. Soft, but distinguishable.

"It's me, Salina. What are you doing here? How did you find me?" The voice was clear, and Amy didn't hear any signs of distress. A small knot of tension loosened. Maybe the whole thing was just a misunderstanding and Jania was down here with a friend.

"Come out, Jania. It's too hard to talk this way," Salina yelled back, leaning over the shaft so far that Amy was afraid she'd fall in.

There was a moment's hesitation, then Jania's voice drifted out once again.

"I can't come out right now. I found something. Come down here. I want to show you. The ladder's safe."

Salina looked over at Amy and Jackson, then reached for the top of the ladder and swung on before Amy could stop her. She started making her way down the rungs. A few creaks and groans emerged from the old wood, but the ladder held, and Salina's head disappeared below the floor of the upper drive.

Jackson looked over at Amy, all signs of humor temporarily erased from his features. "What do you think?"

Amy sighed. "Jania sounds fine. I think we're going to get wet though. I'm pretty sure I heard the rocks fall into water."

"Damn," Jackson said, almost to himself. "And I forgot my water wings."

With that, he reached for the ladder, swung on and climbed down out of sight.

"Crap, crap, crap!" Amy said to herself, then stuck her head over the edge of the shaft. She could see Jackson about ten feet below her, moving quickly downward. Farther down the shaft she could see Salina, standing in water next to the bottom of the ladder. It was hard to tell how deep the water was since Amy was looking at the top of the woman's head, but it appeared to be roughly shin or knee deep.

Amy waited a few more minutes until Jackson had descended most of what appeared to be an approximately hundred-foot ladder, then reached out, and after a moment's hesitation where she very deliberately tried to slow her heartbeat, she swung on and started to make her way downward.

The cold water at the bottom of the shaft took Amy's breath away and for a moment she thought it was much deeper than she'd originally assumed. Finally, her foot found the silty bottom of the tunnel and she was once again standing on solid ground, albeit wet solid ground. She looked back up the ladder, thinking that it had felt much farther than the hundred feet or so that they had descended.

Jackson and Salina were standing there, waiting for her – Jackson, his normal smile having returned, and Salina with ill-concealed impatience that held little of the fear and desperation that had been evident only a few minutes before.

They were standing in a drift which extended into the darkness on either side of the ladder, running perpendicular to the tunnel above. As Amy cast the beam of her headlamp around the walls of the new chamber, she was faced with the same yellow and gray rock they'd seen both in the mine above as well as in the Red Wind mine itself. She could see several areas where the rock was covered with flowstone, the mineral deposits left behind when highly mineralized water runs over the local rock. Several places were currently wet, obviously the site of one or more of the springs that were producing the water lapping at her shins.

The ceiling of the drift was a good five feet above her head, and she could see a large vein of quartz running down the center, probably a gold-bearing vein which the miners had followed when creating this passageway.

"Salina," came Jania's voice from the far end of the tunnel where it and the vein of quartz made a slight turn out of sight of the ladder. "Are you down yet? Come on. I want to show you what I've found."

Jania's voice lacked the excitement that Amy would have expected from her words, but that didn't stop Salina, who turned and surged through the water in its direction.

Jackson waited for a moment, looking at Amy who nodded. He gave her a crooked smile, then turned and headed after Salina, plowing through the water and leaving a muddy wake that washed up against the rough walls of the drift.

Amy took a step through the water, feeling the mixture of soft mud and fist size rocks on the floor of the drive. Everything seemed solid, and she hurried after Jackson and Salina, catching up to them just as they moved around a slight curve in the passageway and entered a large, flooded stope.

All three came to a stop, eyes drawn to the far side of the hundred fifty-foot long, fifty-foot wide chamber where two people stood close to one another. At that distance Salina, Jackson and Amy's headlamps didn't illuminate the figures well enough for Amy to be able to tell which was Jania, and which was the mystery visitor.

"Jania! I've been scared spitless ever since I got your phone call," Salina scolded, the releasing tension making her voice harsh. She started across the stope to where the two figures were standing, Jackson and Amy following close behind.

"Careful, Salina," Jania called to her sister. "The footing is good, but it's deeper in the middle, and there are some boards and large rocks that you could trip over." There was a pause, and Jania seemed to jump slightly, then continued, "Who's with you?"

"Amy Stone and Jackson Wolf," Salina said, sounding out of breath with the effort of wading through the deep water. "I was at the rock shop when you called me, although I guess it was a butt dial. The truck wouldn't start, so they brought me out. We were worried when we saw the strange truck and found your phone smashed - again. Who's that with you?"

Amy had been watching the two people while Salina was talking, the beams of approaching group's headlamps gradually bringing features out of the dark figures. She saw the one that she thought was Jania jerk again as Salina mentioned Amy and Jackson's names.

Suddenly Amy froze and grabbed Jackson's arm. Ahead of them, Salina halted as well. The headlamps had fully illuminated Jania and her companion. A companion Amy and Jackson both knew, and the last person they would have expected.

David Shaw.

Shaw was standing a short distance behind Jania, a bland smile on his face, but something in his eyes told Amy that this was anything but a convivial meeting. Her mind whirled trying to make sense of everything that had happened... trying to remember if Shaw had said he was planning on coming out to the mine when he left. She was sure he hadn't.

"I didn't know you were coming out this way," Jackson was saying, his voice neutral. Amy was sure that he had the same misgivings that she had over the situation. "Strange that you didn't mention it, seeing as Salina was there in the shop and you'd talked to her about getting another tour of the mine."

Something shifted in Shaw's eyes and body language and his smile took on a strange, almost angry edge. Jania jumped again. The knot of tension between Amy's shoulders which had abated at the sound of Jania's voice earlier returned in full force. The water they were standing in was feeling colder in Amy's imagination and she shivered slightly.

"What's going on, Jania? You'd said that this mine was dangerous and never to come in this direction. What did you want to show me? What's in that box?" Salina's voice was taking on an aggrieved tone.

She seemed to be ignoring Shaw's presence until Amy caught her glancing surreptitiously at the man. A slight expression of confusion and worry crossed her face.

Amy looked at Jania and then over at Shaw then back at Jania again. Just as Salina had said, there was a large metal box, almost a trunk, perched on a pile of rocks in front of the blonde woman. A padlock hung from the hasp, and from the looks of the dents and scratches on the rusty metal, either Jania or Shaw had been trying to break it open with some type of tool, probably resulting in the *tink, tink, tink* that Amy and her group had heard from the upper passageway.

"You haven't said anything, Ms. Stone," Shaw said in a soft voice, the strange smile firmly on his lips, "Aren't you wondering what I'm doing here as well?"

Amy felt an undercurrent of menace to his words.

She took a deep breath. "I'm thinking that you came here to get whatever is in that box, and that you didn't know that Jania had placed a phone call to her sister before the phone was smashed," she said, fighting to keep her voice even. "You were snooping for information on the Matthesons when you came to the shop today, and when you saw that Salina was going to be away from the mine for a while and that Jania was alone here, you grabbed the opportunity. How am I doing so far?" She glanced over at Jackson and saw he was also watching Shaw warily.

Salina looked at Jania, then Shaw, then back at Amy.

The brilliant illumination of the headlamp made it difficult to see her features clearly, but her body language shouted confusion and frustration.

Shaw's smile faded for a second, the returned in full force and he stepped back away from Jania, revealing the gun that he'd been holding to her back. Amy realized that the times Jania had seemed to jump had probably been when Shaw was prodding her with the muzzle of the pistol.

Jackson started forward, then stopped abruptly when Shaw raised the weapon and pointed it straight at Jania's head. Salina seemed frozen to the ground, although a slight shiver coursed through her body. Amy wasn't sure if it was from fear, tension, or whether the cold water was starting to affect her as well.

"Very good, Amy," Shaw said in conversational tones. "You're right. I did see an opportunity and took it."

"Why?" asked Jackson. He shifted a little closer to Amy. "What's in that box and how did you know it was here."

"I only came to get what's mine, no pun intended," Shaw said with a small chuckle. "Unfortunately, Jania here hasn't been able to break it open, and I haven't trusted her to stand calmly nearby while I have a whack at it." He chuckled again, and it sent shivers down Amy's body, although she had to admit to herself that the water seemed to be leaching the warmth out of her body at an alarming rate which probably contributed to the tremors.

"Dammit! Will someone explain what is going on?" Salina suddenly exclaimed and took several steps toward her sister. Shaw immediately lifted the gun and pulled the trigger. The bullet struck the rock ceiling of the stope causing a cascade of small stones to rain down into the water below. Jackson grabbed Amy and pushed her down, making them a smaller target. The bullet ricocheted off and struck the wall of the chamber before careening in another direction unseen in the dark.

Finally, the stope was quiet again, the bullet having

spent its energy without hitting any of the humans present... this time.

"What the hell, Shaw!" Jackson exclaimed in fury and started to launch himself forward. As terrified as Amy was, she still felt a moment of surprise having never heard this type of anger from Jackson, even during their run-in with Scott Branson not long ago.

She grabbed his arm and jerked him to a stop, only realizing when he hissed in pain that she'd pulled on the injured shoulder.

"Just so that you know I'm serious," Shaw said, pointing the handgun once again at Jania.

"That bullet could have as easily hit you when it ricocheted," Amy protested. She squinted in the bright beam of his headlamp. "What were you thinking?"

"I was willing to take my chances," Shaw answered. "I've always been a bit of a gambler." His lips twisted in a sardonic smile. "Now, Jackson, if you don't mind, see if you can get that hasp to break. There's a shovel lying next to it, and you may be stronger than my young friend. That trunk is too heavy to carry back up the ladder and I don't intend to leave without my property."

Jackson hesitated, then turned toward the trunk as Shaw stood back, pistol to Jania's spine. He picked up the shovel and hefted it, prepared to strike the hasp, but Amy spoke up.

"Jackson stop!" She turned to look at Shaw, wincing as the beam of his headlamp caught her full in the eyes once again. She ducked her head and squinted. "Jackson broke his collarbone and shoulder blade not long ago. The idiot is supposed to be wearing a sling, but he won't." She looked back at him.

"Do you propose to give it a shot yourself?" Shaw asked. "I don't care which of you gets it open, as long as it is opened."

Amy thought for a moment, looking at the metal trunk, and then around the stope. *Please let Tommy have gotten my message and be on his way.* She contemplated telling Dave

Shaw that they'd called the sheriff's department, but she was worried that he would become even more dangerous if he knew there was a deadline looming.

"Why didn't you shoot the lock off," Amy asked, doubting her ability to break the padlock with the old, rusty shovel.

"With this? Watch a lot of corny action movies, do you?" Shaw laughed as he shook the black pistol in his hand. "Actually I tried. That lock may be rusty on the outside, but it's still solid. Damn bullet only scratched the rust and nearly took my toe off with the ricochet."

Amy's eyes narrowed as she stared at the trunk. She ran her fingers over the surface, feeling the scratches in the rusty metal.

Suddenly a thought struck her. "Dave, help me turn the trunk over. I want to see the bottom."

A bark of laughter burst out of Shaw. "Really, Amy. You almost got me there. Jackson, why don't you help your boss turn the trunk over. You should be able to manage that."

"Can't blame a girl for trying," Amy muttered as Jackson waded over and reached for the trunk.

"We've got to do something. This water is cold, and Jania and Salina are shivering pretty badly," Jackson whispered close to Amy's ear. "Don't know why it's not affecting Shaw."

"Snakes are cold-blooded already," Amy whispered back, then said loudly, "Okay, when I say go, let's flip it toward the wall."

"Ready," Jackson said, then hissed, "but reptiles slow down and stop moving when it's too cold. Maybe there's a smoldering chunk of brimstone shoved up his... "

"Go," Amy said and then grunted as she and Jackson flipped the heavy metal trunk over on its side. Something heavy and soft shifted inside and the sound vibrated through the chamber.

"Your shoulder okay?" Amy said, breathing hard in the heavy, humid air.

"Yeah, I managed," Jackson cradled his left arm in his right, his jaw clenched. As he talked he released his arm, and gradually dropped it to his side, flexing his hand. He nodded, almost to himself then looked up at Amy. "Why did we do that?"

The sound of water moving behind her, as well as the sounds of others breathing heavily, told Amy that Salina, Jania, and Shaw had moved closer to look at the bottom of the trunk.

"So, what was that for?" Shaw asked, the sneering tone making Amy's teeth clench. He stepped closer, yet the gun remained trained on Jania and Salina who stood close together, arms around each other.

"This is what 'that's for'," Amy choked back the mocking tone as even in the strange lighting she saw Shaw tense even more, a look of fury cross his face. She turned back to the trunk and poked at the bottom. The rusty metal flexed, and flakes fell off and dropped into the muddy water. "This trunk has been down here for a long time, and the water has probably been deeper in the past based on the water level marks on the side of the stope; probably deep enough to cover the bottom of the box. The metal is pretty rotted out."

She picked up the shovel and everyone moved back. She swung at the trunk as though she wanted to hit a home run.

Thunk!

A crack appeared in the rusty metal. Another swing, another *thunk* and the crack widened. Amy forced the blade of the shovel on the edge the crack and tried to drive the shovel through. It penetrated a few inches. Amy used the handle of the shovel as a lever, forcing the crack to widen.

Amy was breathing heavily and wondered about the oxygen level in this chamber. She started to reach for her pocket, but one look at Shaw and she stopped. He had tensed and shifted the direction of the gun muzzle a few inches. It was certain that he wasn't going to let her check the lighter. *At least I'm not cold anymore,* she thought, as she forced the shovel in farther, and again wrenched on the handle, leaning on it so heavily that the old wood started to crack and splinter.

Just before the handle of the shovel gave way, a large chunk of the bottom of the trunk ripped off. Amy looked back at Shaw. His teeth glinted in a huge, shark-like grin, lit eerily by the beam of her headlamp.

"Farther. Open it farther. Finish it!" Shaw commanded. He was focused on the trunk, and Amy noticed for the first time, that the muzzle of the gun wavered.

Amy leaned on the shovel, trying to catch her breath. She looked at Jackson and saw him watching her intensely. She made an almost imperceptible (or at least she hoped imperceptible) jerk of the chin toward Shaw, then looked down at the water. Jackson nodded.

With the hand that gripped the shovel handle, she lifted one finger. Jackson nodded again. Meanwhile, Shaw had pushed in even closer. The gun had dropped an inch or two, but was still roughly pointing in the direction of the sisters who were visibly shaking by this point.

A second finger lifted.

Then a third.

In a flurry of movement, Amy grabbed the handle of the shovel, and swung the blade toward Shaw, while at the same time Jackson stooped, scooped an armful of muddy water, and threw it in Shaw's face, temporarily blinding him. Salina, Amy, Jania and Jackson were all screaming, and the sound bouncing around the large stope was deafening.

Shaw staggered backward, arms windmilling as he struggled to keep his footing.

Then the gun went off.

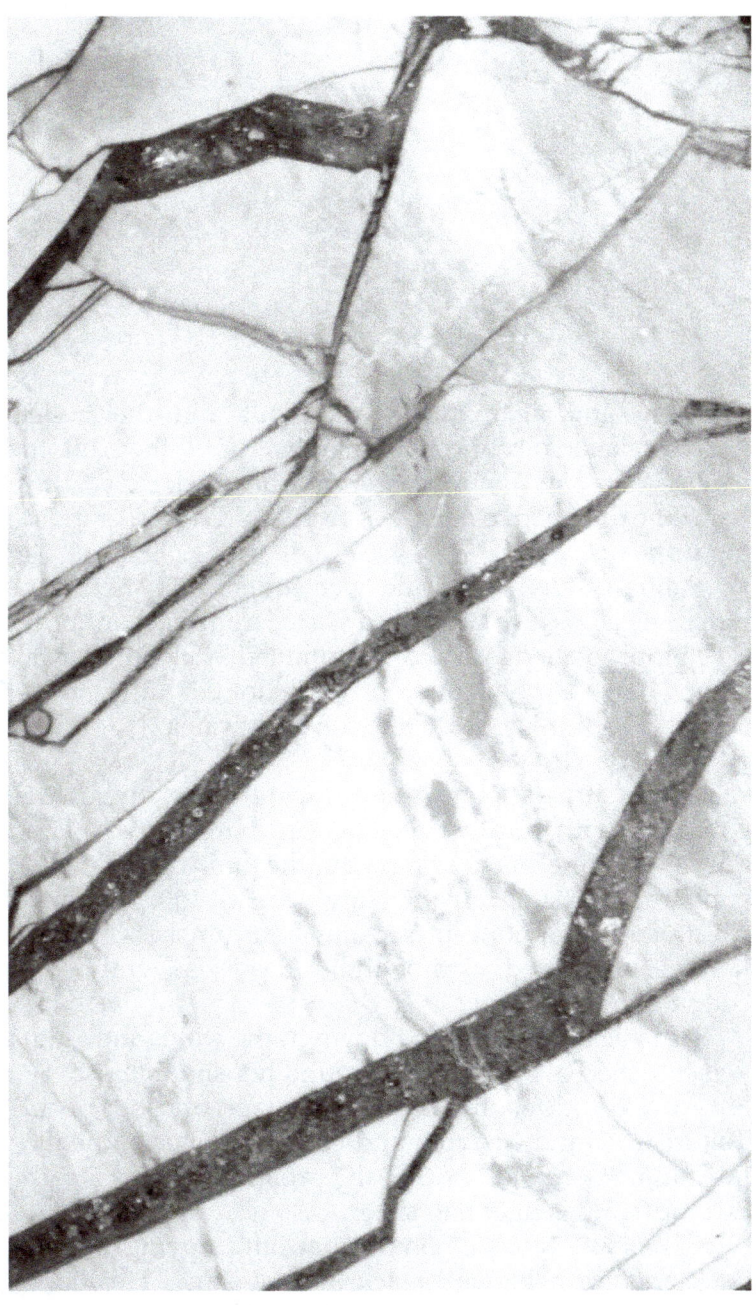

Unknown Brecciated Agate

15

Again and again, shots rang out and the bullets ricocheted around the chamber until they hit the water. Amy saw Jania stagger and heard her cry out in pain. She dropped to her knees in the cold water, grabbing her upper arm.

Salina uttered a cry and went down with her, arms outstretched as if to protect her sister from further harm.

"Stop!" yelled Amy. She stumbled backward, away from Shaw, tripped and lost her hold on the shovel sending it spinning away into the dark water.

Everyone froze.

Amy and Jackson stood facing Shaw who was streaming with muddy water. His mud-brown eyes glared out of the slime smeared face and the gun was trained on Amy and Jackson, causing Amy's breath to catch in her chest. The cacophony of screams and gunshots had left her hearing muted, as though her head was wrapped in cotton.

Jania was still crouched down in the water and Salina was hunched over her, arms around her shoulders.

Amy could feel the mud on her face, and her purple T-shirt was mud smeared and clinging to her body. One look at Jackson told her that she probably looked like the Swamp Thing's ugly half sister.

"That was stupid," Shaw spat out, moving the gun back and forth between Jackson and Amy. He looked over to where Salina and Jania huddled. Jania was leaning against Salina, who was keening softly. "Shut up," he snapped.

Slowly Salina pushed Jania back and rose to her feet. "You shot my sister," she stated flatly. Beside her, Jania struggled to her feet as well, and Amy could see a rivulet of blood trickling through the mud on her left arm.

Shaw spared Jania a glance, then looked back at Amy and Jackson. "It's just a scratch. You two," he gestured toward Jackson and Amy. "Move over there next to the girls."

Amy and Jackson waded through the water over to where the Matthesons were standing. Shaw moved over to the trunk and looked at the large hole that Amy had broken through the metal. Bending over, he started to pry up additional chunks of rusty metal, while at the same time holding the gun in his right hand and keeping it aimed toward the small group.

He reached into the trunk and pulled on something which appeared to be made of material, a fold rising out through the hole. Whatever it was stuck in the gap like a cork in a bottle. Shaw yanked again, and then again. More of the rusty metal broke off, and with a scraping, ripping sound the trunk gave birth to a large nylon backpack. Shaw set it on what remained of the bottom of the trunk.

"How did you know that was in there? What's in it?" Jackson asked. He took a step forward and Amy could hear confusion and surprise in his voice. She felt the same way. What was going on here?

"That's not yours," Jania spoke up without warning, anger hardening her normally soft, wispy voice. "That belongs to our dad." Jania stood next to Salina, her right hand gripping her left arm. Amy noticed that blood continued to trickle between her fingers, but it had slowed. Shaw was probably right that it was a graze, thank heaven.

Salina's eyes went wide in shock as she looked back and forth between Jania and Shaw. "Jania. What are you...?"

Shaw was struggling one-handed with a zipper that seemed to have frozen in spot. "Your dad's?" He laughed.

"Wouldn't you like to know how someone like William Powell got something like this?" The zipper parted with a rusty *gerip*. Shaw reached inside the backpack and pulled out a heavy plastic bag holding several bricks of money.

From her position, Amy couldn't tell the denomination of the bills, but she had a feeling that Washington, Lincoln and Hamilton were not widely represented. Then it hit her. Shaw had left before Tommy called, disclosing the Mattheson's parentage. Yet, he referred to Powell as Salina and Jania's father.

"How did you know...?" Amy blurted out, the bit off the end of the sentence.

Shaw started to tuck the plastic bag back into the pack and started to sort through the remainder of the contents.

"How did I know that the delightful Mattheson sisters here are actually William Powell's daughters?" Shaw pulled the zipper of the backpack closed once again, and hefted the bag, testing its weight. Seemingly satisfied, he set it on the trunk then turned to the four watchers.

"I don't want to hang around too much longer," Shaw said, "but I suppose it's only fair for you to know who your dear dad truly was." Jania started forward at the sardonic tone in Shaw's voice, but Salina grabbed her arm.

"Back in the late seventies and early eighties, William Powell was working for Grand Canyon Engineering. He had a relatively expensive wife, two little girls, dreams of being a great adventurer, and a little bit of a gambling habit. Unfortunately for him, his income didn't cover the things he wanted out of life. Every day, however, he had control over money going in and out of the company, targeted for large, very expensive projects. At least that's what he told me when we met at a conference one year. You see, I had a small company. The type that Grand Canyon Engineering would subcontract with for certain jobs."

Shaw took a deep breath and shifted his position. He looked around, then settled his bony rear on the edge of the metal chest. The cold water was once again sending icy fingers up Amy's legs, and she knew they had to get out of here soon, or they'd all be suffering from hypothermia.

"To make a long story short, William Powell and I came up with a plan, whereby he was siphoning off money using legitimate contracts for services that I never performed, and we split the proceeds. He must have done a good job, too, since when the company finally figured out something was going on, I was the only one fingered. There were suspicions, of course, but by that time, Powell had left his job, bought this mine, and moved out into the wilderness, much to his wife's disgust.

During this recitation, Jania and Salina had remained silent, but Amy could tell that the women were struggling with multiple emotions. Amy could see fury on Jania's face, while Salina's held a mix of sadness and anger.

"So this money was embezzled by Powell?" Jackson asked. "Doesn't that mean you had an equal amount?"

Shaw spat into the water, then fished in a breast pocket of his mud-spattered plaid shirt and pulled out a toothpick, popping it into his mouth. Amy had a sudden vision of Shaw doing the same thing in the diner the night after the field trip. Why hadn't she thought of that when she saw the toothpicks on the floor of the adit above this one?

"There's an interesting story for you. Powell was out here, safe and sound. He'd used his share to buy the mine. There were rumors of something going on at Grand Canyon Engineering, but nothing specific. Some cops came and questioned me, never about Powell, only about some of the jobs I'd done for GCE, and to be fair, some of those were legitimate projects. Powell and I figured that it would be harder for them to pin something on me if they could never find any evidence of any money in my bank accounts or transfers, so I brought my share out here for him to hold a few months after he'd moved out to the mine."

"However, I became more and more worried that they were going to find out that I was involved, and I was sure

I was being investigated, so I decided I was going to make a run for it, abandon my business, take my share and head for Mexico."

"But Powell had the money?" Amy asked, then cringed and glanced over at Salina and Jania. This was their father she was talking about.

"Yeah, Powell had my money. At least he had most of my money. Nice and safe," Shaw said in a sarcastic, sing-song voice. "I came out to get it. He was furious at me. Said I'd exposed him and his family and that the cops might connect the two of us. I told him to give me my money, and I'd book it out of there, head for Mexico and no one would ever find me. He said no. We had to keep laying low for a while. They wouldn't figure out what we'd done if we just played it cool."

"So you fought, and Powell fell?" Jackson said flatly.

Shaw's face took on a distant look, eerie in the harsh light from the headlamps. Still, the gun remained pointed at them, and Amy had no doubt he'd start pulling the trigger again if they made a wrong move.

"It was a nice day. Powell said his wife had taken the older daughter into Kingman for a doctor's appointment, or something like that. Powell was standing there on that little terrace, his little blonde girl playing in the dirt nearby. She got worried when we started shouting at one another, but Powell told her to go back to her playing. While his attention was occupied, I punched him. He stumbled on the edge of the shaft, fell and rolled down that incline. I followed behind. When he got up, he took a swing at me. We fought and he fell backward into the mine, and eventually onto that pile of debris. I'd gone down after him. When he started to get up, I jumped on him, punching. I didn't realize until a little later that he wasn't fighting back anymore."

Shaw shook his head, lips twisted in a scowl. "Damn. I didn't want the guy to die. He was the only one who knew where my money was. The little girl was screaming. I took her back to the tin building they were using as a house and told her to wait for her mommy, and not to say anything or the ghosts would get her. That shut her up pretty damn quick."

Shaw examined Jania with curiosity. "Guess you never did say anything, did you?" He chuckled, then heaved himself up off the trunk and picked up the backpack, slinging it over his shoulder.

"The sheriff's department have wondered why they didn't find Powell during the search after Powell's wife reported him missing," Amy said.

"The search party was mostly made up of local volunteers. I was a 'friend of the family' as far as they knew, and I made sure that I searched the area of this mine," Shaw snorted and shook his head, "Gullible. Well, it sure has been nice reminiscing like this, but I've got to bounce, as the kids say these days."

"Wait," Amy said, taking a step forward. She was coming to the realization that Shaw was going to leave them there, although that didn't make sense. He had to know that they'd follow behind and call the sheriff's department as soon as they were able.

Shaw looked at her. "What?"

"Why wait until now? I mean, why wait until now to come back to get your money?"

"Oh, I was arrested and charged with grand theft. They managed to find enough circumstantial evidence to make it stick. Then there were a few small problems while in prison, which kept me there a little longer than the original charge warranted. I didn't get out until a few months ago. I decided I had to do a bit of research on the situation first. Besides, I didn't know exactly where Powell had hidden the money. I figured it was in this mine somewhere, but I didn't want to tip my hand too early. Wouldn't do to jump in, get caught, and find myself back in prison, you know." He chuckled again, as though making a joke.

"But what about all that money you were flashing at the field trip?" Amy asked, trying to stall the Shaw's next obvious action.

"*That,*" Shaw said in derision. "I didn't bring everything out to Powell. I had a few other deals going, but this," Shaw shook the backpack, "this was my biggest score, and I'm going nowhere without it. Now, if you all don't mind, hand me your headlamps."

Amy's mouth fell open in shock. She could see Jackson's wide-eyed, blue stare, the pupils huge in the dark mine unless the beam from a light happened to catch him full in the face. She started to reach slowly for her helmet.

"You can't leave us here with no light!" she protested. The absolute blackness of the mine loomed on the edges of the headlamp beams.

"Wouldn't want you following too closely, now would I?" Shaw said calmly, hand outstretched. "At least I'm giving you a chance here. I could just shoot you."

Amy's heart plummeted, and she could see from the faces of the others that they also understood exactly what Shaw's request meant. One by one Shaw took the headlamps, wrenched the battery packs loose and flung them off into the water at the far side of the chamber.

"Now your helmets, please."

As each person removed his or her helmet, Shaw took it and threw it out into the water, not appearing to mind if it sunk or not. It didn't matter, Amy knew, since without the headlamps, the odds of them finding any of the helmets was close to zero.

Surreptitiously, Amy patted her pocket. The lighter was still there and she breathed a sigh of relief. *Please don't let Shaw tell us to empty our pockets. Please let him be so cocky that he doesn't stop to think.*

Shaw readjusted the backpack then started to back away from the group, one foot at a time, maintaining his aim. Moving along the edge of the stope, he headed for the narrower drift and the ladder beyond, his one headlamp becoming dimmer as the distance increased.

"Wait!" Amy called.

Shaw paused for a moment. Amy could no longer see

the expression on his face, but there seemed to be a level of expectancy in his body language.

"We know about the Mattheson's father, but why did you push Hazelton last Saturday? That made it almost certain that we'd find Powell as well."

Shaw snorted a laugh. "I didn't push that conceited scarecrow," he said, ignoring the fact that Shaw looked like Hazelton's twin brother.

For that matter, Amy had to admit to herself, neither of them looked anything like the man Bea Hazelton had described.

"I came along on the field trip because I wanted to meet Powell's daughters, and yes, I'd researched the ownership of the mine before I came up here and I knew the Matthesons were Powell's progeny. I didn't figure that the young one would remember me. A lot of years have passed. Still, I thought it best to scout the territory first. Now, if you don't mind..." With that, Shaw turned and vanished into the drift, taking the light from his headlamp with him.

The glow faded as he turned the corner and none of the reflected light made it back into the stope.

Silence fell with the darkness, broken only by their breathing, and the drip of water from somewhere in the chamber.

"We'll be able to get out," Jackson said in a soft voice, but with a confidence that Amy didn't feel. "It's a pretty straight shot as long as we don't get turned around."

"What if..." Amy stopped. She didn't want to voice her fear that they'd miss the ladder, and stumble off down the flooded drive, possibly falling into an underwater winze.

"No 'what ifs,'" Jackson said with determination.

"I'm so cold I can't feel my feet," Salina said, a waver in her voice.

"You'll warm up when we start to move," Jania said.

There was still a note of steel and anger in Jania's voice that surprised Amy.

"Jania," said Salina tentatively, "Why..."

"Not right now," Jania snapped, all of the softer base notes gone from her voice. Then, "I don't want to talk about it right now," in softer, more plaintive tones.

"Amy, do you still have the lighter?" Jackson asked.

Amy nodded, then realizing that Jackson couldn't see her said, "Yes. It's in my pocket. I just wanted to make sure he was gone first." She reached into her front pocket and pulled out the lighter. Her fingers were shaking, but when she thumbed the trigger, a flame burst to life. The yellow tip indicated that there was less oxygen in the stope than in the passageway above, but there was still plenty as far as Amy was concerned.

"Come on. We need to get out of here before we freeze to death," she said. "Shaw should be making his way up the ladder by now, and he won't look back and notice this light." *Please don't let him look back and see the light,* she thought.

"Should we try and find the helmets?" Jackson asked. "Maybe with the light...

"Don't wander into the center of the stope," Jania interrupted. Amy couldn't see her face well, but she could hear a new note of intensity. "There are several deep spots in the center, down toward the far end, and a lot of old timbers and machinery. You won't be able to see them in this faint light and the muddy water."

"You could have mentioned that before, Jay, like when we first got here. What if one of us had walked away from the wall?" Salina said, falling into big sister mode.

"I hoped that piece of toad excrement would fall in, of course. That's why I didn't say anything, Salina. Can we go? I'm so cold." Jania's voice dropped toward the end, sounding more like the Jania they'd gotten to know on the tour, and not the angry woman that had emerged as a result of Shaw's story.

Amy nodded, then hissed in pain as the heat of the lighter made its way to her thumb. She released the trigger for a moment, allowing it to cool down, then thumbed it to life once again and started to move slowly, feeling the footing ahead of her before putting her full weight down. The others followed, the need for concentration, ending any conversation, Amy's thumb started to cramp from the strain of depressing the lighter trigger, and slipped, extinguishing the flame. She brought it to life once again.

Twice as the group made their way across the stope, Amy lost focus on the lighter and the flame died. Each time Amy thumbed the trigger, bringing the lighter back to life, but she began to worry how much fuel was in the lighter. Even if they didn't miss the ladder, climbing it in the dark would be a challenge, and keeping the lighter going while they climbed? Impossible.

Assuming they navigated the ladder without disaster, they still had to make it out of the upper passages. Jackson was right, it was a fairly straight mine, but there were forks, and no one knew what was down those forks: false floors, open shafts, bad air. A myriad of dangers could be waiting in the darkness.

They reached the drift and entered the narrow passageway. Amy breathed a sigh of relief, as it would be much more difficult to get turned around if the light were to fail. She tried to determine how much butane was left in the lighter, but couldn't see through the opaque plastic.

A sudden muffled flurry of noise from ahead startled the four. Indistinct voices raised in anger, the sound of muffled blows, several shots, then wood cracking and breaking as a rain of rocks and dirt splashed into the water below

A scream filled the mine air, sucking Amy's breath from her body. The sound of something heavy falling, crashing into rocks, until it hit the bottom of the shaft with a huge splash. Amy took a quick step back, stumbled and fell heavily in the water, losing her hold on the lighter in the process. The flame winked out and the small group was once again in absolute blackness.

Amy felt tears well up in her eyes and she experienced

the almost overwhelming urge to start bawling like a three-year-old.

"Amy!" Jackson's voice came from close behind. "Are you okay? What was that?"

Amy took a deep breath and tried to steady herself. Slowly she rose to her feet.

"I'm okay Jackson. I just tripped and fell. I don't know what that was. Maybe the ladder broke. I lost the lighter, though." She felt her voice start to waver, knowing that if the ladder broke, they were stuck down there, and without some form of light, they might not be able to tell if the ladder was broken until the first of them attempted to climb out.

"It's okay, Amy," Salina's voice emerged from the blackness.

"You don't understand, Salina." Fear gave Amy's voice an edge to it that she tried to soften.

"No, really. Look toward the ladder. There's a light."

"There's no..." Amy realized she'd gotten turned away from the ladder when she'd fallen and gotten up. When she turned back around, she realized that Salina was accurate, and there was a faint glow illuminating the ladder and shaft.

"Go on," Jackson hissed. "Or better yet, let me go. Shaw must have fallen. Maybe he's hurt, or dead."

"Weren't there voices?" Amy asked, her voice barely above a whisper. "Was someone else there?"

"Let's find out." Jackson pushed past the three women and started to make his way down the drift toward the shaft.

As they approached the ladder, Amy could see more clearly a dark form floating in the water. Jackson slowed his steps, then stopped. There was no way Shaw could still have the gun, if it was Shaw. If it wasn't Shaw, then why was the light still shining from above? Then Amy felt a cold bolt shoot right through her body. What if it was Tommy? What if Tommy had run into Shaw and they fought, and Tommy had been thrown down the mine shaft?

Amy pushed ahead of Salina and Jania, and together with Jackson, they surged the last fifty feet to the ladder. Amy fell to her knees and pulled the body's face free of the water, and then dropped it again.

Shaw.

The body belonged to Dave Shaw, and he certainly appeared to be dead. His helmet was pushed back and twisted, the headlamp missing, the backpack straps still over his shoulders.

Suddenly a voice sounded from above, and the light at the bottom of the ladder intensified.

"Hello? Is someone down there?"

The voice reverberated off the sides of the shaft, distorted and strange, and Amy couldn't place it, although it sounded familiar.

"Who is that?" Amy hissed.

"I think it's Ol' Tom," Jackson whispered back, then moved to the ladder.

"Tom? Is that you?" Jackson put his hand on the ladder and looked upward. A flashlight beam shown down, illuminating the bottom of the shaft, and making it impossible to see the face beyond it. A lone headlamp hung on a broken ladder rung, adding to the light.

"Yeah. It's me. You people all okay down there?"

"Yes, we're fine, Tom. What happened?"

"That there man came at me with a gun. We fought and he fell through them boards covering the hole. He dead?"

Amy looked back at the body floating in the water. Shaw had fallen over a hundred feet, bouncing off the ladder and the walls of the shaft on the way down before landing in the shallow water. "Yeah, he's dead," she called back up.

"Good. Why don't you come on out now? I don't like it much in these mines."

"Can't say I blame him much," Jackson muttered to himself, then he looked at Amy. "We can either send Tom for a rope, and stand here waiting in the cold water for him to come back, or we can start climbing now. I don't think that broken rung will be much of a problem. What do you say?"

Amy knew it would be wiser to wait for a safety rope, but when she opened her mouth one word came out.

"Climb."

In the end, they decided to have Jania climb out first, as she'd been in the cold water the longest. She insisted that she had warmed up as they'd started moving out of the mine, and she'd been up and down that ladder a hundred times, but she was still shivering slightly. Salina went second, and then Amy, with Jackson going last. Amy worried that Jackson's shoulder blade and collarbone wouldn't be able to handle the strain of the ladder following the recent excitement. He pointed out that he'd gotten down the ladder in one piece, and he intended to get out in the same way.

One person climbed at a time, with the next not starting until the one above was out so that if anyone fell, they wouldn't injure the person below. The climb, while long, wasn't difficult, as the ladder was not completely vertical, the slight incline adding a surprising level of support. Still, Amy didn't start breathing easily until Jackson pulled himself out of the shaft and sat on the solid rock of the upper adit, breathing heavily, Shaw's headlamp around his neck.

"Hey there Tom," Jackson said, he squinted in the beam from the flashlight. "Mind switching that light to a lantern now?

Ol' Tom stood there, dressed as they'd seen him days before, wearing the old olive green army jacket, baggy khakis and scuffed black boots, rifle slung over his shoulder. This time, however, he carried a bright LED flashlight which could convert to a lantern. He looked down at it for a moment, then pulled the bottom down. Instantly, the passageway was lit side to side and Amy could clearly see her companions. They were a pretty sad looking group. Their clothing was soaked and sticking to their bodies, and all were liberally splattered with mud. A drying trail of blood trailed down Jania's arm, and a scrape marred her cheek.

"You all okay?" Tom asked gruffly.

"Yes, Thank you, Tom! Shaw took our headlamps and left us down there. How did you find us?" Amy asked.

"I was watching. I'm al'us watching," Tom said, echoing what he'd told Amy and Jackson earlier in the week. "I saw that man in the red truck come. That's the same truck what visited that father, the one who went missing. I didn't remember it though. I didn't remember until after you were gone into the mine that it was the same truck." Tom's eyes had shifted to Jania with that last statement. He sounded sad.

"I thought I should find you and make sure you were okay, but I needed a light. By the time I got back, the rest of you were here and going underground. I was too late." The older man sagged a bit with the last statement, then he stood more upright. "I found this, though. It told me where you went." Ol' Tom held up a dirty, folded stack of paper.

The map, Amy thought, *it must have fallen out of Salina's pocket.*

"I couldn't find tracks in one spot, but this told me I was goin' right."

Ol' Tom started to walk down the adit, heading for the portal. "You're wet. We need to get out." He said, not waiting to see if the other four were following. "You bring that dog?"

Amy hurried to catch up with Ol' Tom, looking over her shoulder several times to make sure that Jackson, Salina and Jania were following. She kept her head low. *Be a shame if after surviving Shaw, I bashed my brains out on a rock outcropping.*

"I didn't bring her, Tom. We were driving Jackson's Jimmy, and not my Wrangler. There wasn't room."

"Too bad. That's a good dog there. I had a dog like that." Tom continued on toward the portal without uttering another word.

In Amy's memory, the trip into the mine had been miles, and taken hours, even though reflection said it couldn't have been that far or taken that long. As usually happens, the trip back went much more quickly. Even moving slowly because they had only Tom's lantern and Shaw's headlamp, Amy found herself trudging up the final incline toward the portal only a half hour after leaving the flooded shaft.

Ol' Tom stooped and climbed out of the mine, then turned and disappeared up the steep slope toward the terrace above. Amy clambered out, then paused to catch her breath. She looked back to check on the others and saw Salina, Jania and Jackson emerging from the portal one at a time, blinking in the bright early evening sun.

Amy edged up the steep slope to make room for the others. Jackson, the last one out, brushed off his clothes and looked up at Amy with a grin on his face. "I feel like the earth just gave birth to the weirdest set of quintuplets ever." He chuckled.

"We're dirty enough for it," Amy agreed. "I don't think there's a square inch of clean on any of us!" She turned and headed up the steep incline to where Ol' Tom was waiting.

Once on the terrace, Amy stopped again, catching her breath. The air was clean and fresh, and she breathed deeply as though trying to scrub the mine air from her lungs. Ruefully, she looked at her arms and hands, then down at her shirt, jeans and boots.

"I think I brought half the mine out with me," she laughed. "I don't know if the washing machine or the shower can handle it." She pulled out the front of her previously purple T-shirt. "For that matter, I'm not sure these clothes can be saved." She let go of the damp material, and it slapped back against her skin. She still felt chilled and basked in the warmth of the sun.

"You should probably stand in a bucket or tub when you shower," Jania spoke up, surprising Amy. The blonde woman hadn't uttered a word since leaving the shaft and heading out of the mine.

"You're right," Amy said, giving Jania a smile. "I'd probably plug up the drain otherwise."

"No... I mean, yes, you might, but I was thinking you ought to use a fine sheet or a big bucket because there might be gold in the mud of that stope. It might be worth collecting it and processing."

Amy stood there, eyes wide and mouth open in surprise as Jackson burst out laughing.

"Jania," Salina said in exasperation.

Jania looked from Amy to Jackson, then over at Salina. "No, I'm not joking. It's mostly flour gold, no nuggets, but I've gotten quite a bit out of the mud down there."

"How long have you been going down that mine, Jania?" Salina asked, giving her sister a hard, brown-eyed stare. "You told me that the mine was dangerous and not to come this way."

"I've been coming down here since we moved to the Red Wind." Jania looked down, her dirty blonde ponytail falling over her shoulder and a shiver that had nothing to do with damp clothes, ran down Amy's back.

"I didn't tell you because Daddy said this mine was our secret, and not to tell." Her voice was placid, almost flat, the word "Daddy" sounding strange in Jania's adult voice, but somehow not out of place.

As a conversation stopper, that comment takes the cake, Amy thought as she met Jackson's startled look.

"Do you remember much about the day your father was killed?" Jackson asked in a soft voice.

"No, not too much," she sighed. "A lot of yelling. I thought Daddy was sleeping." Jania shrugged, then started to walk over to where Ol' Tom was sitting on a rock, waiting for the others.

"But Dad's body was down there and you didn't do anything since we've been here?"

"I wanted to be with Daddy, and if you'd known, you would have taken him away." Jania's voice was so soft this time that Amy wasn't sure what she heard.

"Enough resting. We've got to go back. I have to get home before dark. My headlight doesn't work and this light isn't so good for that," Ol' Tom said, holding up the plastic lantern and shaking it. He turned and started up the trail that led back to the main mine workings.

As the group reached the top of the trail Amy's phone emitted a "message waiting" alert causing Amy to jump. She crossed her fingers as she pulled the device from her pocket. Mud covered the waterproof case, but the phone itself seemed to be in one piece. She looked at the screen. Tommy had returned her call. Instead of listening to the message, she pushed send to call him back.

"Amy," came Tommy's voice after the first ring. "Where are you? What's going on?"

Amy looked over at the others and hit the speaker button. "Tommy, Dave Shaw kidnapped Jania Mattheson and forced her down into the mine. Shaw was... Shaw is... " Amy stuttered to a stop, not sure how to continue. Then, all in a rush, "Shaw is dead, Tommy. He's down in the mine still. He fell into a shaft."

Silence fell for a moment. Jackson crossed the rocky hillside and came to stand by her, putting his arm around her shoulders. Amy felt as though she were going to start crying, and she clenched her jaw, chin rising in its defiant tilt.

"We're on the way," Tommy finally said. "I need everyone to stay there at the Red Wind, got it."

"Yes, I hear you." She looked over at Ol' Tom and saw a frown on his stubbled face, "but Ol' Tom says he doesn't have a headlight on his quad. I don't..."

"Ol' Tom's there?" Suprise was clear in Tommy's voice. "Never mind, you can tell me when I get there. Everyone stays, do you hear me?" Tommy said, his tone leaving no room for argument. "If Ol' Tom needs help getting home, we'll be sure to get it for him."

Amy looked at Ol' Tom and could tell that, while he wasn't happy about it, he was going to comply with Tommy's orders.

"We'll be here, Tommy. Please hurry."

The phone went dead and Amy was left staring at the photo of Laguna lace agate that she used as her wallpaper.

She blew a breath out and looked at her companions who were all watching her with varying degrees of relief, concern, and, in the case of Ol' Tom, downright annoyance. "Tom, you'll stay, right?"

"Got no choice now," he huffed, then turned and stomped off down the trail toward the parking area.

"There's someone who is not happy," Jackson observed as he watched Ol' Tom. He turned back and looked at Jania. He seemed to be debating something, expressions flying across his features. His face hardened, as though he'd made a decision. He took a deep breath.

"Jania, did you push Hazelton into the mine shaft?" Jackson asked, putting into words the feeling that had been building in Amy.

"Yes," came the simple, one-word answer.

"Jania!" Salina exclaimed, grabbing the younger woman's arm, and spinning Jania to face her. "What did you do? Why?"

Jania gave a slight shrug, her expression one of misery. "I saw a man heading toward the mine shaft, and I..." She paused, and then looked at Amy and Jackson, then back at Salina. "I don't know.. I saw him pushing Daddy, and I was so angry I pushed *him*."

Amy thought her heart would break. Tears flowed down Salina's cheeks as she pulled Jania into a tight hug. Amy could see the glint of tears in Jackson's eyes as well.

"The light's starting to go," Jackson said gruffly as he roughly rubbed his forearm across his face. "Let's get off this trail." He started to make his way through the large boulders in silence, then stopped and looked back up at the women.

"The good news is that I bet if you mention to Hazelton that you'd be willing to consider turning the mine into a tourist attraction, he'll drop all charges." Jackson turned back toward the trail. "After all, it's hard to make money when your chief asset is sitting in jail."

With that, Jackson started to move down the trail and the first drops of the late monsoon storm started to fall.

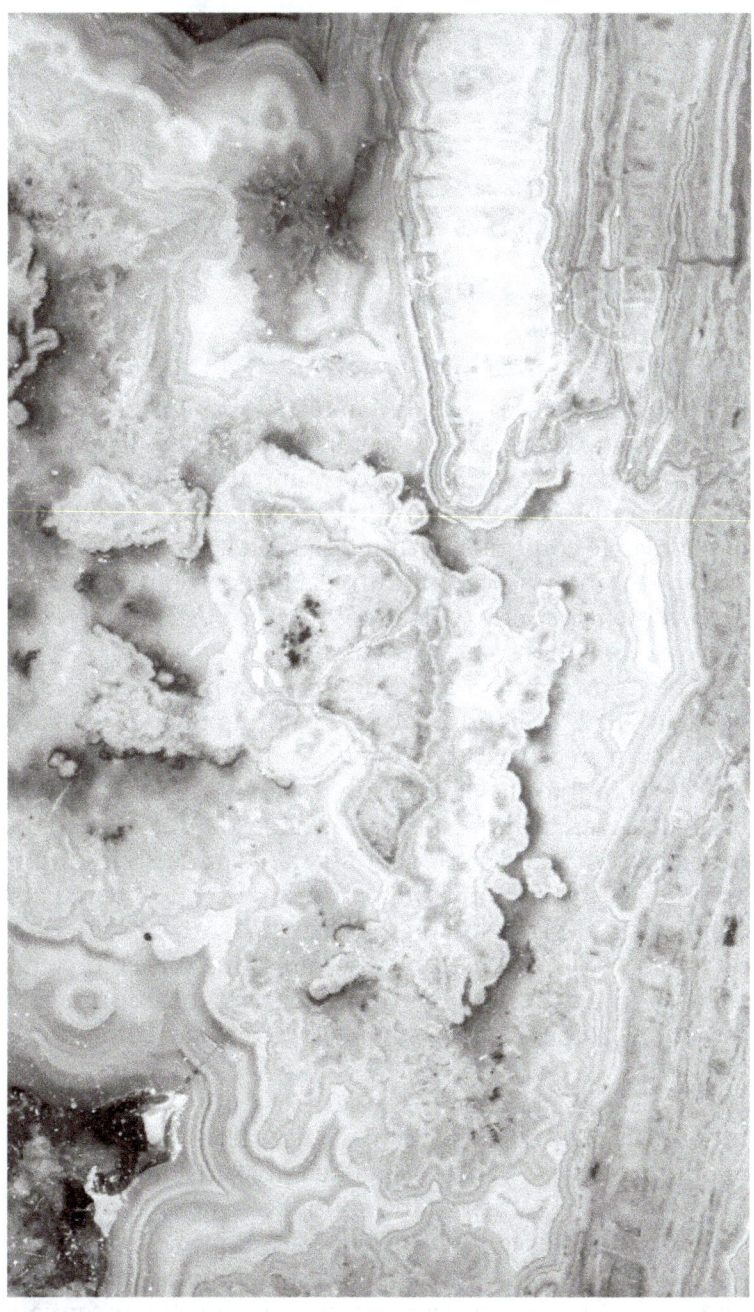

Crazy Lace Agate, Mexico

A my looked around the small apartment above the Stone's Gems and Minerals and sighed. Her dad, Nick, was coming home Monday, and the last two weeks had been unbelievably busy trying to get the apartment into a livable condition. It didn't help that she and Jackson had been interviewed multiple times regarding their involvement in Shaw's death. On top of everything else, they had to run the shop itself.

The community had been practically knocking the door down at the shop, everyone wanting to know exactly what happened from the people on the front lines. A few of the visitors to the shop bought things while there, but most just wanted information. It had gotten to the point that Jackson suggested opening a Peanuts-style booth outside, with Amy playing the part of Lucy van Pelt, dispensing information on the case for five cents a pop.

Jania's confession took the pressure off Pete, who showed up in the shop early on, digging for information on Jania's mine, as that small working had come to be known.

Typical Pete, Amy thought, more interested in the mines and the history of the area, than on the people involved. When he talked to Amy and Jackson following their return to the shop, he seemed downright disappointed not to have been involved in the finale.

Still, the apartment was good enough for now. She still had a lot of her possessions in storage, but the essentials were there; bed, couch, table, some cooking utensils. She'd survive until she had a chance to retrieve her property from Phoenix.

Her phone burst out with *Jailhouse Rock* by Elvis Presley. Jackson's ringtone. Amy frowned. When Jackson left on Saturday evening, he'd said that Ms. Moira had a honey-do list longer than *War and Peace* and had scolded him for spending all that time "playing" in the dirt out at the mine.

"Hey, Jackson. Where's Ms. Moira? I can't believe she's giving you time off to make phone calls?" Amy laughed. "I've got to warn you, I don't hide fugitives. Ms. Moira scares me. Always has."

"She scares me too, but no escape was necessary," Jackson chuckled. "Ms. Moira has a headache, and she said that me banging around the place is too distressing."

"I suppose there was music involved?" Amy laughed.

"I hum while I work. You know that. Actually, I'm pretty sure that the headache has more to do with the Cardinals losing to the Raiders in the preseason game, but I'll take what I can get. I'm heading out to the Red Wind and was calling to see if you wanted to ride along."

"Sure," Amy frowned. "What do you need at the Red Wind?"

"I'll tell you when I get there. I'm at Merri's, so it should only take fifteen minutes or so."

It was closer to twenty minutes by the time Jackson pulled up in front of the shop. After a struggle, Amy was able to open the passenger door of the Jimmy and climb inside.

"So what's this big secret?" Amy asked after catching her breath from the wrestling match with the GMC.

"Did you know that Salina and Jania have invited Ol' Tom to live at the Red Wind? They told him he could have one of the other outbuildings on the property for his house."

"They did!" Amy gasped. "That's wonderful. Did he accept?"

"Salina said he grunted a bit, then went over and sat on the front porch of the old company bunkhouse they were offering, so I guess that means he'll stay."

"That's fantastic. Now, why are we going? Not that I won't be happy to see Salina and Jania." Amy paused and thought for a moment then asked, "Do you think Jania will be okay?" Her voice was soft and sad.

Jackson was quiet for a moment. "I don't know. I don't know enough about how that type of thing can alter a child's mind and development." He broke into a grin, "I think she and Ol' Tom have bonded, though. It will be good for both of them."

"Sounds like you've been out there a few times in the last few weeks," Amy said, not sure how she felt about that. She liked Salina and Jania, but she also felt a little left out.

"Nah. Not really, but I ran into Salina at the diner the other day. By the way, did you know that Ol' Tom's dog actually died several winters ago? Emily said she hasn't seen it for at least four or five years. She said it was a blue-gray thing, similar to Jynx, and that it used to follow Tom around like a shadow. The last two or three years it was so crippled up that he was pulling it in a kids' wagon. Then one day Ol' Tom showed up to buy supplies, and no dog." Jackson's voice was filled with sadness. "Emily said she asked him about it, but he acted as though he'd never had a dog. She says no one even knows what its name was."

"That's terrible," Amy said and frowned as she contemplated Ol' Tom's lifestyle. He'd been like a ghost in the community for so many years, ignored or avoided. She hoped that he'd found a permanent home with the Matthesons.

As Jackson pulled into the parking area in front of the Red Wind, Salina and Jania emerged from their home and started to walk toward the Jimmy.

At a little tin shed set farther away up the valley than the others, Amy saw Ol' Tom sitting on the porch. He didn't react to their arrival, although Amy didn't know what she expected. He never seemed to react to their arrival.

"Hey, Salina. Jania. Good to see you!" Jackson called, as he walked to the back of the Jimmy and popped open the door. He pulled out a large cardboard box, hefted it, and started walking toward where Ol' Tom was sitting, watching Jackson, no expression betraying his thoughts.

Amy frowned in confusion and looked over at Salina and Jania. Both women seemed excited. "What's going on?" Amy hissed as the three followed Jackson. "What's in the box?"

"Just wait," Jania whispered back. She took a skipping step of pure joy.

Jackson walked up to the steps that led to the porch and set the box down. It shook slightly on the uneven boards. "Hi, Tom. I've got a little something for you. Thanks for saving our lives, I guess." Jackson grinned at the old man, and shoved the box closer, the cardboard scrapping across the weathered wood.

Ol' Tom studied Jackson, face expressionless, then looked at Salina, Jania and Amy. He slowly rose to his feet and started to walk over toward the box which shuddered again. He stooped and reached out. Ol' Tom's hand, strong but showing years of hard life, rested for a moment on the crossed cardboard flaps.

Amy held her breath, willing Ol' Tom to open the box, dying of curiosity to see what was inside, but a growing certainty that she already knew. She grabbed Jackson's sleeve and he glanced back at her, a sunshine bright smile on his face.

Ol' Tom slipped a callused thumb under the flap and lifted it, then folded back each of the other folds and looked into the depths. Amy held her breath, and her grip on Jackson's sleeve tightened.

Ol' Tom reached into the box and withdrew a small,

blue-gray puppy, the spitting image of Jynx. Amy recognized the runt of Merri's dog, Lucy's, litter – the one that Amy had played with on that Sunday evening several weeks ago.

For a moment Tom froze, the puppy held up in front of his face. The two stared at each other for several moments. Then, moving as though he were holding a wisp of fog that would disappear at any moment, Ol' Tom brought the puppy close to his chest and rested his cheek on its soft head. A glint of moisture sparkled at the corner of his eye.

"That's a good dog," he murmured in such a quiet voice that Amy wasn't sure at first what he said. "I used to have a dog like this."

Nyssa Plume Agate, Oregon

Glossary

Adit - An adit is a horizontal, or a mostly horizontal entrance to an underground mine. Adits may be used to haul ore out of a mine, and may have rails for ore carts. They can also be used for drainage, ventilation, exploration for mineral veins, or a combination of all of the above. Often in old or depleted mines the rails for the ore carts are removed and sold as scrap metal. Adits often contain either wooden or masonry supports to help protect against collapse.

Agate - Agate is a translucent form of quartz with an extremely small crystalline structure (cryptocrystalline) There are many different forms of agates depending on the other minerals in the area, and how it was created. Agates usually display bands, plumes, dendrites, or inclusions, and these various patterns make it colorful and popular for jewelry. It is often cut into cabs, beads or carved into different forms. There are many different forms of agates around the world.

Botryoidal - Having the shape of a bunch of grapes. Some mineral take on a botryoidal shape, the surface having an almost bubbled look.

Brecciated - A brecciated jasper is one that has been broken into fine fragments, and embedded in another form of rock, such as agate or another jasper.

Cabochon (Cab) - A cabochon (often shortened to a 'cab') is a gemstone cut with a flat back and a convex front surface. It is not faceted.

Cerussite - Cerussite is a mineral consisting of lead carbonate ($PbCO_3$), and an important ore of lead. (Wikipedia)

Coprolite - Coprolite refers to any petrified fecal matter, including dinosaur. Coprolites may differ from one another depending on the organism that produced it and the minerals that replaced the organic matter.

Drift - A horizontal tunnel driven along the strike of an orebody

Drive - A horizontal underground tunnel.

Druse (Drusy) - Druse (or Drusy) refers to a coating of small crystals on another rock, or within a geode. Druse can be found worldwide, and is frequently seen as quartz located in voids in chert or agate. Garnets, calcite, dolomite and a number of other minerals can be a druse coating.

Jasper - Jasper an opaque variety of chalcedony (fine grained quartz) that comes in many different patters due to various impurities and inclusions. Most jaspers are red, brown, orange, yellow, gray, or green or mixtures of those colors. High quality jaspers take a polish well and are frequently used for jewelry and other items.

Mimetite - Mimetite is is a lead arsenate chloride mineral ($Pb5(AsO4)3Cl$) which forms as a secondary mineral in lead deposits. (Wikipedia)

Mineral - A mineral is a naturally occurring, inorganic solid with a definite chemical composition and an ordered internal structure. If it isn't grown, it is probably a mineral that is produced from a mine.

Mohs Hardness - Mohs Hardness is a scale of mineral harness based on a collection of minerals ranging from very soft to very hard. Using items made with these various minerals, or other testing devices deliberately created with the corresponding harness , one can try to scratch the unknown mineral. If it scratches, then the unknown mineral is either softer or equal in hardness to the testing mineral or device. From softest to hardest, the ten minerals are: talc 1, gypsum 2, calcite 3, fluorite 4, apatite 5, orthoclase 6, quartz 7, topaz 8, corundum 9, and diamond 10.

Ore - Ore refers to any rock that contains a mineral that can be mined profitably.

Quartz - Quartz is one of the most abundant minerals in the Earth's crust. It is the index mineral for a hardness of seven on the Mohs hardness scale. Quartz can be found in sedimentary, metamorphic, and igneous rocks and a number of popular gemstones are colored forms of quartz, such as rose quartz, smoky quartz, amethyst, and others.

Rough - Rough refers to minerals or rocks that have been collected, but have not yet been cleaned, cut and polished.

Smithsonite - Smithsonite, or zinc spar, is zinc carbonate ($ZnCO3$), a mineral ore of zinc. (Wikipedia)

Stull - A stull is a timber that is used to support a rock ceiling or a hanging wall in a mine.

Stope - The stope of a mine is the cavity or void left after the ore or mineral has been removed.

Tailings - Tailings are the waste rock that has been removed from a mine, but that do not contain ore. One will often be able to identify where a mine is by looking for piles of tailings which are left near shafts, open cut workings, and opposite the mouths of adits.

Turquoise - Turquoise is a copper mineral with a bright blue to blue-green color. The color is so familiar and liked that the word "turquoise" is used in the English language as the name of a color. In the United States, most of the turquoise is found in the southwest.

Vein - A vein is a fracture in the rock that has been filled in with a desirable mineral. At times a piece of the surrounding rock may be cut out with a piece of the mineral and presented that way. The surrounding rock at that time is called matrix.

Winze - A winze is a vertical or inclined shaft driven downward from the interior of a mine. In may mines they may become places where water collects, or dangerous heavier than air gasses. These gasses are odorless and colorless and are one of the dangers of the older mines that may not be well ventilated.

Wulfenite - Wulfenite is a lead molybdate mineral with the formula $Pb\,Mo\,O\,4$. It can be most often found as thin tabular crystals with a bright orange-red to yellow-orange color, sometimes brown, although the color can be highly variable. (Wikipedia)

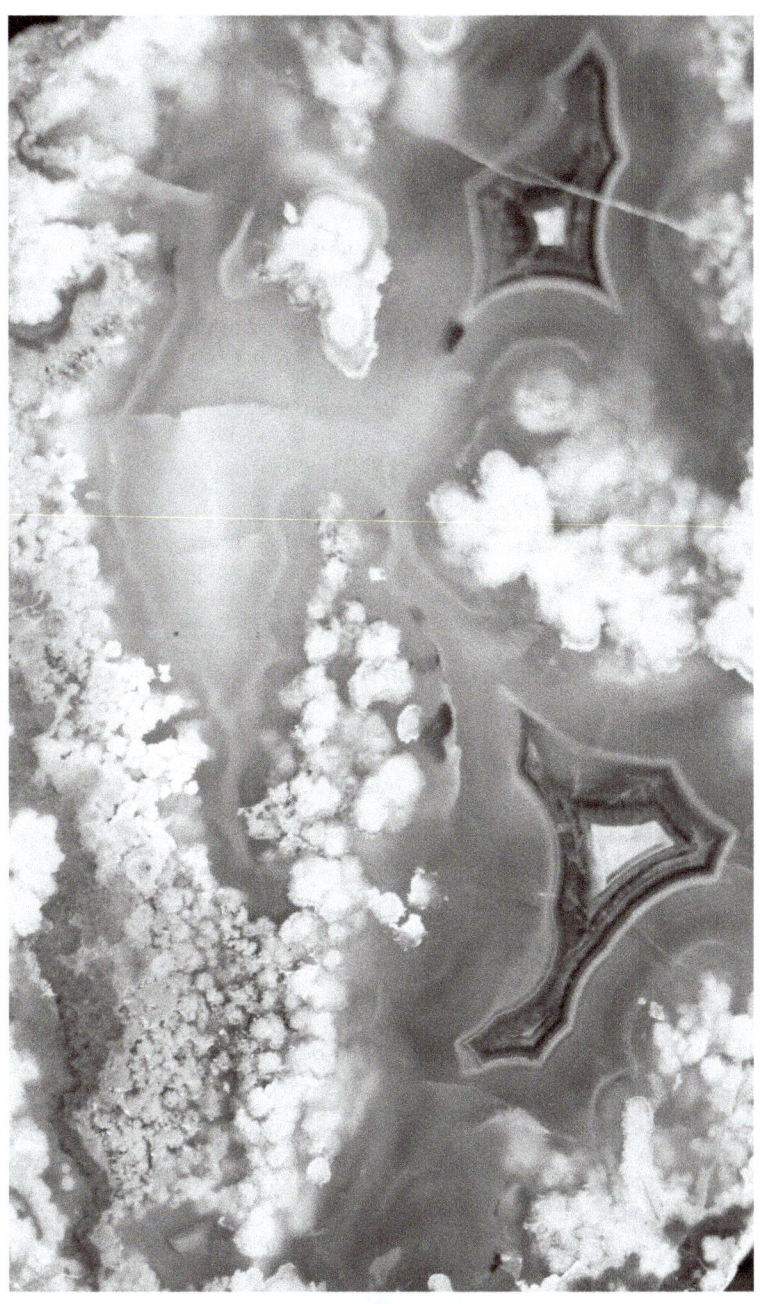

Turkish Agate

Also by Cheryl F Taylor

Amethyst Stone has come home to take care of her father's rock shop, Stone's Gems and Minerals, while her father, Nick, recovers from a broken leg. It's not long, however, before things go awry, as the her father's assistant is murdered, and Amy is suspect number one.

Amy and her new assistant, Jackson Wolf, have to unravel the tangled clues to find out who killed Carl, and why, as well as protect the shop itself from the Copper Springs town council which would like to see it condemned.

As Amy and Jackson dig deeper, they realize that there is a lot more going on than it appears on the surface, and multiple people have a reason to want Carl out of the way. They just have to figure out who actually did it before they become the killer's next victims.

This is book 1 in the Rock Shop Cozy Mystery series

———————————————————

A phone call can change your life forever...

Abigail Williams gets that phone call. Gordon Dorsey, Abby's uncle and last living relative has drowned in the lake on his property, and Abby is his sole heir.

There are a few complications, however. Abby's inheritance is a trout farm in Michigan, but she's a city girl from Phoenix, Arizona.

In addition, Abby doesn't believe the official story of her uncle's death.

And the biggest complication... the four-legged furry owner of the farm who seems to have her own ideas about how things should be run.

Culture shock is the least of her worries.

This is book 1 in the Up North Michigan Cozy Mystery series

GONE TO GROUND

Where do you run when those who say they want to help you won't take no for an answer?

Cheryl Taylor

Following a deadly outbreak of influenza which decimates the population of the planet, the government issues orders that all remaining citizens are to report to designated Authorized Population Zones so that resources may be fairly distributed.

Journalist Maggie Langton, determined not to let her son, Mark, grow up in the dangerous environment of the APZ, decides to run for the empty ranch land of northwestern Arizona. When she runs into O'Reilly, a fugitive ex-Enforcer, she grudgingly admits she needs help developing those skills needed to live on a small ranch camp. What she doesn't expect, however, is that with knowledge of how to live rough, O'Reilly also possesses a darker knowledge: knowledge much more dangerous, and knowledge which the government will do anything to suppress.

Maggie and O'Reilly find themselves in a fight to keep their newly formed family safe and secure, and out from under the rule of the controlling new government. At the same time they discover a conspiracy much deeper than anyone had believed possible.